Frances Marie Norton

The Stalwarts

Or, who were to blame? A novel, portraying fifty years of American history.

Frances Marie Norton

The Stalwarts
Or, who were to blame? A novel, portraying fifty years of American history.

ISBN/EAN: 9783337050283

Printed in Europe, USA, Canada, Australia, Japan

Cover: Foto ©Andreas Hilbeck / pixelio.de

More available books at **www.hansebooks.com**

THE STALWARTS;

OR,

Who Were to Blame?

A NOVEL,

Portraying Fifty Years of

AMERICAN HISTORY,

Showing those political complications which have, in the United States
culminated in Civil War, and even in the

Assassination of two good Presidents.

BY

FRANCES MARIÉ NORTON,

THE ONLY SISTER OF

CHARLES J. GUITEAU.

CHICAGO:
FRANCES MARIÉ NORTON, Publisher,
1888.

To the eternal principles of Justice and Truth; to "vox populi," scattered abroad over God's beautiful earth, and in whom ever dwelleth that spirit of Liberty divine upon which Republics stand; to my imperilled countrymen; to my friends, *adversity proved;* to a proud and honored ancestry; to my children, who are not to blame, are these pages reverently and affectionately dedicated, by the AUTHOR.

PREFACE.

During an extremely trying sojourn in Washington in the winter of 1881-2, I received impressions, which growing into a conviction, impelled me to this work, which I now present to a magnanimous public.

I was persuaded that in many political movements instigated by unscrupulous men aspiring to leadership, who, by trickery, are able to deceive the people, there was danger to the Republic. Notably was this true as to our civil war, ending in the assassination of Lincoln, and of the intrigues which led to the assassination of Garfield—a catastrophe which came near plunging our country into anarchy, which must surely have been followed by a military dictatorship—perhaps an established monarchy.

In order to portray in its true light unwritten, yes, SUPPRESSED history, with which myself and those dear to me are inseparably connected, I was obliged to go into the past for the causes which led to the final disaster, both as to actors and events; as to actors even into pre-natal conditions and misfortunes, as to events into the political excitements antedating our civil war. I was well aware that the mere fact of one man shooting another, even though he were insane, and perhaps unjustly punished, was of little interest to the general public; but when one victim was the Chief Magistrate of a great Nation, and there was good reason to believe that the other was but a " scape-goat " for those who were really to blame, then it possessed undoubted value.

With painful diffidence I approached that historic climax coming so near my own heart—history bloody with tragedy, bitter with prejudice, black with wrong; history which must ever have a world-wide interest—must ever arouse a world-wide regret. And I now ask considerate attention, because never before has it been truthfully depicted; neither can it be except by the unwilling author of this sad book.

At the last moment, after holding my manuscript for five years unpublished, I am still conscious of an uncontrollable timidity at the thought of again coming prominently into view in this connection, and am unspeakably grateful for the company of such names as Dr. W. W. Godding, Senator J. R. Doolittle, Judge Thos. A. Moran, Rev. H. W. Thomas, D. D., Fernando Jones, Esq., Prof. A. A. Woodbridge of Boston, Gen. Wm.

Singleton, J. L. Whitlock, Judge Charles B. Waite, Mrs.
Catherine V. Waite, Rev. Samuel Fallows, D.D., Prof. Jay
Powers, and others—ladies and gentlemen with whom I have
the honor of a personal acquaintance and count my friends,
and who have kindly given me letters of commendation to be
published with this preface, and which will be found attached
to the same.

A sense of grievous wrong could alone have impelled me to
this unpleasant task; of wrong done to the people, to my dead
brother, his honored ancestry, to myself, to my children.

I knew from what I had seen in Washington that a dark
mystery shrouded the assassination of the lamented Garfield;
that a tale which had never been fully told even to me had died
with my crazy brother's last breath; that somebody was using
every endeavor to cover somebody's tracks, somebody's complicity, in the terrible tragedy which had been and was being
enacted.

My brother had given me names and directions as to approaching certain men in his behalf, but, unhappily, I had not
heeded his instructions. After he was gone, I was convinced
by certain developments that he had not "reckoned without
his host." As I looked more into the facts, as knowledge came
to me from watching events, especially the " Star-Route " trial
and the re-investigation demanded by the people who felt that
justice had not been dealt out to the guilty, and when the testimony of Ex-Postmaster-General James was published, my eyes
were opened, and I perceived the clue to the mysterious hints
which had been given me, and recognized the connection between the assassination of Garfield and the final outcome of the
" Star-Route " affair—the virtual acquittal of every one.

*Yes, the " Star-Route" business killed Garfield! The
claim, "The Stalwarts are my friends," hung Guiteau!*

This connection he, in his blind zeal for God and country,
did not see. To his mind it was " The Deity " who called him
to set the affairs of the nation right, by removing the impeding
President, thus preventing the civil war which he believed a
collision between the " Stalwarts " and the Garfield faction
would precipitate. This was the lever used upon his warped,
deranged mind by designing politicians to accomplish their end.

Only the great God can ever know the misery of soul which
I compassed in those weary months when Garfield lay dying,
while those lying messages as to his condition were flying over
the wires; while the doctors were probing, honestly or other-

wise, and the burrowing pus was draining his life away from a blood-poisoned body; while Wall-street stocks were manipulated as cipher dispatches came secretly from that bedside, where a suffering President's pulse went up with rallying strength, or down in deathly weakness—information thus furnished for the benefit of kingly potentates, while to the plebian populace was sent a different story, over those same wires, from the same source.

I prayed and prayed those months, as did the Christian world, with bated breath and stilled heart—praying for that stricken life; but no answer came until at last the midnight cry, "The President is dead! the President is dead!" resounding through the streets, struck our faith dumb with grief. Then came the torturing experience of my three months in Washington, where I sat, day by day, sadly watching the legal chicanery of a criminal trial; watching a crazy brother—crazy from pre-natal conditions, *born to be crazy*, born to be made the tool of crafty politicians—now brought before a tribunal of his countrymen, charged with the malicious murder of his President. Watching the iniquity of that trial, I cried out: "If there be a God, why does he not, from high heaven, smite these evil-doers?" But the time was not yet, and I held my soul in patience, while the wrong progressed to the bitter end—first, the death of Garfield, then the barbarous execution of my crazy brother. And I thought if such an unfair trial is forced by bitter prejudice, backed by the power of a corrupt administration and the money of the United States treasury, upon one man in this republic, what protection at the hands of law can any man expect accused of crime, whether justly or unjustly, should it be for the interest of the ruling dynasty to convict him? And further, if one set of politicians can, by instigating the assassination of a ruler, even in so indirect a way as by the public prints, thus changing the current of administrative events and accomplishing their selfish purpose, what is then to hinder others from doing likewise?

But God is not always mocked. His judgments are just, His punishments sure; and observing carefully the unerring march of His Providence, one after another of those whom the world to-day believes more or less responsible for the tragedy we are considering have already been seen to cross the dark river, may we hope, not unrepentant, not unforgiven. Sad, when life is so short, they had not lived with the thought of Eternity ever in view.

With malice towards none, charity towards all, I send out this

my work, for justice and truth's sake, trusting .the American
people may be warned by the near approach to anarchy and a
military dictatorship, the sure precurser of a fallen republic and
an established monarchy, which they so narrowly escaped, and
which must have resulted from an exposé of the absolute facts
of the Garfield assassination, had a revelation occurred during
the prevalence of the intense excitement succeeding the e¤ent,
and, being warned, may they carefully watch their leaders, those
who aspire to govern, and see to it that only good men are placed
in power, not crafty politicians; and may our beloved republic
live long, and Liberty remain ever firm upon her pedestal.

FRANCES MARIĒ NORTON.

CHICAGO, Sept. 21, 1888.

Mrs. Frances Marie Norton:
   DEAR MADAM—I have read portions of your manuscript "The Stalwarts,
or "Who were to Blame?" and take pleasure in commending it to the public
as a book of more than ordinary literary merit.
   Very respectfully,   WM. F. SINGLETON,
                             Member State Central Com. of Prohibition Party.

CHICAGO, Sept. 27, 1888.

   Having seen some extracts of the forthcoming work of Mrs. Frances
Marie Norton, sister of the unfortunate Guiteau, I shall await its coming
with interest.   It may shed light on the question of his sanity or insanity;
and of the causes which led to the assassination of President Garfield.
                                                J. R. DOOLITTLE,

---

CHICAGO, ILL., Sept. 20, 1888.

Mrs. Frances M. Norton:
   MY DEAR MADAM—I have looked over your forthcoming work in the
form of a historical novel, and am much impressed with the vivid delinea-
tion of various characters and episodes depicted therein.   Your treatment
of the subject of the vicious spoils system of our politics is masterly, and
evinces a deep insight into the character and motives of many of our public
men, and the dangers growing out of the same.   While I can hardly go
with you to the extent you indicate on the question of the responsibility of
the assassination of President Garfield, I appreciate your diatribes against
the system which produced the awful catastrophe, and am persuaded your
work will tend to open the eyes of the American people to the enormity of
that system.   Very truly yours,   FERNANDO JONES.

CHICAGO, ILL., Sept. 20, 1888.

Mrs. Frances M. Norton.
   DEAR MADAM—In answer to your inquiry (made in connection with an
examination of your forthcoming historical novel), as to my impression of
the condition of mind of Charles J. Guiteau, I make the following statement—

You know I was well acquainted with him, and was present at his trial and a witness in it. From my previous knowledge of Guiteau and from the evidence upon his trial I never had any doubt of his insanity, and am persuaded that was the general feeling of all who witnessed the trial. Still, the public furore against the assassination and the assassin was so great that the verdict was in a measure forced upon the court and jury by the strong feeling that pervaded the whole community, even the whole nation. Truly yours,   FERNANDO JONES.

_____

CHICAGO, Oct. 11, 1888.
I have been for many years acquainted with Frances Marie Norton, and, from that acquaintance, and from what I have seen of the recommendations of others, I heartily recommend her forthcoming book " Who were to Blame?" to the reading public, believing it will be a work of unusual interest.
C. B. WAITE.
CATHERINE V. WAITE.

_____

· I have become acquainted with the general scope of the work written by Mrs. Norton, " Who were to Blame?" and shall look with great interest for its publication   I have no doubt the lessons contained in the book will be of great value to the American public.   SAMUEL FALLOWS.

_____

CHICAGO, Sept. 27, 1888.
Mrs. F. M. Norton, 1200 Wabash ave., City:
DEAR MADAM—We have gathered enough from the original manuscript of your book to confirm us in the opinion that the work will prove most interesting and profitable reading to the young and old alike. We trust the book will soon find its way into the library of every home.
Very respectfully yours,   J. L. WHITLOCK.

_____

CHICAGO, Oct. 1, 1888.
Mrs. Frances Marie Norton:
I have read some extracts from your book—about to be published—and I have no doubt that all who may read the book when completed will find much to admire in it, and will learn much from it. The historical novel may be made the means of illustrating phases of our National life, and of pointing out factors in political movements that are known to but few. The period which you propose to draw your facts from, the last fifty years of history, bristles with significant events.   T. A. MORAN.

_____

The tragedies of the world are never forgotten, they are studied by all minds, and hence live not only in history, but in art, in poetry, in fiction and the drama. Seven out of ten of the Roman Emperors of the first Century were assassinated; only two presidents of the United States have died violent deaths, and hence there has arisen in our country so very little of this peculiar form of tragic literature; if, indeed, " Who were to Blame?" is not the first. From her peculiarly trying and intimate relation to the events of which she writes, the author felt their fullest, saddest force, and hence the work naturally shows traces of deep feeling; but, at the same time, it is calm and aims to be fair. From the few selections examined, I judge it possesses more than ordinary literary merit.

H. W. THOMAS.
Chicago, Oct. 4, 1888.

CHICAGO, Oct. 15, 1888.

I have read the manuscript of "The Stalwarts; or, Who Were to Blame?" and regard it as a story of thrilling interest, which should be read by every American citizen. The writer has chosen scenes of our own country and characters of our own times, and into the warp of historical fact has interwoven the woof of a pleasing fiction. Through scenes the most thrilling of the past fifty years, and with characters the most conspicuous of modern times, the writer takes us to where we may see the dangers underlying our party prejudice and political madness. No book brought out since the publication of "Uncle Tom's Cabin," is, in my mind, destined to create such a sensation

J. W. POWERS.

———

Dr. W. W. Godding, Superintendent of the St. Elizabeth Insane Asylum, at Washington, who attended daily the noted trial referred to in this book, even examined the so-called assassin, by official request, soon after the shooting, reporting to the Government that the man was undoubtedly insane, and should be tried by a lunacy commission, *not as a murderer!* now says, by letter sent the Author for publication:

ST. ELIZABETH ASYLUM, WASHINGTON, D. C., Oct. 14, 1888.

Mrs. Frances Marie Norton, 1200 Wabash Ave., Chicago, Ill.

DEAR MADAM—We may admit that the shooting of President Garfield was the legitimate outcome of the "Spoils System" in our politics, and yet allow that his assassin was insane. Herein we may find the lesson, find also the only consolation for that martyrdom. It ought to make the very name of "Spoils System" odious to the American public, while for us—we can still be thankful that no *sane* man has yet been found to lift his hand against the President of the Republic, that people-crowned king. That Guiteau was insane is hardly seriously questioned now. This is one of the instances where the world has not had to wait for the verdict of history— contemporary opinion having acquiesced in the reversal of the decision given at the trial, even within the lifetime of those whose testimony went to the making of that verdict.

Truly yours,   W. W. GODDING.

———

Prof. A. A. Woodbridge of Boston, the life-long friend of James G. Blaine, writes the author under date of July 15, 1888:

MY DEAR MADAM—Your book is one I would like to see published and circulated. You know there are some historic points I would like changed somewhat, so as to conform more closely to actual history, but the whole work, as a historic novel, is *full*, literally *full*, of situations and incidents that go to make a thrilling tale. The style is admirable. Get your book on the presses *somewhere* at once; the country is ready for it.

With distinguished regard, I am,   Yours sincerely,

A. A.-WOODBRIDGE.

To FRANCES M. NORTON, 1200 Wabash Ave., Chicago.

THE STALWARTS;

OR,

WHO WERE TO BLAME.

CHAPTER I.

MYRA'S TROUBLE.

A clean deal-table of polished whiteness, a fair-faced woman, neat and trim, walking briskly to and fro as she takes from the moulding-board, where she has rolled them out, the light, sweet cakes, and deftly drops them into the kettle hanging over the bright fire built of solid maple sticks, crossed upon the gay brass irons standing on the old-fashioned hearthstone.

No odor of smoke or burning fat offending, but all borne in circling wreaths up the wide chimney to the air outside, suggesting only beauty; nothing foul or unseemly in this model kitchen of the olden time, being also dining and sitting room of the family, comprised of husband, wife and child, loving and loved.

As the mother works, singing a soft refrain, the child, a little girl, sits in a tiny rocking-chair, holding her kitten and much-loved doll; the kitten, as are kittens now, a purring gray and white lump of warmth and comfort, but the doll grotesquely made from the homely corn-cob supplying bone and sinew, somewhat of shapeliness added by strips of cloth wound round and round, and with rare artistic inspiration the semblance of eyes, nose, lips and hair, by rude markings in ink or paint—a veritable rag-baby, uncouth, but calling forth the mother instincts of by-gone years as do the life-like imitations provided for the delight of young misses to-day.

Rocking her doll, the kitten purring its quiet song, in all the world could not be found content more perfect than by that chair encompassed. It was an *old-time chair*, too—no superfluous curves or carvings, no cushioned abomination full of dust

9

and moths, but a clean, hard-seated, wooden rocking-chair, with hard, straight rounds at the back and for the arms and feet—a chair with no nonsense about it, and placed upon a smooth, bright floor; no dust or moths there, either, for all in this old-fashioned home is neat and healthful, and Gertrude, a winsome child, its joy and delight, beguiling the time with wise remarks and odd sayings, has such housewifely ways, the neighbors shake their heads and say, " You'll not keep her long." How little know we of the fateful future!

· Our story commences on one of those perfect days of the later spring months, when this old world seems young, and new, and pure; when Nature outside, as well as the matron inside, has finished her drenching and cleansing; when the April showers have completed their mission, and all is fresh and sweet, awaiting the joyous summer-time; when the birds have built their nests, and are ready for love-making; when the seed for the harvest is sown, and longs for the ministry of the life-giving sun; when the roses have budded and are bursting into bloom, and in Dame Nature's domain, at least, all is purity, happiness and peace.

The young mother, preparing for a morning walk, calls to her child: " Come, Pet; mamma's going to see auntie; do you want to go, too?"

" Yes, mamma; can I take my kitty? She's so lonesome when we're gone."

" Never mind, dearie; leave kitty at home. You can bring your doll; she will keep still."

And tripping along together, hand in hand, they are indeed a happy pair; out from the vine-covered porch, over cool stone walks shaded by thrifty maples, past flowering shrubs—on they go; past well-kept beds of flowers arranged on either side, where bloom in early spring the crocus, the pure lily of the valley, the gaudy tulip and the modest violet; not the audacious hot-house pansy, but the sweet-scented, hardy, faithful violet— the first to peep from beneath winter snows, the last to succumb to his cold blasts—nature's type of a true woman's love. And later, where were found the bachelor button, coxcomb, marygold, nasturnium, hollyhock, poppy, the (until of late) despised sun-flower, and many another posey esteemed by our grandmothers, but well-nigh banished, if not exterminated, by the fastidious modern gardener.

In the old days these carefully-tended flower-beds helped keep women young, healthy, contented, and happy. Give the average woman a passably good husband, a child or two—ever so humble a home, with the surroundings making it worthy the name—and she will not go far astray.

This little home was one of many in the country village containing but one church or meeting-house, one academy, one store (where might be found everything a man, woman or child ought to need, from a leather shoe-string to a wash-tub), one blacksmith and wagon shop, one tavern, clean and decent, for the accommodation of the few strangers who came that way.

No competition, no strife or brawling there—each doing for his neighbor, according to his calling, straightforward, honest work for straightforward, honest pay.

No use for lawyers; not much for doctors, except in the ordinary course of accessions to the population, or, in the sure decay of extreme old age, weak humanity needing help and comfort now and then. Seldom a case of real disease, rarely an accident, one physician doing the work required for a circuit of thirty, forty or even fifty miles, and that often until overtaken by the allotted threescore years and ten.

The women, dear souls, imagined then, as now, they were sick when only ailing—when all they needed was a cheering word and a few bread-pills—the doctor then, as now, humoring their notion, spending a little time, not unpleasantly, feeling the beating of the life-giving pulse in the warm, soft wrist—listening to the melodious voice revealing its tale of headache, heartache, and various woe.

The hard-worked country doctor of those days was not unlike the modern city article, in that he was human, and would take a morsel of the good things of life as he went along, sometimes sending the bill to the other man.

The world never has and never will get along without a fair amount of humbugging. Everybody likes it now, as when Eve coaxed Adam into eating that pesky apple.

However, nothing very much amiss often happens; as a rule, men and women go in a respectable, jog-trot sort of way to the end of the chapter. Loved, honored, trusted was the doctor; indispensable while human folk *must* sicken and die; faithfully ministering to the disabled bodies until death, then, at the last, side by side with those who sacredly labor for the sin-sick souls of men; for after death comes Eternity, for weal or for woe.

What space shall we give—what shall be said of the sainted preacher of that distant day? How shall we recall him at this hour? Who among us gifted to look back over the long years, and, with vision undimmed by all that is compressed between, see standing out, beautiful, grand in his unselfish devotion, the minister of the gospel of that time? Wants so simple, heart so loving, taking no thought what he shall eat or wherewithal he shall be clothed, but seeking to preach the truth as handed down to him, and to do his duty as he understands. No thought of looking for a better place than the one in which he found himself, as people now say, by chance, but as he believed where Providence had cast his lot—steadfastly, patiently continuing in well-doing, teaching the little ones, comforting, admonishing the youth and middle-aged as their needs required, smoothing the downward path of the old and infirm; occasionally, and with sad wonder in his heart that in such a path his duty lay, preaching a morsel of that hell and damnation which he found in the dry books and creeds of centuries-old theology—theology venerable enough to be most respectable, *not* old enough to draw its inspiration from the Fountain-Head of Truth, from Him who was *in the beginning*, but a one-sided, crooked, warped, human theology; not the perfect Divine theology whose beginning and ending is love.

This sainted man dwelt mostly in his sermons upon the loving-kindness of the Lord; His mercy, which endureth forever; His watch over His creatures, caring for the sparrow when it falleth, teaching that the hairs of our heads are numbered. As a type of the quiet, stable, unselfish ministry of the olden time, he has passed away. The sweetness of his Christ-like spirit is in the heart of many a preacher of to-day, but they, with all the rest of us, are in the seething cauldron of investigation. We seem rushing after the Truth pell-mell, as though fearing she might elude our grasp. We are saying, " Lo! here, and lo! there is Christ; believe this or that and ye shall be saved, or believe nothing at all, and it will be well."

Yes, the good old quiet times are for the present gone beyond recall; we *must* go forward, lest we perish *under the wheel of progress.*

The little girl of our story, fortunately or otherwise, came into this world when society, having been for a long time quiesant, was now stirring with a great ferment, and westward, ho! was the cry which was beginning to be heard. The male members of her family had already caught "the fever," as it was aptly termed, and with the grand caravan of " movers " it was ordained that she must go; traveling along we may watch her destiny.

While we have been investigating our surroundings and finding the manner of place we are to start from, making the acquaintance of some of our companions perhaps, our little girl and her mother have pursued their way towards the home of aunt and friend.

What can be more lovely? Almost a counterpart of the one they have left; the beautiful flower garden at the right, the velvet lawn about the house, the old trees, the climbing vines and roses.   •

As they near the house, comes through an open door the song of a cheerful canary, and, mingled with its notes, the low, sweet crooning of a young mother's lullaby.

Peace, happiness are within and around.

" Why, good morning, Myra, and there's little Pet, too. Come in, come in, Auntie's glad to see you this morning; never mind the baby, he's not asleep yet, and I think does not intend taking a nap just now, the cunning rogue. No, indeed, he wants to see his aunt Myra and little cousin, too!"

At this Master Robbie straightened backwards full length in his mother's arms, for he could not raise himself up owing to a lack of vetebra which his utmost endeavor and youthful am · bition had not yet overcome, and was forced to twist his fat neck nearly out of joint in the frantic attempt to get a good look at the latest arrivals.

" There, now, sit up sir, don't squirm so! You shall have a nice frolic." And Master Robbie was safely bolstered up on the floor, with the help of a couple of pillows, the two young-sters left to entertain each other, while the mothers engaged in a friendly chat.

" Well, Myra, how is everything getting on at the Maples?"

" Oh! very well, but I came over to have a talk with you about something which worries me just a trifle."

" Why, what can be the matter? You are looking sadly disheartened."

" Well, the fact is your brother Eben is getting uneasy, wants to go west, and I cannot bear to think of such a change; we are nicely settled here and are so happy."

" Can it be? Why, he has not mentioned this to us."

" No, he is very well aware neither yourself or your hus-band, with his cool head and plodding ways, would second such a venture; but he and father talk a good deal together at home, how much easier a young man can rise in the world by locating in a new country; while here it is such a treadmill life, working in the same old ruts. I believe they are surely making up their minds to go, and I am more distressed than they can imagine at the thought of leaving our dear little home and the church and all our kind friends—and you "—now the lips were trembling, the sweet violet eyes full to overflowing with tears.

Emily, who had since first they met, been a true sister to her brother's wife, took Myra's hand in hers, comforting her as best she could.

" Please, dear, don't grieve so, altogether likely they will evaporate their scheme in talk. Your father ought not to be easily infatuated at his time of life; his blood should be cool. I'll send Edward over to talk them out of the notion if possible."

"I doubt if he can," answered Myra. " The fact is father took some land on a bad debt a long time ago, which heretofore being unproductive property, now that a town has been laid out adjoining it he wants his whole family to emigrate, that wild brother of mine included. Eben and father insist there is a great speculation before them in corner lots located on a bleak western prairie, under water half the year, out in Illinois; perhaps there is, sometime in the future, for our grandchildren; but Emily, we'll all be dead long before it amounts to anything.

" Father hopes by getting brother John away from his bad associates here and interested in business to reform him, and really it is mainly on this account he wishes to go; but I have no faith in a good result while his coarse, heartless wife treats him as she does; poor John, he deserved a better fate, but like many another man he fell in love with a gay face and married without knowledge of the character of his inamorata. I dread that even they should go, although I have hoped father would return after he had seen John comfortably settled. But why can't they let Eben and I alone and dear sister Lucille? A dreary life surely must a young girl lead there. If we remain here I'll keep Lucille with me. My brother's wife can attend to the comfort of John and father. From what I hear and have seen (which is very little as they live in Stubenville), it will be no hardship for her to go—she was born and raised in the west and would enjoy a rough life."

" But, Emily, I am tiring you with my complaints, and besides must be getting home."

" Oh, no you are not, dear! I am sorry you must go, and sorry for your trouble, but do not despair. Let us hope better counsels will prevail. If they would give your wise little head its due prominence all might yet be well; but we women must brew and bake, and boil and scrub, and make and mend, while our lords contrive how to accumulate a great deal of money in the easiest possible way, as they think, and then forthwith plan how to spend it again."

" Well, good bye, Emily. My visit has helped if only in giving vent to pent-up feelings. Eben will be home soon, and I *must* be going. Come Pet."

And when Gertrude had given Robbie a final hug, nearly squeezing the breath out of his round, fat body, auntie a farewell kiss, they started on their homeward way, but the shadow did not leave Myra's thoughtful face; even the prattle of the child failed to cheer her, for the longer her mind dwelt upon the proposed change, the more she felt opposed to it.

As they walked towards home a glimpse of the village grave-yard came in view, and a pang shot through her heart as she remembered two mounds, one very, very small, but they had been her special care; in the far west she should never see them more—and she dropped a tear as you or I might have done—for her heart was sad and sore.

Soon Myra reached her home, and quickly laying aside bonnet and shawl, proceeded to prepare the mid-day meal as best would please her husband.

Her wonted cheerfulness returned as she worked, and by the time he appeared the trouble at her heart could not be seen upon her face.

The little girl descried him and ran out to meet " Papa;" prattling along, her hand in his, they came up the walk together.

" We's been to see auntie and 'ittle Robbie, we has."
" Have you, Puss? Well, what did auntie say? "
" Auntie glad to see we, but mamma cry. Auntie say don't cry, dear, you shan't go away. Edward say so."

The open face clouded in an instant, a hard look came into it.

Although Eben really wished his sister and her sensible husband to know that he intended going west, he did not care to have them see how his wife felt about it; still, now that they knew he was relieved, even though they did disapprove. Now he would not have to tell them, as he had purposed that very evening; really he was quite well pleased as he considered what the little one had unwittingly told him. Just then Myra came to the open door; the frown was gone in an instant, his arm around her, for Myra in her best moods was a bright, sweet, utterly irresistable woman.

Gathered around the table in the neat kitchen—sitting and dining-room as well—before the open door of this wee home nest, shaded by grand old maples—containing besides this living room a pleasant parlor and one cosy sleeping-room, they were a happy family, a pretty picture.

Our little lady, as you have seen, did her housework with the help of a day now and then from old Betsy. In time of sickness sister Lucille and aunt Emily were within easy call. "What more of comfort or worldly good could mortal wish," thought Myra.

Not so Eben—he had visions of stately halls, grand equipages, servants at his beck and call, all the et-cetera going to make the daily life of a wealthy metropolitan merchant.

He had no intention of spending all his life a store-keeper in a country village! Not he—nothing was too good for him— going west was but a stepping-stone to fortune. Thus had Eben planned. Shunning consultation with his wife, or with his sister and her careful husband, for he well knew they would weigh all the pros and cons before giving their consent, he had long before determined to go west whoever opposed.

He had not directly mentioned the subject to his wife, much less consulted her; he had fully trouble enough convincing Grandpa Gascoigne without bothering with the women folks, and besides, such was not the common practice of those times. Occasionally a man would travel out of the ordinary line and habitually confer with his wife about business matters, and she become the envy of all her acquaintances. As a rule husbands and fathers laid their plans, carrying them out without question from wives and mothers; women of stolid nature quietly acquiesced and it did them no harm; but women of finer grain, more intensity of love, capable of deeper hurts, lost heart under such treatment, grew into saddened lives, quietly grieving, *unknown strangers* in their own homes to those nearest and dearest.

This husband and wife, loving truly, but letting estrangement creep between, each thinking their seperate thoughts, except for the little girl would have eaten the meal in silence. Neither could speak without effort on any but the subject uppermost in the mind, and that Eben carefully avoided.

At last, rising from the table, turning to Myra, he said: "My dear, your father, brother John and myself have made arrangements to join the party going west one month from to-day. We start on the first day of July, and if we have good luck shall reach our destination by the middle of August, certainly by the first of September, depending upon how long we remain in Chicago and the condition of the roads beyond there. Freelawn, where we shall locate, is about a hundred miles further on, and sometimes the roads, when there is much rain, are very bad. You and your sister Lucille will have a great deal of work getting ready for the long journey. John's wife is delighted at the idea of going; they are coming over to join the party here. Good bye, I must be off for the store."

Imprinting a kiss on her now ice-cold brow he hastened away.

And she, when he had left her, seemed like one upon whom a heavy stone has fallen, or who has been shot, pierced to the heart, only she did not cry out, or fall, or die; but sat silently, motionless, all joyous life and animation gone, with hands folded listlessly in her lap, looking sad-eyed through the open door, away into the graveyard, beyond the church near by, where lay sleeping beside the mother, long gone, her own little one, his tiny mound close wrapped in its netted covering of dark-leaved, azure-eyed myrtle and sweet-scented violets, planted by her hand, nourished by her tears, every twining tendril, each bright blossom an outgrowth and symbol of maternal love.

And thus sitting, musing of the happy past, deploring the grievous present, trying to reach out into the future for needed hope and comfort, until the waning light and little Gertrude's " Mamma, I'se tired, I want to go bed," roused her; then she rocked the child in tender arms to rest, and in the evening lullaby her crushed and wounded love wailed forth its dying requiem.

Bodily, Myra lived long years after, but the loving heart life which had permeated her whole being was departed, and to the end she remained the same as on this fateful day, quietly mourning, covering from sight the bleeding hurt, cherishing sacredly memories of glad hours forever gone.

Such episodes oft repeated, *killing love*, culminate now-a-days in divorce—that monster of the 19th century—an evil which cannot be strangled by stringent laws, seeking to rivet the chains binding the outward lives of those whose every thought and impulse is antagonistic. We contend for marriage as against divorce, but for an inseparable marriage of soul as well as body; the nature of men and women being to attach themselves permanently when congenial attributes arouse love. But the surety of possession which is now a part of the marriage bond makes all the difference between courtship and marriage, when only love doth bind. Each must carefully cultivate and cherish love and respect lest they die and the bond be broken.

In those days, when divorce was considered a disgrace which no excuse or atonement could extenuate, sensitive women who felt themselves governed by a master's will, not cherished by a husband's love, would sometimes sink dispirited under the load every wife and mother must assume unless she shirks her duty; and men, finding themselves encumbered by a thankless, unappreciative wife instead of encouraged by a helpful companion, would sometimes desert wife, home and children, fleeing to distant lands.

Even now, when lagal separation is easier of attainment, the opprobium less severe perhaps, the rupture and dismemberment of family life is felt to be so terrible an alternative by all right-thinking people, none but the coarse natures will hastily resort to such an expedient, those of finer grain preferring years of unhappiness, oftimes physical torture, to opening noisome closets, exposing ghastly skeletons for the inspection of the public; continuing after the love and respect constituting true marriage has departed—inwardly though completely divorced as by the decree of a court of justice—yet patiently enduring for long years, living in spirit separate and independent lives. Some, goaded to desperation, rise up and shake off their shackles, break the hateful bond asunder.

But is this the better way? Why cannot men and women so live that wives may yield to their husbands not a stolid obedience, a slavish help, but hearty, willing assistance in every emergency; a loyal allegiance, akin to hero worship, for the womanly soul her chief delight, and women win from their husbands honest admiration, deepest love, instead of the shallow affection given in return for ofttimes shallow, heartless lives?

Not that her husband had been inconsiderate, severe, arbitrary, different from his wont; not that they were to go far away and must leave much which could not be replaced, many things very dear from long association, or that she perhaps disapproved of the change for financial reasons; but that he could be altogether careless of her wishes in so important a matter, affecting all their home and business interests, making a final decision without mentioning the subject to her directly, or by the least effort endeavoring to have her see it in the same light as he did. This was partly what had shocked and grieved every atom of her sensitive nature. But, as Myra pondered, certain recent incidents, scarcely noticeable when they occurred, now assumed new meaning and importance, and she became sure that her husband had suddenly and irrevocably decided upon the removal because of a hidden purpose more easily to be achieved with the opportunities offered by the peculiar manner in which the journey must be accomplished. Could she have been convinced that his own business prosperity and the welfare of his family were the sole objects in view; had Eben, this old-time husband, instead of pursuing a dictatorial course, been even as considerate as is usual among men of ordinary enlightenment now-a-days, Myra would have assented cheerfully, had he insisted, though her judgment were averse to the project, for she was by no means an unreasonable, stubborn woman.

But that her husband should entirely ignore her preference, should regard his wife and child as chattels to be moved at his convenience or pleasure, was more than she could comprehend.

Surely some radical change must have taken place in him, for the tenderness which since first they met had been constantly present towards her was certainly wanting of late, and in this instance had been substituted by actual unkindness and heartlessness. The absolute knowledge of her husband's indifference coming suddenly upon her had agonized every fiber of this affectionate woman's heart beyond repair. Oh! those telltale words—"John's wife!"

Deluded man! that he had at once dispelled from his mind a silly infatuation for one he really cared not a whit about—a woman immeasurably inferior to his own wife—and giving his whole attention to the gentle companion who loved him so dearly, regarding her as friend and comrade, consulting with her as he would have done with a partner in business, more necessary when for life—thus must these two have been drawn inseparably together.

The real obstacle to such conference was the headstrong nature of the man, unused to asking advice of any one, much less a wife; a man perfectly sure he knew what was best, under any and all circumstances, and with a determination of purpose when his passions were aroused to carry out his plans, have his own way, though the Juggernaut car of his will should crush the life out from the hearts of those who loved him, or eventually wreck his own happiness.

Because of this strength of character the man was capable

of loving with an impassioned tenderness, commanding the deepest, truest love in return. A man who had but to let his own heart go out and the object of his desires must of her own accord come to him.

Such a man a wife will worship, clinging to him alone through good and through evil report alike, even after repeated unkindness; and alas! oft times a woman, loving though erring, drawn irresistably to his fond embrace, exhibits not one atom less of devotion.

Eben Grieveau was a handsome, manly fellow, and Myra, his wife, had deemed herself a queen among women during the three years of their wedded life, each day binding her closer in allegiance to her king; especially through this beautiful spring time as she had watched him coming up the walk leading to their cottage home, with free, springing step and bright, genial smile, her love had increased to adoration until she felt her chief joy must ever consist in following him to the ends of the earth did he but say the talismanic words, " Come, my darling, come!" And he, as the sweet wife came tripping to meet him day by day, her soft arms at last about his neck, the dainty mouth upturned to his, had thought, " Was there ever such another little woman? "

But now, *very lately*, a wily siren had discovered this fruitful Eden, and her own garden being barren had wickedly coveted her neighbor's apples, with the result apt to follow when a man of warm temperament and strong nature is encountered by a coarse, passionate woman full of the fire of youth, strength and health, but lacking in the refinement of principle, the sense of justice and right living which should pre-eminently distinguish woman, causing that she prefer any torture rather than reach out after or accept that which belongs to another, rather than estrange the affection which every wife has the right to expect from her husband.

But this woman, thoughtless, robust, with a certain animate beauty—striving her utmost to crowd between these two—had little delicacy of feeling or just principle, and the fateful wrong progressed unhindered to the end.

Now where had been joy and peace, discord and sorrow have entered. Eben, nearing his home at the close of this pleasant summer day so long ago, no one comes to meet him as of yore, no one is stirring within, but such sad, unearthly music strikes upon his ear as he has never heard before; anon the notes rise wild and free as though the soul of the singer would burst its bonds and soar away to the very skies, and sinking lower—with an unutterable sadness—yet lower, until it seems the breath must surely be stilled in death.

Eben comes nearer, hoping to distinguish the words, it is only a lullaby, and greater wonder, the songstress is his wife! He knew she could sing indifferently well, but *such* music! What can it mean? And she sitting alone with only little Gertrude for company!

Hark! His step has roused her, she hears him coming, instantly is the wierd melody hushed, nevermore to be resumed. She lays the child quickly upon its bed, and with bewildered, dazed manner goes about her neglected household work.

Eben waits a little, thoroughly alarmed by her strange conduct; he watches her movements, but she proceeds methodically as is her custom.

There is a very tired look, a hopeless expression in her face, otherwise she is the same as usual.

He enters—Myra meets him *almost* in the old accustomed way—a shadow there is possibly of indifference and coldness in her tone as she mentions that "little Gerty was tired, and after rocking her to sleep she forgot herself."

He answers nothing, but wonders at the strange manner women have of showing it when they are grieved; for he very well knows that the heart of his wife is profoundly chilled, and wherefore, but he does not at all comprehend the extent of the defection or the depth of the pool of anguish which has been stirred.

Though he did, would he relent? Likely not. He'd think, " Women are so queer, but she'll get over it, they always do."

And thus men reason to this day, the best of them; men who would not hurt a fly, much less a woman, physically, see those they love sorrowful, growing cold towards them day by day, because of their own thoughtlessness or downright unkindness, and yet they do not mind or trouble in the least about so trivial an affair as a woman's preferences and notions, much less over her jealous whims, as they are pleased to say.

As for Eben and his wife, from that day when the abrupt announcement of his intentions had been made to her, they traveled their separate roads; he attended to his business in his own way, with no effort to know aught on her part beyond her special domain, the household work and the care of her children.

Each labored faithfully in the sphere marked out, though contracted and circumscribed through lack of concerted feeling, with such results to themselves, their children and their home life, as might have been expected, the misfortune not lessened by the fact of one party reserving the right to selfish action or arbitrary interference upon any occasion at his option.

Notwithstanding the heartache and the sadness, preparations were made for the long journey, and the family started according to the original plan. Eben Grieveau, Myra, his wife, and the child Gertrude; Myra's father, Dr. Gascoigne; her sister Lucille, brother John and his wife, Julia; besides aunt Debby Jones and the good deacon, her husband, also several others not connected with our story.

In the course of this narrative the reader can judge whether the removal was in the interest of wisdom or of cruel destiny.

CHAPTER II.

PREPARATION FOR THE JOURNEY.

" Why, Mrs. Grieveau, you don't say you are really going away out west? "

" Yes, that is what my father and husband have decided upon."

" But how do you like the idea, you and your sister Lucille? "

" To tell you the truth, Mrs. Sykes, we have no choice in the matter; father and Mr. Grieveau have made up their minds to go, and as nothing we could say would influence them in the slightest, we think the wisest course will be to keep still."

"Keep still! You don't seem to be following your own counsels if what I have seen since coming here is a sample of the work you do."

" No," replied Myra; "in all these changes, though we women have no voice in planning the main event, the detail comes upon us just the same whether the heart be sad or gay, be the circumstances pleasant or otherwise—isn't that as you find it? "

" Oh! yes, woman's lot, I suppose. Life is pretty much the same wherever we go I sometimes undertake to have my way, but yield sooner of later for the sake of peace. I never quarrel with my husband. If there is anything I detest it is wrangling. But it is just too bad that we must lose you. We shall miss you all so much in every way. I shall never forget your kindness when I had that poor spell last winter. I shall think of it every time I go by this dear little house. Who's to have it? Has it been sold yet? "

" No, but my brother Edward will attend to the sale. Please don't speak of it, my heart is fairly broken at the thought of leaving all that is so pleasant here." And Myra could no longer control her choking sobs.

" My dear little friend, do not worry so. Cheer up, cheer up. You must try and look on the bright side. You'll like it out there better than you think. I know ever so many who are going in the fall or next spring; you'll have us all out there before long. Old Barrytown'll be empty. The men are wild now about that new place over across the big lake—Chick-ca-

go or She-ka-gy, or some such a name they call it, some outlandish Indian name. They say it is a miserable poor location
as ever was, set down in the mud on a level with the lake, so
that when the storms come and the waves are high, the water
sets back into the dirty river and there is danger that the whole
town will float off away out on the big prairie beyond. I am
glad you are not going to stay there."

"Yes, so am I. Why, I've heard that in the spring when
the freshet—as they call the early thaw—floods the land, people
actually go about in boats on the main street, there is but one,
well-named, Lake street, and for weeks after the water sub-
sides, you'll find poles set up to show where the bottom has
fallen out from one of those deep black mud-holes, the street
being well nigh impassable."

"I declare, Mrs. Grieveau, you don't say. It is a mystery,
sure enough, how any one happened to think of building a
town there. I've heard the Indians first started it as a trading
port, and then the government had to build a fort—Fort Dearborn, I believe — and station soldiers to keep the Indians
straight, and so the place commenced, and now it is growing,
and growing like a great coarse swamp-weed, rank and nasty,
but so strong and vigorous nothing can kill it out, and there's
no end of the stories they tell of the money to be made investing in corner lots under water half the year. That is the kind
of place it is."

"Yes," said Myra, "we go through there, and only think,
a hundred miles beyond, over prairies, through sloughs, *where
horses go down*, sometimes, *sink entirely out of sight*, and are
never rescued. Oh! dear, oh! dear, why can't men let well
enough alone? And then the people are sick half the time or
more with a fearful disease in which they get freezing cold and
you can't warm them with anything applied externally or in-
ternally; they shake and shake with the cold, they turn blue
and their teeth chatter and rattle, until you'd think every tooth
would fall out, and they are in such misery they want to die
but can't.

"After hours of dreadful suffering the fever comes on, the
patients are just burning up, and you can't cool them with any
thing. They often remain delirious for hours, until at last,
when the climax is reached, and the time has come for the
change, all quiets down, the fever abates, sleep restores the exhausted victim, and for a short period of a day or more there is
comparative comfort, and then another attack.

" The most aggravating thing about the disease is that it does not often kill, and because of this unfortunate circumstance, people make sport of each other and try to laugh it off, calling the terrible affliction 'having the shakes,' but I'm told it is a serious matter when the fit is on, and almost every person going to new countries when the virgin soil is being broken up for cultivation is sure to suffer from this disease. The children and even the dear little babies have it too."

" You don't say, Mrs. Grieveau; well I never heard the likes of that."

" But, Mrs. Sykes," said Myra, " it is of no use spending time in repining, for we are to go, and sister Lucille and I have decided to make the best of what we cannot prevent. Perhaps, at any rate we hope, if father and Mr. Grieveau do not succeed there as they expect, we shall return after a while. Eben says he intends coming back when he has made his fortune, and will spend the remainder of his life among his friends here."

" Well, that'll be nice, I'm sure."

" Yes, but now we must make ready and go as they wish, without commenting or parleying; it is the only way of getting along peaceably with men."

" Yes, I suppose so, Mrs. Grieveau. You are right; so sensible and good. Just like your mother. I remember her looks very well, though she died soon after coming here from Vermont. Marrying as you did, in a short time, and taking her place in the household, you seem always to me herself over again. She was a dear, good woman, we all loved her the little space she remained with us, and you are more her counterpart than even your sister Lucille."

" Please don't, Mrs. Sykes," said Myra, quietly wiping her eyes. " I'm not very strong lately, and cannot endure any more heart-breaking thoughts to-day. Lucille and I are to be very busy and must save all our strength, for there are no end of things to be done in preparing for the journey and for use after we arrive in Freelawn. They tell us no kind of fruits or luxuries to which we have been accustomed can be procured there at any price, and we intend carrying all the dried fruit we can secure and other choice articles for our comfort during the first winter. After that is over, we shall start a garden and an orchard, and in time hope to have these and many of the pleasant surroundings which have made our home here so enjoyable."

" Yes, though at first no doubt you will miss many things you have been used to, and your lot will seem very hard; but you must keep up courage. This trouble may all be for some good end beyond our present comprehension."

"Perhaps so," answered Myra despondently, with that faraway look in her eyes, for the shadow of doom was upon her; "or to consummate some evil. I have had from the first mention of the intended change a premonition of such result, but do not allow my mind to dwell upon this view; for we shall have enough perplexities to engage our attention and activities in the present, without drawing upon the imagination for the troubles of the future. Why, do you know, Mrs. Sykes, we are not at all sure of even a house to live in upon our arrival, and father and Mr. Grieveau are starting thus early in the summer that they may build comfortable quarters for occupancy before the the winter comes upon us if they find it necessary. We may be obliged to camp during the whole month of September, sleeping in our wagons, as we must while journeying. Lucille and I have already commenced making strong, coarse garments for father, Eben, little Gertrude and ourselves, which will bear the wear and tear of the rough traveling. You would never recognize us in our queer costumes. Come, I'll show you our sun-bonnets—'prairie schooners'—they are called."

And the dainty woman arrayed herself in an ungainly thing made of brown gingham, cords and pasteboards, turning about for her friend's inspection. But the lovely eyes, of darkest, velvetly, purpleish blue, peeping timidly out from under curtaining lids, as does the modest violet from its hidden retreat, the dimpled mouth and chin, the smooth, fair brow, the rippling golden brown hair, of sweet Myra Greiveau could not be concealed or even disfigured by this outlandish toilet.

A hearty laugh they had at her expense, and then the kind friend, throwing her arms about her impulsively, kissing her gleefully, declared she'd "know that face anywhere, inside any sort of headgear that could be contrived. But it's growing late, must be near about noon; so good bye for to-day. My husband will be home soon, tired and hungry, and a man is not himself until he has his dinner. I hope *he* won't take any such notion. You are to be pitied, Mrs. Grieveau, and your little sister Lucille—bless her heart. I will see you again to-morrow, and perhaps can bring something for your journey that may add to your store and remind of a Barrytown friend."

With another kiss and warm embrace the good neighbor went her way, not neglecting the task of spreading the newly acquired information that "the Grieveau's were going west! The whole family! Myra's father, Dr. Gascoigne; her sister Lucille, her brother John and his wife." For what woman inhabiting a country village, having a particle of enterprise or snap about her, ever let the sun go down on such a startling piece of news?

And before night it transpired that the more garrulous women of this quiet town were shaking their heads ominously, wagging gossippy tongues, throwing up hands in amazement, exclaiming, after the fashion of such· "Do tell! You can't mean it! Well I never! I wouldn't go one step if I were Myra Grieveau or Lucille Gascoigne, so I wouldn't. What a headstrong fellow that Eben Grieveau is, to be sure, and dear old Dr. Gascoigne must be losing his senses leaving his home and practice here going away off out west with nothing to depend upon in his old age but that good-for-nothing son of his. It's just a shame to drag those two dear girls, Myra and Lucille, out there, away from all their friends. Reckon if their mother'd lived and their father hadn't got so broke down things would a been different."

As for the men of the village, if the truth must be told, nearly every one had the "western fever" with an intensity equaled only in the case of Eben himself—and of course offered scant criticism.

However, after the first excitement, all set to work doing what they could in giving the movers a good send off—assisting in every way possible, even though many regretted the change and disapproved of the venture.

CHAPTER III.

HEREDITY.

During the conversation between Myra Grieveau and her kind neighbor, the young sister to whom she had been counseler and comforter, since the dear mother was laid to rest years before, sat quietly in the adjoining room, her heart too full for idle talk.

She could not reconcile her mind to the thought of the new project, and regarded it with extreme aversion for a special reason known only to herself.

When Mrs. Sykes had gone, Lucille, breaking over her usual composed demeanor, threw her arms about her sister, sobbing: " Oh! Myra, Myra, must we go?"

" Yes, dear," answered Myra, soothingly. " I fear there is no other alternative. Father and your brother Eben have so decided, and I am sure not one word we can say will move them; besides our consent has not been asked. It is hard indeed, my dear, for you to leave your comforts, friends and lifelong associations, but I have in addition to all this, the grief caused by the knowledge that my husband, whom I have adored, cares not enough for my desires to give them a moment's consideration when they antagonize his plans and intentions. I would gladly yield my preference did he deem it worth while to ask the concession; that he does not is evident, and so long as he continues to avoid it I cannot approach the subject.

" My dear Lucille, I fear I shall never regain the feeling of trustfulness in my husband's love and devotion which has made life so happy. A barrier, seemingly insurmountable, has arisen between us"—and sorrowful, downcast Myra laid her face in her hands and wept as only women can.

Soon regaining her composure and looking up, she was surprised by her sister, who was quietly sobbing, almost convulsed with grief, trying, but in vain, to conceal her distress.

" Lucille, dear, forgive me; how selfish my own trouble has made me. I have been blind and stupid not to notice before this the change in you, which certainly betokens something more serious than our moving west. My poor girl, how strange and white you look. What *is* the matter? What *has* happened?"

And Myra took her weeping sister tenderly in her arms.

Mystery of life! Here were two beautiful women, either all any man could desire, and yet estrangement had come between them and the loved one. Now each was supremely miserable.

We have seen how Myra's unhappiness commenced; Lucille's trouble was even more trying. In a thoughtless moment she had made some laughing remarks, of no account in themselves, but intended to lead her bantering companions astray as to how much she really cared for her lover, which being repeated by those envious girls with added coloring, had shocked, and, she feared, alienated him forever. And he had given her no opportunity for explanation, but, man-like, simply kept himself away, not even condescending a recognition when they met, as often happened, he in the company of those same frivolous girls who had caused the difficulty.

Just so cruel and hard-hearted are men when they take a freak, just so proud and stubborn.

And she, her strong love controlled by maidenly reserve, sensitive, wronged, could make no advances towards a reconciliation; he would then consider her unfeminine, bold, and be still more antagonized.

She could only wait patiently, hoping her sad face, quiet dignity, and a belief in her steadfast love which she thought must surely influence him when his resentment had time to cool, would after a while touch his heart and he would of his own accord come to her.

This was the only course Lucille felt she ought to pursue; the only advice her elder sister could give. This their training, the invariable usage of those times, it did not occur to either that it would be proper to solicit an interview. Such a forward and immodest proceeding was not to be for a moment considered.

Lucille's heart throbbed wildly and sobs choked her utterance, as she recounted how, when they chanced to meet, Henry Armstrong did not deign a look towards her whose love was as ever still so true. And now they were to go away into the far west; the separation might be final.

"Oh! Myra, sister," cried Lucille, wringing her hands and pacing the floor of the little sitting-room; "I *cannot* give him up. I can *never* let him go. He was so good and true and noble every way before this dreadful trouble came; but now he won't speak to me; scarcely even look at me. Oh! sister, what can I do? I shall surely die. I *know* I shall die."

But Lucille did not; instead she learned to endure what could not be cured, as has many another woman.

The question now was, would Henry, putting aside his wounded pride, come and see her before she went away and it might be forever too late?

Lucille hoped, prayed that he would; but he did not come. Of course not, no man in love ever acted in so sensible a manner.

For Henry Armstrong was in love, madly, desperately, and this is why he allowed jealousy, fed by those foolish, unfairly repeated remarks, to make him play the despicable fool, and actually let the dear heart-broken girl go away without so much as a good bye. Such is life. Notwithstanding, afterwards when she was gone, regret came in and grew until Lucille's sad face haunted him night and day.

Could he have seen her then all would have been well, but to apologize in writing for what he then felt to be his cruel injustice was more than his pride would let him do, and although Henry longed for Lucille years and years after with a love which increased with his strength, and was at times overpowering, he too, as well as Eben, allowed much of sorrow to result from his mistaken willfulness, so nearly alike are men in disposition. Henry reasoned whenever he thought of Lucille in the after years, "Women are heartless and fickle, separation and time always dissipates their affection. She should see that he could forget too."

Did she forget? Did either?

Not in the least.

And many there are like these two, memory-tortured, carrying bleeding hearts, still bleeding to their dying day.

Some, after a while perhaps, unite themselves with other mates, for no loving nature can destroy its desire for the close companionship of marriage, the comforts of home, the love of children, and thus it happens both men and women when they cannot find, or have through some misfortune lost the needed completement, at last content themselves as best they may with an available substitute.

But these are rarely satisfying, never to the extremely sensitive; breeding unhappiness in the present to themselves and entailing lifelong misery upon their children; even their children's children.

The offspring of such unions, or where discord has entered, being born in many instances, not only with distorted moral natures, but with physical deformity for their inheritance; insanity in their brains, murder in their hearts, the only possible result—bitter, blighted lives.

How much better for individuals and the race, did men and women deal fairly and openly with each other, from a standpoint of equality as to privileges in all their intercourse in every circumstance of life, and when a true, pure love rises up in the heart letting nothing short of death interpose to prevent the final consummation of right living and fulness of joy.

Humanity, even when begotten of congenial and enlightened love, being disabled by ages of ignorance and prejudice not yet dispelled, coming to maturity, the two halves unequally yoked together, still further enthralled.

We see two babes in one cradle, a boy and a girl—they grow apace; the boy full of strength and ambition going out into the world's open field equipped for conquest, and to gain happiness; the girl, hampered by adverse customs, doing what she can in the same direction, but with body, mind and heart cramped—her life oft times wrecked because of the lack of suitable opportunity for the exercise of her powers, the acheivement of her aspirations.

The boy, too, missing the best things of life because his sister has been roughly ignored in the race, no friendly hand extended to keep for her an honored place by his side, and when dire emergencies come, she who should be, is not there.

Out in the world he sees little real equity and truth, or brotherhood of feeling; but instead, self-seeking hypocrisy and deceit, cruelty, temptation, sin.

He finds that since the human race came forth by the thought of God, asserting individual being, each man, as did the traditional Adam, has with few exceptions, taken care of his own immediate concerns, the dearest ties of which he is capable continually sacrificed upon the altar of self-interest; and woman, who should be his cherished companion, too often overwhelmed in trouble and suffering, without power to remedy wrongs, which, though inflicted primarily upon herself and offspring, must surely also react upon him.

For even our mistakes and unintentional errors follow us in consequences more or less detrimental to the end of time.

And further, making matters worse, the laws of society being arranged upon the basis of self-preservation by those who have thus been able to protect themselves, claiming the best good of mankind demands that the weak should be left to the tender mercies of the strong as has been taught and believed for hundreds and thousands of years, when in reality those laws and practices breed only injustice, and ruin to individuals both men and women and detriment to the race because grounded in selfishness.   Pre-eminently is this true of relationships between men and women, and of the laws governing those ties held of all others most sacred.

By slow degrees has woman, as will be conceded, in spite of various disabilities, worked her way up until the loving-kindness of her nature, careful prudence, and pure instincts have permeated the pulses of being through all the channels of life—the race improved and benefitted in just so far as these influences have predominated.

But woman's inevitable lot is to love, and because of her yearning heart to suffer.   Only an affection as pure and enduring as her own bestowed in return can compensate; less radical remedies but modifying or partially improving her estate; there is no other real *panacea* for her unavoidable griefs.

Not *passion*—but love!

For passion devoid of love burns, consumes, destroys.

Love purifies, exalts, ennobles, bestows life and youth eternal.

Every emotion of love, every enthusiasm of being, lifts and helps mankind into the light of that perfect day where is joy forever more; by love shall every good be restored, all that is beautiful and great be acheived.

Love!   Transfixing every atom of humanity with a heavenly thrill of delight; transfiguring the face with the beams of an angelic radiance.   Love!   Which baptises the soul in ineffable bliss and peace; sometime, somewhere, this consummation of the joy of living must reach every human creature, else the purpose of all existence comes to naught.

In the balance of Infinity *souls are measured by their power of loving!*   Those having loved much the more worthy they; and one whose attributes have called forth this most holy and divine passion from another, judged to have thereby conferred an inestimable blessing, and each to be forever weighted with responsibilities sacred beyond estimation.

Life in an atmosphere of love constitutes the Heaven of the eternal ages, which has been, which now is, which ever shall be.

Oh! Love!   Thy power is infinite, but ofttimes thou art a wavering flame, a tender flower, a breath can quench thy light, can blight thy growth; with what assiduity should we tend thee, with what care shield thee.

Once, possibly twice or thrice comes to us this dearest boon, but with what trifling do we receive and roughly handle the priceless treasure; would some power discernment bestow, that having more wisdom, and growing happier, the race, as a sure result, better, ourselves and our children generation after generation.

Here were two beautiful women, with woman's lot upon them to love, to yearn, to weep, so soon to be removed from the refinements which were to them an essential of happiness; for they were capable of enjoying as well as suffering more intensely than coarser natures.

Sad enough could they have had the consolation of appreciative love, in life's closest and most satisfying companionship. But this boon was denied them; it may have been in the interest of destiny.

Industriously were the preparations made for the weary journey by the sisters, assisted in their task by friendly neighbors, the whole village astir and interested in the work. The coarse garments needed were made, fruits dried, even roots and herbs medicinal; good grandma Guenther preparing, sorting and labeling them all nicely for use in every ailment, as she thought, not knowing the disease more dreaded than all others on those distant prairies was the quaking, shivering, teeth-rattling western ague for which her mild herbs would be about as efficacious as so much water. Only the bitterest of bitters could suffice for this cure, as our friends found.

Quickly the weeks flew away, at last all was ready and they were to start on the morrow notwithstanding the sighing and the grieving.

Lucille still hoped that Henry would come to her at the last moment, but Myra's heart grew heavier each day. Eben now absolutely avoiding his wife, for he could not endure the sight of her reproachful eyes.

Sadly the neighbors came to bid them good bye and cheer as best they could. "I'm coming out to see you," and "You'll be back next summer perhaps." "You must write and tell us all about how you like it, and everything concerning yourselves, and whether we can do well there, for we're coming too, you may be sure," were some of the messages heard on every side; but alas! with one or two exceptions, those friends so true met not again on earth—broken ties are seldom reunited. When we part it is for aye.

3

When the leave taking and commotion were ended, the
village hushed in slumber, Myra stole out from the little home
which she had loved as though it were a human life, and alone
walked rapidly to the church-yard where lay in the still light
the grave of mother long since departed, and of her own little
one, both so dear; not until then did she pour out her broken
farewell of all that must inevitably be left behind.

Softly came Lucille also to her mother's last resting place,
and the stricken sisters wept in each other's arms.

A grave may be of less account than some other things, but
for years past sacred memories had clustered about this treasured
spot, and these two felt they were taking final leave of that
which to them was very precious, and as the sisters turned
away they dropped scalding tears.

The coming morning putting aside dreary contemplations
Myra and Lucille arose betimes, bright and cheerful to outward
seeming, and joining the others busily prepared for the starting.
Before the sun reached mid-heaven the last words were spoken
good byes said, and the moving train of wagons had passed over
the western hills, beyond the little village with its pleasant
homes, its friends tried and true, and our travelers were fairly
on their way, had entered upon a new world, an expanded life.

CHAPTER IV.

REMARKABLE INCIDENTS.

From day to day without serious accident or hindrance our friends pursued their journey, determined to make the best of whatever happened now that the die was cast, and although a sigh of regret and occasional homesickness would come to some of the party, they all agreed without dissent, to cheer, help and comfort one another.

The out-door life gave increased strength to those who were depressed or ailing, the fresh breezes were soul-inspiring, imparting elasticity of spirit and consequent health, sleep had never seemed so restful nor food eaten with better relish, the sun was bright, and the free sweep of clear air untrammeled by roof, wall or shutter, relieved all sense of oppressive heat; existence was a joy, to be—was Heaven.

The enthusiasm of these pioneer travelers was boundless. They said, "Why will people remain cooped up in houses all the beautiful summer-time, when broad prairies—green woods—rippling streams—placid lakes—and God's pure air say come."

Even Myra and Lucille found partial compensation for the comforts they had left behind, but for present trouble there came no relief.

Lucille felt hope dying, her heart sinking within her, as they journeyed on, farther and farther away from Henry; and Myra's pale face grew sadder, her manner more abstracted each day, for Eben still avoided his wife.

The way of our movers lay directly across one of Nature's inland seas, ever glorious Lake Michigan, forever singing, moaning, tossing, dancing, raging, always beautiful.

Beautiful water, now light cerulean blue, now white with misty paleness, now dark and green with jealous wrath.

Anon rocking gently as a mother her sleeping babe the many sheeted craft upon her bosom, and again lashing their sides with her wild waves in unreasoning fury.

Gently sigh the summer winds across her placid breast, until gathering strength and passion, whirling, whistling, shrieking like demons, they come rushing on, mercilessly driving to destruction and death many a fated ship with all on board.

Beautiful, glorious, treacherous Michigan! When wilt thou give up the ghostly army of thy dead, the debris of untold wealth, buried deep out of sight beneath thy cruel waters? Nevermore—and yet we love thee, we worship at thy shrine.

As our travelers neared the wonderful lake of which they had heard so much, and knew the time had come for embarking and crossing, many misgivings filled the timid hearts of the women and children. In those early days of lake navigation a safe journey without unpleasant accident was the exception, and our friends wished themselves back in their eastern home before the transit was finished, for it proved a remarkable voyage not devoid of danger.

A storm arose whereby some peculiar incidents were developed, and besides they were for hours tossed about at the mercy of the waves until terror was in every breast illy concealed.

The anxiety of the crew and at last of the older passengers as they became aware of the trouble which threatened them, was intensified to a sickening dread when it was known the captain had lost his course and could not find his soundings.

From a cause never explained a light which should have been near some rocks, and indispensable to safe navigation, had disappeared, and they were now close upon the coast with a dreadful gale carrying them on to destruction, one of those summer terrors breaking unexpectedly from out a clear sky, when the weather is unusually hot and sultry.

As all these rumors were spreading and the belief was growing that they might at any moment go to pieces on the rocky shore, a panic among the passengers was imminent; even the sailors, when they could not see the accustomed light, were frightened, unruly and mutinous.

The waves were now dashing over bow and deck of the little tub-like craft of the olden time, washing away every moveable thing, and as she struggled along her course, chopping across the terrible sea, now rising on the foamy crests, then plunging madly into the deep, dark trough, her masts stripped of every rag of canvas—her yards dipping into the seething waters as she lurched, then righting herself bravely, coming heroically up again on the highest white-capped wave, shaking her drenched and dripping sides, quivering in every atom—but still not dismayed, not overcome—on went the little ship, seeming a living thing in her staunch striving to reach a place of safety for the precious freight entrusted to her keeping.

As the vessel was now deluged in every part except the pilot-house where the captain was stationed, himself working the wheel, the whole ship's company were gathered there awaiting their expected doom, the excitement momentarily increasing; women and children crying and screaming; men shouting and cursing; the captain and officers calmly as possible giving orders, the crew trying but in vain to obey.

Just then appeared in their midst a large, lank, loose-jointed individual, lantern-jawed, with high cheek bones, unkempt hair, prominent immense nose, and otherwise of ungainly feature, and with long, bony hands and feet and limbs; but having withall a pleasant eye, of wonderful intelligence, lighting up the whole face with magnetic kindness, a genial smile, and a voice full, strong and deep; of that penetrating, out-going, lofty quality, clear and ringing, yet tender and calm, which can be heard above the loudest storm, can still the wildest tumult; the voice of a man born to comfort the distressed, no less than to command obedience from the unruly.

He came forward from no one noticed where, and amid all the terror and confusion, seated himself quietly up by the captain's side upon a coil of rope, and commenced, no one knew exactly when or how, telling them a story in a slow, measured, monotonous tone, but loud enough to be distinctly heard and to attract attention.

The absolute indifference which this strange man apparently felt as to his surroundings of danger and excitement, could not but arouse the interest of those who saw and heard him. Just who he was talking to no one could say or did they care, but in a little time he had gained the wrapt attention of all, and the people, gathering about him, looking up, straining eye and ear in nervous intensity, were listening to the weird yarn he was telling them; a story of deliverance from expected disaster by the intervention of an instrumentality fully as remarkable though more humorous than their own experience proved.

Very serious was the narrative at first until the spell became painful, then with wonderful tact and skill he led them into the ludicrous, and before they knew what was coming those frightened people had forgotten their fear and were roaring with laughter, loud and long, joined by the man who afterwards achieved the distinction of being the champion story-teller of his time.

A man of uncouth presence and backwoodsman's ways, but with sagacity, moderation, calmness and courage, which then

helped rescue from peril and long after carried a Republic safely
through a period of stormy wrath, when grievous crime to individuals and to the State seemed likely to end in National
shipwreck and ruin.

A man possessed of great power over his fellows, bred from
a sympathetic nature and an honest purpose through a personal
gift with which few are endowed in the same degree, capable
of controlling excitement in each breast as though by magic,
entrancing all at his will.

Little Gertrude, who, if always timid, had quick perceptions,
and seldom made mistakes in her choice of friends, had, when
the story began, slipped from her terrorized mother's lap, and
clambering up the short ladder to the top of the pilot-house, installed herself, without hindrance, upon this wondrous story-
teller's knee.

Was it a childish liking which drew these two together,
or something deeper, far-reaching and beyond our knowledge ?

Certain it is that their paths in life led each, by devious
ways, to the center upon which riveted the eyes of a great
Nation, in the enactment of similar tragedies, and in which
each was a sufferer.

The storm now abating and confidence being somewhat
restored, partly at least, through this man's influence, the passengers and crew becoming again manageable, a dire calamity
was averted.

Averted? Yes, that a greater than any dreamed of might
rest upon some of those in that little party, might overtake a
doomed man, might come to a babe yet unborn; for Fate never
allows herself to be defrauded of her prey!

But to the good Methodist Captain, noted for his extraordinary experiences, was decreed the episode which proved to be
the climax of this remarkable voyage, for as the storm and the
panic were together subsiding, and they hoped soon to reach
the desired harbor, it was found that the ship had sprung a
leak and was well nigh disabled. The Captain, passengers
and crew were again terror-stricken, when suddenly he shouted, "See there! See! There she is: *My angel child!*" at the
same time pointing to the top of the highest mast. Instantly
every eye was fixed upon an apparition which we will discribe
to you in the Captain's own words, as we heard the narration at
his fireside, related in proof of his right to believe in the recognition of friends after death, he insisting that loss of identity
would amount to annihilation, and unjustly defraud the Chris-

tian of the promise made in Holy Writ as to Immortal Life. In corroboration of his faith he said, "Let me tell you a sailor's yarn, in a sailor's old-fashioned way:—Several years ago we lost the darling of our flock, a dear little girl. There existed a peculiar bond between the child and myself, different from any I have ever experienced, and after she was gone, the conviction grew until I could not shake it off that she was often near me, especially in times of extreme peril, and as my life was beset with dangers, I came after a while to regard my lost child as a guardian angel.

"One of the most wonderful manifestations of her presence occurred during a severe storm on Lake Michigan, which I was crossing, my vessel loaded with passengers and freight bound for Chicago.

"The day had been hot and sultry, and at nightfall when nearing the coast we were overtaken by a fearful storm and blown far north of our intended destination, narrowly escaping shipwreck.

"As the night advanced towards the morning, the wind and rain, the thunder and lightning ceased; and although I had been able so far to control the crew and passengers, as to work the ship for the best advantage, by the help of a man then a stranger to us all, but since become world renowned, and who seemed to to possess unbounded influence over them, thus preventing a fatal mutiny; I discovered at the moment when our prospects began to brighten, our minds to feel relief, that the ship had in the terrible gale sprung a leak, and to make matters worse a light near some dangerous rocks, outside the harbor we were trying to make, could not be seen. All on board were in despair, when casting my eyes Heavenward, I saw plainly as I see you now, my angel child standing on the tallest mast-head, her long golden hair streaming in the wind, her outstretched hand pointing imperatively towards the shore.

"Against the dark clouds her luminous body stood out bright and beautiful, the whole form distinctly visible, even the expression of her face.

"Hesitating not a moment I righted the ship about, changing entirely our former course, for I knew by other similar experiences there was safety only in following her guiding finger, although directed toward what appeared to be a solid wall and certain destruction, besides we could not be more sure of disaster if I obeyed her than we already were. On we went, bound straight for the rocky shore where apparently was not a seam

or crevice, the water coming through the strained timbers of
our doomed vessel at every plunge—we must be speedily saved
or surely perish.

"Still at the mast-head stood the luminous child with the
bright flowing hair, the imperative gesture; we were now close
upon the shore, when by the moonlight breaking through the
clouds, we could discern a fissure in the rocky wall, and coming
through a running stream, narrow but deep; we followed its
course and discovered not the well known harbor we had hoped
to enter, which was afterwards proven to have been beyond
our reach in our disabled condition, but we found inside that
rock bound coast, the snuggest haven that ever blessed a storm-
tossed mariner.   A harbor not then upon any chart and believed to have been entered for the first time by civilized navi-
gators as the result of this miraculous interposition of Providence.

"As the light broke over her the wonderful child gradually
faded from view; but" said the Captain, "nothing can convince
me that I did not see her really and truly, and I know she still
guards me when danger is near.

"We dropped anchor, making all safe as possible, just as the
morning sun broke in glory across our deck, and I am sure
every one on board was impressed to thank the God of the
living and the dead, (*dead as we say*) for our deliverance."

And thus after much tribulation, though storm-tossed,
angel-guided, our travelers reached the land, to them of golden
promise.

But the events of that memorable night were not soon
forgotten, and those who passed through its terror, gloom and
peril, ever after believed in the supernatural.   This belief colored all their lives, even the life of an unborn babe, whose
mother enduring these thrilling experiences, witnessing this
extraordinary phenomenon, transmitted to her offspring impressions culminating in destiny, and fulfilling the behests of Fate.

CHAPTER V.

CHICAGO.

Although not coming as they had expected directly into the harbor of Chicago, our friends, but a day's journey north of their destination, were too thankful for their miraculous deliverance and to touch land again, for complaint.

As the Captain did not advise further risk upon his badly strained vessel, a day was spent in disembarking, drying stores and equipage, and preparing for their journey in wagons to the much talked of and even then famed Chicago.

The second morning after the landing they arose with the sun, and while the men were loading and getting the teams ready the women prepared a delicious breakfast of fish caught from the treacherous lake, and some wild strawberries the children had gathered.

By six o'clock they were on their way, leaving regretfully behind the Captain and his crew, each wagon making room for an additional passenger or two, thus accommodating those who had reckoned upon reaching Chicago by boat.

. As Gertrude had become inseparable from her friend of the storm, Dr. Gascoigne invited him to a seat beside himself and little granddaughter, and the two men were soon conversing like old acquaintances, the child cuddled between them.

Over roads not the smoothest, they went jolting along, cheerfully catching at any trifling incident serving to break the monotony or raise the gay laugh, not a grumbler to be found— they from the start vetoed.

Eben was inclined at first to be rather cross, but Grandpa Gascoigne held him in check; he knew how sore were the hearts of his motherless girls, and he did not intend they should be unnecessarily annoyed.

Though this really affectionate father meant always to be indulgent and kind, judging from his standpoint, which was that men should consider, make up their minds and act; that it were unmanly spending time trying to persuade women, who had only to acquiesce in any arrangement made, without argument or comment, he did not realize the situation, or know of the secret grief, wearing visibly upon each of these so dear to him.

Eben, with more modern ideas as to womanly duties and privileges, and also as regarded a man's obligations towards his wife, and besides understanding the real difficulty, was aware that an injustice had been perpetrated, and the gentle, sensitive nature of his wife outraged beyond repair.

This knowledge disturbed and angered him; he was vexed with himself, but the manifestation came upon others.

Eben had become thoroughly disgusted with his folly, but was too proud to withdraw from the entanglement and of his own accord solicit his wife's favor and confidence; his unnatural position irritated him extremely, for he found himself in the dilemma of caring only for his lawful and lovely wife, while, from mere stubbornness at the last, he bestowed persistent attentions upon another, immeasurably her inferior in attractiveness; finally his annoyance was rendering him decidedly disagreeable. Even Gertrude noticed the changed disposition of her dearly loved papa, and sometimes shrank from his caresses, filling him with chagrin; and when a harsh word sent her sobbing to her mother, he was still more angry.

Only for the soothing influence of Grandpa Gascoigne, distressing scenes must have occurred in this estranged and miserable family; such a slight thing, a breath of unkindness and mistrust at first, can, growing and gaining strength until it becomes a great black cloud, fill all the air of domestic life with sorrow and dismay.

This trouble in the once happy family of Eben Grieveau could not keep brewing without attracting other eyes as sharp as Dr. Gascoigne's. Aunt Debby Jones, a good-natured woman who came with them from Barrytown, thought she saw something amiss, and undertook the task of setting matters right.

When the teams halted at midday she went around where Eben was moodily standing, and accosted him thus:

"I say, Eben Grieveau, why don't you go over there and cheer up that little wife of yours a bit? Anybody can see she needs it bad enough; she's the patientest, helpfulest woman of the whole lot, always doing something for somebody, but I declare to it, if she don't look like she'd left her heart in her mother's grave. And Lucille, too; why under heavens didn't that beau of hers come along? There is nothing in particular to keep him in Barrytown, *I* know, and he'd be a 'nough sight better off out West. If he ever intends to stand by the girl, now's the time, I should say."

And thus the well-meaning but injudicious woman spoke her mind.

Eben felt keenly the reproof, but as nothing could be said by way of excuse he did not reply, and this unwise meddling brought no benefit.

Aunt Debby's husband, a quiet man, as unlike as possible to his bustling wife, comprehended her blunder in exposing a carefully concealed wound, and remarked impatiently:

" There, now, Debby, hope you're satisfied, always putting your fingers into other people's pie, and only getting burnt for your pains."

Gertrude came along just then, and, hearing the word pie, said eagerly, " I want a piece of pie." Her childish mistake and Deacon Jones' remark set them all laughing, and good-nature was restored, if not peace. Hastily eating their luncheon without the pie—a luxury not to be secured until at their journey's end they could have their Yankee cooking-stoves in which to bake their Yankee pies—they jogged on again.

Just at sunset they came in sight of a square block-house, or fort—old Fort Dearborn—near the shore of the lake; and situated on either side of a sluggish river, whose perfectly flat, low banks seemed scarcely sufficient to hold the water in check, a few small, mean-looking houses.

The whole country, south, west, north, being flat and on a level with the immense body of water at the east, there seemed danger, should a storm arise, that houses, fort and people would be swept away.

For some distance back from the shore was loose sand— deep, well-nigh impassable for man or beast—a barren waste of sand.

One lone tree stood near the mouth of the river—a scrub oak, knarled and seamed and twisted—*only one;* and it stood there defying every vicissitude and change, through sunshine and through storm alike—*immovable*, though the rains and the winds beat upon it for years and years; stood as men and women sometimes stand and battle against fate—against the world; as Gertrude afterwards stood for the brother then unborn, against the *whole world*—battling *alone.*

After the sandy waste came the black loam of the prairie, and if there has ever been anything darker or muddier than this prairie loam after a heavy rain, our travelers had not seen it; neither has any one else to this day, unless it be modern scandal.

As the storm on the lake had been accompanied by rain,

there was a surfeit of mud in Chicago, also plenty of mosqui-
toes, and of course no end of Indians at that early day. The
new-comers found only a few white folks, but those came greet-
ing them so heartily, they seemed a host.

If anybody would make sure there exists a warm, throbbing
heart, full of sympathy for his fellows, in the breast of man,
let him go into a new country and he will be convinced. The
people will tell you they are glad to see you, and they'll mean
it, and prove it, too. Although many things about the country
and the town they had ·reached were extremely uninviting,
there was much that was pleasant and desirable.

The earnest welcome received comforted their hearts; the
broadness of the prairie gave a free sweep of air especially invigorating, calculated to banish the feeling of depression and
desolation which the barren flatness at first inspired.

After getting used to the absence of trees and hills, the
extent of view, the ever-changing color of the green expanse
caused by the shadows of the shifting clouds overhead, forced
the new-comers into conceding that a flat prairie might have a
beauty of its own not elsewhere to be found.

And the sunsets were different from any they had ever seen
—certainly unexcelled in magnificent glory.

And the lake—the ever-changing, rolling, tossing Michigan—was a continual joy.

Before leaving the little trading-post which has since become one of the great commercial centers of the world, our
friends became interested in the village and attached to the
people as they scarcely thought possible in so short a time.

They remained but one week, resting and making inquiries
as to the wisdom of investing in the swampy little town, instead
of going on as they had intended, and settling in the rolling
prairie country towards the north-western portion of the State
of Illinois.

Several of the party, with long-headed calculation, understanding the necessities certain to result in making this trading-
post a great mart of commerce and enterprise, decided to put
their money into the black, sticky corner lots offered them at
sums too small to be believed if told, and they, or their heirs, if
not squandering their birth-right, are now the millionaires of
the north-west; but the majority of these people unwisely concluded " the place would never amount to much, and even if it
did they wouldn't live in the nasty mud-hole for any consideration," and they left their golden opportunity behind them.

Our "aristocratic movers" partially deserted their wagons when in town, and stopped at the only hotel, or tavern, as it was called—the old Lake House—which until within a few years was left standing.

Everybody called to see them during their short stay, and among others they made the acquaintance of a peculiar man, who had before been a pioneer, and as he was about returning to the place they were going to, he gladly joined them.

You will like him when you know him well, notwithstanding his oddities, as our travelers did. .

Dr. Gascoigne and the congenial companion he found the story-teller of the storm to be, spent the few days of their stay in Chicago pleasantly together, and a bond was formed which each carefully cherished during the after years.

They did not meet again for a long time, when the same spontaneous kindness, the strength and originality of character, entranced Dr. Gascoinge as before; and towards this courteous gentleman of the olden time, refined, elegant, white-haired, a Frenchman by birth, by education an American—the man who had then risen from frontier life to be one of the first lawyers of his State—was strangely attracted—for Dr. Gascoigne was one of those who draw the best to themselves from the people with whom they are thrown.

Leaving the village and their friends behind—except the queer man before alluded to—our party started once more on their journey, over those wonderful prairies, commencing at Lake Michigan and stretching on, broken by occasional wood-bordered streams, to the great Mississipi, whose broad waters move quietly out to the sea; their final objective point being the village of Freelawn, situated mid-way of this vast country, on an insignificant river bearing the Indian name of Picka-tonica; and where circumstances occurred culminating in events which in their inevitable sequence moved the world, and with which some of the persons mentioned in this narrative, especially Myra, are inseparably connected.

CHAPTER VI.

THE ARRIVAL IN FREELAWN.

A queer individual indeed was the acquisition of our party during their short stay in Chicago. From an impediment of speech, between a stutter and a drawl, he had been dubbed by the nickname of " Tutty," and " Tutty " Swanson he was ever after called. But if talking troubled him, seeing did not, and what Uncle " Tut " failed to notice was of little account.

It happened that on the morning of leaving Chicago, he observed Eben Grieveau, after scolding his little girl until she cried, leave his wagon to the care of Dr. Gascoigne, while he took a seat beside brother John's wife, quite fascinating certainly in her way, a handsome brunette though somewhat coarse, surely the mouth was large, the lips not well formed and of that hard, decided cherry-ripe color, nothing soft, velvety or sweet about them, but just an aggressive bright red.

For amusement only, to pass away the dreary time, came Eben, thus he insisted in his thought, to sit and chat with the brother's wife, for he could not converse with Myra, as neither were able to think when together of anything but the one trouble which had separated them—namely his heartless, inconsiderate conduct in planning this removal without so much as consulting her wishes in the matter—and which he was determined to ignore.

The brother's wife was lively, full of fun and animal spirits, and in her company Eben soon forgot his discomfort.

He was dissatisfied with himself, and, as a consequence, with every one around him who served to remind of the unpleasantness which existed.

He could not endure Myra's patient sadness, or little Gertrude's clinging way with her mother, or Grandpa Gascoigne's shielding, protecting manner towards his girls; Eben's family life was becoming unbearable, and he persisted in looking upon the fictitious instead of the real cause.

From a beginning, which was simply asserting his just prerogative, without waiting to bother by explaining every reason which influenced him to the women folks—making up his mind and acting upon his convictions, as he had a perfect right

to do—so he reasoned, had grown this complete estrangement
between himself and wife of whom he still believed himself
very fond, not acknowledging the new enchantment.

How easily could this unwise husband have bridged the
gulf before forever too late, by conciliating and if necessary,
treating his wife with more than ordinary consideration; but he
was stubborn and would not; boasting in his mind that he had
given no adequate cause for the coldness which he could feel in
spite of Myra's effort to conceal it. He had chilled her love
and the flame was burning low. He had hurt her, and the
wound refused to heal, and as the woman's despondency increased, the more unkind became the man. For such a nature
as Eben Grieveau's, brooking no opposition, rebels with all its
force against the slightest manifestation of patient suffering
from a woman whom he knows he has wronged, be it ever so
little.

Women think quiet gentleness appeals to a man's chivalry,
but sometimes they are mistaken; for one who would deliberately wound the feelings of his wife, never cares very much for
a woman who allows herself to be stricken down, either figuratively or actually. When men lack tenderness they are sure to
be cowards.

Experience proves that both men and women of a certain
grade treat exacting, tyrannical partners with more consideration
and respect, often seeming to love them better, than they would
those of a self-sacrificing disposition.

Sad comment upon human nature, but true in many instances.

And thus it was that instead of being drawn together, these
two were thrown assunder, and into the widening breach came
another who, in no particular of person or character, could
be favorably compared with either.

Julia had never liked her husband's sisters over well—she
too fully realized her own coarseness in contrast with their refinement—and it was a triumph in which she did not conceal her
pleasure, that the handsome husband of Myra should seek her
side frequently as he did of late.

Her own consort had shattered his manhood by dissipation,
and was in no way satisfactory to her now, whatever he might
have been when they were married. It was mainly on his account—hoping to change the current into which he was fatally
drifting, by getting him away from bad associates—that Dr.
Gascoigne had undertaken the uprooting of his own life, seeking
a home in the far west, giving up those comforts to which he

had been accustomed and depriving himself of needed consolations in his old age.

As we have said, what Uncle Tut failed to see was not worth looking after; but it transpired that he soon discovered a considerable flirtation going on between Eben Grieveau and Julia Gascoigne; deciding then and there to watch their maneuvers for his own edification, which he did, with astounding results.

Flirting was not so alarmingly prevalent in those days as now, but was a pastime occasionally indulged in by both sexes, as has been the case since that unlucky day when the wily serpent beguiled Eve in the garden; sly old mother she, telling Adam they were only eating an apple together and cooly invited him to take some too—no wonder the race has gone to the bad with such a mother.

Tutty Swanson and Grandpa Gascoigne soon became fast friends, although as unlike as it is possible for men to be.

Uncle Tut was short and thick set, with stubbed hands and feet; hands that had done many a hard day's work, feet that had walked many a mile. His broad shoulders were surmounted by a small bullet head, a neck he was supposed to have but it was scarcely preceptible; the little round, hard head was circled by a crop of short, coarse, straight, reddish yellow hair just turning grey—not the soft, silky, auburn locks whose gleaming waves are so beautiful and rare, but the carroty yellow which is only repulsive.

Poor Uncle Tut was homely to the extreme, that his friends pitied while they loved him. His features were like those of the famous man in the moon; with eyes of the whitest, dullest blue-grey, utterly stupid, expressionless—blank---when he chose to have them so, which was whenever he did not intend any one should know what he was at.

When no one was noticing, those same eyes would sometimes give a sly twinkle. Uncle Tut had also a peculiar way of chuckling to himself.

But this twinkle of the eye, this quiet chuckle, was usually reserved for the exclusive satisfaction of the man himself, not shared with another except upon rare occasions with a specially favored friend—some one in whom he had perfect confidence. And the confidence of Uncle Tut was not easy to gain; those of his acquaintances who had been allowed to participate in the peculiar chuckle, upon whom had been bestowed one of the knowing glances, considered themselves favored, and that not lightly.

Grandpa Gascoigne was one of these—yes, Grandpa Gascoigne, the elegant, refined, courtly gentleman that he was, had already come to regard the condescension of this new acquaintance as an honor not to be despised.

For Tutty Swanson if an ignorant, uncultivated man, was shrewd and practical, possessing the faculty of concealing his ignorance and producing the impression of knowing more than he chose to tell. A fool often passes for a wise man by keeping his own secrets; but Uncle Tut was no fool either, as some people found out in the end.

Being quick to see and hear, if not to speak, he soon discerned the trouble that was brewing between Eben and his wife, and having a tender spot in his heart left there by the memory of his own dead wife and daughter, all the sympathy of his rough nature went out towards the motherless girls of Grandpa Gascoigne, especially to Myra, after he knew her hard lot.

While Eben was chatting gaily with Madam Julia, Uncle Tut had noted an observation for future reference, and when the first halt was made, he went over to the wagon where little Gertrude was still grieving at the unkind treatment she had received, and her mother was sadly trying to comfort her.

Uncle Tut seated himself beside Grandpa Gascoigne where he could look occasionally in the direction of Gertrude and Myra, and commenced talking in his peculiar style about the country they were passing over, the town they had left and the place to which they were going.

He had been out the year before and entered a "claim"; his wife and daughter having succumbed to the climate and the unaccustomed hardships during the summer, and soon both dying, he felt he could not endure the loneliness of his cabin life after they were gone, and had returned to his Eastern friends hoping to find consolation with his old neighbors; but he grew more and more restless, until finally a longing for the wild, stirring life he had found in the West took possession of and forced him back again.

Fortunately, as our travelers thought, who were journeying to the same section, for they availed themselves of his invaluable experience upon more than one occasion.

He was most excellent company, too, for if it was difficult for him to talk, he persisted until he made himself understood—the impediment he suffered from seeming to arouse his combativeness.

4

And just now Uncle Tut had something special to say for Grandpa Gascoigne, besides the topics of general interest which have been alluded to; he soon commenced:

"I sa—say, Mis-ter Gascoigne, you-your con-con-founded son-in-in-law we must be looking after a-a-bit. Th-that Mistress Ju-Julia Gascoigne an-and he are ca-carrying on to-to beat all dem-dem-na-tion."   •

And Uncle Tut's eyes twinkled, as he ended with his characteristic chuckle, but this time he added a dissatisfied grunt, as was his custom when angry.

While he had been getting out this sentence his eye was fixed upon little Gertrude, and he now reached up and forward, beckoning with the forefinger of his upturned palm, until he had attracted her attention, for he always made people look at him too, when he wished to have them.

The little one scrambled down from her mother's lap and over intervening obstacles until she reached the front seat where the two men were sitting, where she crowded herself contentedly between them. Rough and uncouth as the man was, he had succeeded in winning the child's affectionate trust, no less than her grandfather's confidence, and as she cuddled close down by his side, he, well pleased, placed his arm around her, continuing the conversation.

Not getting any further special attention the little girl finally volunteered a remark, and peering up quizzically into his face, she broke in abruptly, "Say, Uncle Tut, what makes your winkies so white?"

The two men, engaged in conversation, failed to notice the funny question, but Gertrude did not propose being put off without an answer; she saw something strange about Uncle Tut's eyes and wanted to know what made them look so different from other people's she had seen.

Waiting a moment she commenced again—"Uncle Tut, what makes your winkies so white?" Still no reply; and the persistent child reiterated her question at intervals, for a full mile of their journey. Securing no response, she at last snuggled her head down in his lap, and sleepily drawling out "win-kies-so white?" dropped off into blessed oblivion;—and to this day she does not know *why* Uncle Tut's "winkies" *were* so white, neither does any one else.

While Gertrude had been talking herself asleep, the two men conversed of the country they were going to, the climate, the streams, the occasional timber, the grand expanse of rolling prairie so admirably adapted for farming, the rare springs which were considered invaluable by the owners of the land upon which they were located—and many other things interesting to a newcomer.

Homesick Grandpa Gascoigne found himself cheered and encouraged by the glowing account Uncle Tut gave of all he knew about the land and the people. "You-'ll find every th-thing migh-ty rou-ugh and like-ly be sot ba-back mor-morn wonst by some-thing dif-er-ent fr-from what you-you've expected, but every bo-dy'll try to he-help you the best th-they know how, and after a-awhile you-you'll find you could-n't be be hired to stay East of Lake Mi-Michigan, if you under-take to go ba-back as I did."

The morning had not passed so very unpleasantly after all, although Dr. Gascoigne was much chagrined by the hint Uncle Tut had thrown out as to Eben and Mistress Julia.

When they halted for dinner and to feed and rest the horses, the anxious old father went to where Eben was alone, and lying stretched full length upon the soft, sweet, green sward, under a tree, the picture of easy content, but really seething with dis-satisfaction and annoyance; saying to his son-in-law, "Eben, as a true friend, I feel it my duty to warn you that your coldness, I will not say unkindness towards Myra, coupled with the marked attention you are pleased to show John's wife, is already attracting the attention of our fellow travelers. I believe you innocent of any wrong intention, but as Myra's father, I wish to say that I have the honor of my daughter's husband, no less than my son's wife at heart, and cannot quietly see things go-ing on, which are liable to detract from the fair name of either or both. Pardon me, Eben, if I seem to meddle, but I trust a word in time may not come amiss to you."

Eben started up angrily, and answered, " Thank you, sir, for your interest in me, but I desire you to understand that I am fully competent of attending to my own business, and prefer doing so in a manner that suits myself," and the irate man stalked ungraciously away, leaving good Dr. Gascoigne grieved and astonished beyond measure that the trouble was so much worse than he had imagined.

After a rest of an hour or more and partaking of a dinner as palatable as could be asked, everything being packed snugly away again, they started and jogged along as before until the glorious sunset admonished them to prepare for the night.

Gertrude was the first one to try the bed made for her in a

far corner of their wagon, close by mamma and grandpa, where
not a breath of wind could reach her should a change of weather
occur at night as was often the case after a warm day, when
the cold wind and rain accompanied by heavy thunder and
sharp lightning would sometimes wake the little girl from her
sound sleep, and cause her to creep still closer into her dear
mother's arms, no harm could come to her then she thought.

These rains frequently even in mid-summer made the sticky
prairie loam heavy for traveling, and in places exasperatingly
near together there were the deep sloughs which never disappeared in the dryest weather, and were at times almost impassable.

For this reason, principally, emigration was timed as near
the middle of the hot dry season as possible, and the dread
which a " mover " experienced when approaching one of those
swampy sloughs is incomprehensible to us who now rush over
these same prairies whenever convenience, business or pleasure
dictate at the rate of forty, fifty, even sixty miles an hour.

Our travelers of only a few years back were just one month
in journeying from near the middle of southern Michigan to
the center of northern Illinois, and their trip was considered
rapid and successful.

The day we have described was a sample of every other,
except that upon several occasions they found themselves stuck
fast in the mud holes of the sloughs which they encountered,
and this notwithstanding all their care in attempting to cross
safely. Often they were obliged partially to unload the wagons,
the women and children sitting patiently on trunks and boxes,
while the men brought rails from adjoining fences and sometimes horses from the settlers along the route, who willingly'
assisted those asking for aid in any emergency. Sometimes
hours were spent in prying out the horses and wagons, un-
loading and getting under way.

They had one of these experiences on the afternoon of the
last day of their journey, just in sight of their destination; the
village only hidden by a bit of rolling prairie, and there, between them and their Mecca, was a terrible slough which must
be crossed.

All had been cheered at the prospect of arriving before dark,
and having plenty of time to look around and prepare for their
first night in the place which was to be their future home.

It must be confessed they had expected their arrival would
make quite a sensation, their outfit being more than ordinarily

complete, and showing at a glance to the eye of the western settler that no trouble or money had been spared in securing every
comfort compatible with the circumstance of moving at all.

In this case, as in many another, when success seemed assured, disappointment came, and our friends·found what had
appeared to be only a "soft spot," as inconsequential sloughs
were termed, one of the very worst they had essayed to con-
quer in all their journey.

Elated at being so near the end of their tedious travels, they
neglected to use the precaution which they had learned to be
indispensible in crossing one of those diabolical black mud-holes.

Uncle Tut warned them, for he knew the place of old, but
not heeding, they drove gaily along without waiting to lighten
the load, until suddenly down went the horses up to their knees
in soft slush where the bottom had fallen out.

The whips were applied to no purpose, hallowing did not
help the matter at all, either; there they were, at three o'clock
the last afternoon fast in the mud. What wonder if every man,
woman and child was thoroughly disgusted and exasperated.

The women sat on the unloaded trunks and scolded the
children and cried; the men lashed their horses, and one or two
swore; no doubt every one of them felt like it. Eben was one
of those who refrained from swearing, but he wished in his
heart that he had never started from Barrytown.

At last sense and patient reason gained the supremacy, the
women and children became quiet and reconciled to the situation, the men unhitched the horses and pried them out with the
rails, also the wagon wheels; and adding fresh teams to their
own jaded animals, with combined strength and effort succeeded
in hauling the wagons out of the hole; dragging them across
by a slightly different route from the one they had at first
chosen, the people, children as well, being obliged to walk
across, although the rains of the night before had rendered the
road, if such it might be designated, very "muddy." The men
had besides to carry all the heavy articles of baggage across as
best they could.

Just at nightfall all were reloaded, and, tired, wet with dew,
which fell upon them as they waited, bedraggled, discouraged
and uncomfortable beyond description, our forlorn travelers
came into the small village of twenty houses all told—no more
—the village which was to be the only home the majority of
that party should in the future know—the home where they
were to live and from which they were to be buried.

Immediately when it was known that some " movers " had arrived from the east, every one hastened to meet and welcome them. And this means they took them to their houses, to their tables, and shared with them their beds—that they opened wide their hearts, their homes and in true western fashion " took the strangers in "—sharing all they had with them.

The dreary, homesick, hungry travelers were soon provided with food, and made comfortable for the night; the worn horses were not forgotten.

A public house had not yet been built for the accommodation of people coming to this new town, but no stranger was allowed to feel himself such for very long among the genial settlers of those early days.

Patiently enduring every hardship, carrying many heavy loads of sorrow, our fathers and mothers labored to establish homes, and lay the foundation of our present prosperity.

Although the exterior sometimes became hard and rough, they somehow kept the heart tender and the feelings fine.

CHAPTER VII.

JULIA'S SCHEME.

The morning after their arrival in the little town of Free-lawn, our friends were out early, even before the sun had dissipated the fog which arose dense and wet from the broad prairie as far as the eye could reach, everywhere covering and hiding from view the green expanse beneath – wood-bordered stream, farm-houses, all except the nearest objects.

It was a strange sight, differing from any they had ever seen before, imparting the feeling of having gotten above and away from the world. As the sun rose in the Heavens his rays penetrated the clouds of mist, until, permeated by a rosy hue, they were wafted upward on the morning air and finally vanished.

When the fog lifted from the landscape, a break here and there revealing the verdure below, the effect, looking off over the vast prairie, was most enchanting, resembling a sea dotted with green islands.

Very beautiful was the poisonous, malarial fog, and deadly, as our friends learned to their cost. The old settlers cautioned them against again indulging in such early rising: "You must not do it, you'll have the ague sure if you do; but must stay in doors night and morning until the fog is gone. It's the only way for new comers to escape, and even with this precaution you may have it."

Besides the beauty of the misty sea dotted with islands, the suffering of the ague and many other things new to them, our friends found in this very small village a strange medley of people.

There were a few ladies and gentlemen whose equal can scarcely be met with even now, there was also the gossip who meddled with everybody's business; the rough, uncultivated bore; the loud-mouthed, sanctimonious hypocrite, who thanked the Lord daily that he was not as were other men; the dishonest, pettifogging lawyer; the doctor, who never ought to have been a doctor; all the discordant and disagreeable elements to be found in older and larger towns, no less than the people capable of doing well their part and whose influence was help-

ful, improving and ennobling; those of different vocations and
degrees of refinement, who, for one cause and another, had
seen life in the communities and surroundings they had left to
be for them unprofitable and uncongenial.

The society of the village of Freelawn was gathered from
miles around, and on Sunday everybody came to meeting; it
was the only change to be had from their week-day life.

Before the Court House was erected these meetings were
conducted at the houses of one, and another of the more respectable and comfortably quartered settlers, among whom were our
friends the Gascoignes and Grieveaus; after that they were
held in the Court House, until in the progress of events a
Methodist meeting house was built, and when the place was
recognized as old and established a Presbyterian church, then a
Baptist, and finally a *very* high-toned Episcopalian—" *The
Church* "—but a number of people were born in our little
village, and died, and went to Heaven or some other place, before " *The Church* " came along or its clergyman arrived.

Ere this happy consummation of church building and a
settled ministry, these people, who had been accustomed to
regular attendance upon religious services in their eastern
homes, uprooted as they felt themselves to be, torn from old
and dear surroundings, would not willingly have dispensed
with the comfort derived from meeting together—singing,
praying and exhorting one another.

Ofttimes those men and women through much tribulation, ·
developed a saintliness of character which we search for almost
in vain in these latter days of frivolity, worldliness and self-
seeking.

One dear, white-haired, sweet-faced woman, our motherless
girls, Myra and Lucille, made the acquaintance of very soon,
who from the hour of their meeting became a true friend to
them—Mother Brewster she was called throughout all that
section. In a short time after their arrival both Myra and
Lucille were attacked with chills, and immediately Mother
Brewster was on hand with good cheer and advice, as was her
custom when anybody was sick or in special trouble.

Grief weighed heavily upon them now that the excitement
of the journey was over, and had much to do with their falling
an easy prey to the malarial climate.

They both had the chills regularly, but for an unaccountable
reason or for *no reason*, their sickness occurred upon alternate

days; some people do not believe in Providence but little Gertrude did.

"God will keep your shakes away to-day, Mamma, it is Aunt Lucille's turn," she would say.

It seemed hard that these two who were least able to bear it, and were sadly tried in other ways, should be the ones to have this affliction.

The brother's wife was never stronger or happier in her life, and she continued her desperate flirtation with Eben, partly for the excitement and the spite, but also because she really liked Myra's handsome husband better than she had ever any one before, and fully as much as her selfish nature was capable of caring for any one.

Poor Myra, pale, weak, forlorn, was in no condition to compete for her husband's favor with the robust, jolly, red-lipped beauty; for a beauty she would be called, possessing a certain attractiveness which might take temporary hold of a man dissatisfied with or estranged from his wife.

And Myra did not act the part of wisdom; she should by every means have concealed her coldness from her husband; even though the hurt was sore, the wound deep, she should have sedulously kept it from his sight, perhaps after a time it might have healed, for true love will accomplish wonders.

At any rate Eben would not recognize her present mood, and had no patience with his wife, persisting in feeling that *she* was changed, refusing to acknowledge *he* had given any real cause for the estrangement.

Long years after as he looked back, remembering her pitiful white face those days he blamed himself—oh! how bitterly!

Myra's mistake was in brooding over her grief until she lost her wonted vivacity, and consequently the power of pleasing her husband; had she crowded down her sensitiveness, putting on a kind, cheerful air, he would after awhile have himself realized how much dearer she was to him than any other, and shown his regret by his actions if not in words.

Such a course might have cured the disposition for straying, which all the circumstances of the case now encouraged.

Men being fickle and prone to wander, it behooves wives as well as maidens that they use every endeavor in keeping any influence they may have over those they love.

Dissatisfied husbands and lovers then, as now, had no difficulty in coming across women quite ready to go fully half way in pleasure with men who belonged to other and better women than themselves.

Myra learned this when too late.

An incident here occurred which, with a hint from Uncle Tut, started her thinking seriously of the situation, and she determined upon going about the business of regaining her lost place in her husband's heart forthwith.

This is how it came about.

Shortly after arriving in Freelawn, finding no suitable home, the men of the family, with the help of a carpenter, an old settler, had erected a comfortable house, also a shed for the horses, and completed arrangements for living through the winter.

The building being store and dwelling combined, was on a corner, giving one front for the store on the main street, and one for the dwelling which was a continuation built on the side street, less traveled than the other.

The goods arriving were snugly placed upon the shelves of the store, which being patterned after the one they had left in Barrytown, contained everything necessary for the comfort of man in the line of merchandise.

Grandpa Gascoigne, Eben, Myra, Lucille, little Gertrude, John and his wife Julia, besides Uncle Tut, took possession of the new home with thankful hearts.

Uncle Tut declared he could not live alone in his cabin, even though he lost his "claim," and he had become so helpful in every way, Dr. Gascoigne's family were very glad of having him with them through the winter. In the spring he might feel better about the cabin and the claim.

Whenever he would say anything about going away, Gertrude, putting her little fat arms around his rough old neck, and snuggling her curly head on his shoulder, would insist, "she couldn't spare her own dear old Uncle Tut, not a bit."

And thus Providence, or Fate, ordained that he should remain through the winter with his friends, a decision which changed the current of all their lives—the affairs of a great nation as well—a decision the results of which are not even yet fully foreseen.

Myra and Lucille, so it happened, busied themselves with the housework and the care of the child, and with many kindnesses from grandpa and Uncle Tut, who were not so busy as John and Eben, they managed to accomplish the necessary work between them.

Julia being the well and strong one, volunteered to do the
washing and ironing. She said, "she'd rather have a good day's
work and be done with it, but could not endure puttering around
all the time."

The fact was she had a scheme she was particularly anxious
of carrying out, and which would take her away from the
kitchen, where Myra and Lucille were mostly occupied, and into a far part of the house. About this time, very obligingly, as
a cold winter was prophesied, Julia offered to tie some comforts,
and make some quilts for the beds. The large front room over
the store not being much used, Uncle Tut sleeping there, but
being unoccupied during the day, this place by mutual consent
was devoted to the quilting and tieing, when the work had
been suggested. The apartment was warmed by the heat from
a sheet-iron drum, connected with the immense box-stove, large
enough for holding cord wood, being in the store below, and
by the pipe passing through the floor into the drum and thence
into the chimney of the room, producing an even temperature
night and day.

In this secluded spot, away from the noise of the family,
there afterwards occurred illness long and grievous, nigh unto
death—even death itself—*and a birth, which had better have
been a death.*

A memorable room, filled with sad, gloomy histories connected with never to be forgotten tragedies. Myra's unhappiness was at last rendering her very restless, but no one suspected how much she was suffering, outwardly she remained so
calm, so sweet and patient.

Even Lucille failed to notice the tempest, the whirlwind,
the tornado of passionate longing and regret which was rack-
ing her sister's inmost soul.

Lucille was aware Myra did not take kindly to their new,
rough life any more than did she. They were both too utterly
disheartened and sick much of the time, and incidents which
would have amused, had the sisters been well and happy, now
seemed dreary and uncomfortable.

Lucille knew Myra talked longingly when she conversed
at all, which was seldom now, of going back to the old home
and to the friends they had left, but she had no idea of the
turmoil agitating her sister's mind and heart. Her own trouble
absorbed her whole attention, and perhaps dulled her perceptions.

While busy with her work, Myra would partially forget,

but a delicate woman cannot be incessently busy, neither will
the society of a child compensate the heart for the idol lost
either by dethronement or death, or cure its utter loneliness.

Myra felt that the work did her good, the prattle of little
Gertrude was a relief, but there were times when all failed to
subdue her unhappiness, and it seemed she could not endure
her life or her surroundings another moment. She sometimes
feared she should lose control of herself—should go wild.

As she wandered from room to room looking dejectedly
from the windows, she was conscious of an almost uncontrollable impulse to spring through, and fly away—far away—from
all the trouble.

She longed to get back to dear old Barrytown and throw
herself upon her mother's grave and weep her life out there.

This intense desire to get away from her surroundings—to
fly away—*anywhere*—only to get away—was increasing until
it was becoming an actual torture.

Myra rarely sought her husband's presence now, and he
did not seek her, he had found more entertaining companionship, at least for the time being, and at last his anger and resentment towards his wife were taking the form of antipathy.

Marvelous as it may seem, this man who had been a loving
husband, was so annoyed by his wife's persistent sadness, which
he was pleased to construe as a reproach to himself, that really
he would have been glad never to have seen her more.

Her wan face nettled and exasperated him beyond measure,
he could not drive her from his mind a moment except when
intensely occupied by business or pleasure—because he still loved
his wife, and knew in his heart he was not doing right by her,
but he was too proud to yield and make the first advances towards a reconciliation. Little did he realize the bitter sorrow
he was storing up for himself and for her, by his unreasonable
willfulness.

Poor Myra did not understand her own condition, she only
knew it was now becoming impossible to overcome her sadness
and restlessness, strive as she would—she was a mystery unto
herself.

If she could have appreciated the effect of all she was passing through—of all the happenings—if her husband had been
apprised of the facts, Fate might yet have been cheated of her
prey—but ignorance spoiled lives then, as ignorance spoils many
a life to-day.

The fall rains were now rendering the roads impassable, at

least for women, and the necessity of remaining indoors had increased Myra's nervous irritation almost to the pitch of frenzy. She *was* at last losing self-control, and Lucille was surprised at the unusual harshness several times manifested towards little Gertrude. Soon Myra must have developed symptoms which would have aroused the family as to the state of her health, and a dire calamity and the grief of a lifetime might possibly have been prevented.

But just here an unlooked for occurrence brought her condition to a crisis, and changed the whole situation.

Of course the quilts and the comforts at which Julia was working industriously, must be marked, which was done with a chalked cord held by two persons one on either side of the frames, holding tightly, and when all was ready in place, one lifting the cord and letting it fall suddenly, a mark would be left for the guidance of the stitches.

Uncle Tut noticed that Mistress Julia often came down into the store for Eben to go up and help mark her quilt; sometimes a rap on the floor would be her signal, and that Eben seemed ready at any moment to leave what he was doing and obey her call, and he did not hurry back either.

One day Eben was gone so long that Uncle Tut thought he'd go up to his room and change his coat—while he took an observation; opening the door without knocking, (for why should he knock at his own door?) he surprised the marker, "taking toll" from the quilter over the frames.

The lips, yes—brow, cheeks, neck of the red-ripe beauty were even redder than usual, when Uncle Tut opened the door—so were those of Myra's husband.

Eben got himself downstairs to his work as quickly as possible, neither of the men saying a word, and Eben entirely in doubt as to whether a discovery had been made or not.

Uncle Tut had seen enough to cause alarm as to the state of affairs between Eben and Mistress Julia, and made up his mind he'd do a little scheming himself, and if necessary give Myra a hint, perhaps also Grandpa Gascoigne, before it was too late for reclamation.

He contrived after this to have Gertrude in the quilting room as much of the time as possible, upon the pretext of its being a nice, warm place for her to play, now that the weather and the ground were unfit for her to be out of doors, but Uncle Tut kept an eye out and was getting more worried every day.

He had lately found Myra several times wandering alone from room to room, looking strangely, he thought, gazing with an expression almost desperate through the windows, over the broad and now dreary prairies, which stretched as far as the eye could reach; and once or twice he had seen her throw up her arms suddenly, press her hands convulsively upon her head and rush from the window with a cry, almost a shriek, away into another room, far from the family.

Said Uncle Tut at last to himself: "I'll speak to *somebody* this very day, to Grandpa Gascoigne or to Lucille, perhaps to Eben."

But he had come to dislike Eben so thoroughly, he could not endure to talk with him about anything, much more such a matter.

Finally he concluded, "I'll give Myra just a hint and let her manage her husband as she thinks best." And Uncle Tut taxed his brains for another day as to how he should communicate in such a manner as to shock Myra as little as might be what he wanted her to know, namely, the danger she was in of losing her husband absolutely, unless something was done to break up the intimacy between himself and Mistress Julia.

After all the delay and cogitation, when he did tell her it was in the clumsiest manner, abruptly, without immediate intention of doing so; exactly as people nine times out of ten approach a delicate subject.

He had made an errand up to his room, where, as often before, Eben and mistress Julia were having a gay time laughing and chatting (to say nothing of anything worse) over the marking and the quilting; coming down exasperated, he was yet more annoyed at finding Myra, who had just finished her morning work, sitting listlessly, tired, pale and half sick, her hands folded hopelessly in her lap, and tears falling quietly from those sweet violet eyes.

Not one word of repining had she uttered through all her sorrow; she was too heart-broken for complaint. As Uncle Tut looked upon the dear little woman he felt like shooting somebody, but, instead, he marched up in front of Myra and stammered out: "I—I say, Myra—Grie—Grieveau,—quit that, an—and go up and lo–look after that hus–band o' yo–yourn;" and off he went, knowing that at the last he had blundered and stumbled head foremost into the hidden trouble, making matters even worse than they were before.

Alas! that Uncle Tut had not realized the extent of the mischief he was doing, for his thoughtless precipitation may surely be blamed that a beautiful life was wrecked, destroyed; yes, more than one, more than two—many more—before the end was reached.

At first Myra was bewildered by Uncle Tut's strange speech. She had not believed her husband really cared for the society of such a coarse-grained woman as she knew her brother's wife to be; she had never suspected his honor or doubted his truth; she had hoped that eventually he would be touched by her patient sadness, and that somehow they would be reconciled; would understand each other, and be once more happy as they had been before the dreadful estrangement. She knew Eben neglected her, and spent more time chatting with Julia than he ought, but the thought that her husband would desert her for another had not entered her mind. And such another!—utterly heartless and frivolous, not to say unprincipled—perhaps immoral!

The blow was crushing, and, coming unexpectedly, nearly took away her breath; but as a hard fall, a hurt on the head, or a severe shock, to an insane person will sometimes restore reason when all else fails, so Uncle Tut's abrupt hint had the effect of bringing Myra to her senses, and she resolved to put away her despondency, giving her whole and immediate attention to the object of regaining her lost place in her husband's affections.

Leaving Gertrude in charge of Aunt Lucille, who, after having passed through the ordeal of a chill, was feeling somewhat better now that the fever was coming on, but not at its height, Myra acted upon Uncle Tut's advice, and betook herself to the quilting-room without delay.

It was a terrible mistake—weak, heart-sick, worn woman—she overestimated her strength sadly when she essayed to go up for her recreant husband.

Her only thought was that something she loved more than her life was drifting away from her arms, beckoned on by a "will o' the wisp" as false as it was alluring.

Save her husband she must at any hazard; she would go directly to the room where she knew the red-lipped, unprincipled siren was busy weaving her charms about him, and, making some excuse, get him to come down with her, and henceforth she would devote every energy of her life to her husband's pleasure; he should lack for nothing in the power of woman to bestow.

How bitterly now she blamed herself for her cold, exacting reserve; that she had not ignored self entirely; abnegated her own personality, if need be, in the effort to retain her husband's love. She knew now, when she feared it might be too late, that she had not understood a man's nature more than ahd he a woman's, that the mischief *was indeed beyond repair.*

CHAPTER VIII.

MYRA'S DISCOVERY.

Myra's imagination had not pictured what her eye beheld through that opened door—her own husband, her life's darling, his arms around another woman, his lips pressed to hers!

Unhappy Myra—one moment she stood spell-bound—then fell headlong upon the floor—not a sound, not a moan escaped her, she lay as one dead.

Instantly Eben disengaged himself, more angry than he could express that his wife should have discovered his folly. He lifted her in his arms and placed her on Uncle Tut's bed.

Both Mistress Julia and himself hastened to use every known means for the restoration of the wronged woman to conciousness. At last she breathed, she opened wide her beautiful eyes, but stared vacantly in her husband's face.

Overtaxed in body, distressed in mind as she had been for months past, having besides the unfavorable climate to contend with, and more than all, a dear, sweet, cherished secret which only mothers can understand, and which she had carefully concealed, even from her husband, feeling in oversensitiveness that he did not care for her now, but hoping by a glad surprise to win him to her side again; overburdened little woman, what wonder if heart, strength, life, failed her.

For weeks and months after that day those vacant eyes when they opened at all, only stared reproachful from their sunken sockets, while the thin lips muttered in delirium of things which no one but the guilty husband, Mistress Julia, and Uncle Tut could comprehend. Eben and Julia vied with each other in their ministrations. Grandpa Gascoigne, sister Lucille and John were surprised and thrown off their guard by the unexpected devotion displayed on the part of those heretofore deemed incapable of deep affection, and regretted the supposed unjust estimate of their characters in times past; especially did John blame himself, thinking he had not fully appreciated his wife; for long before the project of moving west was broached she had come to be regarded by him as the embodiment of selfishness and heartlessness.

He had been, when very young, thrown in her way and cap-

5

tivated by the pronounced though decidedly animal style of
beauty, married hastily, neglecting consultation with his father
and sisters; the mask was soon dropped, the illusion roughly
thrown away, and the young husband found in the place where
should have been a wife tender and true, a loud-voiced, heartless, exactingly selfish woman, one of those who care for a
husband but as a provider for their wants.

He being of the same fine nature which his sister possessed,
inherited from both parents, soon, from having his sensibilities
daily shocked, became reckless, dissipated and hopeless; a tithe
of the man he should have been, and was now fast becoming a
besotted drunkard, health, ambition, self-respect almost gone.

But at the perception of apparent goodness in his wife
which perhaps had been overlooked, he was ready to take her
lovingly in his arms, trying once more, and be a man worthy
of a true woman.

Although a mischief had accrued for which no earthly
power could now find a harmless remedy; naught but the death
of an unborn babe could checkmate Fate, and it was forever too
late for the cure of all the evil which had resulted from the sad
mistakes; yet just here was a place in the lives of this badly
mixed family, where, had they gotten hold of the true end of
the tangled thread, the gordian-knot might have been untied,
the skein of their destiny unravelled, the broken woof reunited,
and a garment of beauty, the work of sweet charity, woven
from their daily lives, gently covering from view the past,
lovingly enfolding the present, bestowing comfort and peace
instead of the sorrow to all, the remorse to those in the wrong
which was coming irretrievably upon them.

Repentance, restitution, prayer unceasing, might have lifted
prostrate Myra from her sick bed, and possibly brought the
good angels to bear the little shattered life tenderly away in
arms of love to its Paradise home, where restoration comes to
all who desire the attainment of that purity and goodness of
which misfortune or inheritence has defrauded them here.
Restoration—Paradise—Joy—to the innocent unborn babe, and
to those who meekly, trustingly as little children enter in,
patiently waiting until Christ shall send to their sin-sick souls
His ministering spirits—Chastisement—Purgatory — knashing
of teeth, to those who defiantly ignore the true, the right, the
just, seeking their own aggrandizement.

The Lord's helpful angels coming evermore alike to the just
and to the unjust at repentant, suffering humanity's call, coming

in answer to prayer; for prayer is to blessing what the bursting longing in the heart of the bud, bound tightly leaf by leaf in waxen coldness, is to the sun benignantly waiting ready to impart warmth and comfort, while the imprisoned bud strives to absorb its invigorating beams; until, at last, penetrated by the blissful life-giving rays, bursting forth in eager aspiration, leaf by leaf is unfolded, expanded, giving back hues rich in the radiance of glowing happiness; and thus are both filled with ineffable joy, for it is even more blessed to give than to receive.

But the desire must precede benediction, mark the injunction, "Ask and ye shall receive."

No man's prayer can darken the sun, or cause the rain to fall perhaps, the Ruler of the Universe chosing good for the whole creation, as seemeth best, but special need causes special asking, and special disease requires special treatment—hence prayer as a means of benefit—prayer! whereby even the behests of Fate, the edicts of destiny may be overruled.

Uncle Tut, with his unfathomable, know-nothing grey-eyes, saw all that was going on, and knew what it meant, but earnestly as he longed to set matters right, he felt himself unable, and a Higher Power he did not invoke. Prayer was not in his creed, the thought was to him incomprehensible.

And the stoney mill of Fate kept grinding, round and round, a steady, slow, but sure and unrelenting grind.

The one thing which Uncle Tut could, and did do, was to tend by Myra's bed-side constantly—literally night and day, dozing occasionally in the old fashioned straight backed rocking chair Myra had brought from the Eastern home.

Eben and Mistress Julia were not more vigilant, much as they feared exposure from Myra's delirium.

Fortunately for them it was mainly of the low, muttering kind, in which words can only be distinguished with the greatest difficulty. A person not knowing what was in her mind, could not understand her at all; but Eben knew and Mistress Julia, and Uncle Tut, although he kept so still.

Poor Myra lay now day after day, with shaven head drawn back deep into the crushed pillows—shorn of all those rippling waves of golden brown hair, her eyes closed, half open or staring vacantly, sometimes appealingly, then again wildly, the thin, parched lips muttering so pitifully, so low, only *they* could understand:

"My darling, *oh!* my darling! how *could* you do it? *How could you do it?*"

"Come back to me, husband dear, I'll be *so* good, I really will, if you'll only come to me."

Then opening wide her glassy eyes, raising her trembling hands, white and wan, reaching for his face, she seemed to be stroking it tenderly, muttering; "Eben, dear, Myra's sorry she vexed you, Myra'll be good, Myra loves you—just the same."

And then in a sudden frenzy, raising herself with unlooked for strength, trying to strike an imaginary foe, screaming now in wild fury, "Get away you serpent! She's got her coils around him, her fang is on his throat. Take her away—she'll drink his blood! Take her away—he's mine—he's mine! Let me kill her—let me kill her!"

And falling back exhausted into the strong arms of Uncle Tut or Grandpa Gascoigne, or of her sorrowful husband, who had each or all been trying to hold her, she would sink again into a stupor, breathing heavily with half shut eyes, and shaven head drawn back deep into the wet pillows.

These attacks of frenzy were rare, and came when they thought her better, and she seemed almost to *know her attendants.* Those who were aware of what was in her mind, noticed that they occurred, if at such times her eyes settled upon Mistress Julia, and she, guilt stricken, learned to keep out of the sick woman's sight, fearing an outbreak.

Twice during this long, memorable illness, Myra seemed to rally, and then a relapse would come, discouraging those who loved her so well—but not once did she regain her reason—not until the sad wail of a little new born babe was heard in that chamber, where the mother had lain so long prostrate in the valley of the shadow of death—in the shadow, but not overcome—for not yet was her mission fulfilled.

The little boy-baby was tenderly cherished, day by day, his feeble life watched over, and the flickering flame gently fanned into a stronger, steadier glow, for was he not to fill the place of the first-born, the dearly loved one, whose grave they had left behind nearly a year ago?

Even Eben was proud and elated at the thought of another heir to bear his name, and his heart warmed with somewhat of returning affection towards his broken wife. Had Myra recovered rapidly, regaining her former health and buoyancy of spirit—chief among the charms which had first attracted him—Eben might have been entirely weaned from his new fancy, perhaps, but she remained in that sick room nearly a year, and there are few men whose fidelity can endure such a test.

After the novelty of the new baby wore off, and Myra still continued an invalid, both wife and child requiring much care, he began to consider his visits to the sick room as annoying episodes in his daily life. Soon they were so far apart as to cause remark from the members of the family, and finally from the gossips of the little town.

As for Myra, she had been near *death's* door, and could now be reconciled to life, even though accompanied with sorrow and much tribulation.

From the day she had seen another woman in her husband's arms, her heart-strings had loosed their hold of him—she did not fully realize this, but such was the fact.

The babe being very delicate, absorbed her attention, and the poignancy of grief gradually wore away, although at times her love struggled with terrible violence for the possession of its lost idol.

If she could have filled the vacancy as men do with another object, it would have eased her suffering, but she could not; even the devotion she felt for her children failed to close the gaping wound in her sore heart—nothing can compensate a true woman for a lost love.

Little Gertrude's quiet, gentle ways, and her cheerful prattle, were much company and comfort to her lonely mamma. Sister Lucille was her attendant and constant companion, but not even to her did this loyal wife confide what she had seen on that day, when the whole family had been summoned to her bedside, scarcely leaving it for weeks and months after. Whatever her husband might do or leave undone, his wife would not betray him; with her, come weal or woe, his secret should be safe.

Myra, as does many another heart-broken mother, clung to life for her children's sake. She tried steadfastly to overcome her weakness, and lived on for a time, growing lovelier each day, to all who knew her; especially to the sad old father, Lucille and Gertrude, the memory of her last days on earth was as the dream of an angel's presence.

CHAPTER IX.

MYRA'S STRANGE CONDITION—EBEN'S TROUBLE.

While Myra was confined a close prisoner all those weary months in the seclusion of her chamber, the world outside did not cease from moving on. Many changes occurred in the village, new people kept coming, several houses were erected and every living thing was stirring in this growing western town.

One of the questionable improvements was the establishment of a grocery for the sale of liquors, containing also a drinking bar, on the corner just above Eben's store, he dealing only in general merchandise.

Dr. Gascoigne had been appointed post-master, and the idea of putting up a Court House was being broached. A tavern or hotel had been actually built; one of the long, wide upper rooms, ordinarily containing a dozen or more beds for the accommodation of travelers, could, when occasion required, be turned into a ball-room, and the sitting room upon the first floor was used on Sundays for holding the meetings before mentioned; a needed convenience most surely was the tavern.

When the stage, drawn by four horses, even six, driving up to the front with a flourish of long whip and loud tin horn, after leaving the great leathern mail bag with Dr. Gascoigne at the post office, the passengers alighting upon the broad tavern stoop, all the people of Freelawn felt that they were the inhabitants of quite a town.

Gertrude delighted in going behind the counter and watching Grandpa while he sorted the mail. She was a pet with the people who came to the store, and seldom did anyone neglect asking the child the oft repeated query: "How is your mother to-day, little one?" Her invariable answer being: "As well as usual, thank you." For in Myra's condition there was no material change, although the winter had passed and the spring come again.

Not the clean, sweet spring-time they had enjoyed in the pretty eastern village, with its stone walks, graveled roads, magnificent shade trees, velvet lawns, flower beds, roses and shrubs; they missed all these sadly and the blossoming fruit trees, too, besides many a comfort and joy. Myra, in her lonely

sick room, would sometimes forget-herself, and imagine she
could smell the fragrant apple blossoms of the old tree which
had grown by her window in the Barrytown home; the exquisite perfume from the delicate pink roses of the sweet-brier
bush her own hand had planted, came to her as a reality: she
was sure it was not the scent of the wild crab-apple, or the
thorn bush, although they were lovely too, in their way, growing near the kitchen and wafted up to her on the fresh prairie
air, and she could hear the bell pealing from the tower of the
church over by the grave yard, where she had left the dead
mother and the child. Nothing could convince her these impressions were not real, dear little woman, her head was not
quite right yet.

Doubtless, had she lived in these latter days of wonderful
scientific pretension, she might have been consigned to the tender
care of some asylum superintendent, as a victim of insane delusion. A man, astonishingly wise, who having his own cranky
eyes set corner-wise, could see a lunatic in every fifth person he
chanced to meet; a man who it will be remembered, gave this
sort of testimony in a celebrated criminal trial, not many years
ago; a man with most scholarly air intensified by the high,
white forehead and piercing black eyes set toward the shapely
nose with the peculiar inward slant alluded to, and a habit of
always looking down at something he seemed to be holding,
and closely studying.

Should he glance up at you as you talk to him, it is only
with an amused quizzical expression, as though he said,"You
may know something, but *I* have the whole subject right here
in my hand."

You speak of mankind, meaning an animal to be sure, of
the genus homo, but an animal with a soul, an animal who
can think, who can love, who can plan and act intelligently,
who can look forward to a future life, where all thinking, loving,
planning, acting is bliss forevermore. This wise Doctor stares
at you with an incredulous, almost contemptuous manner, and
asks, "Will your man of the future world have bones, blood,
nerves, flesh, heart, brain, if not I know nothing about him.
I have a man here before me on this dissecting table, I have cut
his flesh, sawed his bones, torn his nerves, stripped. his brain,
uncovered his heart—know all about him through and through."
You answer, "Sir, you know nothing or nearly nothing, about
the animal called man, for all that. You have not caused his
blood to flow, or a nerve to quiver, you have only been handling

what he formerly inhabited; him you have not touched. If *he* were here, I could cause his heart to throb, his blood to course through his veins, electric thought to flash from his brain through all his nerves, 'till they should tingle with the pain of wild desire, by just one look of my eye, one touch of my hand."

The cold, earth-groveling scientist stares at you again, but only a sidelong, soulless stare, not the quick, honest recognition of spirit squarely meeting spirit in debate, and he concludes, "here's another lunatic, another of the *one in five*, we must see about this, and forthwith confers with an enemy he knows of, also a fellow scientist, (reduced to the necessity of managing a private asylum since being removed after an investigation from the state asylum) and soon has the satisfaction of acquiring notoriety as well as fees for himself and friend—the asylum superintendent—in a celebrated insanity trial. For the less real insanity in the victim, the more famous the trial becomes; occasionally, by rare adroitness, are the prosecutors outwitted; but to-day, in free America, an individual has more reason to dread being placed upon trial for insanity, than if for murder, so little do we understand this subject, so fearful are we when once the cry of *"mad dog,* catch him, chain him!" is raised.

Had gentle, sensitive, loving Myra, been subjected to the inhuman treatment now common in similar cases; the mere fact of being separated from her children, deprived of the care of those who loved her, missing her accustomed surroundings, the thought of being deserted by friends because they did not wish to be troubled, the knowledge that night after night she was under lock and key, helpless in a prison cell, where, cry and moan and call as she might, no one would come at her bidding, unless perhaps the attendant—prison-keeper—who should be placed over her, might from inherent kindness of heart heed her distress, bring a matter of option with no one to know, no one to tell; the consciousness that any neglect, unkindness or cruelty might be practiced, and complaint, when made, regarded as only the imaginings of a maniac, if happily not altogether suppressed; these wrongs and outrages surely must have hastened the pitiful ending of a beautiful, devoted life.

Certainly had feeble, shattered Myra lived in these latter days, she might have been the victim of such wicked incarceration, and by the advice too of the family physician. Under this regime, her tortured sensibilities must have wrought upon the brain, until a true frenzy were developed, ere death came to her relief, and thus ignorance have basely claimed its inhumanity justified.

Happily, in that olden time people had not yet learned to shirk responsibility in this fashion, but cared patiently, intelligently, with loving service, for their sick and disabled, whether the nerves, the stomach or the brain were at fault.

And most tenderly was Myra watched over day and night, not for a moment was she left alone, they dared not, for none could predict future developments.

Lucille, Julia, Eben, Grandpa, John or Uncle Tut were one or another constantly with her, but she could not get used to Julia; her attendance, they said, made her nervous, the sight of Eben often set her crying. How strange! thought the neighbors and those of the family who did not know the truth and all that had happened.

Mistress Julia and Eben continued their intimacy, though carefully concealed, especially from the eyes of Uncle Tut. He kept his own counsel and their secret, now that the mischief was done and Myra's health and happiness destroyed, he did not much care; her intense sufferings were ended and she was settling into an apathetic indifference from which nothing had power to rouse her; all force, vigor, animation gone, only her matchless sweetness and marvelous patience remained. Father, husband, sister and all her friends could see as well as Uncle Tut, that Myra's life was wrecked; there was no help for it now, but only he and the other two knew all, understood the wrong which had been done.

More mischief was brewing in another quarter. It might not be too late there for a remedy, and to this Uncle Tut turned his attention, determined upon preventing the only son of his friend, Dr. Gascoigne, from ending his life as a drunkard.

Although John had partially recovered himself after the shock of Myra's illness, and the seeming change for better in his wife, since the drinking bar had been started on the corner and was the resort of the town loafers, he was a constant patron, and the poison and debauchery were beginning to tell upon him sadly, as in the case of several others;—more than one wife was watching and grieving, more than one mother in that little village, no inhabited place being too small for a rum-seller's thriving, or to contain its drunkards, certainly no western town.

Uncle Tut meant, if possible, to change the current into which John was drifting, and as a preliminary step essayed to break up the infatuation between Eben and Julia, and arouse some feeling on her part towards her husband.

This was not so difficult as he had feared. Now that the novelty of getting Myra's handsome husband away from her had worn off, Julia was beginning to tire of him; there was scarcely enough excitement in keeping a man from the side of a sick wife who made no resistance, and whose patient sweetness appealed to the most callous heart. And Julia could scarcely be called hard-hearted, she exhibited usually a good-natured kindness towards those of whom she was not envious, was seldom vindictive, but just ordinarily selfish and narrow-minded. While lacking depth and tenderness of feeling, she was never malicious, surely not towards a fallen foe, and since it was apparent how Myra had taken the loss of her husband's affection, she would most gladly have remedied the evil she had helped bring about.

Watching faithfully over Myra as she had at the first for her own protection, afterwards because she came to love her in her helplessness and suffering, she found all her sympathies turning away from the recreant husband, to the woman they had sorely wronged.

And Eben too, man-like, now that nobody troubled about or tried to keep him away from the forbidden fruit, found he did not want it after all.

How he regretted in those days when he was awaking from his delusion, that he had not discerned the truth before his wife became the wreck she now was in body and mind, and how those happy days in the pleasant Eastern home haunted him. Myra was continually before his eyes as she used to be, her manner of doing things, the way she dressed, the sprightly, cheerful, amiable speeches she would make, all passed before him as the vision of a dream.

His tribulation was upon him now; *his* time had come, he was never more miserable in his life; at last he could not bear the sight of Mistress Julia, neither could he endure the thought, or to look upon Myra's pale face; truly was Eben between two fires—Gertrude his only solace; he was more considerate of the child than he had ever been before, and was winning back her love, she could see her father's unhappiness, doing her best to comfort.

Just then Uncle Tut discovered the opportunity for doing good, and he went at it in his own direct way.

His claim had remained unmolested during the winter, but

now the spring had fairly opened and something must be done. New comers would not scruple at taking possession of his claim, cabin and all, unless some one occupied it, and even then vigilance might be necessary in keeping all the land, for a rough fellow had settled beside him, driving stakes to suit himself, and neighbors reported had encroached upon Uncle Tut. Quite likely violence might result from any attempt at regaining his rights; not unfrequently were people murdered in those early days, when enforcing possession of disputed claims.

With Myra's sickness and all the rest, so many things had occurred in the family of his friend during the winter to occupy the attention, that he hardly thought of his own affair at all, but some ideas of a personal nature, which we shall hear more of further on, coming lately to his mind, he naturally turned to his claim, his cabin home. *He might want a home* again before very long

Yes, he must look after that claim, and thinking over the matter he concluded upon asking John and Julia if they would live with him during the summer. Julia was a good housekeeper. John could by this means be removed from temptation, and Eben, who was rapidly getting over his infatuation, would be given an opportunity for recovering his equilibrium.

Uncle Tut never delayed after he had decided about a project, and that very evening John and Julia had consented to the change and to live with him through the summer.

Grandpa and Lucille were only too glad that the son and brother could be placed under better conditions. They hoped Uncle Tut's influence, his wife's improved behavior and the out door work, would make a reformation and restoration in his life.

Julia seemed really benefitted by the lesson of Myra's sad illness, and truly sorry for her part in the wrong, and though she never became a refined, tender-hearted, unselfish woman, this could not be expected, she tried to atone in every way, especially as regarded her husband, not without good results.

After they were gone, Eben devoted himself more and more to his invalid wife, resolved to remedy, so far as possible, the injury done.

The babe was growing stronger, but the mother preceptibly weaker each day. Do what they would for her, the shock had been too severe, recovery impossible. She had improved for a time in the early spring, but now was again declining.

The climate was adverse, and she pined for the air of the

far away Eastern home where she was born, longing for old Barrytown too, and all the kind friends there; but her native air was what she needed most, nothing else could restore her lost vitality.

But a journey for one in her condition was not to be considered, even had their finances allowed of the expense.

People could not then, as now, travel round the world on easy beds in swift steam-drawn coaches, containing the comforts and conveniences of every day life, thus slipping away from the clutches of the grim monster when almost at death's door.

And Myra pined and longed, growing feebler each day; not even her husband's tender care could bring her back to life—*it was too late.*

Mother Brewster, who had been absent visiting one of her daughters, returned when Myra was visibly failing, the family exhausted with long watching; calling upon her friends and finding the invalid sinking, every one in great alarm at this new and unfavorable symptom; she forthwith installed herself at the bedside, and remained with them until the end came.

Myra declined so rapidly now day by day, her friends knew nothing could save her. Eben and the others went about sorrowfully doing what they could, but it was not much.

One day they called the sad husband to come in haste, but before he could reach her bed-side the patient little wife was gone—gone to her rest—a saintly smile on her wasted face.

Had a dagger struck him to the heart Eben would not have cried out—he did not then—but the wound was deep nevertheless.

He knew at last how much of happiness his own willfulness and recklessness had lost him.

Lucille and Gertrude were for a time inconsolable, and Dr. Gascoigne grieved as only a wifeless old father can when he buries his favorite daughter.

Uncle Tut took Myra's death almost as much at heart; he understood better than any one except those who were guilty why she died, and it was hard to forgive them. Julia truly repented her conduct, and her frivolous nature seemed deepened and softened; whether the change would be life-long none could tell.

CHAPTER X.

LUCILLE.

Her sister's death came with crushing weight upon Lucille, adding another to her own special sorrow which never left her for a moment; that face, those eyes, his presence were with all her waking hours, and at night they haunted her.

During the first year of the cruel estrangement she had been comforted by Myra's sympathy until, becoming delirious in her sad illness, and then Lucille found that pent-up grief is ten-fold harder to bear; when Myra partially recovered and they could sometimes converse as of old, she had again experienced relief; but now her loved sister was far away in the Great Beyond, and Lucille could speak to no one. Her one resource consisted in the question asked each day—" Any letters for me?"

She was almost sure when she had been disappointed more than three hundred and sixty-five times, that the one letter she had longed to see would never come. She heard frequently from Barrytown and of the marriage of one and another of her former mates, and occasional rumors reached her that Henry Armstrong intended taking on the yoke matrimonial; but as none proved true, Lucille continued hoping that sometime she should receive the long looked for letter; or that some day when the stage drove up Henry would be one of the passengers.

She could not get rid of the idea that he cared for her after all, and finding she did not marry, he would at last know she was true and waiting for him; till finally his heart must be touched, and he would come to her; and thus, day by day, she grieved over her lost love, hoping still.

Outwardly she was calm and cheerful, maidenly pride assured this, and when the first intense grief for her sister's death had passed she seemed to the eyes of strangers almost the same bright little Lucille she had been in Barrytown.

Lovers, even offers of marriage, came in plenty, that is as many as the village and country round could muster, for Lucille was one of those rare women, a man looks upon but to love, they would offer themselves in marriage before she even felt acquainted; but she had nothing to bestow upon any one of them all, and could not understand their feeling towards her, for she avoided giving the slightest encouragement.

Neither could they comprehend her, always lonely they were sure to imagine an especially tender regard towards themselves on her part, and their avowal not being reciprocated were sorely disappointed, but she would remain firmly of the same mind yet entirely kind, and they could not be vexed with her. Lucille had that unusual faculty possessed by some beautiful women, of making her repulsed lovers life-long friends, and they estimated her, after the first ebullition of passion had passed away, as a veritable saint whom no man could approach beyond a certain well-defined limit.

Poor little girl, could they have seen her in the pangs of heart sorrow, walking the floor, wringing her hands, pressing them on the aching head, over the struggling heart, heard her cry out in agony:

" Henry, oh! Henry my own beloved! when will you come? when will you come? My God! my God! I shall surely die;" then they might have understood why the peerless Lucille was to all unapproachable.

This one love absorbing her whole being, how could she give aught to another? It was impossible—but instead, she grieved and agonized, enduring stoically—giving no sign. No sign? She thought not, but her old father's love-quickened eye discerned all that was in his daughter's heart. He could not but notice the sudden paleness overspreading her face; upon receiving the answer: " No letter to-day," or if one were handed her, glancing at the superscription, missing the hand-writing she longed to see; nor how eagerly she watched the the passengers alighting from the coach each day, and when Henry was not among them with weary footsteps turning to the seclusion of her own room; he had seen her stagger, almost fall several times of late before reaching the door.

Dear old man, life was growing very sorrowful in his declining years; he needed a tried and true counsellor, in whom he might confide; such he found in Uncle Tutty Swanson. The more intimately he knew this rough, uncouth man, the less his hesitancy in trusting him. As his heavy burden pressed hard, and he felt unable longer to carry it alone, he told his faithful friend all he could of Lucille's trouble.

At first Uncle Tut was very angry with that "fool fellow," as he called Henry, then he cooled down and set his wits working to unravel the tangle, but before he got through he

found it a task fully his match. When a man or woman un-
dertakes to change the edicts of Fate, we won't say but they
sometimes accomplish their desires; but if so, it is like commanding a mountain, "Be thou removed, and cast into the sea," this
the Good Book says can be done, "if ye have faith," and Uncle
Tut had great faith in God's goodness, and faith in himself.

Laboring long and patiently, sometimes hopefully, then again
despairingly, at his self-appointed task, he would, as he thought,
seize the right end of the skein, and proceeding, attempt un-
tying the knot, when a power beyond his ken would grasp
another, and he would find the net of events snarling tightly
in his hand, until suddenly the mysteriously twisted threads
slipping away, eluded him altogether.

And what had seemed at first but a simple misunderstand-
ing between young lovers, grew, as the years went by, to be a
momentous affair, dragging down and involving these two and
many others, in the slimy meshes hidden beneath those slums
where political intrigues love to wallow, and in this instance by
their mischievous working, came near wrecking a prosperous
nation.

After Myra's funeral, the family resumed the routine of
their daily lives undisturbed, aside from the anxiety caused by
Lucille's unhappiness.

As for Eben, whatever he thought, nothing escaped him,
but by kindness towards Grandpa Gascoigne and Lucille, and
devotion to his children, he proved his regret. From Gertrude
he was inseparable, holding her fondly in his lap when he
could spare time, looking into her eyes, stroking her bright
hair, listening to her ceaseless prattle, thinking how like she was
to her mother.

Gertrude talked a great deal about her lost Mamma, and
Eben liked to hear her. Myra was sadly missed by all, but
Aunt Lucille had a philosophy of her own, perhaps not in ac-
cordance with the received opinions of those distant times, or
indeed as yet of these latter days, which she was able to impart to the little one comforting both herself and the child.

Before Myra's release, her mind became preternaturally brilliant, active, spiritualized, and Lucille thought her sister as near
being an angel as humanity can possibly attain on earth, and
now as she recalled their conversations about the future, and
the life both hoped for in the hereafter, she could scarcely realize that she had passed from her side; her presence had so savored of Heaven, the very air of the room she occupied so long

seemed filled by the balmy breezes from the better land. What
wonder if the one left to mourn, believed in the near-approach
to us, at times, of departed friends, after they have passed behind the veil of death.

Lucille was obliged to spend much time in Myra's room,
which, now that she was gone, was appropriated to the use of
herself and the delicate babe; the infant requiring constant care;
and there were days when her sister came to her so life-like,
she felt she could almost see her, hear her speak, and these
wonderful experiences during those months gladdened her heart,
steadied her faith, causing her to rest upon the promises of
Immortality they corroborated, and the reality of things unseen,
as upon a mighty rock, for safety.

Only for this, Lucille thought she never could have lived
through the dreary summer and desolate winter; and for years
after, the memory of those days, when she went back to them,
fell upon her as a wierd spell.

While the babe was awake, demanding her care, she could
endure the loneliness and sorrow, but when the boy slept, or
during the long evenings and the still nights, memory goaded
without mercy; then Myra's mystic talks would fill her mind,
comfort her breaking heart, and she seemed almost to hear her
voice, to see her heavenly smile. *Almost*, ALMOST, oh! how she
longed for the *real* presence, the actual touch of the dear hands,
the living fleshly body to be with her once again.

But this could not be, no prayer or love would restore the
lost one just as she was before the change had taken place;
there could be no stepping back to the same conditions; *all life
must go forward, stagnation is actual death; the only death;*
and there is no such thing as positive standing still in spirit or
in matter, therefore—*there is no death*—but alas! when the
thin veil intervenes it is as effectual in separating loved ones as
the iron bar which cannot be broken, the chasm which cannot
be bridged.

And Lucille, as does every bereaved heart to-day, philoso-
phised, and theorized, trying to reason and become reconciled
to the inevitable, but, in spite of all, grieving, agonizing, rebel-
ling just the same. And to her mind the separation from her
lover was quite as effectual, causing the same suffering in kind if
not in degree as the death of her sister; only that she believed
him to be alive, as we say, still in the material body, and that
some day he would in reality come to her, this was her hope,
her solace—this the difference between life and death.

Lucille had heard nothing for a long time, even incidentally, from Henry, no one who wrote from Barrytown mentioned anything about him, and she had been very uneasy and anxious. Soon after Myra's death, when the blackberries were ripening, she received such an impression she could not shake it off, or divest herself of the idea that some calamity was impending relating to herself and Henry and which would separate them yet more completely.

It came to her in this wise: On a sultry day, the babe taking his afternoon nap slept longer than usual, Lucille too dozed in her chair, the old wooden rocker Myra had brought from Barrytown. Suddenly she awoke with the feeling that her sister stood by her side calling her attention to something she wished her to know, and immediately her sorrow came upon her with unwonted force—loneliness at the loss of Myra, intense longing for Henry.

She had been unusually cheerful during the day, for it seemed to her that at last her loved one was surely coming; but now she had awakened in an agony of apprehension and could not dispel the thought that Henry was going further away even than he had been—*a long way off*—and the distance widened, the space lengthened into years, until a great gulf yawned between.

Lucille seemed to herself reaching out after her vanishing idol, trying to span the abyss; at last drawn by an uncontrollable impulse, she stood upon her feet and with out-stretched arms and beseeching voice, cried aloud: " Henry! Darling! do not go away *so far*, come back to me! Come! *Come!* COME!" and exhausted she sank down, a wonder, a mystery to herself. Recovering from the bewilderment caused by her strange condition, and trying to reason, she could think only of one event likely to widen the breach—Henry's marriage—yes, this must be what ailed her; and in some mysterious manner the fact had been conveyed to her mind, her heart. But, as she pondered, less willing was she to consider this the truth, or that Henry had any desire stronger than his wish to reach her.

Then why did he not come? Here was the puzzle, surely he had but to put forth a man's indomitable will and any obstacle, however stubborn, must yield.

Perhaps he was dangerously ill—dying—or dead. Poor Lucille was again in extreme distress, but her sufferings intensifying her perceptions, she could not ignore the knowledge obtained that Henry was neither dead, dying or married. The
6

estrangement was certainly less than it had been, still she could
feel her loved one drifting further away on the current of
events though outside his own volition.   And now there
seemed a real and tangible *something* that was more than a
mere sentiment, coming between them, yes, a slender, delicate,
beautiful woman and Henry standing side by side.   Nor could
she believe it was Myra her own sister who pushed her away
beckoning Henry to go with her, until Lucille, trembling with
grief, was left standing—alone.

Dr. Gascoigne came up for a chat with his lonely daughter
and to see how the babe was getting on.   Finding her in an extremely nervous state, he prescribed valerian to quiet and give
better sleep.   Throwing her arms about her old father's neck the
little woman sobbed as if her heart would break: " Oh! father,
father, medicine for the nerves is not what I need; but peace
for my heart, rest for my mind!" and the white-haired man
who had himself passed through grievous sorrows, wept with
her.   Full well did he understand that not one of his favorite
remedies could reach her ailment.

"My child, my poor child"—was all he could say.

Soon after the remarkable episode of that summer afternoon, Lucille learned that Henry had left Barrytown about this
time, going to a place in York-State, for the purpose of attending to some property devised him; whether he returned she was
not informed, and could not under existing circumstances inquire, what other foreshadowing of events was meant to be
conveyed, she received no immediate intimation, but at the last
all was made plain.

CHAPTER XI.

UNCLE TUT AND AUNT DEBBY.

At the time Myra was taken sick the family of Dr. Gascoigne had secured the services of Aunt Debby Jones, an excellent but gossippy woman, she assisting with the housework, who will be remembered as the officious friend trying to set matters right between Eben and his wife, in the commencement of the trouble, making such a botch of it as to call for reproof from her usually quiet husband. He, poor man, yielded to the unfortunate climate, dying from malarial fever, the fall of their arrival in Freelawn.

Aunt Debby remaining with them through the sickness and death of Myra, was regarded by the stricken family as a special providence. She had not failed to discover with those eyes of hers, black and brilliant—they could snap and sparkle too upon occasion—not one bit like Uncle Tut's, nearly as much as had he of the trouble; and Aunt Debby never entirely forgave Eben's neglect of his wife, during the convalescent period of her illness, declaring *privately* to a dozen or more intimate friends, that "Myra Grieveau might have recovered then, had Eben attended to her instead of spending his time flirting with Mistress Julia Gascoigne;" and when she saw his remorse, said "it was just good enough for him."

Many a knowing look had been exchanged between those dull, blue-grey eyes and the snapping black ones, while these things were transpiring; Uncle Tut even condescending to give an occasional chuckle in Aunt Debby's presence, and a few times attempted talking with her, but "law sakes," as she would say, "I couldn't keep my own rattling tongue still long enough to listen, while he drawled out one of his stammering speeches."

Dr. Gascoigne surprised them one day when Myra was better, soon after the babe was born, trying to converse, and heart-sick as he was, could not stop laughing, though it was the only sense of jollity he had known in months.

Here is a specimen of what they were saying: "Miss Jo-Jones," began Uncle Tut, "ca-can I ge-get yo-you some kin-kind-" Aunt Debby catching the idea, "Kindling-wood? Yes if you please, I shall be glad to have you."

"We-well where's th-the-"

"Ax? You'll find it behind the wood-box. Scat, you cat, there now, get out will you; you're always poking your nose into everything; I declare to it, if you ain't licking your chops now, for all I watch you every minute—scat, get out." And after poor pussy went the irate woman with the broom.

"Lo-look out, Mi-Miss Jo-Jones, yo-you'll hi-hit-"

"Hit you, no I won't, if you'll keep out of the way; there now." And bang went the door after the retreating cat, and also Uncle Tut, he, ax in hand, for the needed kindling-wood; firmly of the opinion he should never be able to keep "Miss Jones" as he called her, quiet long enough to tell how he thought her about the smartest woman he ever met, and had a notion, if she did not object, to try if they two could pull together the remainder of their lives.

And he continued thinking it over, how he'd like to have her keep house for him, on the claim, through the summer and longer; but as he dared not undertake the job of asking, it happened that finally John and Julia went with him—but this was only for the first summer.

After her mother's death, Gertrude was a great comfort, and furnished much amusement for them all, with her peculiar ways and odd speeches, her dollies and kittens, which she loved dearly as ever, managing to have a multiplicity of both. Being old enough now, she might be trusted in Aunt Debby's kitchen, and they were becoming fast friends, although Gertrude carefully kept her pet cats out of the way as much as possible.

The hard working woman liked the child, she was so quiet, orderly and winning, "no one could help it," all the neighbors said, and besides Aunt Debby pitied her because she was motherless, bestowing many a kindness on this account.

Gertrude, like all little girls, was fond of playing with dough, and would watch patiently while Aunt Debby rolled out whatever she was making, bread, pies or cookies, when, getting her own little bread board and rolling-pin she had coaxed Uncle Tut to make for her, climbing into a chair at the end of the table, she would peer up in her face, with those violet eyes like her mother's, saying in a queer, lisping way:

" Peathe, Aunt Debby, dive me a 'ittle piece of dough to make a pie wiv."

No woman with a heart could resist her, and Gertrude secured many a scrap to roll and muss with, Aunt Debby letting her bake and actually eat the brown, dirty lump although she declared "It went agin her stomic;" but, said she, by way of excuse, "that young 'un has a way with her as would soften the heart of a stone."

Besides her cooking accomplishments she was learning to sew and make dollies' clothes, and they were tailor-made, too; at any rate manufactured in a tailor's shop; this happy aristocratic consummation being thus achieved: Gertrude, spending much time in the store for the edification of Grandpa, Papa and herself, saw here different gentlemen; one especially friendly was her fancy, and, being the village tailor, often took her home with him, teaching her to sit cross-legged on his table as he did, and here she would sew contentedly for hours, he threading her needles.

Years after, when he had become one of the wealthiest men in his section, and Gertrude the most sorrowful women living, meeting in Washington, these two recalled the good times they spent together when she was a wee little girl.

Diverted by these and other immaterial incidents, our friends soon found the winter had passed and spring come again. * * *

While Myra had been sinking away in that quiet chamber, and those left behind were grieving after she was gone, a very different existence was coming to our friends on the claim, one full of activity, some excitement, even danger.

Mistress Julia was installed as housekeeper, and Uncle Tut and John were busy breaking up the deep prairie soil, using heavy ox-teams instead of horses, and planting in the newly-turned sod potatoes and corn, the first resort of agriculturists in tilling virgin soil; wheat, oats and other products coming after, with the crops adapted to older farms; this, with the building of sheds for one purpose and another, preparations for fencing and the care of the stock, kept the men well occupied; while Julia's dairy and garden filled in her spare time.

Besides the regular work, one whole side of the claim had to be restaked, and this more than once, for no sooner were they in place than little by little they disappeared. Unaccountably? Well, not exactly. Uncle Tut felt sure how it was, and why the same thing had occurred during the winter.

The claim being a very desirable one, situated on high, rolling prairie, sloping to a nice piece of bottom land near the river, wooded on either side, giving a strip of timber, quite a disideratum, and close by the cabin home was a large spring, from which flowed a clear brook, another rarity; these unusual

advantages causing a new-comer, a hard, grasping, ugly customer, to covet his neighbor's possessions; for though there
was plenty of land to be had for the taking up, such farms as
this were far apart.

Much trouble was caused in those early days by men who
maliciously endeavored to secure choice land already entered.

A man would honestly comply with the requirements
of the Government that settlers taking land must improve and
live on the same, pay his fee, driving stakes to mark the
claim, build a cabin, and with his family commence farming
in earnest; when something occurring to discourage, sickness or
unusual hardship, he would temporarily abandon his new
home, as did Uncle Tut.

This often happened in the fall; having obtained more comfortable quarters, and likely employment during the winter in the
nearest village, intending a return in the spring. If no one removed the stakes, took possession of the cabin, *jumped the claim*
while the rightful owner was absent—all was well—but frequently this took place and then trouble followed.

Or the stakes being partially broken down by accident and
neglect, a prospector not finding them, would, by mistake, lay
out a claim over on his neighbor's, and then a disputed bound-
ary would cause much bitterness. Sometimes dishonestly, from
pure avarice, the same thing occurred as in Uncle Tut's case,
and on one side of his land he could not keep the line defined,
work as he would.

This new neighbor had decided upon taking possession of
the vacant cabin, when Uncle Tut and party arrived to reoc-
cupy, and, coming a day too late, made no effort at concealing
his disappointment.

Being one of those unreasonable persons who are sure to
consider themselves aggrieved when the fault is their own, he
had been heard more than once to vow vengeance and declare
that under the law the whole land belonged to him, as he lived
in the cabin during the six months of Uncle Tut's absence; but
of this there was no proof, and his assertion was not credited;
nevertheless his threats boded mischief, for not unfrequently
were lives lost and property destroyed in these contests.

Meantime John and Uncle Tut possessed their souls in patience, working steadily at the contemplated improvements.

CHAPTER XII.

THE PIC-NIC.

As everything is moving smoothly at present, if not entirely satisfactory, both with our friends in the village and on the claim, at any rate, as we can do nothing to help them, we will go back to Barrytown, which they left nearly two years ago, and ascertain the changes which are taking place there, no less than in the Western home, also tracing the outcome of some unexpected events.

Dr. Gascoigne has been sadly missed; his place poorly supplied by young Dr. Bankson, who came from near Boston to Barrytown, soon after the good Doctor and the Grieveaus had departed for the West.

The young doctor, possessing money, was of course considered decidedly a better catch than Henry Armstrong, and the wildest of those giddy girls, who had caused Lucille's grievous trouble, deliberately laid siege to the citadel of his affections. Being somewhat of a beauty, and one who could be demure as a saint when she choose, the gentleman was soon in her toils; they were married in a hurry, and *he* had all his life before him for leisurely repentance, really deserving a better wife.

Edward had not sold Myra's snug home when the event occurred, and Dr. Bankson purchased the cottage, installing his wife therein, expecting many days of comfort and joy to follow; but alas, her slatternly ways soon played sad havoc with the appearance of everything inside and around the house. As time passed, dirty, crying children about the front door, broken crockery and rubbish at the back, told the tale of discomfort and waste within.

Here was a husband who had most excellent cause of complaint, here a most unsatisfactory wife and home; as they number but one in the myriads of criss-cross matches thickly scattered throughout the world, we will follow their history no further, introducing them here to show what Henry Armstrong discovered as to the stuff such girls prove to be, and the kind of wives into which they grow.

Every time he passed Dr. Bankson's door, it was to contrast the difference between the motherless daughters of Dr. Gascoigne and the silly girls he had allowed to prejudice him against Lucille, the one he truly loved.

Jealousy had ailed him, and now as the months, even years, were passing, bringing no tidings of her marriage, or that she was receiving special attention from old or new admirers, he began to realize what a simpleton he had been, and how much of sweetness and devotion foolishly thrown away.

Although at times his sense of loneliness and loss, the desire to see Lucille and take her in his arms, was overpowering, his pride would not let him acknowledge this mistake, at least in writing, but promising himself that after a little, he would go West prospecting, find Lucille, and if she did not resent his unkind treatment, bring her back, or even settle there himself; he would consider the idea.

Henry's friends noticed he was very uneasy, was getting a touch of the "Western fever," and surmising the old liking for little Lucille Gascoigne had something to answer for, they did not hesitate to banter him accordingly, but soon stopped that, the spot was too sore for careless probing, they found Henry was not a man to be trifled with, though so genial and good natured.

About this time, the latter part of the summer after the Grieveau party had left Barrytown, as Henry was firmly resolving to go West that very fall, and before he returned see Lucille, he received news of the death of an uncle who had lived in eastern New York, or York State as people used to say; a wealthy man as riches were estimated in those days, and being a bachelor, had left the bulk of his fortune, a few thousand dollars, to the only son of his only sister; Henry must come *immediately*, the letter said which had been a month on the way, postage twenty-five cents, and attend to his inheritance, being as some might think, encumbered by the old mother of the legatee, who must be looked after and cared for.

And thus nothing remained for Henry but to turn his head towards the rising instead of the setting sun. Thus does Fate blow us about as the shuttle-cock—the battle-dore, at the mercy of every breeze; or is it Providence directing our devious course? Let us choose the latter belief, it will make us happier—perhaps better.

And Henry's pill was not so hard to swallow as those ungilded or not even sugar-coated; his western trip must plainly be deferred; but when he did go he could establish himself to his mind or come back, as he chose; perhaps he'd remain, select a suitable location, lay out a town and call it by the respectable old name of Armstong.

Disappointed, but not altogether discomfitted, Henry made preparations for turning squarely around and away from the road his inclination prompted him to take.

Waiting Lucille! I fear your heart will break before he comes.

Now that he had inherited a fortune, Henry Armstrong was the "Lion" of the village, and several of those same wild girls tried to fix their fangs upon his heart with utmost endeavor; not accomplishing their purpose, for there was more transparency than wisdom in their scheming.

It was Mr. Armstrong, and *Mr.* Armstrong, and now please *do Mr. Armstrong* do this, and come here, and go there, and invitation to tea, to luncheon, to parties, to pic-nics, and adulation, and flattery, and flumery until he was sick with disgust, annoyed beyond measure from attentions he knew to be heartless.

All this only brought sincere, quiet Lucille, with her honest affection and modest ways, more vividly before him, and he realized how deeply in love he had been all along and that the love was growing now day by day.

Occupied with preparations for leaving Barrytown not to return again, having concluded to go directly west from Bentonville, his new home, when he had arranged his business there; busy as he found himself, Lucille was before him every waking moment, and at night she came to him in dreams.

How he longed to see her and tell her of his sorrow because of the grief he knew he had caused her; but not even with the addition of remorse did he suffer as she; a man's nature is so different from a woman's. With her, love is all—with him, only an incident; often multiplied, and so near alike in intensity he is puzzled to know, dear soul, which it shall be, Mary or Jennie.

And is it not always as with Henry? Was it not really a question of his own determination? Could he not go, or at least communicate with her whenever he strongly willed to do so? No social requirements held *him* to a line which could not be overstepped, and it may well be doubted whether any man fails to win a woman whom he truly loves if he sets himself about the task, unless another already occupies her heart. Women so need sympathy and protection.

Although Henry had been jealous of what he believed Lucille's want of appreciation, and the thought did occasionally obtrude itself that someone else might secure her affection, yet strangely enough his faith in her steadfastness grew with time.

The only way to solve the whole problem was to get away from Barrytown and proceed on his eastern journey at once.

As the time of leave-taking drew near Henry's friends, the aforesaid young ladies, among others, planned a picnic in honor of his departure—a sort of "good-bye-for-luck" affair.

Some two or three of the most inveterate flirts the village contained, those who upon approaching the uncertain line dividing young ladyhood from old maidenhood, were weighing and counting their last chances; grasping desperately after every stray ticket in the matrimonial lottery, had determined if possible to secure something *tangible* and *decisive* before he left them, from the handsome, gallant and very desirable Mr. Armstrong now that he was to have property; and they hoped by their bewitching toilets, fascinating manners and the opportunities for unwonted freedom to succeed upon this occasion. They commenced, each trying for a special invitation to accompany Mr. Armstrong, but he preferred just going along with the crowd; and besides, his mother required close attention, for this was to be a turning out of·the whole village, both old and young, seeking an afternoon of enjoyment.

As the blackberries were ripe in the woods on the hill-sides they proposed making a profitable excursion of it also, and, locking up the houses, leaving a few who were infirm, too old or young for the jaunt. With these exceptions the whole town piled into vehicles of every description, drawn by any sort of a horse, and started for the deep green woods, carrying pails and baskets for the ripe, luscious berries, and jugs of cool milk from the cellars, and jellies, preserves, and pickles, and hams boiled, chickens fried, and pies of every description; and sweet cakes, caraway cakes and doughnuts; and cheese, sage-cheese and cream cheese, dried-beef and every known kind of bread; hop yeast bread, emptins bread, salt rising bread, every style except bakers' bread, the ever available relief of modern housewives; and biscuits from the raised dough, and delicious, tender, toothsome, oldfashioned biscuits of generous proportions, made with sour cream and saleratus, such as only our grandmothers could mould—*a lost art*—and eaten on them, genuine maple syrup and white clover honey, made by the real bees, not the article manufactured from glucose, sorghum and the like. All this for luncheon in the woods, substantial and bountiful truly, and the people were as old-fashioned and comfortable as the edibles.

A merrier party seldom gathered, than rode over the hills and along the edge of romantic ravines, on that summer day, reaching the heavy woods by the river, a few miles from the town, before noon.

The Rev. Father Stebbins was along, the recipient of extreme attention, and young Dr. Bankson with his pretty wife; village Pastor and Doctor, honored guests, dividing privileges with Mr. Armstrong, the hero of the hour.

Henry had placed his mother in their roomy rockaway, drawn by faithful old Charley, with a dear friend of hers on the broad, easy, back seat, and when all were ready for the starting, found *himself* squeezed in between two of the aforesaid young ladies; how they came to be there, he never knew, but *they* did.

One, a dark beauty gorgeous in furbelowed pink calico, the other, a cross between a blonde and brunette with no color hair, dingy complexion, and eyes neither blue, brown nor honest grey, with no freshness or decided color about her, yet exhibiting the imbecility of attiring herself in solid cottony white, without one bit of filminess or airiness of texture to redeem the unfortunate selection; the only pleasing item about their costumes or appearance, being the rather good looking necks and arms possessed by these healthy country girls, displayed to advantage in the low-necked and short-sleeved dresses universally worn by all females in those days, whether babes, misses, young ladies, even married women of mature years, on all occasions; a shawl, cape or mantle added for out-door protection.

A fashion, happily for the health of the race, not mentioning quite chaste manners, long since abolished, unless recent innovation be an attempted revival by the recherche select few.

. But then *everybody* wore them, that is all who aspired to *be anybody*, as the distinctive mark of a gentleman must be his black suit, silk hat and uncomfortable, high, stiff stock encasing his neck; the world has certainly moved on in these regards.

Henry Armstrong enjoyed his ride? Well, yes, he was at least amused.

On one side being entertained by Miss Amanda with squeaking voice pitched in the highest treble:

"Now, Henry, let me drive, do; I know how, see if I don't," and taking the reins in each hand, woman fashion, slapping first one and then the other on the back of the patient animal, and

producing a peculiar noise from her mouth, such as only a fe-
male devoid of horse lore, ever essayed, with an occasional
"git up, there now." 'Manda imagined *she* was urging on the
slack jog-trot of the old horse; the fact being Charley drove
himself, as does many a human drudge, ganging his own gait,
while some one carrying the whip and holding the lines fancies
by this arrangement every impulse and movement is controlled.

"Get up," squeaked 'Manda, until, as the horse was trotting
leisurely down hill, she dropped both lines and whip under
Charley's feet, and then screamed.

"Whoa!" called Henry composedly but decisively. Instantly
the docile creature stopped still although the carriage was crowding on his heels.

Out jumped Henry, picking up the lost articles, and patting
the good horse affectionately on the neck, giving his nose a little stroke or two by way of reward for good behavior, thinking the while, how much more knowing and companionable
most horses are than some girls.

'Manda did not again obtrude her accomplishments upon his
attention.

While she had been trying to drive, Miss Mollie on the
other side of the much enduring Henry, was lisping soft com-
pliments into his ear.

"How much better you *do* look Henry, since you have had
your hair cut for the warm weather. I like to see a man with
short, curly hair; Jim Smith's hair is so long and straight, such
a mean color, too; I never could bear Jim Smith, anyway."

"Oh, I don't know, Mollie," answered Henry, "Jim is a good
fellow if he isn't very handsome."

Miss Mollie was glad a few years after to take Jim Smith
"for better or for worse."

Laughing and chatting as they went, talking about nothing
at all, they soon reached the spring in the woods, at the foot of
a high hill with over-hanging rocks, near where the black-ber-
ries grew in plenty.

The company alighting, unloaded, tied the horses and prepared for luncheon, boys bringing water from the gurgling spring,
men making fires from brush and dry leaves, that the women
might boil the tea and coffee they had provided. A cloth was
spread here and there, and a few grouping about each impromptu
repast, all hastened to refresh themselves before commencing
the real object of the day—berry-picking—and possibly too,
love-making.

When they had eaten their fill, everything was packed carefully away, and leaving those disinclined for fatigue in charge of the wagons and teams, the workers gathered about any heavily laden bush they encountered, and commenced in earnest, each intent upon surpassing the others.

Gradually, and possibly prepense, the groups dwindled to three or four in a place, as a new bush would be discovered. Eventually, the whole party paired off in twos, for there were *lovers* of every age and stage of development; little cupids of seven summers or less, and those stirred by the sacred fires at seventy years of age; there were wee ones, just commencing to twitter, others contentedly assured, those soon to be united in wedlock, some *few lovers still*, though years had intervened since they had entered the holy bonds of matrimony; every one a lover of somebody.

Such was life in the olden times, and human nature is unchanged to-day.

The two young ladies who by some strategy rode in Henry's carriage, each used their practiced wiles in the effort to draw him away from the company, but he proved in no mood for being enticed; others tried the same plan, but his mind was fixed upon one far away, and he could not, flirt that he had been, interest himself in any one else, and in spite of all inducements, just stayed by his mother and her friend the live-long day.

The picnic was, to Henry, decidedly tiresome though contrived in his honor, but like all mundane events, it came to an end at last, as the earth revolving and the sun disappearing, reminded them of night and home. When they were arranging for the return, Father Stebbins came forward leading by the hand a timid young Miss, and accosting Henry, said, "Allow me Mr. Armstrong, to present my niece, Miss Effie Stebbins. She arrived only last evening from my brother's, who lives south of Barrytown, and as she leaves by the same stage which I suppose you take to-morrow, for her home in Bentonville, I beg you will act as her escort, knowing we may securely trust her in your care."

"Certainly, Father Stebbins, I shall be most happy to render the young lady any service in my power, and doubt not she will require all I can bestow, ere we reach our destination, for the journey is long and tiresome. If you wish I will order the morning stage for her to-morrow at 7 o'clock."

Neither of the three suspected that Destiny was playing a trump; but it was even so, and this was partly, though not the

whole by any means, of the trouble which impressed Lucille
that summer afternoon, hundreds of miles away, dozing in
Myra's old arm chair, *worked upon by unknown forces, seeing
visions of the present, led into futurity.*

The next morning saw Henry and Miss Stebbins starting by
stage towards Detroit, where they were to take the boat for Buf-
falo and Erie, and thence proceed by the famous canal to the end
of their journey. The quickest time they could hope to make
would consume fully three weeks, and provision had been made
for the comfort of each, by friends stowing away in their baggage, the requisites for any emergency they could imagine.

Such extensive preparations were necessary in those days,
people delaying for weeks, that new suits, linen, stockings, shoes
might be manufactured for the occasion. *Journeys were events;*
now at a moment's notice we start with a change of clothing,
and man's best friend, a well filled purse, traveling round the
world.

After a month or more of anticipation, without unusual incident, unless we call the placing of a young girl in the care of
a man not many years her senior for so long a time, out of the
ordinary course of propriety, Henry Armstrong arrived with
his little companion one sunny afternoon in September, at the
door of his dead uncle's homestead, and, as Effie knew the
family, both were cordially greeted by the aged Grandmother,
overjoyed at Henry's coming. She had been quite a long time
dependent upon a young niece for care and company, assisted
by a man named Cronksey, who, living with her son, attending
to his business during the illness, had after his death continued
looking to the affairs of the estate; which now, with the responsibility of providing for the old lady, belonged to Henry; he,
finding the niece tidy, capable and kind, the man competent
and shrewd, retained them in his service, little thinking the influence this decision would have upon his whole after life.

Besides the farm, his uncle had left many matters unsettled,
requiring attention all the winter following at least, if Henry
would make the most of his patrimony; there was no alternative,
he must remain in Bentonville instead of going west in the fall
as he had intended.

Sorrowing Lucille, how tedious and dreary the time will
seem to you before he comes.

If the winter after Myra's death dragged wearily to Lucille
so also did it to Henry; and when reminded by the robin's first
song, the running brooks of the hillsides fed by the melting

snow and ice of the uplands, and the few blades of bright verdure appearing here and there in the warm nooks, of the near
approach of spring, his thoughts turned more impatiently than
ever towards her western home.

Other matters of business being arranged he had decided
upon leaving his uncle's old mother in undisturbed possession
of the homestead during her life, in charge of the man Cronksey—the niece acting as housekeeper—at least while he prosecuted his contemplated trip to the new and distant country so
often discussed. He had become acquainted in the course of
the winter, through manifold transactions, with several eastern
men commanding capital, and the subject of going west, investing some money, and perhaps laying out a town had been
talked of between them.

The " Western fever," instead of abating, seemed more
wide-spread than ever, the fact being that a financial panic was
imminent, and many beginning to feel the premonitions, were un-
easily endeavoring to better their condition.

To be sure, " going west " had not yet come to be regarded
a panacea for all the ills which the renowned advice of the
lamented Horace Greeley afterwards suggested; but, nevertheless, was then considered quite the thing for young men or
those wishing from any cause to improve their circumstances.

Long-headed, calculating men, were constantly going out
prospecting, taking up quarter sections in good localities, laying
out towns and starting settlements.

Persons with even a small amount of capital and sufficient
enterprise, could from the start draw some of the best people
of older communities with them.

Early in the spring Henry inaugurated such an expedition,
and a half dozen or more formed a party whose destination was
a short distance beyond Freelawn; though he carefully avoided
mentioning a further interest in its inhabitants than would be
indicated by the information that a number of his Barrytown
friends had gone there, and quite likely he might stop a day in
passing were circumstances favorable. Far was it from his intention that any should suspect a tender regard on his part
towards anyone in that quarter, until he was sure how Lucille
would receive him. She might be married for aught he knew.
Information was transmitted slowly in those days, and scarcely
anything had come to him except that of Myra's death, and
this only casually; but the thought of losing Lucille now that
he was certain of his own feeling, the fear that she might al-

ready belong to another made him sick at heart, and he promised himself, after the party accomplished the end for which they
had organized, he would contrive some excuse for leaving
them and return by way of Freelawn.

What a circuitous route it seemed for reaching Lucille.
Now his mind was settled he was impatient of delay. Steam
or compressed air would not be too swift in these days for so
ardent a lover.

But Henry must content himself with a mode of travel like
the pace of a snail; first the Erie Canal to be traversed, horses
drawing the boats along a path on the brink; then proceeding
in the cumbersome stage-coach for weeks over roads rough,
often muddy—going always slowly—the monotony broken
only when in due time the Lakes were reached, the party crossing Lake Michigan, as did our friends from Barrytown before
them, and also stopping a short time in Chicago. This wonderful town had made rapid strides even since the Grieveaus
and Gascoignes passed through; but to Henry it contained
nothing of interest, and remaining over night, taking the morning stage, he pushed on, finding the remainder of the journey
especially tedious and unpleasant. When once seated in the
stage there was no relief for cramped limbs and aching head,
except as they waited for meals or to water the horses. Should
any desire they rested by night at the taverns along the road,
but many proceeded without interruption. From day to day
new passengers were taken up, others dropped; and as they
traveled on all were thumped about in a fearful fashion; shaken
up inside the vehicle like scraps of tin in a baby's rattle-box,
furnishing an abundance of exercise.

Fortunately there were no hills, only a gradual rise and descent now and then over a bit of rolling prairie; but pitch-holes
and mud-holes were often encountered into which the horses
would sink, and the stage bounce, the passengers being jerked off
their seats into each other's laps, then again coming up standing, jamming their already sorely abused heads against the roof,
as the top was called.

A trip by stage was exciting, tiresome and even dangerous
when the road was rough or the driver had taken a drop too
much of stimulants, and would crack his long whip over the
horses with a flourish, in his endeavor to make a stir in the
world.

The passengers were entirely at his mercy as he well knew,
feeling his importance hugely.

Swearing at the horses and the road, with cracking whip, loud tooting horn and the bouncing, thumping, rattling stage coach, he managed to make more commotion and fuss, as they passed along at the rate of five or six miles an hour, with ten or twelve passengers and a trunk or two, than forty heavily laden cars drawn by resistless force do now-a-days.

In one instance we have much ado and very small results; in the other, great achievement with little noise or pretension. Thus the world progresses, opportunity coming to all, when the fortunate circumstance presents, *wisdom* discerning, speedily acting, reaps the rewards; though Omnipotent Power will not do all for a man, he must himself see and execute, working out his own salvation.

Opportunity came to Eben when he might have straightened the tangled thread of his life, and saved disaster and much sorrow, but he failed to perceive the crisis, until the time had passed for administering a remedy. Opportunity is coming to Henry Armstrong; will he prove wiser, and benefit accrue to himself and Lucille?

CHAPTER XIII.

JULES.

The summer was following close upon the spring, the increased heat acting upon the swamps and low boggy ground
of the prairies and wood-bordered streams, which had overflow-
ed their banks early in the season, covering the country for miles
on either side with water, besides other discomforts causing
malarial fever, ague and dangerous sickness, most liable to
attack the weak and disheartened; for this reason Lucille's
friends were becoming very anxious because of her failing
health.

Although keeping up bravely since Myra's death, now that
the hot weather was again becoming intense, she showed unmistakable signs of wearing out, and her symptoms were ag-
gravated by the constant care bestowed upon the little boy. He
was over a year old, requiring more attention than is usually
necessary with children of that age, because of his delicate constitution, and having peculiarities, the result of the mother's
condition shortly before his birth; especially connected with the
brain fever from which she had suffered, affecting the child in
such a manner as to render him extremely nervous, irritable and
troublesome.

He was bright enough, even too quick in understanding for
one of his age, but uneasy, restless, dissatisfied, though affectionate and not difficult to control, unless when he fixed his mind
upon attaining something desired, and then his persistency was
phenomenal, seeming absolutely without calculation as to consequences, leading him always into trouble, unheard of predic-
aments and dangerous places.

He had, before a year old, enough hair-breadth escapes to
prove conclusively he was not born to die of an accident, and
he surely came through the ailments of infancy wonderfully
well for a child not naturally strong; the doctors said soon after
his birth that he inherited a tendency to consumption, for he
had coughed incessantly from the first, and they fully expected
him to die, but he disappointed them and lived; in spite of every
thing which happened, the poor little fellow held to life with

the grip of Fate, the pertinacity of destiny. Was it Fate, was it destiny?

Be that as it may, the whole family watched and tended him untiringly for Myra's sake; at last they ceased to fear he would die, and instead came to think nothing would kill him, but as the natural result of continual solicitude their hearts were wrapped up in the welfare of the unfortunate, motherless babe, and it was plainly seen that this in addition to her other troubles, was wearing sadly upon his Aunt Lucille.

Mother Brewster declared she must have a change. Her father and Uncle Tut knew that more than the oversight and worry with the child was telling upon her, but they kept their own counsel.

Sad eyed, wearily she watched for the incoming Eastern stage, and the opening of the mail.

As the hour arrived she would arrange her hair unlike any one else, but becoming to her sweet face, don the neat gown, displaying by its very simplicity, her trim, round, perfectly developed figure to the best advantage; the small, white throat rising from the close collar, bearing the symmetrical head as a drooping flower on its stalk; for Lucille tried to hide her tell-tale face from view, but the bowed head and shaded eyes only said the story plainer.

Day after day, as the time drew near for the expected stage, Lucille was ready, herself, and the pleasant Western home, wild branches, vines and flowers, wherever a place could be found for decoration; every room and article in perfect order, *for possibly Henry might come at last.*

Patiently, with heart full of love and trust, hoping against all past experience, the little woman looked eagerly forward to the arrival of the stage, but when the rattle and flourish subsided, and she neither saw Henry or received any message from him, prostrated with grief, broken-hearted, she would get away to her own room, avoiding the notice of those who loved her, and, alone, give way to emotion uncontrollable; then, after a time recovering, go about her duties quietly as before.

But such a life as this was past human endurance and could not last much longer, they all understood the trouble now, and grew to be very considerate. When she had experienced her daily disappointment and gone away grieving by herself, one of the family would come up softly with the boy or Gertrude as an excuse, and divert her attention.

Eben was kinder than ever, often contriving a ride for her

and the children, sometimes he would accompany them; but
Lucille being an accomplished horse-woman, preferred holding
the reins herself, as she found the drive more exhilarating.
Many a pleasant jaunt they had, and this recreation was of
much benefit; but all the efforts of her friends could not restore
her feeble strength. Nature asserted itself at last and Lucille's
health gave way. After consulting together in her behalf, the
unanimous decision of the family was that she must go out to
the farm for a while. Her consent could only be obtained by
insisting that the boy should have a taste of country living and
country air; the atmosphere of the little town situated on the
sluggish stream being very different from the sweeping breeze
of the rolling prairie where Uncle Tut had located his claim;
and the cool spring water was wonderfully invigorating, not
mentioning the foamy milk fresh from the sleek, contented
cows; even this, they all declared, was better than that from
their own, because Julia's cows had free access to the brook flowing from the famous spring. All these enticements prevailed,
and Lucille concluded to go for a few weeks; ashamed to own
the only comfort in life for her, consisted in watching the daily
arrival of the eastern stage; but she was sorely tried at tearing
herself away from the place, her own chamber window, where
she should see Henry the instant he came—if *he ever came!*
She was beginning at last to entertain this view of the case, and
to let the thought obtrude occasionally upon her sick heart, that
possibly after all, Henry might not come—but she was too
weak—she dared not dwell upon it for more than a moment, and
drove it away so soon as it came to her mind. She still believed
that some time Henry would surely come, she was certain he
did love her once dearly, and could not understand how love
should entirely die out, even from the heart of a man, but in
her sorrow would cry beseechingly: " Why are men so fickle?
Why do they wreck the lives of those whose love is constant
and pure? "

Dear, tormented little woman, sadly was a change needed,
and the very next morning after she agreed to make the visit,
Eben brought the spring wagon to the door in good time, that
they might accomplish their short journey before the noon
meal.

Lucille had been over to the farm since her brother lived
there several times, and the pleasant views stretching as far as
the eye could reach, spreading before and around them, from
the summit of each rise in the land over which they were driv-

ing, was not new to her; but the lovely expanse of picturesque
greenness, and the fresh morning air, were cheering and restful
to her feeble body and fainting heart.

Upon their arrival all made haste to welcome them; the
really kind-hearted Julia stirring busily about, prepared a comfortable dinner of the best the place afforded.

Brother John seemed a different man now that he had recovered from the effects of dissipation; Julia acting the part of
a true wife so far as she was capable.

His friends had advised him to remain away from the village
and temptation, and thus it happened he had not seen his sister
during the time she was visibly failing.

Dr. Gascoigne had been out a few days before, telling them
what he surmised of Lucille's trouble; but John was not prepared for the recent change in her appearance, she looked like
a drooping flower, so weak and sad, yet patient and lovely.
The strong western farmer took his little sister in his arms and
burst into tears, his honest heart throbbing with indignation at
all she must have suffered. He was sure she did not deserve
this sorrow, for Lucille was not one to be unreasonable with a
lover. Henry Armstrong must have turned from his sweet,
loving sister because of mere fickleness, and this devoted brother
thought of pistols and horse-whips; he'd teach the good-for-
nothing fellow to trifle with a woman's affections if he ever had
a chance at him; but, strangely enough, when the opportunity
was unexpectedly presented, John failed to perceive it or that
villainous Fate looking over his shoulder chuckling.

After Julia's well-cooked dinner was disposed of, Eben made
ready for his return.

Julia must needs send for Aunt Debby and Grandma Brewster a roll of her choicest butter, and some fresh wild strawberries, which she had gathered that morning for preserving.
John brought a dear little kitten for Gertrude; Uncle Tut insisted on providing a pair of young banties for her, and a magnificent shanghai for Grandpa Gascoigne.

Pleasant good byes were said, and having innumerable messages intrusted to him which he forgot before turning the lane
into the road, Eben drove away; Julia proceeding to install
Lucille in the neat room reserved for her adjoining the sitting
room.

The fresh, white curtains, edged with dainty ruffles, at the
window; the half-circle toilet table placed under the old-fashioned mirror with its gilded frame, which had been handed down

from mother to daughter for generations, was of home manufacture, and finished with the same cool looking, white ruffled
drapery; the clean bed, the comfortable chair, which Julia with
John's help had made from an old flour barrel, cutting it down
the right height, fitting in the head for the seat, leaving half
still uncut for the back, covering all with pretty chintz; with
these simple articles Julia had neatly and ingeniously furnished,
—and rendered her guest's room very inviting.

In this retreat, while Julia looked after the boy, Lucille
rested, pondered, dozed, finally slept and dreamed. Dreamed
that Henry came and looked at her with the old love-light in
his eyes, that a dark, dreary shadow passed between, and then,
Henry turning away—she saw him no more forever. With a
start she awoke to find herself prostrated, almost fainting with
the heat of the summer's day; and the sad memories stirred by
her dream, did not serve to strengthen her.

They all realized how weak she was, and great her need of
help. John especially exerted himself for his sister's entertainment, taking her that very afternoon when the sun was low
and the evening breeze gathering, to the spring, where they
had built a dairy house for the milk and cream and butter, of
which Julia was justly proud.

Lucllle enjoyed watching her strain and set the milk as she
brought it foaming, drawn by her own hands from the gentle
cows, John and Uncle Tut doing their share with the hard milk-
ers; afterwards when her strength allowed Lucille assisted in the
care of the dairy, skimming the luscious cream into the cool,
stone jars placed on the pebbly bottom of the running brook,
where every article needed for the milk and cream and butter,
must be rinsed immediately when used.

Lucille also interested herself in the cows themselves for
their own sakes, as well as the products yielded. Each of the
family had their special favorite in the herd, and she soon learned their names and peculiarities. They were not what are called high-bred, five thousand dollar cows, in the ownership of
which fashionable city dames sometimes indulge as well as
fancy farmers; but just ordinary cows, brindled, white, spotted,
and red, with curved, crooked or crumpled horns, sometimes no
horns at all, "mooley cows" they called them. But Julia's
cows were well pastured, kindly treated, and with the pure
spring water to drink their fill, winter and summer, what wonder with such cows, and facilities for the manufacture of their
rich product into golden butter and choice cheese, if Julia Gas-

coigne's dairy was famed far and near. And she never scrimp-
ed her family of cream either. Cows were cheap, pastures
broad, the butter market overstocked, transportation impossible,
and cream was freely used in many ways long since forgotten,
which an epicure might envy. The white, mealy potatoes when
baked, spread with thick cream instead of butter, with the addition of a little salt, could not be surpassed; and they had cream
gravy for the crisp, sweet, fried pork, corn fed and healthy;
with tender chickens fried as only southern or western housewives know how, on lettuce fresh from Julia's well tended
garden; of course on all berries in season; as for green peas
and string beans picked with the dew on the vines and served
with plenty of rich cream, what could be more delicious?

Certainly there was some compensation in the prairie home,
for all they had left with so much regret two years before in
Barrytown. Everything grew thriftily in the black virgin loam,
there was enough and to spare, so much land to be had for the
taking up they could not cultivate it all even should natural
avarice prompt, and this was not a trait of these early settlers.
Their life on those vast prairies broadened their hearts, making
them generous and hospitable. Much of the same spirit has
descended to their children. A man or woman growing up in
the West with a stingy, contracted soul, must have inherited
these qualities from some away-down-east Yankee, who lived
where they had to raise their crops between the stones, on the
side of a hill at a slant of forty-five degrees. No wonder they
count the beans.

Besides the spring, the dairy and the garden, Lucille was
greatly pleased with the poultry which Julia had raised; turkeys,
ducks, geese and no end of chickens.

Every morning and evening the two women, accompanied
by little Jules, as they had named Myra's boy, would scatter
corn and oats for them, not forgetting the nice pan of wet meal
for the young broods, the callow turkeys, ducks and goslings,
and for the little chicks.

Jules felt himself quite a man, now that he was allowed to
run about out of doors, and they no longer called him the baby,
and would fill his blue checked apron with corn and oats, spill-
ing nearly all before he reached the barn-yard, but tossing what
remained gleefully in his now chubby hands, jumping up and
down, yelling with delight to see the eager crowd picking up
the kernels. Partly too, with fear, when the great cocks flap-
ped their wings and crowed; when the ducks and geese came

with their clatter, clatter, squak, squak, and when the old tur-
key-cocks streached their hideous red and blue necks, spreading
their enormous wings and tails, strutting about with their ugly
gobble, gobble, gobble, the little fellow would run screaming
and hide his face in Aunt Lucille's apron.   But next time he was
just as eager to go with them, when the poultry were to be fed.

Though dismayed, not conquered, though frightened, not
overcome; a persistency which became a predominant characteristic as he grew to maturity.

All this diversion, change of surroundings, and the pleasant
occupation, took Lucllle's mind in some degree from her trouble.
Brother John and Uncle Tut were fond of children, and looked after the boy when they could do so without interfering with
their work.   Soon Jules would stay with no one else, if he had
his way.   Lucille found this a relief to her overtasked strength, .
which she hardly realized the need of until the change came.
The diet furnished by Julia must have nourished one less able
to assimilate, and soon from these combining causes, Lucille's friends saw, with extreme gratification, that she was beginning to improve in health—really gaining flesh, and looking
somewhat "like the plump little sister of old," John said exult-
ingly.

Jules, too, was enjoying his visit; there were so many ways
for him to get hurt or into mischief at home, he had been kept
most of the time in Aunt Lucille's room, and he now more fully
appreciated his freedom.

He had not been allowed to run in the store or the street,
for they could never keep things out of his reach in the store,
and small as the town was occasional teams were passing, and,
if in the street, he was sure to be under the wheels.

Aunt Debby would not have him in the kitchen, she declared " he was worse than the cat," and she came near killing
her a dozen times a day; no indeed, you may be sure Aunt
Debby would not be bothered with a "young 'un"—she was too
much of a " worker and driver " for such nonsense as coddling
children or petting cats; even Gertrude's kittens were continually disappearing, she managing to supply the place of each as
they died or strayed away.   As for poor little mischievous Jules,
he had not yet developed the winning ways necessary to con-
quer Aunt Debby.

The result of all this had been that at home after Myra's
death, Lucille devoting herself to the child to keep him out of
everybody's way, scarcely allowing herself any recreation and

brooding over her trouble, had come near following her beloved sister to the last resting place. Now she was gaining
cheerfulness and strength, and seemed almost her former self,
but the sore spot in her heart was still there, and the slightest
probing would set it bleeding again.

Unfortunately, the old wound was opened wide before Lucille finished her visit.

CHAPTER XIV.

THE FIGHT AT THE CLAIM.

Uncle Tut was all this time full of anxiety because of his disagreeable neighbor, and gave little attention to anything else. He had done all he could for his friends and now left them to care for themselves and amuse each other as they pleased.

His neighbor never forgave him for returning just in time to prevent the "jumping" of his claim, and had threatened all the spring to go to law; finally bringing suit for possession.

The case soon coming up for trial when Lucille went for her visit at the farm, Uncle Tut was spending much time in town with Dr. Gascoigne and Eben Grieveau.

At last the trial commenced, and the man, Silas Smith, swore that he had lived in the cabin with his wife (as he called the woman who kept house for him) during the winter; and also early spring, but that they were away visiting when Uncle Tut arrived. The woman testified to the same facts, explaining that the few articles necessary for housekeeping had been packed in a large box and left with their comrade, Doc by name, who lived in the cabin on adjoining land, for safe keeping, and that some repairs might be made on their own cabin before their return.

The man called Doc. corroborated these stories, and swore in addition that he owned the land adjoining and also the cabin. No one believed this testimony to be true, but the man Silas Smith had made out his case and Uncle Tut had no contrary proof.

The story was plausible as to the housekeeping, for in those primitive days in furnishing these cabins, beds were simply bunks built against the wall, tables the same, and a short board with sticks driven into the four corners, slanting out a little, served in place of chairs. These articles were left in the cabin by Uncle Tut surely, and he found them upon his return.

Notwithstanding the earnest efforts of the lawyer and story-teller of the storm on the lake and his buisness partner, who happened in Freelawn (it being the County seat) on other court business, and whose services were secured for the defendant through their mutual friend, Dr. Gascoigne, the Judge was obliged on the proof to decide the case in favor of Silas Smith, and nothing remained but to vacate the premises or appeal. Uncle Tut pursued the latter course, hoping something would eventually occur to reverse the decision.

You may be sure Dr. Gascoigne did not neglect tendering the hospitality of his home to his friend the lawyer and his companion during their stay in Freelawn, and it was difficult to say whether little Gertrude clung more closely to Grandpa, Uncle Tut and this genial and wonderful man, or to the new friend she found in the gentleman who accompanied him. You will remember the bashful child who usually feared strangers trusted her friend of the storm-tossed ship as she did Uncle Tut, men so unlike, *implicitly* from the first moment, as she now did the new-comer. Time proved that a strong bond existed between these men and the timid little girl, developing a life-long attraction and understanding of each other, which helped them in searching out and unraveling a great mystery.

After the conclusion of the trial, the Smith party, elated with their temporary success, left the court room, vowing "they'd have the claim, live or die, without waiting for another law-suit either," and off they went to the grocery on the corner, filling themselves to the brim with bad whisky, taking a jug and bottle or two besides, then starting for home, women and all, roaring drunk.

Uncle Tut did not like the out-look; he was not a coward, and had no intention any one should think he was, but he took Eben quietly one side, and requested that he accompany him home. Eben consented, and prepared to do so without unnecessary delay, being careful to place his trusty rifle in the wagon with plenty of ammunition, and also Dr. Gascoigne's old gun, in case Uncle Tut should need to use it before they reached the cabin where his own hung suspended from iron hooks driven deep into the logs.

The men were soon on their way, having avoided arousing apprehension on the part of Dr. Gascoigne, who was quite feeble and could not endure much worry; neither did they care to have their town folks know they felt a shadow of fear regarding the drunken rabble which had preceded them.

After starting, the two men drove rapidly along and were soon out of sight of the village; for they wished to reach home before the reckless crew, and prepare for any mischief they might concoct.

They expected it would be about sun-down when they arrived and hoped John might have the chores done, the cattle and horses taken care of, and that the family would be together, in or near the house.

The country being open prairie, broken by a slight rise now and then, barely sufficient to hide a team traveling along the road, but giving no opportunity for outwitting an enemy by strategy, their only hope consisted in having the lightest load, the fastest horses and no liquor on board, outside or inside.

Eben had suggested as they were harnessing up, that Uncle Tut's hard worked animals be left in the stalls, and that they take his fast bays; fortunate they found the change, for the difference in speed became a matter of life and death before the race was finished.

Not wishing an open encounter, they kept far enough and yet near, behind the rowdies, so that an occasional eminence might cover them from view, until the dusk of evening coming on, hoping thus to evade discovery while overtaking them, when a dash ahead would enable the preparation of a warm reception, should the villains attempt to vent their wrath upon arrival.

This plan 'was easy of accomplishment, for quite a distance after leaving town the country was somewhat rolling, and the river which must be crossed, bordered by a piece of timber on either side, so that they could follow closely without being seen.

The men rode along anxiously, and at dusk were so near the drunken load in front, they could hear them bragging what they'd do for mischief, after reaching Uncle Tut's claim.

Threats of violence could be plainly heard wafted on the still, dewy air. They were intoxicated to ugliness, but not yet incapacitated for planning evil. Uncle Tut's blood grew hot when he heard them tell how "they'd string him up to the rafters of his own barn, and turn whiskey down the gullet of that whining temperance teetotaler, John Gascoigne, until he couldn't stand, and scare the women near about to death, and send them running into town, little brat and all; oh! they'd have lots of fun before morning."

Thus the scoundrels rattled on with their bragadocio, unable fully to understand the enormity of their own wicked folly.

Uncle Tut was boiling over with rage, "Da-dam the vi-villains," he whispered to Eben, "gi-give me th-that gun o' yourn I-I say, an' let me put a bu-bullet through the rascal-ly crowd."

"No, Uncle Tut, I won't, you must keep still for awhile yet," answered the cooler headed Eben—"we shall have need enough of powder and bullets before we get through, I fear."

Finally, just as they passed the last rise of land and Uncle Tut was about to break out again, Eben gave the word, and a peculiar, low noise, which the team seemed to understand, sent them flying pellmell past the surprised load of drunken desperadoes in front, who plied their whips vigorously and yelled with all their might, but to no purpose; they had the heaviest load, a lumber wagon, tired horses, and though using strenuous endeavor, keeping up the race until Eben drove into the yard, his spirited team could not be overtaken.

Fortunately John saw them coming, and divining at a glance something serious, immediately at his command, the women rushed in doors, carrying the child, who had been watching Aunt Lucille feed the poultry, with them.

John, in the twinkling of an eye, put up the bars after Eben had entered, before the others could get through. Uncle Tut sprang from the light wagon at the instant when Eben had reined in the excited horses to a stop, opened wide the barn doors, and in they went, wagon and all. Not waiting to unhitch, they had barred, bolted and locked the barn, succeeding in reaching the house when the marauders drove into the yard.

Quickly the doors and windows were fastened, the windows covered with heavy wooden shutters, and by the time the last one had alighted the little home was in a state of seige, for possession was, in this case, nine points of the law.

Those inside labored to be sure under the disadvantage of being on the defensive; while those on the outside, could without hindrance start almost any imaginable deviltry that bad whisky could help men devise, and they improved their opportunity.

First they attempted battering down the doors and windows of the house, then they assailed the barn doors, and failing in these projects, started to slaughter all the poultry, but really only killed a chicken or two, and set the ducks and geese squaking, and the old turkeys cocks gobbling and strutting about with the importance of the idea that they were to protect the whole barn-yard brood.

Then they tore up the nicely tended garden, even destroying the flowers and shrubbery about the house, twisting off the young fruit trees of which John and Uncle Tut were so proud, in pure spite and vandalism.

At last they began to talk of setting fire to the barn; at this Uncle Tut and Eben made ready to shoot from the little attic window above the living-room, should they attempt an execution of their threat.

The party being so drunk as not to realize all they were doing, Eben insisted upon refraining from firing unless the emergency of some greater outrage than had yet been perpetrated demanded such action.

His was the mistake so often made in war, legal and otherwise, of not fighting hard enough at the beginning, with the result almost invariably following as in this case, that leniency before the end costs dearly. Had a shot or two been fired at the first, showing the villains they meant to fight in earnest if pushed to it, the fright would have cooled their angry, drunken ardor perhaps, and they might have desisted; but Uncle Tut and Eben were content to watch them quietly from their station at the window, John attending to the women and child below, at least for the present. The evening was now advancing into the night, and though fussing about for a while longer, threatening what they would do, but accomplishing nothing serious, the assailants, after a noisy, unintelligable consultation, getting into their wagon drove away.

John, Eben and the women thought the trouble was over; but Uncle Tut said, "No, they would come back, he felt certain."

After waiting a little to make sure they had gone at least as far as their own claim, Eben and John went to the barn, took out the horses, still hitched to the wagon, and drove down to the far-pasture, where they unharnessed and tethered them securely to some stakes which had been driven for that purpose before the fence was built; taking this precaution in view of a possibility of the barn being burnt.

Barely had they reached the house again, where a terrible noise was heard outside, tin-horns, tin pans, cow-bells, dogs barking, men hallowing and swearing, and with an occasional shot fired towards the house; pandemonium seemed let loose.

Soon the marauders commenced battering the doors again, evidently intending to frighten the beseiged party into a surrender.

John and Uncle Tut could be kept still no longer, and in spite of the cool advice of Eben, they insisted upon firing into

the crowd; someone was wounded, and instantly the people outside became fearfully excited, exasperated to frenzy, and commenced mischief in good earnest. They placed their guns
wherever they could find a crack between the logs, at the key-
holes, anywhere, and fired away. The cabin being so small
there was little chance of escaping the bullets which came thiek
and fast. Those outside had, it was plain, provided themselves
with plenty of powder and shot as well as whiskey.

At last Uncle Tut took Lucille and Jules up the ladder into
the loft, Julia following, for they hoped thus to escape harm.
Uncle Tut again stationed himself in the attic window, thinking
to get some good shots at the rascals from this quarter should
they come round to execute their threat as to the barn. John
and Eben remained below, fearing the wretches might break in
the doors, strongly as they were made and bolted.

Lucille, in her weak condition, was now nearly dead with
fright; but neither of the women made the slightest noise, although it required all their tact to keep little Jules even passably
quiet; strangely enough he did not scream or seem frightened
by the confusion as most children would have done, but persisted in trying to run about, clapping his hands, jumping up
and down, laughing with glee, really enjoying the excitement.
They succeeded in controlling him after a while, and the women
and child crowded into the farthest corner of the dark attic,
while Uncle Tut noted an observation from the window.

Very soon a man came round with a lighted wisp of straw,
attempting to fire the barn. Uncle Tut covered him with the
muzzle of his trusty rifle, the man dropped quick as thought,
groaned and lay still, but was not dead.

When the crowd heard the shot from this new quarter, and
the groans from their fallen companion, they came rushing
around to the side of the house wildly, and upon realizing the
situation were furious. At that window they were determined
to come cost what it might.

As this was impossible without a ladder, and none could be
found outside, they tried breaking into the barn, which, failing
to accomplish, but finding a low shed with a thatched roof of
straw built against it on the side farthest from the house where
the shots could not reach them, they soon had the threatened
fire under headway, and forcing their way through the shed un-
daunted by the flames, secured a short ladder. Elated and
shouting curses at the top of their voices, they placed it without
delay under the attic window and proceeded to mount.

The situation of the defenders was now becoming desperate. The heat of the burning barn was intense, several men were crowding at the foot of the ladder, more were coming round the corner. Reinforcements had evidently arrived; how many could not be seen, but surely two or three to one of the besieged party.

Since several of their number had been wounded the assailants were mad as demons, and bent upon revenge; the effects of the whisky had partially worked off and they were able to do some rational thinking, only increasing their capacity for harm. As the result of a little calculation two or three aimed at the men in the open window, seeking to retaliate and also protect those trying to reach the top of the ladder. Up went one, weapon in hand, and another soon followed.

The women, now pale, trembling and cold with terror, cowered in their corner with compressed lips and glistening eyes, hushing the boy as best they could.

The men within the window were prepared to give the villains a warmer reception than they thought.

When John and Eben saw the fight was to be in the loft, they ascended, carrying besides their rifles each a strong, sharp knife; the long, sword-like blade used by western farmers for slaughtering. As the men outside came up they were at a disadvantage with their guns, not being able to use them on the ladder, or until fairly inside the room, and the defenders dodging the shots from below had an idea of taking good care the besiegers should not get in safely, or more than one at a time.

The first man who put foot on the sill of the window received a terrible gash, and as the blood spurted from his wound, the fellow on the topmost round staggered back appalled, draging his injured comrade with him.

They had not expected such work. Fortunately the early morning stage came rattling along the road a few rods from the house—the burning barn, the rifle shots, the yells and curses told the story—some settlers were fighting over a contested claim.

In a few moments the stage had driven up to the house and ten or twelve passengers, springing to the ground, entered into the melee with a vigor which soon terminated the contest; by an intuition comprehending the situation, throwing their forces on the side of justice and right.

The assaulting party hastily placing their wounded companions (one, the ringleader, Silas Smith, having received what

seemed a death blow just at the close of the fray from one of
the stage passengers) at the bottom of the wagon, the others
jumping in, drove furiously away.

After extinguishing the fire, the men, new-comers with
them, came pouring into the house to see what had become of
the women and talk about the trouble. They found Julia
laboring with the now unconscious Lucille; over-taxed nature
could endure no more, and had given way again. She had succeeded in placing her on the only bed in the loft, which had
been set apart for the use of Uncle Tut since Lucille's occupancy of his room below, and Julia was striving in every way
to restore her, but she lay in a faint, seemingly dead; the boy by
her side sleeping. Those who had championed their cause with
the men of the family coming up at Julia's call, some by the ladder outside and others from the inside, all expressing sympathy
and offering their services—among them who but Henry Armstrong!

For Fate had brought him at last in spite of himself to Lucille's very door, even to her side.

But alas *she* was far away, only her wasted body with its
stilled heart, and wan, white face was lying there before him—
herself gone—departed.

Henry gazed with the others upon the passive form, so different from his Lucille as she used to be; and at the thought,
the fear that she might be surely dead, his heart gave a bound,
and a great sob burst from his heaving breast; but with the will
of a strong man, repressing every sense but that of seeing, he
looked again, and if a dagger had struck him sharp and deep
he could not have been more agonizingly transfixed.

Yes, there lay Lucille, his own true love, and by her side—
a babe—her child—every feature like its mother, and the fine,
handsome fellow bending over her so tenderly was the father
certainly, and her husband. For who that had known him of
old could recognize in the stalwart western farmer the once dissipated brother John? And Henry had never seen John even
in Barrytown, for he had married and gone away before
Henry's advent. John himself was too busy with Lucille, as
were all the family, to notice the stage passengers individually,
though truly grateful for their assistance.

Was Lucille dead? No—for very soon she opened wide her
eyes, fixing them upon Henry Armstrong with a supernatural gaze
—a look he never forgot to his dying day—such instant recognition, devotion, appeal; he could not endure the emotion it

8

stirred within his heart for another moment, the love, the regret, the remorse.

How could he now right the wrong he felt he had done her and himself?

Was she not a married woman, her babe owning another than himself its father?

What now could aught avail?

Out—out into the cold morning air he must go or he should fall.

Wearily, as John leaned over her, shutting Henry from view, Lucille closed her eyes again; restfully, peacefully, for had *he* not come at last? Had she not again seen his dear face, the love-light in his clear eyes—a light once seen never to be mistaken?

And Henry following his fate turned from the group of people, and from Lucille, going out into the grey light of that chilly, foggy morning.

The red streaks of the coming dawn in the east intensifying the dreariness which enwrapped both landscape and desolate traveler as with a funeral pall.

Weak, and trembling in every limb, paralyzed with grief, Henry reached the waiting stage and sank into his seat, ten years older than when he left it two hours before.

Not one word did he speak until the stage stopped for breakfast, when, to avoid remark, he must rouse himself, and explained by saying he was very tired; not well! No—not well indeed! Henry Armstrong was never again as he had been.

Now that he had lost her, how strong and yearning was his love for Lucille; growing day by day continually, year by year. Over the world he traveled for change and forgetfulness, seeking another woman who should be to him what she might have been, but he never found another. And what of her? After a few moments rest she opened her eyes, expecting to meet those of one she loved so well, butHenry was not there, and scanning each face inquiringly, she turned appealingly to John, who was bending over her. "What is it Lucille, dear?" For John knew his little sister wanted something. But she, too weak for speech, could only look, with intensest love and longing in her eyes.

One by one the passengers went out and soon the stage was on its way.

It was a long time before Lucille recovered from the excitement, the fear, the final shock and disappointment of that eventful night. Her nerves were unstrung, strength exhausted, vital force gone, said her friends; and sadder than ever was Dr. Gascoigne. For months she remained very weak, nigh unto death; though not like her sister, delirious, she would murmer as they watched her sleeping—a few words, a name now and then, Myra's name and Henry's.

All those who loved her so dearly and would have shielded from every sorrow, knew at last what ailed Lucille. Gradually, with persevering tenderness, they nursed her back to life and a degree of health.

After she had partially recovered, and no one mentioned having seen Henry, although she could hardly believe he had not been before her eyes really and truly, she finally concluded that what had appeared to be her lover of by-gone days, must have been a vision of her own excited brain.

" But it was so real, so exactly like flesh and blood, bone and sinew; in every way as a live man—how strange, how strange."

"And yet, if it were himself, why did he not speak? Why did he not stay? How came he there? Where did he go to?"

These questions Lucille revolved over and over again as she lay sinking and prostrate those weary months; sometimes almost touching the verge of the dark valley through which flowed the cold stream waiting to engulf her; but the mystery was not fully solved until long years after.

And Henry went on and on, from place to place; never returning that way as he had intended.

Thus does Fate defraud us when happiness is at our very door, just within our grasp.

Ever enticing—ever eluding.

CHAPTER XV.

REMOVAL.

When the Freelawn people learned how the drunken rowdies who tormented Uncle Tut and his family for so long had
wound up with the outrageous attack upon him the night after
the suit was decided, which every one believed won by false
swearing, they made up their minds the villains should leave
the country.

Judge Lynch was a popular man in those days, and many a
coat of tar and feathers, if no worse treatment, was administered
by his decision; in this instance little mercy would have been shown
only that three of the party were wounded, the leader, Silas
Smith, dangerously. He received scant sympathy in his distress, for there were several witnesses to his deadly aim at Uncle Tut, which he was prevented from executing by one of the
stage passengers grappling him just in time, inflicting serious injury as the issue proved.

Notwithstanding the extreme provocation received, which
it will be allowed would have instigated most persons to revenge,
Uncle Tut, John and Eben each urged that the men be left unmolested until all had recovered.

None of the wounds proved fatal, and soon those disabled
were in condition for traveling, a change was no great hardship, as they had not improved their claim, but spent the time
drinking and carousing with the women and such neighbors
as were like themselves; they were tendered a quiet but effectual
notice to move on—and they moved *speedily*.

Years elapsed before any one in that vicinity heard from
them, when they again came before Uncle Tut as central figures
in a tragedy most extraordinary; at least the woman, Silas Smith
and the man they called Doctor or Doc.

While Uncle Tut was staying with his friends in town, attending his law suit, he did not omit making himself as agreeable and sociable as was possible for a stammering man, with
Aunt Debby. The fact is, he was becoming thoroughly disgusted and dissatisfied living without a mate, as was she.

There being no one else near, eligible for either, it was not
necessary that Uncle Tut should do a great amount of talking,

and when he essayed to "pop the question," Aunt Debby accepted him before he got half way through the first sentence.

"Why, yes, to be sure, of course I will. What day are you going out to the claim, and how soon are you coming back for me? I'll want to know so as to be all ready. Law sakes, who'd a thought two such queer ones as you and me, Uncle Tut, 'ud ever have made a match? But, I reckon, if you do go slow, while I *must go fast*, we'll manage to pull putty well in double harness after all; perhaps we'll check-mate each other, and both be better for it, at any rate we'll make the venture, if you say so," answered Aunt Debby, wiping her eyes on the cornei of her clean checked apron.

More soft-heartedness than Uncle Tut had seen from Aunt Debby since he had known her. "Women are queer creatures," said Uncle Tut to himself.

A strange, queer woman was Aunt Debby, truly. Never had sorrow brought from her a tear, and here was she rubbing her eyes because an honest man had asked her to marry him. But it was settled that he'd come for her the next week, and they'd be married and go back to the farm together, the wedding being celebrated in Dr. Gascoigne's parlor according to programme, without the least hitch or delay. For the Evil One never troubled himself in the slightest about the affair. He knew very well that once the knot was tied, Aunt Debby'd make lively times for Uncle Tut without any of his assistance, it being one of those unions, though bringing a fair degree of comfort, nevertheless sure to evolve enough discomfort, before the antagonistic elements assimilate, to be entirely satisfactory for his Satanic Majesty.

After this change of base, John and Julia took possession of the claim deserted by their bad neighbors, paying them a fair sum for the same before their departure, and Lucille returned to her father, leaving little Jules with them in their new home, as they had formed such an attachment towards him and he for them, while Lucille lay sick, they begged Eben to let him remain—awhile.

To this he readily consented, for he never felt at ease when the child was near him, being unwittingly reminded by the boy of the wrong he had done its mother, and there was also an uncontrollable shrinking on the part of Jules from his father, which Eben knew and felt.

Lucille, although fond of the motherless little fellow, found her strength unequal in the care of him. She had seen how Julia tried by kind treatment of the child to atone for her former folly, and felt certain John was devoted to him for his own sake, and because he naturally loved children. Thus the arrangement proved satisfactory to all concerned.

Gertrude, who was quite mature for her age, would rather her brother had returned with Aunt Lucille, but she was not accustomed to having her own way, and could adapt herself to changes, finding contentment, or even pleasure, where a child of more restless, unhappy disposition would see cause for dissatisfaction.

She was a quiet little girl, trusty and capable, whom everybody liked, her friends declared, and the kindness she invariably received proved the assertion. As she grew older, incidents much the same as have been recited, marked the months and years.

She as a matter of course attended regularly the ordinary day school, and besides the evening schools for singing and spelling intended to benefit adults and older children, and on Sundays the school for religious instruction.

Also parties without end; in spring, summer and fall, nosegay parties, berry-parties and nutting parties; in winter, sleighing-parties and coasting-parties, and apple-paring bees, and candy-pulls, and quilting-parties, and *kissing-parties* all the year round, where the little lads and lasses met to play games and give forfeits, to be redeemed by the inevitable, innocent kiss. Gertrude long remembered the disappointment shared equally by her mates of either sex, consequent upon the superintendency of the aged maiden sister of a young miss, at one of these gatherings, whose extreme prudishness frowned upon, and exterminated for the time being at least, the harmless kiss. That party was privately voted an unmitigated failure by every little miss and young gentlemen in town.

Gertrude, as a child, surely had her share of good times, plenty of sweet-hearts, and was a general favorite with her play-fellows as well as elders, though perhaps experiencing more sorrow than some others.

Another grief was just now on its way, coming into her life, Grandpa Gascoigne becoming feebler each day, and Gertrude was ever afterwards glad that she gave him cheerfully her loving attention in his declining days.

She was his chosen companion whenever accessible, and would sit for hours by his side, her head resting upon his shoulder, the bright, golden curls mingling with the soft, silvery gleam of his snow white beard and flowing locks of rarely beautiful hair, listening eagerly while he told stories of his younger bygone years.

How his father had been physician to Queen Marie Antoinette, of France, and in the days of the persecution when a mob followed her carriage through the streets of Paris, the ignorant populace demanding only blood, the members of her household had escaped as best they could, well satisfied at saving their lives, so unreasonable was the wrath of her subjects.

And how his father, the Queen's physician, succeeded in reaching the coast in disguise and putting out to sea with a younger brother, in a fisherman's boat, sustained by a loaf of bread and a jug of water, until finally taken up by a ship bound for America. And then he would take from his pocket the old watch which had belonged to the French savant, and removing the time-keeper from its huge silver case, show her the beautiful pictures it contained, carefully packed away in the capacious cover. Some on velvet or satin, others on velum or on a parchment fine and smooth, thin and silky as the red poppy leaves in her own garden; but strong as they were frail, fit foundation for the exquisite likenesses of friends long dead, or flowers, leaves and strange artistic tracings in pencil and water colors, or oil, executed by friends, sweethearts, or members of the household, and presented as keepsakes to be placed in this receptacle of choicest mementos.

Gertrude ever after carried the memory of her grandfather's queer old watch—its history, all the strange stories connected with it, and those last days spent with him, through the vicisitudes of her eventful life—even to the end.

The sad trouble was very near Gertrude now, grandpa sat day after day in the dear old chair Myra had brought from the Eastern home, and dozed his life away. At last they came and found him quietly sleeping—sweetly resting—in the not unkindly arms of death. Although long expected, it was a shock to the good doctor's friends, especially to Lucille and Gertrude—the very event we are looking for, often coming as a surprise.

They placed him beside his loved daughter Myra, and both Lucille and Gertrude were comforted with the thought of a helpful and honored life, fittingly ending in peace; but even so, after he was gone, his wasted body laid away, these two wandered drearily from room to room of the desolated house, grieving together.

But a change was coming to them, which, though resulting from a misfortune, would benefit and surely divert the attention from their affliction. Soon after her grandfather's death, Gertrude, child as she was, noticed an unusual irritability on the part of her father, no one could please him; the cause proved to be financial embarrassment. From their first coming to Freelawn it had been a struggle for existence, and in the mercantile business, almost impossible to have the accounts balance; the past year being extremely unfavorable, sickness universally prevalent, and the crops poor, for the farmers could not work, consequently they could not pay their debts, scarcely current expenses; at last from this combination of adverse circumstances, her father was on the verge of bankruptcy, in a few weeks when the fall goods were to be purchased, the crisis can.c, and Eben failed utterly, even the home was swept away.

What to do next was the question, John was not prospering on the new farm either, and the idea of removing to Wisconsin was considered.

At a little town on Lake Michigan, called Port Ulao, situated twenty miles north of Milwaukee, Dr. Gascoigne had left some real estate, taken shortly before his death, in exchange for an equity in Eastern property.

A wooding-pier and a store and dwelling house combined, like the one in Freelawn, constituted this transfer.

After consulting together, it was concluded that Eben should try what he could do there first, and if he succeeded, John was to follow when he sold his farm.

Preparations were commenced at once for the change, old ties were severed once more, and the new venture entered upon.

Julia having now a boy of her own, and neither Lucille or Eben being willing to part with the child, or separate the brother and sister permanently, Jules was brought home to be taken with them to Wisconsin.

As Myra had requested that Lucille should care for her children, she was loth in yielding the charge to any one, even their father. Owning an interest in the Wisconsin property, and for so many years a member of the same family with Eben, nothing strange was thought of the arrangement that she should go with them, especially as Grandma Brewster, burying one after another of her own family, had lived with the Grieveau's since Aunt Debby's marriage, and now declared her wish of accompanying the family to their Wisconsin home.

She said they seemed dearer to her than any one living, and

having saved a small competence could do as she desired, and no advice of other friends or relatives should hinder her from going with Lucille and staying near Myra's children.

When the final day came and good byes must be said, they were surprised at the strength of attachments formed in Free-lawn. Their hearts had wandered so persistently to old Barrytown, speaking of it as home and of going back, they were now unprepared for their own feelings.

The farewells were finished at last, and the family started away in much the same fashion as they had arrived in Free-lawn a few years before this time, directing their course towards the wilds of Wisconsin as the State was spoken of at that early day.

Being further north, more rugged, heavily timbered, not easy of cultivation as Illinois, Indiana, Ohio and Michigan, Wisconsin was several years behind these States in filling up with settlers. But as our friends traveled across the State from southwest to northeast, they passed through Janesville, Beloit, Whitewater and other prosperous towns before reaching Milwaukee, a flourishing city situated at the extreme eastern limit of the State and on the western shore of Lake Michigan.

After leaving Milwaukee and proceeding north a short day's journey, they halted at their destination, the lake port before mentioned; finding the place settled entirely by Norwegians of the lower class, with the exception of two or three American families. These hardy emigrants were honest and kind though indigent, much poorer even than the new-comers, who, greatly to their surprise, found themselves looked upon as aristocracy. For did they not own one of the three or four frame houses which the village contained? Many of these people occupying at best a log cabin of one room, however large the family. Some being content with mud huts dug deep into the side of the bluff and floored with the smooth, flat stones from the shore of the lake; cedar slabs forming the front of the mansion, while others supporting the mass of earth and gravel which composed the hill above them furnished a roof; one small window and a door, also a chimney built of brush, stones and mud-mortar against the front in one corner completing the structure. This rude arrangement answered for heating and culinary purposes in winter, while during the few hot days of summer an open fire against the hill-side, among an ingeniously contrived pile of stones, was the cooking-range used by these thrifty people.

Many a thick slice of rye-bread baked in the hot, clean

wood-ashes of these fires and spread with the delicious Wisconsin butter, did Gertrude and Jules accept after they had made
them friends, from the kind dames to whom these humble homes
were a kingdom.

The change from Freelawn to Ulao was accomplished in
the early summer, and but a short time elapsed after their arrival before the brother and sister had visited every hut along the
shore.   Aunt Lucille could watch them from her own door as
they strolled about picking up curious stones and pebbles sometimes flowers, as they went, until hands and aprons were running over full.   When tired they had permission to avail themselves of the invitations to rest in the neat little homes.   For
the Norwegian woman keeps her family comfortable be her resources ever so limited.   The men, too, are industrious and
careful.

During the summer they worked from sunrise till sunset in
the heavy timber upon the bluff, chopping and piling long rows
of cord-wood ready for hauling down to the shore in winter,
for the use of the steamboats which would stop at the pier the
next summer, and also for shipping.

While the men labored in the deep, cool woods, the women
attended to their house-keeping and their gardens; raising potatoes, rutabagas, cabbages and others vegetables grown in cool
climates and easy of storage in winter.

The lake and the woods also contributed to the support of
these simple, economical people.

Fish were salted or dried, berries and nuts gathered in the
woods, a few hardy apples secured from the gardens, and all
carefully put away for winter use, except snch as were immediately needed.

With this provision and the fowls, pigs and sheep, an occasional calf or beef for slaughter, with the eggs and milk, the
butter and cream, they managed to exist and enjoy their full
quota of happiness.

For clothing, the women in addition to their other work,
carded, spun and wove the fleecy wool into warm cloth for
winter use; manufacturing flax also in the same manner for
summer wear.

When the winter evenings were long, after the day's work
was done, after the men had hauled their loads of wood down
from the hills to the shore on the great ox sleds, after the
women had attended to their housework and the children, getting them off to school betimes in the morning, being sure that

not a moment was idled away when home, the whole family at eventide assisted in the careful feeding and housing of the highly prized animals, horses and cattle, sheep, pigs, and fowls. When the day's work was finished, men, women and children would gather around the open fire-place piled up with immense logs of blazing wood, each knitting so rapidly, on stockings fully a yard long for the adults, the steel needles, but for their glistening brightness could not be seen. As they flew the men smoked their clay pipes, often the women did the same, while one and another of the elder ones related some marvelous narrative handed down from generations back about the wraiths, the brownies and the elfin bands who had for ages past disported themselves and played their pranks among the Friths and Fjords in old Norway; of which the following, told by a woman whose grandmother had when a little girl served a lady in the capacity of servant, is a sample:

"When my grandmother was a little girl, she lived with an old widow lady and helped her with the house-keeping. One Christmas Eve the lady made up her mind to go to church and hear the morning mass, and as it was to begin at half-past six in the morning, they fixed up the breakfast table the night before—for she wanted her breakfast before she went. Then they went to bed, and when the lady waked up, the moon was shining on the floor, and she got up to see what time it was, but the clock had stopped at half-past eleven, and she could not tell the time, so she looked out of the window to see if it was daylight, and was surprised to see the church lighted up. She called the girl to hurry and make some coffee while she dressed, for she did not want to miss the mass. She drank her coffee, took her prayer-book and went to church.

"It was very still in the street, and she never saw a human being on the way. When she got to church she went straight up to her pew, but when she looked round she saw the people looked so pale and curious, just like they were dead, all of them. There was nobody she knew, but a good many she thought she had seen before, but when and where she could not remember. When the preacher went up to the altar she saw that he was not the regular city preacher, but a tall, pale looking man she remembered she had seen somewhere before. He spoke splendidly, but she noticed it was not so noisy, and not so much coughing and whispering as before they always had in meeting; it was so quiet she could almost hear a pin drop on the floor, she became nearly frightened. When the singing commenced a woman sitting next her bent over and whispered in her ear, 'Put your cloak on your arm and get away as quick as you can, for if you wait till the end you are lost. This is the dead having their prayer meeting.'

"The widow lady was awfully scared, for hearing the voice and looking at the woman, she saw she was an old neighbor who had been dead a long time. She looked round and saw that the preacher and a good many of the people she had seen when they were alive; but they had all been dead a good many years.

"She was so scared she was most crazy, and drew her cloak over her shoulders as the woman had told her, and got away as fast as she could. But the dead people all tried to stop her, and her feet trembled under her and she nearly fainted, but she flew along and got to the door. As she was coming out of the church she felt somebody pulling her cloak and she left it behind her and ran home as fast as she could.

"When she got back to her room, *the clock in the church tower struck one*, and she jumped into bed—clothes and all—most frightened to death.

"In the morning when the people came to church they found the cloak torn to a hundred pieces. My mother has *seen one of the pieces* and *knows* it was all true, as the widow lady and my grandmother told it."

Yes, as true and as well authenticated as is many another venerable tradition controlling the faith of the world.

At these ghostly tales the little grey eyes of the young Norwegians would be distended wide in intensified amazement, and every straight, flaxen white hair stand on end, until shivering with a comfortable fear, a pleasurable horror, they slyly crept away, awestruck, to their cozy little cots, and crawling between the ample feather beds, hid their heads in the downy pillows.

This wierd amusement was not reserved exclusively for the evening entertainments, and Gertrude and little Jules never tired of listening to these strange stories, sat many an hour with a group of tow-headed youngsters around some old granny's knees, whose tongue flew not less rapidly than her needles, until all were shivering from head to foot, even on the brightest summer's day.

These with other experiences, which seemed a part of their fate, produced in the minds of the two children a predeliction for and a desire to investigate spiritual phenomena, which became a marked characteristic of their mentality.

Especially was little Jules affected in a peculiar manner, and the worship of the supernatural already engrafted upon the child by the events of his pre-natal existence, was greatly intensified, coloring his whole life, mayhap developing his destiny.

Among other things to be learned from these poor and certainly ignorant people, as the world's knowledge goes, our friends from Freelawn came to know how few of the artificial surroundings costing so much money, are really needed for making people comfortable and happy, if only they would come down to nature and the use of their own hands; for in these humble homes was contentment, thrift and peace, which the millionaire of to-day may well envy.

CHAPTER XVI.

AN EPISODE.

Lucille, although very lonely, received much benefit to her health from the change of scene and climate. Mother Brewster declared Wisconsin air would put life into the dying, and there are many now who will agree with her; surely if with the pure invigorating air, is combined the water of those medicinal springs found everywhere at near intervals in this wonderful State, worthy to be distinguished as Nature's sanitarium.

Even the forlorn town of Ulao, under the great overhanging bluff, lying flat on the sand by the shore of the lake, could boast of as good a spring as the famed Bethesda, whose healing waters bring so many every season from far and near to the beautiful city of Waukesha for health and pleasure.

Gertrude would take her pitcher in one hand, her brother Jules holding by the other, and go up through the deep ravines, rocky and romantic, thickly studded on either side with fragrant Cedar, Tamarack and Juniper trees; the Cedars growing with close, straight branches, Tamaracks tall and slender with a feathery grace, Junipers down by the ground, spreading out broadly, tangled in with the briars and white starry blossoms of the blackberry bushes, thick green mosses, and delicate wildwood flowers; up through this fragrant bower, this dell of delights, following the gurgling stream, jumping across from side to side as better footing required, the happy sister and little brother went every day, bringing fresh, cool water from the spring in the hill-side, but so *nasty*, they thought in taste and smell, for Aunt Lucille to drink.

Auntie throve on the horrid spring water and pure air, feeling more strength and vigor than for years; although her grief over her lost love did not leave her but she was becoming accustomed to carry her burden.

She heard in the strangest manner through Uncle Tut's investigations, just before leaving Freelawn, that Henry Armstrong really was a passenger in the stage on that eventful night, and that he *did stand by her bedside;* this much Uncle Tut ascertained, even tracing him as one of a party going to San Francisco, crossing the Rocky Mountains, where he lost the clue, and time proved that years were to elapse before he should find it again.

Lucille was more than ever puzzled, and longed to know why Henry had looked at her with such passionate love and tenderness in his eyes, and then left her without a word.

She tried in every possible way to solve the mystery, and finally concluded that Henry must have formed another tie which could not be broken without causing the same pangs to another which she had felt so keenly. This thought partially reconciled Lucille to the sad fate decreed her, she said unselfishly, " If some other woman loves him as I have loved, for her sake I will banish his image from my heart;" and then, that last, warm, entrancing gaze, from those deep, dark eyes, which had laid hold upon, engulfing her very soul in bliss and peace, coming back to her, Lucille would cry out in anguish, " How can I let him go, when I know he loves me truly even now, for I'll never believe I did not see it then. What can it mean? What is the trouble? What *has* he done? What have *I* done, that we should be so cruelly separated, estranged, parted forever, and without one word of explanation?" And Lucille would be again overcome as of old.

About this time, one of the three families comprising the society of this Norwegian hamlet, was the recipient of an unexpected visit. Some business requiring the signature of a member necessitated search, which resulted in the arrival one day by the afternoon boat, of a man refined in appearance, who enquired " If a family by the name of Glenn lived anywhere about?"

He was directed to one of the frame houses near by, but before reaching the door encountered Lucille returning from the spring with the children, pitcher in one hand and a large nosegay of beautiful yellow flowers in the other.

On the instant a pleased surprise each saw unconsciously revealed to the other, for how could they conceal the sudden admiration felt at unexpectedly meeting a lady or a gentleman, a fact easily recognized by the free-masonry of congeniality.

The last place he had thought to find such a vision of lovliness as little Lucille presented, and far from her mind the idea of seeing a thoroughly bred gentleman outside her own family.

The stranger proceeded to the house of the people he was looking for; but although the needed information was shortly acquired and nothing hindered him from leaving by the morning boat as at first intended, he suddenly discovered himself

very tired from long continued travel (for he had crossed an
ocean in the interests of his clients), and accepted the invitation
to remain a few days with his new acquaintances, who were
very glad of a visitor breaking in upon the monotony of their
lives.

He afterwards concluded to lengthen his stay indefinitely,
and insisted they should accept a suitable remuneration for any
trouble he might give them.   To this they had no objection, for
small help was thankfully received by these people in this out
of the way place, where a comfortable living was difficult to
secure.

Of course Lucille was the enticement, a fact the gentleman
in no wise attempted denying to himself, whatever he might
aver to others,   He said, "Here is a woman who would attract
wherever one might meet her, did she speak never a word; for
though not faultlessly beautiful, she possesses a charm none can
escape."   Coming across this rare flower in a wilderness, he
was even more interested to know and talk with her, to learn
where she came from, and what manner of woman she might
be, than if finding her under ordinary circumstances.

He had traveled much, was a man of the world, and also
quite a gallant among ladies, had engaged in flirtation more or
less serious, but his heart was still untouched.

By the afternoon following his arrival he had gained an introduction, not a difficult undertaking in a place where there
were so few people, and everyone was fairly obliged to know
everyone else.

A walk along the shore, an invitation to enter the pleasant
parlor upon their rerurn, a chat upon almost everything under
the sun, and before they bade each other good evening the acquaintance was commenced which induced the gentleman to
remain in this desolate little village a full month, well entertained every moment of the time at any rate when beside Lucille—a happiness which he managed to enjoy pretty constantly.

He could never tire of walking, riding, boating, visiting
with her; talking and listening to her replies.   He found her
sensible, quick, witty, well-informed, amiable, easily-pleased,
agreeable to look upon, magnetic and sympathetic as only those
can be who have been touched by sorrow.

Lucille never alluded to her sore disappointment in the
slightest manner, not even after their acquaintance grew to be
an acknowledged friendship; but somehow her new friend felt
sure he did not get near her heart, and this was just what he

was trying to accomplish, staying here in this dreary place all these weeks.

He was coming to realize more and more every day that when he went into the world again he must take this dear little woman, whom fate had thrown so unceremoniously in his way, along with him to be his own forever.

And yet he almost knew that although she had become indispensable to him, no lasting impression was made upon her heart or life by his presence.

Why, he could not divine; she liked him he was sure, for she brightened at his approach, was contented in his company, and loth to have him go. But she would not allow him to approach her in the least way that could be construed as tender, or draw from her more sympathy than she displayed towards the children, members of her family and other friends. Of all the women he had known she was the only one over whom he felt absolutely no power; others had been ready to fall into his arms at the slightest provocation, but Lucille was immovable as the pure white marble. He failed to arouse her enthusiasm in any degree, and yet she was uneasy and dissatisfied if he left her long alone, always restful by his side, but when he tried to induce some return of the yearning passion which was consuming his own life, he could never gain more than the admission that she was very lonely—glad of his friendship and company.

And this was all the bond between them on her part; she had basked in his companionship, as does the consumptive in the rays of the life-giving sun; she seemed powerless to turn away from the invigorating, saving influence which had come to her unsought, in her desperate despondency and grief; she believed it had perfected her restoration to health, and was truly grateful for his kind devotion, but fully understood, notwithstanding all, she could never love him as she knew he desired. Lucille had tried her utmost to rest in the sense of possession, which, it was plain to be seen, this man had towards her, but was more and more entirely conscious she did not belong to him in the least, but to another.

It mattered not what that other might do, or how long he should stay away—sometime, somewhere, they would meet again and she be his forevermore.

Lucille was aware she could never forget Henry Armstrong, though having purposely given every opportunity that his image might be displaced. She had allowed the experiment for her own sake, and because of the one to whom she believed

Henry in honor bound; also to gratify, if possible, this man whose happiness she knew was in her hand; but her wilful heart could not be brought to love him, and now she was ready to answer the question which she was conscious he intended asking, and wished no longer delay.   She should miss him sadly, but there was no help for it, she must send her kind friend away.   Still, day after day passed and the denouement did not come, something seemed to hold it back.

When her friend called, or they went for the accustomed walk, he would resolve upon ending the mystery of Lucille's conduct towards him, but each day they met and parted, his chains the while tightening hopelessly; the one wish of his heart unaccomplished.

At last their stroll one afternoon was more extended than usual, a storm overtook them, no alternative remained but shelter under the inevitable tree; sharp lightening, terrific thunder, hail and wind, *a fearful storm* had come upon them unawares.

Lucille was thinly clad even for a summer's day, the previous hours being hot and sultry; not a shawl or wrap at hand wherewith to shield the woman he loved, and she so frail the exposure might be fatal.

Before Lucille could remonstrate he had removed his coat, and placing it about her, lifted her from the drenched ground, doing what he could to protect from the gale.

The moment he had her in his arms the strong man was wild with love and passion.   Not now could the raging elements drown his words of love.   He entreated Lucille to be his wife, he begged for one kiss from her sweet lips, one love look from her dear eyes; kiss *her*, he did, how could she prevent him?   In his arms he held her tightly, he showered kisses on her face, but not one in return.

As she felt his passionate breath upon her cheek, heard the endearing words whispered in her ear, no chord of her being thrilled at his loving caresses.   There was no response, only apathetic indifference; noticing this at last, his ardor cooled. She lay in his arms helpless as a child, with eyes closed, lips tightly sealed.

"Lucille, sweet, look at me," he cried.   " Kiss me, darling, kiss me."   She opened wide her eyes, and gazing full in his face, answered, " No, I cannot kiss you, and you *must not* kiss me."

If a thunderbolt from Heaven had struck the man he could not have seemed more certainly sent to his death.   He staggered, reeled against a tree, almost fell, then recovering himself, as the storm had abated, they quietly walked home without another word.

The next morning saw him take the boat as he had intended doing a month before, but now years older, carrying a sadder face, a heavier heart, than when he came.

Lucille knew, without a shadow of doubt, that *her heart* would ever refuse another than Henry Armstrong, and she should die an old maid. A woman by every attribute of mind, heart and body, who should have been a loved and loving wife, doomed to such a fate! Thus do men defraud women—entering the sacred citadel, stealing away their choicest possession, naught returning.

Lucille bitterly reproached herself for encouraging affection from one so truly honest as her lost friend, when she found it impossible to reciprocate; and gladly would have rectified her unhappy error, but regret could not mend the evil wrought.

The drenching of the cold rain, revulsion of feeling, and subsequent dreary loneliness told upon her health, and again was Lucille cast down.

The sudden departure was commented upon in the wee little hamlet, a lover's quarrel surmised, and also as the cause of Lucille's alarming illness following, just as would have been done in more fashionable society. But the gossips did not know *all* about their neighbors' business in this instance, any more than they would in the other probably.

Finally Lucille rallied as before, regaining health and cheerfulness, notwithstanding all the strain imposed upon her body and her spirit.

CHAPTER XVII.

COMMUNISM.

After a year's sojourn Eben was glad to dispose of a part of the Ulao property, and dividing the proceeds with John and Lucille, the family moved again, this time returning to Michigan, and locating not far from Barrytown, which Eben had left, a happy man with a loving wife, and a good start in life not many years before. Now he returned wifeless and poor, and would have been destitute but for the fortunate outcome of Dr. Gascoigne's last investment. His old neighbors said when they came to visit him, that Eben Grieveau was a good deal broken down with all he had been through since he went away; and they whispered among themselves, the chances for being better off in every respect, had he kept still. As for Eben, he gave the invariable advice to restless men, when asked his opinion about going West, 'Let well enough alone, you can live where you are, if industrious and contented."

Their new home was the site of a flourishing university, and an academy or preparatory school for both sexes. As Gertrude and Jules had been hindered in their education by the time spent in Wisconsin, they were placed immediately in school. Mr. Smythe, the gentlemanly principal, displayed much apparent interest in the Grieveau children, and soon called upon the family. In a short time he became very attentive to Aunt Lucille, and people were beginning to evince curiosity, when a different fate was evolved by the circumstance of her receiving a sudden summons, and proceeding at once to Freelawn, where her brother John was dangerously ill of a western fever, begging constantly for his sister whom he dearly loved. Her visit was prolonged beyond all expectation, Grandma Brewster attending to the household during Lucille's absence. The kind teacher continued his visits without abatement, helping the children with their lessons of an evening; they making rapid progress, being apt, even precocious for their years. Gertrude, especially, though so very young and of delicate organization physically, was acknowledged to be developed beyond her years in mind and character.

When she became a woman and was called to pass through

seas of trouble, she remembered with wonder how old and sedate were her thoughts and feelings at this immature age.

For the child really imagined herself capable of loving this teacher who treated her so kindly, with the love a wife should have for a husband; he doing his utmost to encourage the delusion, and before Aunt Lucille could make the long journey and return to her charge, the poor, foolish, little girl was actually married to a man many years her senior.

Grandma Brewster united with a strong force of old ladies, who remonstrated earnestly, Lucille had done the same by letter, but nothing prevented the consummation. The man was determined to wed the child-woman, and easily obtained the consent of Eben, who becoming absorbed recently in religious speculation, was oblivious to everything else.

From having all his life been an erratic, headstrong man, he had of late grown to be very strange in many of his ideas, and was drifting into an opinionated fanaticism.

About this time, happening to make the acquaintance of a member of an association, believing among other peculiar doctrines, that the common ownership of wives and families as well as property, was expedient, wise and religious, some of the men of the "Community," as it was usually styled, traveling about the country in the interests of their faith, also the mercantile part of their scheme, sparing no pains in making proselytes; they were invited, and often stopped in the Grieveau family, and soon Eben was an outspoken convert. These men argued the truth of their theories from certain passages of scripture, which could not be gainsayed, for almost any assertion may be proved from the Bible, by taking it piece-meal instead of as a whole.

Quoting isolated texts, such as "In Heaven they neither marry or are given in marriage," they concluded, the best way to start a Heaven on earth, would be to commence by abolishing this holy rite, and establishing free commerce between the sexes. Many were easily made to believe this extremely human, and not at all divine doctrine, and a large institution was established, which has continued to this day, showing forth by its inner workings, not a *Heaven* below but a fair sample of the other kind of place.

People will assent to almost any impious, unnatural, absurd religion, as instance: Communism, Mormonism and other vagaries, if plausible theories are preached until an impression is made on the mind before bringing the practical workings and hideousness resulting into view.

In this manner was Eben dominated by the new creed until he believed the principles taught true, and the life led, the best for individuals and for the race. And there was besides an element of sociability which captivated his heart. While not in any sense licentious, he was, in spite of his willfulness and unreasonableness, an affectionate lovable man. Little children, those in any trouble, domestic animals, every weak, dependent or distressed creature, turned to him with implicit trust, as by instinct. Such a man must from his nature enjoy the society of pleasant, decent women, and they confide in him, some more, some less; and this without a thought of wrong. Although there is for every honest man, one woman comprising within herself all gratifying attributes, as there is for each true woman, the man who could be to her more than any in the world besides, it often happens that men and women. miss or lose their mates, and then no one else, not even many combined, are sufficient to appease the hunger of the heart, to satisfy the requirements of being. Neither men or women understand this as a rule, hence they try sipping sweets from one, two, or a dozen, with the result of universal demoralization.

Eben ceased not to grieve for Myra, his lost wife, and the trouble grew as he advanced in years.

To his daughter Gertrude he expressed himself thus: "My love for your mother increases each year, and at times I long for the presence of her sweet spirit with unutterable desire. I am sure she has before this forgiven me the unkindness with which I treated her when your brother Jules was born, both previous and after the birth; but I cannot forgive myself. Every peculiarity of the boy is a reproach to me; poor fellow, I, of all others, should be more patient with him, knowing he is not responsible for any strange thing he may do; but there is something about him which exasperates me beyond measure."

Gertrude made no answer, for her father was not less a mystery than her brother; each becoming, as the years went by, more unaccountable to their friends. Father and son were nearly the exact counterpart of each other, in personal appearance, manner, general characteristics, and workings of the mind; the difference being that anything peculiar or only slightly disagreeable in the father, was intensified in the child.

Seeing the distorted reflection of himself in his son, who had been defrauded of his birthright, a healthy brain and even-

ly balanced mind, by his father's mistakes, was what annoyed
Eben; but this he did not understand any better than some
other of his own experiences.

It is said a wise man knows himself, but Eben Grieveau's
self was a riddle he had never solved, and therefore failed to
comprehend why it was that the more lonely and grieved at
the loss of Myra he became, the more ardently he wished for
the society of women. He sometimes thought of marrying,
but had never yet seen the one whom he could endure to enstall
in her vacant place. Now, he was offered, through his new
friends, and their strange faith, the intimate association with
women; or, if he chose to avail himself, even their affection;
but devoid of the tie which binds for life, and which under some
circumstances is so irksome that any desolation is preferred rather
than submit to its demands.

Embracing the new life one could enjoy this companionship
subject to certain restrictions, or, let it alone. He could be the
friend of agreeable women without being either husband or
lover; this was one of the elements which enticed him, but only
one.

Eben really believed with others the community of family
and home, of property and labor, of education and amusement,
of all the interests which go to make up life, to be the true idea
and the plan intended by the Creator for human living.

How they came to all these conclusions from any premises
found is past comprehension, but to this end had these men read
their Bibles, warping their judgment to suit their own notions
and desires.

We have yet to know a true-hearted woman of sound mind
who upholds communism of the sexes, or Mormonism, when
she has learned the practical outcome of these "isms." Women
unless demoralized, preferring starvation to being fed at whole-
sale, even though the food be the sweet honey of love. *Sometimes*, when thrown upon their own resources for support,
women of the worst type enter houses of prostitution; others,
perhaps not much less abandoned, aim by some sort of make-
shift, at keeping up a show of respectability while they prey
upon society, undermining the very foundation of domestic life.

Set apart from both these classes are those rendered desperate by wrongs, over whom let us throw the pure, white
mantle of charity.

But we will not believe that woman, with her inborn, devout, consecrated nature, can ever go to Communism or Mor-

monism; or in any way use religion, knowingly, purposely, willingly as a cloak for her sins; they enter upon these unnatural, repulsive ways of living because their fathers, their husbands or lovers influence, perhaps coerce them, and they remain enthralled for the same reason.

However, Eben was prevented from entering community life, although he held to this faith until his death, probably because he never tried the system by experience.

He was saved in this wise: About six months after the marriage of Gertrude to Mr. Smythe, Eben became acquainted with a lady who approached nearer his ideal than any other since Myra's death, as she seemed to love him dearly, they were married, and he was more cheerful and contented than for many years.

With returning happiness, his mind acquired a healthier tone, and the fanaticism which had possessed him, was held in abeyance. *   *   *

While these things were transpiring, Jules was growing, studying and thinking.   That crooked brain of his, *born* crooked, was leading him into many strange ways.   He was progressing rapidly with his studies, when suddenly, in spite of all remonstrance, he dropped them, and devoted himself to the investigation of the new religion of which he had heard so much discussion in his father's family before his recent marriage. His mind once directed to obstruse dogma, nothing else satisfied.

Eben being a believer, did not discourage this turn of affairs, but allowed the boy to leave school and give his whole time to this pursuit; helping him to all the books needed, furnished by the Community.

Since Eben's marriage, Jules had lived with his sister whose husband still superintended the Academy.   Mr. Smythe never liked him over well, and his growing peculiarities and sometimes disagreeable ways were antagonizing him still more, and it was often difficult for Gertrude to keep peace between them.   This caused her much unhappiness, for she had been convinced by close observation that her brother was the victim of defective mental organization, rendering him to a certain extent irresponsible, and calling for unusaal forbearance from his relatives.

One day in a sudden fit of excitement, the usually docile and affectionate boy, at least to his sister, whatever he might be towards others, raised an ax with which he was chopping wood, attempting to strike her; only that she sprang away, he would have felled her to the ground. Frightened and astonished, Gertrude hastened into the house, going to her own room, trying to collect her thoughts and make up her mind what course to pursue under this extraordinary development, for, though Jules was often uneasy, fussy and easily irritated by anything which rasped his nerves, she had never before seen such a demonstration. Not daring to tell her husband what had occurred, full well knowing from past experience that his ungovernable temper would be roused to such a pitch, unreasonable vengeance would come upon poor Jules, she at last decided to go immediately and inform Grandma Brewster of what had transpired, asking her advice.

Since Eben's marriage she had bought a little home at the other end of the village, and here lived alone. Without delay, Gertrude putting on bonnet and shawl, walked over to her house, and with flushed face and streaming eyes related what had happened. They agreed that not a word should be said about the trouble either to Mr. Smythe or Eben.

His father could not take Jules home if he desired, for his wife disliked the boy extremely.

Homeless unfortunate, upon him were falling the consequences of wrongs inflicted before he was born. Eben would gladly have done more for the boy, but since the change in his family, it was impossible, and his conscience distressed him in regard to Jules as never before. He had come of late to believe with Grandma Brewster and Gertrude, that something was radically wrong and twisted in the make-up of the boy's mind; that he would always be, growing more so as the years advanced, erratic, hard to get along with, and though well intentioned, to some people disagreeable and troublesome. That he was doomed to be one of those impractical geniuses who fail to get a good grip on life, are unable to cope with their fellows in the race, sure to fall behind, sure to go under.

He had a fair amount of ability in certain directions, and was at times the extreme of good nature; then, suddenly, without warning, would become unruly, even violent. When not moody he was apt to be restless and changeable, could not be kept long enough at one employment to accomplish anything worth while, but, on the other hand, if he took a notion of himself, would persist contrary to any advice or remonstrance, until he had gained the object undertaken however unwise or ridiculous.

No one could predict what would come of it all, or how the

strange, unhappy boy would turn out. It was long years before the inside of that remarkably constructed brain was looked
into, and as yet none dreamed of the catastrophe which was to
culminate as the result of its morbid workings.

Although Gertrude and Grandma Brewster tried to keep
the knowledge to themselves, a man employed about the place
had seen the ax raised in the hand of Jules to strike his sister.
Eben soon heard of the trouble, and that Mr. Smythe refused
longer to be annoyed with him.

Eben and the rest, knowing it was not his nature to be vindictive, revengeful or cruel, were more than ever anxious about
the boy, really at their wit's ends, trying to contrive how to dispose of him, and thankfully accepted Grandma Brewster's offer
that he should stay with her for awhile. She said, " She could
manage him, and they'd get along nicely." All were pleased
and the transfer was made.

Those few weeks when he lived with Grandma, cut her
wood, built her fires, milked her cow and went errands for her,
was the most comfortable time he had spent since he used to
walk up and down the lake shore with Gertrude in Wisconsin.
Knowing all the circumstances of his birth, and taking into account recent events, she watched him closely at first, and with
just the slightest fear; but he was so quiet, affectionate and docile, she was encouraged and began to prophesy that " Jules
would take a turn," which he did shortly, and an unexpected
one it was.

Without consulting any of his friends he abruptly started off
for the " Community," as the new religionists had named the
place of their abode, and was missing several days before they
learned where he was; then the news came by letter of his
whereabouts.

It seemed he had saved a small sum of money from the pittance given him from time to time, and as railroads were then
built through the country, he was soon at his destination, well
satisfied with the performance.

When Eben heard what had occurred, he felt relieved of a
heavy load which he knew himself incompetent to carry, and
placed the boy as soon as the papers could be made out, irrevocably, during his minority, in the custody of the leaders and
rulers of the association, transferring to them the property designed for his education by his grandfather, Dr. Gascoigne.

Foolish Jules, when he was at last fixed in his chosen home,
tied hand and foot, a prisoner under a cruel despotism, found

what had been done—the kind of life he was expected to lead, and why the emissaries of the Community had worked upon his father and himself, until their object was accomplished; but there was no helping now the mistaken action.

Nothing could ever convince his deluded father of the real state of things at this place; where without any actual knowledge of their practices he had decided his boy should remain.

Once only during the time her brother was at the Community did Gertrude unasked intrude upon their privacy, and during the day she spent with him they were so closely watched, not one word of special conversation was secured, and all she ascertained of his feelings or condition was, that he seemed like one dazed and cowed down by fear. She never knew until he became of age, and she could interfere in his behalf and he was finally released from their tyranny, to what cruelties he had been subjected, and then only in part.

His mind being full of imaginations she gave little credence to his stories until they had been fully corroborated by other testimony horrible as true, and as *true* as horrible.

When the proof came to her which could not be gainsayed, that a woman, induced by her husband to go with him and enter this Hell upon Earth, had been found by her brother, a respectable farmer, imprisoned in a cellar of one of the Community buildings; she a raving maniac, her lacerated back from neck to waist, welted, marked with festering gore from the lashes administered to drive the "Devil" out of her, as they said—a "Devil" which would not allow of her giving her husband up to strange women, or permit her cohabitation with strange men. When it was found that it had cost ($25,000) twenty-five thousand dollars to suppress this testimony, which years after came out in court, when least expected, and was fully proven under oath of the woman's near relatives; then Gertrude and others who had before been skeptical, believed what had been called crazy Jules' wild stories. And that discipline had been administered in this *socialistic home*, after the fashion of the modern reformatories for criminals, and even resorted to oftener than is ever known in those places where brain-sick people are secluded from the world for treatment. Yes, *secluded* from their friends, too, quite as effectually by the watchful regulation of "visiting day," the supervision and retention of their letters, and other ways and means by which organized power can blind even the solicitude of true love, can cover, when occasion and ample pay demands, the doings of Demons. Can make it appear that sane people are crazy, and render crazy people still more insane by treatment which includes the diet of bread and water, chains, handcuffs, straight-jackets, dungeons, the cold douche, sometimes beatings which bring the blood at every blow.

In the modern insane asylum the plea for using these *remedial measures*, is, restraining the insane impulse, destroying delusion, restoring unbalanced minds.

The Community excused their brutality by averring that the *Devil* must be driven out of refractory members—women and children were the usual victims—occasionally a demented man or a boy received chastisement.

In both cases the inhumanities practiced should be investigated and punished by the severest penalties of the law.

Finally in the bitter Winter weather at midnight Jules escaped from a third story window, walking for miles to reach his sister and make accusations against his tormentors; but these things had not been established, and they, making excuse as to him that he was erratic and unruly, which was in some degree true, his deluded father also siding with them, his best friends not believing him entirely responsible for all his sayings, the matter as to him was dropped.

After Jules returned to his sister Gertrude's home, either from the natural development of his case, or from the cruel treatment he had received at the "Community," he was still more shattered and incapable of anything practical. His friends tried their utmost to set him right, but his mind was full of vagaries and they could not control him, seldom would he be advised.

As Gertrude's husband had turned from school teaching to the study of law, becoming a successful practitioner, Jules was induced to enter his office as a student and clerk; the usual time elapsing, he was admitted to the bar, much to their surprise, upon answering *two* out of the *three* questions put to him —so slack was the examination in those days, conducted by one of the three judges appointed for the work and engineered through proper influence; which Jules astonished them by securing as the result of his own efforts, for he had an unusual faculty of ingratiating himself into the good will of those with whom he came in contact.

When it was over, he came rushing into Gertrude's little sitting-room where she was sewing, with her three year old Elsie by her side, shouting, " I've got my license, I'm admitted, hurrah!" flourishing the important paper in the air above his head.

" Why, Jules," said Gertrude, " how *did* you manage to pass?" " Oh!" answered Jules, "Charley Rush only *asked me three questions* and I *knew two*, and he let me go. Ha! ha! ha!" ending with that strange, indescribable, hideous laugh, a sure indication of insanity. and which Gertrude recognized as the same she had heard the day he raised the ax to strike her (an occurence of which he afterwards seemed entirely oblivious). At the sound her blood curdled in her veins, she hardly knew why—but she said nothing.

After Jules was admitted to the bar his unnatural egotism, a trait also often indicating insanity, and which had all along been a marked and disagreeable characteristic, increased to such an unbearable degree he would listen to no advice, endure no restraint, and was sure he knew all that was necessary about everything; yet he could not earn his own food or clothing, and was incompetent to provide for himself.

Gertrude and his other friends worried along with him for a while, striving to keep him near them; but after a time he drifted away notwithstanding all their endeavors, ceased to communicate, and for years they did not hear from him. Poor Jules, little did they imagine his true condition, or that he was growing crazier each day—an inevitable result of his pre-natal misfortunes. When at last tidings came to them of their wanderer, the ghastly message froze the blood with an untold horror, of those who still loved him for his mother's sake, and they were struck dumb, quaking with a deadly fear.

Eben was gone, and Grandma Brewster, only Aunt Lucille and Gertrude remained to do battle for him against a whole world.

CHAPTER XVIII.

LUCILLE'S VISION.

Going in retrospect a few years to about the time when Jules had entered the "Community," we will take up an important stitch which was dropped in the yarn we are manipulating.   As will be remembered, Lucille was some time before summoned to the bedside of her brother John, whom she succeeded in nursing back to life through one of those low, malignant fevers which often shatter the constitution beyond repair.

As he did not regain his health and strength sufficiently to endure farm labor, they disposed of the place as soon as an opportunity presented, purchasing the old Grieveau homestead in the village of Freelawn, and Lucille having consented upon their urgent invitation to remain with them after hearing of the marriage of Eben and " little Gertrude," as they still called her, had as her own the very room in which Myra died.

Here she had agonized in years gone by as she now felt she could never again suffer for her lost love's sake, but although the acuteness of her first grief had passed away, the heart hunger was not appeased.

While she occupied this room, saturated with memories, until faces seemed to stare at her from the very walls, and voices to vibrate through the air, Lucille had an experience which tore open the old wound until it bled afresh.

On a warm summer day, as before, when she had that vision of Henry going far away—just such a day over again— a day when her soul had been tortured almost to the verge of escaping from the body, Lucille was again brought to the climax when spirit and matter well nigh part company, the angel of sleep now mercifully tempering her sore distress.   She dreamed of Henry Armstrong, and he at the altar, a beautiful young bride by his side, flowers, music, all beauty and joy were there; the betrothed pair stood before the sacred man in somber gown, the ceremony was commenced; at the proper time, Henry essayed to take the hand of her he would wed, but a deathly pallor overspread his face, and the strong arm dropped for a moment powerless by his side, when, proceeding, the words were said, " *I pronounce you husband and wife*," a figure exactly like Lucille's own self, in form and feature, stepped between the united pair, which Henry seeing, turned whiter still, staggered, and fell.

People were now running to and fro—"The bridegroom has a sudden illness," they said; and Lucille sat dreaming in Myra's old arm chair, as she had done fifteen years before that very day.

Appalled—shuddering with terror—she awoke, and for days afterwards she could not shake off or dispel the sense of dreary foreboding caused by her remarkable dream. But this is scarcely or fairly altogether retrospection.

CHATER XIX.

CIVIL WAR.

While these things were transpiring, the whole country, east, west, north and south, was becoming excited more and more as the years went by, over the question of negro slavery at the south. Agitation had been inaugurated by a set of soft-hearted fanatics, called Abolitionists, and kept up by designing politicians until Mrs. Stowe's story of " Uncle Tom's Cabin" had aroused the moral sentiment and sympathies of a majority of the northern people in behalf of these enslaved negroes, and they determined the favorite southern institution should never be extended into the new Territories of the Union, even if it could not be exterminated from the Southern States.

The people below " Mason and Dixon's line," from having become accustomed to the injustice and hardships inflicted by the sanction of the peculiar slave code, ceased to regard with horror the daily spectacle of the cruelties and inhumanities practiced.

They insisted the institution was permitted by Divine writ, was patriarchal and protecting in its character, best for the colored race, and further, when they chose to occupy any portion of Uncle Sam's domain, they should take their goods and chattels, that is their slaves, with them; the Northerners said, " You shall not," *and thereupon was war.*

Before this final catastrophe there had been much commotion for several years.

The slaves knew from intuition, as well as by rumor, it seemed, that liberty and the pursuit of individual happiness existed for them at the North, and to the Northern country they were determined to go, leaving their *dear masters* far behind.

So many runaways were harbored, encouraged and helped to reach the Canadas, by the residents of Northern States, that the Southern politicians finally succeeded in establishing a U. S. Statute called " The fugitive slave law," which required that all persons should give up escaping slaves upon legal demand and provided severe penalties.

But notwithstanding this law, fugitives continued running away from their masters, who never resorted to more earnest

measures than fifty, one hundred or more lashes, as they happened to fancy; or hunting down with bloodhounds, the animals often tearing their victims limb from limb; or burning at
the stake, and other similar mild means for the reclamation of
their cherished bondsmen.

And although the severe punishments were promptly en-
forced upon anyone convicted of violating the law, the queer
set of soft-hearted fanatics, before alluded to, contrived what
they called an underground railroad, and in various ways assisted
the escape of these men, women and children, who, even if
covered by a black skin, they foolishly believed entitled to all
the political privileges and protection enjoyed by their whiter
complexioned brothers and sisters.

The people of the south would not give up their slaves, but
with true southern, headstrong, unreasonable passion and grit,
declared through their leaders, " They'd fight for what they
considered their rights, until the last man lay in the last ditch."

These southern slave-holders had grown, generation after
generation, rich and powerful by the labor and suffering of their
fellowmen, until they were proud, arrogant and in this matter
unprincipled, freely boasting withal of their honor. "A southern
gentleman's word was as good as his bond," said they, " be it a
gambling debt or what not, did he owe any man, the obligation
should be paid at maturity." *Why not?* All he need do, sell
a slave or two and the money was ready! Easy enough to be
honorable at the expense of some one else suffering. These
men hated labor and the laborer. " No northern mud-sill should
dictate to *them* as to the right or wrong of their actions or manner of life, that was their own affair." Was it? The sequel
proved it to be an affair which concerned forces far above either
northern mud-sill or southern gentlemen, moved by a Power
controlling the destiny of Races and of Nations, no less than individuals.

There were, as is always the case in political and civil contests, conservatives both at the South and the North, trying their
utmost to restrain wrath and induce peace, but they found it
impossible to control or influence in any great degree, either of
the extremes to which reference has been made.

The Abolitionists should have arranged some plan whereby the slave-holders might have received compensation for their
slave-property, or a system of gradual emancipation and emigration should have been established.

And yet it is doubtful, had such a proposition been made, if
10

it would have been favorably received; the ownership of human beings was so profitable and satisfying an investment, that scarcely One less than The Omnipotent could have wrested them away.

And the wrongs perpetrated under the delusion that Divinity gave sanction, were at the last atoned for in blood and dire agony, such as only the carnage of war can bring.

For several years, while these contending parties were ranging themselves on either side for the final battle, during each political campaign, the points at issue would crowd to the surface, and neither the peace-makes North or South could prevent or retard for any length of time the imminent catastrophe.

But instinctively feeling if ever the extremes met face to face, a long and bitter war must be the result—in sheer dread they used their utmost endeavor trying to stay the calamity, and might perhaps have been successful had not foreign influences, as the sequel proved, been added to the already disturbed condition of our politics.

Finally, Abraham Lincoln, the pioneer rail-splitter, the renouned story-teller, the hard working lawyer of Illinois; a man who quietly, persistently, *honestly* had worked his way from an illiterate, over-worked, back-woods-man to be one of the first lawyers in his state; a man who could cope with the giant intellect of a Douglas in debate, and not be overcome, but rather bear away the laurels; a man without spot or blemish to detract from the beauty and purity of his character; a man of whom every honest northern working man was justly, and ever will be proud; this man, *a King among men!* was nominated for President of the United States, by the party lately consolidated from the old-time Whig, the recent Free-soil and other abolition parties, and aptly named to catch the popular fancy, Republican.

The new coalition swept the country, and Abraham Lincoln was elected President.

At this, the southern slave Oligarchy and the northern Demagogues were rampant.

They declared "The low-lived mud-sill, the black-hearted abolitionist," as they named him, should never take his seat in the presidential chair, or occupy the White House at Washington, and his assassination was freely threatened.

The Southerners were in dead earnest and forthwith prepared for war, though not openly. *When they were ready* a-test case was forced at Sumpter, and the Fort was fired upon by the Rebels, as they were now styled.

In the mean time the journey had been safely made by the newly elected President, from his home in Springfield, Illinois, and the inauguration had taken place in Washington.

Only after the Rebels commenced glaring hostilities, did the North awaken to the fact of civil war. Before this the majority North and South believed all the menaces and commotion to be but the idle, violent talk of politicians determined to gain their point;—*now* they realized that cannon were to roar and musketry to rattle, that armed men were to march to and fro in conflict; that sons, husbands, fathers were to leave their homes; that widows and orphans were to fill the land; that there was to be suffering dire, and death, aud broken ties, and grief unutterable.

And women held still their hearts, while men went forth to battle.

One of the very first responding at his country's call was John Gascoigne. Leaving Lucille and Julia with the boy Charley who had grown quite a lad, in the old place to attend the store and post office as best they could, John started for the headquarters of the regiment, then recruiting in their vicinity. He had received the assurance from friends and neighbors, especially from Uncle Tut and Aunt Debby, that they would have a care for his family, and Julia who had always been a stirring sort of woman, he knew would find no difficulty in managing the business. Lucille, at John's request, was appointed in his place as postmistress, an innovation inaugurated during the war, paving the way for the after prominence of women in national affairs.

John entered the Western Division of the army, volunteering as a common soldier, and some time elapsed before he was brought into special prominence. The Bull Run disaster had occurred, also the partial victory of the second Bull Run fight, before the Western Division accomplished anything of note.

Both the northern and southern armies had advanced and been repulsed time and again, many battles been fought, and the war was extending into years instead of terminating in a few months, as had at first been predicted, and nothing was heard except by his family and neighbors, concerning John Gascoigne; he had, to be sure, been in a good many engagements of more or less importance, enduring his full share of hardships, but was yet only an atom in the great whole, only a soldier in the Army of the Republic.

At last a hardly contested battle was fought on the Mississippi, the result being a surprise to the country, when it was known a decided gain had been made for the North.

It was also found that John Gascoigne, who had risen from the ranks to an honorable place without attracting particular attention, was the hero of the hour, and he was given a high position as his hard earned reward, with the title of General.

Soon after he was transferred to the Army of the Potomac and placed in command of a division. As he was to be permanently in the East and could have his family near him, they decided upon removing to Washington where his headquarters would be; and Lucille, Julia and the boy Charley, all who were left of the family in Freelawn, made preparations for the change. Ere the departure, his towns-people were made happy by a visit from Gen. John A. Gascoigne, now without doubt carrying with his name a proud renoun.

A glorious reception they accorded him, prompted by hearty good will, compensating for many a sorrow and hardship.

In the midst of the rejoicing a telegram announced a conference of the Generals of the Eastern Army with the President and Commander-in-Chief, the revered Lincoln; and Gen. Gascoigne must hasten away.

Farewells were hastily spoken, and the next morning they had started by rail on their way to Washington.

Again passing through Chicago, they saw not the sloppy, muddy, little Indian town of the years before, but a flourishing, enterprising city with its comfortable hotels, its blocks of iron, and stone and brick for business and residence, with its paved streets and stone side-walks, its marvelous water works, its centering rail roads, its commerce and trade—one of the wonderful young cities of this great but still new country.

Our friends remained over night and after dining at one of the hotels, Gen. Gascoigne, who had a matter of business which needed looking after, and was also curious to note the improvements, strolled out leisurely examining some of the former landmarks and more noticable recent buildings.

As he stood gazing upon the old Court House, long since passed away, born swiftly in the Fire-King's flame wreathed chariot, but which was at that time considered an achievement in architecture not to be despised; Gen. Gascoigne presented a type of manhood seldom seen.

His frame of grand proportions was symetrically formed, his carriage strikingly noble, and there was something indescribable in the free springing stride, and lofty, independent manner of throwing up his head, shaking back from the massive brow the superb shock of long and heavy jet-black hair, entirely different from any other, reminding by its strong, straight, ebony masses, of the Indian chiefs who ruled the tribes of the wilderness in olden times.

Hair the same in color and in its luxurient growth, as the remarkable mustache reaching down, over, and almost covering the dark-hued beard, sombre as midnight.

Hair, beard and mustache matching the magnificent far-seeing, passionate eyes; not those ordinary black eyes, small, bead-like and repulsive—but the glorious, uncommon eyes, speaking from soul to soul, and which are so very rare.

Altogether, Gen. John A. Gascoigne was a man scarcely to be encountered in a life time, and when once beheld, never forgotten.

Whether his unusually handsome and distingué appearance had attracted the strange creature at his feet, can not be said, but suddenly an unmistakable negro "Hi, hi, hi! massa!" called his surprised attention to the most ludicrous figure the general had ever seen; kneeling before him on the stone sidewalk was an old darkey wrapt in admiration, his bald head thrown back, the coal-black, velvety eyes displaying a wide margin of glistening china-white, the great, thick, red lips parted in wonder and adoration, revealing the whitest of teeth; the clasped hands uplifted as in prayer;—who was known to every one about town from his pitiful condition and grotesque appearance, as "Crazy Leonard." His dress was even more remarkable than his strange conduct; by his side he had carefully placed his hat, when in mute admiration falling prostrate at the feet of the General, and this was in itself a curiosity, ever changing in the light of each new day as the chameleon of many hues. A silk hat, though dilapidated, nothing less suited Leonard's aristocratic ideas, but the decorations surpassed anything before attempted in the line of millinery under the sun.

One day an immense bunch of artificial roses, a tin-star, or tag, such as are used for labeling various articles, a long feather from ostrich, peacock, turkey or shanghai, as he had the fortune to find; bows of ribbon of different gay colors completed the trimming, but never twice alike did this eccentric head-gear appear in public.

The other garments comprising a man's apparel were always of well worn black doe-skin or broadcloth, this also being his idea of gentility, and were set off in the same outlandish fashion; the effort being mostly expended upon the front of his coat and vest.

All will concede that the personelle of this poor fellow was quite strange enough, but when that enormous mouth opened the astonishment and interest increased.

" Hi-hi-hi, massa, praise de Lord dat poor Leonard see you. I's lub struck, I is, but I's a good boy. Leonard come clean back-yard if massa say so. Leonard nebber do any harm. I's lub struck, I is, dat's what ails poor Leonard. Massa down in ole Virginny take my 'Liza 'way wid him, neber see her no mo, neber no mo, for *shuah*. 'Liza, mighty nice gal, yellow as a sunflower, but she done gone 'way, *shuah*. Leonard'll come clean back-yard, stay to dinner if massa say so. Leonard's lub struck, 'scuse poor Leonard, hi-hi-hi, massa." This speech was delivered with a pitiful pathos of intonation, impossible to imitate, ending in attempted merriment, still more pitiful. Making a very low bow, he arose, placed his wonderful hat on his empty head, and then apparently reconsidering, took it in his hand, waiting patiently for the General to speak.

So surprised was General Gascoigne at the spectacle before him, he could not immediately recover himself, but at length taking in the man's condition, that of a harmless lunatic, he thrust his hand in his pocket, drawing out some loose change, which he offered him.

To his amazement crazy Leonard drew himself up with great dignity, lifting his hat again to his head, and with a most courtly bow, a gracious, condescending smile, he answered, " No massa, no, keep dem yourself, Leonard don't want no such trash; he's got plenty jinglers too—see hyar—" and taking a handful of odd buttons, bits of tin and little trinkets which he had picked up in his wanderings, from the deep pockets in the tails of his long frock coat, he proudly displayed his treasures.

After a little, being satisfied at the interest manifested by his auditor in his stores, crazy Leonard walked away; but a few minutes later the General was conscious of some one following, and looking round, saw his admirer walking behind him at a respectful distance; keeping right along, when General Gascoigne reached his hotel Leonard seated himself with the utmost complacence near by on the piazza.

A group of gentlemen soon had the General in conversation,

for he was a favorite wherever he went. Leonard sat still drinking in every word that fell from his lips, and as before, wrapt in admiration. General Gascoigne prevented the servants from molesting him, and moved with pity, handed the porter a quarter to find a bed, and another for supper, to be furnished the harmless demented creature.

At the usual time the hotel guests went to their rooms and crazy Leonard was forgotten.

The next morning early, the General and his party took the train for Washington. When all were settled in their places, and the conductor was passing through for fares, a commotion was raised by an effort to put a colored man off the cars because of non-payment. He screamed and struggled until the attention of the passengers was attracted. The man proved to be Leonard, who insisted he belonged to the General's party, and must remain in the same car to wait upon him. General Gascoigne recognizing his adorer of the night before, rather enjoying the joke and the ludicrousness of the situation, came to the rescue, paid half fare and had him placed in a second-class car upon his assurance that he would "Keep quiet and be a good boy," deciding in his own mind to take him to Washington and if necessary place him in an asylum.

Leonard caused no further trouble, but when the company disembarked for meals, was introduced to the ladies and gave them much entertainment; to Julia especially was he attracted, as he had been to the General, seeming to be fascinated by the pronounced and strong type of physical beauty for which the couple were celebrated.

Julia declared she would keep him near her, and ever after General Gascoigne's establishment was adorned by crazy Leonard, and, in many ways he became useful, after they got him toned down as to dress and some other particulars; Julia humored his caprice for bright colors and decorations, and when dressed in the English lackey style, with his own daily additions which he continued to pick up, his taste for the grotesque was fully gratified.

Little by little they learned his strange history, as he had lucid intervals and could remember and talk with some degree of rationality.

He was a fugitive slave, having in bondage a good enough master, as masters are, allowing his slaves more privileges and better education than was usual. Leonard being body-servant, almost even a business manager, (for he had possessed more than ordinary intelligence) being about the house and his person constantly, it happened that he fell desperately in love with a comely yellow girl whom his master had as a mistress.

This fact coming to the eyes of the master, for love cannot be concealed even under a black skin, he ordered his faithful servant to be severely flogged for his impudence, as he called it, also the poor girl, because he said, "She had encouraged a lover."

After the man had recovered from his terrible punishment, he did not cease, night or day, to revolve in his mind how he might escape from this cruel thralldom, and rescue his love from her desperate fate.

At last the opportunity came, and giving the girl assurance that he would steal or buy her, after he secured his own freedom, he started on his perilous journey for the Canadas, reaching his destination with the usual risks and vicissitudes.

Several years elapsed and by hard work Leonard accumulated a small sum of money. Hearing of the John Brown expeditions which had been organized for the purpose of running slaves off to Canada from the South, he joined them, and started, full of hope, for the heart of the southern country where the old plantation was situated, intending by secret negotiations to buy his lost love. If this failed, carry her away by force.

The party reached Harper's Ferry in safety, where they stopped for rest and arms. Here they were joined by their chief and a small squad of his men, among them, as turned out years after, the son of Eben and Myra Grieveau, who come across and naturally affiliated, with these intensely conscientious Abolitionists, when he had drifted away from his friends. For all his inherited tendencies prompted Jules Grieveau to sympathy with the oppressed wherever found. Although at that time he was considered a strange man with queer notions, his real *insanity* had not developed to the marked degree which would attract attention among a concourse of zealous fanatics, certainly themselves could not recognize a disease so nearly allied to their own condition.

This visionary brain was quick to grasp the scheme of their leader, the noble-hearted and philanthrophic, though mistaken, John Brown, and he went into the work with an enthusiasm unexcelled by any of the others. He took a special interest in the case of Leonard, who was seeking his lost love; for Jules had himself been disappointed and defrauded even before entering the "Community," and a boy's love is sometimes as pure and earnest, if not intense to the degree of those passionate affections of later life. Many a man carries the ineffaceable scar of a wound inflicted in the years so full of tender memories, of youthful endeavor, of honest purpose, before he has passed from the teens into the twenties. Jules Grieveau's brooding fancies and morbid tendencies were not dispelled or cured by this, to him, sad experience, and possibly it had much to do with the after developments in his case.

Soon the raiders secreted in the old barn at Harper's Ferry were surprised, surrounded and captured after a desperate fight with United States troops; a few only escaping, among them Jules Grieveau, who, as afterwards transpired, wandered still further away towards Ohio and Kentucky, with the vague idea of finding Leonard's girl and bringing her back to the North; at least, this seemed his first idea, but his mind soon turned to its wonted fanaticism. Years after, in the course of testimony given under oath by various persons, Jules' friends, from whom he had disappeared during this time, were surprised to learn he had been a constant traveler throughout the Eastern, Western, Middle, and Southern States; actually traversing the Continent from ocean to ocean. How he managed will never be known, but it is certain that he had no settled or visible means of support; his story being that he was "getting in his work for the Lord," lecturing and distributing pamphlets, both of the intensely fanatical type, which characterized his insanity more and more until the end. He said, when under oath in his own behalf, "I reckon some of you would call me a tramp, but I only did as the Lord told his disciples to do, taking my staff and going from city to city, giving no thought as to what I should eat or what I should wear. I had a hard time getting in my work for the Lord, I can tell you, and was often hungry and cold, and knew not where to lay my head; but then it was no harder than Paul and the Master had, and it's all right, I am satisfied. *I'd rather be one of the Lord's 'tramps,'* than any of those rich men who can no more enter Heaven than a camel can get through the eye of a needle." And thus at the last the poor crazy fellow unwittingly reproved and convicted the selfish, worldly crowd, gloating in his torture. But all those years the homeless man wandered and wandered, growing more forlorn and insane each day.

John Brown and several of the captured men, convicted of inciting an insurrection and of treason, were hung; martyrs to the cause of Human Freedom.

No proof was adduced convincing to the unprejudiced, that

they *intended* arousing the southern slaves to insurrection or violence of any kind, but only to help those who were cruelly treated in gaining their freedom, furnishing arms for defense should they be attacked, but not for the purpose of *commencing* hostilities.

This jnst and philanthropic plan might have saved the desolation of a civil war; however, it proved not to be the order of Fate or Providence, as you will.

While Leonard lay in prison, the girl he loved was so severely punished for some trifling offense, by the master who hated her since finding she preferred another man to himself, (for a licentious man is invariably wickedly jealous), that after excruciating torture, she died.

When Leonard learned what had happened, this, together with the execution of his loved commander, John Brown, and the immediate breaking out of the war, dethroned his reason, and he became the wreck, the harmless lunatic we have shown you.

Even crazy Leonard was afterwards avenged; the fatal doom falling upon one at least, *who was surely* concerned in the sad outcome of a national tragedy, receiving just punishment through his instrumentality.

CHAPTER XX.

IN THE "ROCKIES."

Fifteen years had now elapsed, not one of his former friends receiving any word. from Henry Armstrong, since the night when he stood by Lucille's prostrate, sadly wasted form, and in her pale face saw the unutterable love, joyous peace and trust, which settled upon her heart at sight of him; and then in sheer weakness, closing her eyes, they both by Fate had been defrauded. For, was not another man seen bending tenderly and with an unmistakable air of ownership, over Lucille; looking after her welfare; standing between Henry and his long lost love, whom he had so nearly regained only to be irretrievably and bitterly disappointed?

For this man must surely be Lucille's husband, and the child lying by her side, their own, the image of its mother.

It was fifteen years since that memorable night when the stage passengers had alighted and taken part in the fight over Tutty Swanson's claim, but the picture of Lucille, her husband and child, was indelibly inscribed upon Henry's mind.

No change of scene, no occupation, or power of his will had effaced that heart-rending sight, all these years. Goaded on by memory it had been impossible for him to remain very long at a time in any place, and he had become a restless, intrepid, indefatigable traveler. Going back to this period, we will follow him in his wanderings.

The destination of his party being only a few days' journey beyond Freelawn, the plan had been to remain here for some little time, taking up land and perhaps laying out a town. After this was accomplished Henry would return to Freelawn and find Lucille; but the adventure at the claim changed everything and very soon Henry declared, after looking about for a few days, his intention of starting immediately and going further West, a resolve from which his friends could not dissuade him. In fact he had been so queer since the night of the fight at the claim, they could not make him out, and were puzzled to know what had happened to him. He said he was sick, but they were sure something more than physical illness ailed him; he was depressed, absent minded, and so disagreeable, moody and fretful, they scarcely cared how soon he and they parted company.

The bantering and surveilance of his companions was becoming unbearably irksome, and he determined to leave them and every reminder of the sad past behind him, traveling while his money lasted; by what route or the final destination was to him of little consequence; things old or new could have small interest, only serving to help his despondency and grief, perhaps temporarily, he was well aware.

Henry realized that a mistake not to be rectified had been made, and the only woman he ever really cared to make his wife, was lost to him forever.

He had liked many women, enjoyed their society in certain ways, but he at last fully understood that no other one could satisfy entirely, or appreciate him as Lucille would have done; but it was of no use now repining; by action, business, change, he would drive her from his mind. Such advantage do men have over women; for a time they suffer more intensely possibly, with an actual physical misery, but they succeed in overcoming and forgetting sooner; and besides they have the whole field of sweets to sip from, when they choose to avail themselves of the privilege.

Henry disconsolately determined to sever all connection with his past existence, pressing on and hoping for a better future; when he bade his friends good bye, feeling himself entering upon a life-long journey, and this, time proved. Drifting aimlessly, his first rest was at a new place called Galena, because extensive lead mines were found there. As he still had some money left, and was sure of a regular remittance from the estate bequeathed to him by his Uncle in Bentonville, New York, Henry invested in a new mine just opened, and in after years yielding a fair income. Through this enterprise he formed and retained a number of pleasant acquaintances; one to whom Henry was especially attracted, was a man of medium size, rather stout in build, possessing an honest face with good, blue grey eyes. This new friend had recently married an amiable lady, and they were starting in an humble way, working out their destiny together. Many a social hour did Henry spend in their comfortable home, oblivious apparently of former ties, finding rest for both body and heart, chatting cheerily, ruminating, smoking, always together, for these men were even then most inveterate smokers, though still young.

A habit growing with years, and to which one owed per-

haps much of his success in life, though in the end causing a
painful death; for his subsequent great opportunities came to
him in such shape, that only quiet, plucky, bull-dog grit and
nerve would win. A man of quick perceptions and intense
nervous force adequate to understanding his chances, when they
come thus, requires a strong, continuous nervous stimulant and
sedative, to keep him in the necessary condition, enabling him
to hold on until the final victory is achieved. Fortunately for
this man he acquired the power of consuming a large amount
of the "weed" with little apparent injury to his organism, before the emergency arose, requiring its hero to be a constant
and thoroughly seasoned smoker, who could sit and puff cigar
after cigar, calmly, persistently—while cannon roared about him
and comrades were dying.

But years after the great crisis was triumphantly passed, the
instrument thus prepared for the accomplishment of an end, fell
a victim to the deadly poison steadily imbibed, no less a sacrifice
upon the altar of God's Providence, than if slain on the field
red with the blood of Liberty's sons.

As the fateful wheel of Destiny revolved, and new scenes
were to be enacted requiring a remarshaling of forces, higher
powers, (whether good or bad we will not say), working upon
him, Henry became uneasy in a few months, and bidding his
Galena friends adieu he boarded a Mississippi steamer for Rock
Island, one of the oldest towns on the river, where a Fort was
located and Government troops stationed. He remained here
for a little time, picking up a good thing now and then in the
way of speculation, for Henry Armstrong was a money-making
man whether he would or no, everything he touched turned to
gold, his fellow towns-men said; but though successful, it benefitted him little in the real enjoyment of life. Henry felt the
need, as the days went by, more and more, of a good wife; but
he came across no one who suited him, and feared he should
become a dissatisfied, crusty old bachelor. He knew he was
getting soured as well as old, for he fairly despised the women
who "set their caps" for him because he had money, and the men
who toadied to him for the same reason. He was thoroughly
tired of civilization and what people call society, with its shame
and pretences.

About this time a great wave of excitement came surging
over the country. Gold had been discovered on the Pacific
slope, and the "California fever" was raging. Thousands
mortgaged their homes for the means to make the venture

and started for the gold-fields, expecting to bring back
bushels at least, of nuggets as large of their fists or their
heads; but as a rule, they never returned at all.   Many
seemed to forget mortgaged homes, wives and children when
once away — "out of sight, was out of mind" with them.
Families and homes deserted for a myth, becoming estranged
by absence, forming new ties, even when success crowned their
efforts, leaving those behind to take care of themselves as they
could with perhaps an occasional remittance from the land of
gold.   Some few returned, bringing fabulous wealth; but these
were the exception, and were ever after known in distinction
from those who only *went* as "*returned Californians.*"

When the incoming wave struck Rock Island, Henry Armstrong was just in the mood to grasp this excitement as a drown-
ing man the floating straw, and with others, organized an expedition going by the overland route to the Pacific coast.

The journey proved tedious, and Henry experienced full
enough of adventure to drive away any past trouble by present
trepidation, before he reached the golden gate, the land of the
setting sun.   Adventure which colored his whole after life
even more than his disappointment with Lucille, causing him
to change his name and launching him upon a sea of trouble.

The trip made by Henry's party was one of the very first,
even before "the great path-finder," General Fremont, had ex-
plored the route and discovered one of the true passes through
the Rocky Mountains—the discoverer of new political high-
ways as well, over which enslaved millions eventually traveled
to freedom, a man whom this nation has forgotten to honor,
but destined to a place in history beside, not below, that of the
revered Lincoln, who, following this opened way, finally, when
the crisis of war pressed hard, gave to the colored race of
America, Emancipation.   Since that time several passes have
been found through the "Rockies," but in the beginning
men would start for the south-western portion of the United
States where California is situated, from any point where
they happened to reside, and struggle past every obstacle, across arid plains and trackless wastes, over mountains,
rivers, lakes, until they reached their destination, if happily in this they succeeded.   Impeded by hostile Indians,
broad rivers, unbridged and unfordable, the hot "simoons" of
the Desert, the cold "blizzards" of the plains, the "cyclones"
of the prairies, and the terrible snow storms of the famous
"Rockies," saying nothing of minor discomforts and dangers

encountered by these early gold-seekers, what wonder that many perished by the way?

The expedition to which Henry belonged started rather too late in the fall, but they found no special difficulty until arriving at one of the high mountain passes, which they essayed to cross on foot, foolishly leaving their mules below by the advice of their guide, who proved inexperienced and incompetent. A heavy storm overtook them, they lost their way, and at last became entangled in a wild labyrinth of snow-capped peaks and treacherous canyons from which it was impossible to extricate themselves. They wandered about in the snow and ice and blinding storm, hoping, but striving in vain to find the trail, until their rations gave out and they were upon the verge of starvation, in real danger of perishing with cold and hunger, with neither ammunition or strength sufficient for hunting game in their weak and bewildered condition—scarcely to defend themselves, if attacked by Indians or wild animals.

After floundering about in the deep snow for several days, the storm not abating, until completely exhausted from hardship and want of food, their last morsel eaten twenty-four hours before, they gathered around the few burning sticks which they had managed to bring from the steep, rocky, ledges, and counciled as to what should be done in this crisis. It was plain that food must be provided, or a horrible death confronted them all. There seemed no alternative, and it was decided that they should draw lots to settle who of their number must be sacrificed to save his comrades from starvation; who suffer death to save his fellows.

At the first drawing the lot fell upon a genial, dark-haired, sad-eyed man, who had become a general favorite. No one knew his history, or where he came from, but all had a suspicion some mystery attached to him. When the drawing was announced not a dry eye was among that group of desperate men, for this man was endeared to every one.

Without dissent all refused to consummate the terrible tragedy, hoping against hope that relief would come in some other way.

The man himself regarded his fate with the utmost indifference, even courted death, insisting he was " Entirely satisfied to go, that he had lived too long already, that life held nothing dear for him. If he could serve his fellows by giving up his body they were welcome to it." Another day's delay, but the more willing he, the more loth his comrades that he should be sacrificed—*if we except one man*—and, strangely enough, this was the proverbially kind-hearted Henry Armstrong.

Why this exception? Simply because Henry had made a discovery in regard to the man, one which concerned his own life at a vital point, and which in his present condition induced by starvation, had the effect of rousing his natural latent jealousy to the pitch of an insane frenzy.

The day after the drawing by lot, during the interval of delaying and hoping, Henry had accidentally picked up a picture of Lucille, and also a slip of paper falling from inside the well worn morocco cover, on which were the words in the doomed man's hand writing, "Oh! how dearly I love her!"

Henry Armstrong was a man in whom his fellows were apt to confide, and before the fatal finding of that tell-tale picture, the man, Wm. Smith by name, after the drawing, while waiting for his doom of which he seemed sure in his own mind from the first, had prepared a hastily written letter, including his last will and bequests, which he intrusted to Henry without explanation, it being sealed and directed to Silas Smith, Freelawn P. O., Ill.

Henry placed the letter away not noticing the superscription, in fact he had no curiosity in regard to this man's private affairs, but it was the regret of his whole after life, that he had not known the contents of that epistle at the time; soon, under the fierce pressure of hunger, he forgot the matter altogether.

The man also entrusted the fact to Henry that a childless old uncle who had resided in Australia, dying recently, had made this only nephew his heir, with the proviso that he should bear his name, and as neither had any ties or relatives to be injured by the arrangement, he intended upon arrival in San Francisco, to have his name legally changed to that of Gerald A. Johnson, and proceding at once to Australia, take possession of his legacy.

"But," said Smith sadly, "That will be of no account now, I feel my time has come, and as a special favor to me, I ask you Mr. Armstrong, to take the name, if you can do so without wronging any one, and with it the property; if you have no need of it use it in benefitting others."

And in spite of Henry's remonstrance he insisted, and to pacify and humor his caprice, Henry finally promised to do as Smith desired, should death overtake him before the end of their journey, caring nothing for the property, for he had already a fortune, but really wishing to lose his identity and separate entirely from his past life.

The change of name to Gerald A. Johnson involving the Australian property, was a secret known only to Wm. Smith and Henry Armstrong; their mountain comrades understanding that for some mysterious reason, the man had requested in the event of his demise before reaching their destination, that Henry should assume his name of Smith, and with it his effects.

Had Henry considered the matter as of much importance at the time, the idea "What's in a name?" would most likely have been suggested, but long afterwards he realized the responsibility he had assumed in consenting to take another man's name and property—dead, under such peculiar circumstances; when it was impossible to undo the error, however embarrassing, even serious the consequences.

Almost immediately when these matters had been arranged between the two men, Henry had the misfortune of finding the picture before alluded to; at sight of which his first and only thought was *joy* that the deadly lot had fallen, *if fall it must*, upon one whom he believed the husband of his lost Lucille, and whose "removal" might restore her once more to his arms, and wickedly he brooded over this sinful suggestion until finally circumstances having given him the opportunity of putting his dark thought into execution, he did not hesitate to avail himself of what seemed to his distorted conceptions a "Providence"—so easily can men believe their desires right.

The catastrophe had been postponed for two days, no sustenance was received during that time except such as could be derived from frozen snow.

At last, with the fever of starvation upon them, with parched tongues, dry skins, insane staring eyes, the glassy balls fairly starting from their sunken sockets, these men driven to such dreadful straights, several of their number half stupified in the snow, sinking surely down to death, the others knowing full well that soon their condition would be the same, held a final council, hastily ordering another drawing of lots, including every man.

And now to Henry's diabolically jealous insanity came his "Providence." It was easy for him to whom had been entrusted the preparations for the drawing, to decide that the fatal slip of paper should be blood-marked, and to arrange the posi-

11

tion in which the men were to stand; in the confusion and distress no one noticed (if we leave out a dark fellow with snakey,
evil eyes, and Henry was not sure that even *he* understood the
ruse, or saw what followed, only there was a *peculiar look* in
those eyes, certainly,) that Henry Armstrong placed himself
at the right hand of the brown-eyed, genial man upon whom
the lot had previously fallen, and that in making the drawing,
the first man who reached his hand from the circle in which
they stood, bringing forth the little slip of clean, white paper
from the old fur cap, stood at Smith's left side, each following
from left to right, with the same result, *white paper everyone*,
until it was Henry's turn, and after him the doomed man.

No one noticed or gave any attention to all this unless possibly the man before alluded to, or if they did all kept silence
as did he, only too glad of their own escape, for sometimes men
lose all natural feeling, becoming veritable beasts, and they were
now ravenous as wolves.

Henry in his younger days as a clever pastime, had practiced some sleight of hand tricks, and now when his temptation
was before him, listened to the Devil's own suggestion, retaining
in his hand the bloody slip until his turn came for drawing,
when he took from the cap the two white slips remaining, leaving behind the blood stained one for his comrade following him,
who could only be the fated Wm. Smith. Of course the drawing was finished with the same result as before and all were
awe-struck by the wonderful "Providence," none suspecting
Henry, knowing the friendship between the two, for those who
are seemingly our nearest and dearest, sometimes betray us.

And the man Wm. Smith, whom all loved, with the dry
joke "That it *must be Providential*, certainly for them, his being
in better condition than the others," cheerfully prepared to meet
his fate.

Finally, when all preliminaries were finished, just as the setting sun threw its lurid light across the dreary waste of snow,
the deadly shot was fired, each man pointing a gun that no one
might know the real executioner, and the brave hero passed
away without complaint.

Ere the pall of midnight fell upon them, the ravening hunger of each was appeased, the horrible debris cleared away,
buried under the deep snow out of sight of the heart-sick sur-
vivors, and all lay in the stupor which comes alike to the proud-
est man no less than the lowest animal after engorgement.

For thus are we, when dire necessity comes upon us, beasts of prey every one; each creature devouring his fellow, if not bodily, oft times crushing the life out no less unmercifully as selfishness dictates.

During the night another heavy fall of snow covered forever from view all traces of what had passed, and when the morning sun broke over glittering peak and deep gorged canyon, changing the late scene of bloody horror and savage carnival into a pure, white, diamond-sparkling fairy-land, each tall, slender, ice-bound tree along the rocky ledges of this retreat, standing sentinel over the sleeping men resting under snowy winding-sheets below, were not more silent and passive, than were they every one.

In that sleep, like unto death, all must have perished but for the timely arrival of a party bound for the same gold-fields, better equipped and guided than were our unfortunates.

Henry Armstrong, now known as Wm. Smith, to his companions old and new, bitterly with the others bemoaned their haste in quenching the pangs of starvation at the expense of their dead fellow traveler. No longer hungry, they soon forgot their sufferings, and were horrified by the crime perpetrated at the instigation of self-preservation. To Henry especially, when he had recovered from the insanity of starvation, did his wicked jealousy and its result fill him with agonizing remorse.

Each man had taken an oath coupled with a bloody penalty swearing to lock forever in his breast the secret of that night spent high up in the "Rockies," and it was years after, before it became known that the Gerald A. Johnson who was constantly getting into such strange dilemmas, was the Henry Armstrong who had that night assumed the name of Wm. Smith, and that he had by agreement with him dropped the name of Smith, changing to that of Johnson, upon his arrival in San Francisco.

The further mystery regarding their dead comrade which had come only to Henry's knowledge, he concealed safely in his own heart, at least for a time.

Though finding the picture of Lucille with the words written, "Oh! how dearly I loved her!" in the hand-writing of the dead man, had filled him with jealousy and wrath, he secreted and placed this relic carefully away with the letter which was to be forwarded to Silas Smith at Freelawn, still thinking that Wm. Smith had been the husband of Lucille, the same whom he had seen leaning over her on the night which turned his own fate.   To be sure he never mentioned a wife, or left any thing to be sent his family.   Evidently had he pos-sessed wife or child, they must have been estranged—all was in-volved in mystery which doubtless could be solved by the letter in his possession.

Comparing notes and information with the new-comers, the unfortunate travelers who had so nearly met their death, found themselves not far from the regular trail, but bewildered by the blinding sleet, they had missed their landmarks from not wait-ing quietly beside some one of the scored trees or blasted rocks which marked the way, until the storm subsided and they could safely proceed.

When overtaken and rescued, the whole party were ex-hausted, freezing, sinking into the stupor of death; but by care-ful management, were soon restored, and reached their destina-tion without further unusual incident.

Henry remained in San Francisco for several years known only as Gerald A. Johnson.   After a time the rumor went back to his friends in Rock Island and the east, that he had been lost in the perilous trip across the Rocky Mountains, just how or where was not definitely stated.   As Cronksey continued look-ing after his Bentonville affairs, providing for the Uncle's old mother and her neice who was next of kin after Henry, the property reverting to her at their death, and whom Cronksey had taken the precaution to make his wife, upon receiving an epistle from the *supposed dead man* instructing his agent to use the property exactly as though it belonged solely to himself; asking no questions, making no inquiries, as for reasons of his own, Henry informed him, he wished to remain perpetually in-cognito and *as though* dead, under the name of Gerald A. John-son, adding that he should probably soon leave the country never to return.

This was certainly a satisfactory arrangement so far as Cronksey was concerned, who had all along *been using the property as though it were his own,* under an unlimited Power of Attorney given by Henry before his departure for the west; and Cronksey had also been appropriating so much of the pro-ceeds of the estate to furthering his private ambitions, he quite feared to face an accounting of his agency.

His marriage with the neice, the rumored death of Henry Armstrong, and afterwards the letter from him referred to—the death being corroborated in the minds of his neighbors by the developments of time—all conduced to end his anxiety.

Henry having no other relatives, his mother dying soon after he left Barrytown, no one troubled themselves further about the settlement of his estate; as for himself, he cared not one whit how Cronksey disposed of the difficult problem, if only his secret was safe; for he had already accumulated more wealth since coming west than could be comfortably handled.

CHAPTER XXI.

CRONKSEY AND SPIDELER.

Upon arrival in San Francisco, Henry had assumed the name agreed upon, and in due time, as Gerald A. Johnson, taken measures to have the will of his Australian namesake proved and himself identified as the person intended in the document, coming into possession through a properly appointed agent of the property which doubled his former riches, and besides had made a large fortune since arriving in California and was now a millionaire; but still more dissatisfied, unhappy and conscience stricken than ever before.

The scenes of that terrible night in the "Rockies" continued to haunt him without mercy; in every breeze he fancied he could hear the whispered question, "*Where is thy brother?* Where hast thou laid him?" And at night the pure eyed stars of Heaven looked down upon him with accusing, fiery glances that seemed to burn into his soul, *that man's name.*

Few that had known Henry Armstrong, the innocent boy cherishing his first young love, would recognize him now; his very countenance was changed and marred, and seamed, by the internal conflicts which had racked him since that night, until *he*, at least, imagined the mark of Cain who slew his brother Abel, was branded in his forehead to be read of all men; one of the most miserable of miserables was the Hon. Gerald A. Johnson, the millionaire.

He was especially troubled in regard to Lucille his old-time love, for he had not only defrauded her of a true woman's dearest possession—her heart, but also unintentionally diverted from her a valuable estate. Circumstances conducing, his inclination impelling, he had opened and read the letter entrusted to him, fully expecting to find that the deceased man had been Lucille's husband, but discovering instead that he was her Wisconsin lover. Gaining no knowledge of the year or place of their meeting, Henry still supposed her the wife of the one he saw bending over her that night of the fight at the claim, and that this lover must have been an acquaintance of her maidenhood.

In the unfortunate letter Henry also found enclosed a will properly prepared and witnessed, several years before his death,

in which this friend so devoted, had given the larger share of
his estate to Lucille, making Silas Smith, who it seemed was a
distant relative, the administrator; a small pittance to go to Silas
himself.

These bequests did not of course include the legacy after-
ward left him in Australia, and for the possession of which he
had yet at time of death to take the nécessary steps, but which
by his wish had devolved upon Henry. The complications were such that any action in regard to the letter must
be secretly done; and, after attending to the request of his
mountain companion (bravely meeting an untimely end) as to
changing the name assumed of Smith to Johnson, and securing the Australian inheritance, Henry had carefully in-
tructed a lawyer to communicate with the Freelawn Post-
master making inquiries for Silas Smth, intending if he
could be found, to send him the letter, but the answer came
back that Smith had disappeared leaving no trace behind. Fortunately thought Henry, for now an excuse offered and again
he imagined a "Providence" was assisting him to bring about
his desires, and immediately decided upon opening the letter,
ascertaining as has been related that the dead man was not
Lucille's husband at all, but leaving him with a properly executed will on his hands, the provisions of which it would now be
almost impossible to carry out, without revealing his connection
with the affair, even should his own wicked plot against the man's
life not be disclosed. Everything had been different from his ex-
pectations, filling him only with regret and consternation. He
dared not make direct search for Lucille in the circumstances,
his identity would almost surely be discovered; certainly during
the necessary investigations for proving the will and transferring
the property to her, should he attempt to do so; and since knowing her to be, as he supposed, still a wife, he did not care to
risk any denouement by prosecuting further inquiries.

While brooding over this and his other troubles until almost
distracted, Henry received news requiring that himself or some
trusted agent should go immediately and attend to the Australian
estate; always longing for change, he concluded to proceed
directly to Bentonville, as secretly as possible, and after consulting with the agent who had managed his eastern affairs, as
he thought honestly, depart for a sojourn of several years in
Australia, possibly he might not return at all.

Henry Armstrong would never have ventured this visit to
his old home, had not the trouble in regard to Lucille and his

uncertainty as to her conditions of prosperity or adversity, so preyed upon his mind. She might be in poverty, actually suffering for the comforts to be derived from the estate left her by one who had proved his love to be ten-fold more than his, who was now withholding fraudulently that which belonged to her, and himself possessed of more wealth than one man could use to advantage. No wonder he was haunted by remorse, and could neither rest night or day, and determined before leaving the States to arrange with Cronskey some plan for finding Lucille and transferring to her, whether married or single, a regular and liberal remittance from his own abundance, not allowing any knowledge of the donor to escape, except the fact of a lover dying, and making this provision for her welfare.

Arranging his California business hastily, and taking a steamer round "the horn," as from its peculiar shape the southern extremity of South America is called in sailor's parlance, Henry reached New York about six or seven weeks after leaving San Francisco. Desiring to avoid recognition by friends in New York, he went without delay by the night express to Bentonville, being met upon arrival at the depot by Cronskey in his private carriage; who having now a large practice as a lawyer, and amassing considerable property through his connection with Henry's affairs, was a man of much importance.

The night was dark, but when Henry entered the vehicle, the door held open by the stylish coachman, he noticed the man gave a start, and sudden upward look into his face, both immediately suppressed. Upon alighting under the lamp of the carriage way at the door of the remodeled old house, which had been his home, Henry also looked sharply at the man, and into his face and was even more startled than the other had been. In fact he trembled from head to foot and nearly fell, for those snakey black eyes certainly belonged to the little fellow who had stood uncomfortably near him when the fatal lot was drawn up in the "Rockies" so many years ago. Neither of the men spoke a word, and Henry was glad to go directly with Cronskey to his private study or office, and enter immediately upon the business which had brought them together.

The more important matters were hastily scanned, Cronskey managing to evade going into particulars or showing papers. Soon the investigation, although cursory, disclosed clearly that the agent had become rich, either from the practice of law or the stewardship of Henry's affairs; it mattered little to him so that certain important facts remained covered. But he was hardly prepared for a demand upon the part of Cronskey, that he should immediately transfer to him all right, title and interest in his Bentonville property, for which transfer he had the papers already made out even before Henry's arrival, upon learning of the proposed visit; "Just as a precaution against any trouble in case of *your death*," said Cronskey.

"But," answered Henry, "the property is to revert to the old lady's niece at my demise, I cannot consent, and will not defraud her of one penny which rightfully belongs to her or any other woman, if I can help it." "Tut, tut; you needn't worry about that," broke in Cronskey, "the niece and *I are one*, we were *married* soon after you *informed me of your death*" —dryly—"it is probably needless to tell you, knowing me to be a good lawyer, that she long since merged all her interest in mine, and that I have the legal papers to that effect. There's nothing quite so good as a paper properly signed and delivered to prevent difficulty. Oh! you needn't worry about the niece, there's another matter about which you should concern yourself—a little affair which occurred up in the Rocky Mountains, a disagreeable episode, surely—unpleasant—*very* unpleasant, and I say to you as your legal adviser, that it will be difficult—*very* difficult to dispel from the mind of any one knowing all the facts, the suspicion that a deliberate murder was committed solely for gain."

Henry Armstrong was now shivering from head to foot, his teeth fairly chattering with nervous fear; and the thought of those snakey little eyes so recently glaring upon him, was anything but soothing; it was needless to ask how Cronskey had received the information evidently in his possession. Henry could only gasp, "For God's sake, Cronskey, what do you want? Where are the papers? I'll sign them, and then we'll drop the subject forever." Partly recovering, "No, not until I have asked you to help me rectify a wrong entirely unintentional on my part, connected with that sad affair about which you seem so well to know; the source of your knowledge I can easily guess, but never mind that now. My business here is really more on account of a woman whom I once loved, than for any other purpose. I care nothing for property, and am heartily sick of money getting, every thing I touch turns to gold only to curse me. GOLD *cannot love me*; GOLD *cannot comfort my soul, I hate* gold! A cold, heartless, glittering tyrant is gold."

"And now, Cronksey, I want you to search the country over, cost what it may, until you find the whereabouts of a lady

who was once Lucille Gascoigne, daughter of Dr. Gascoigne,
of Freelawn, Ill.   I cannot do this without revealing my identity—and when you have found her remit to her regularly the
whole income of my Galena lead mine, also the proceeds of my
stock in the Comstock mine, which property I have arranged
to transfer to you to be held in trust for her—and have brought
the necessary papers with me for that purpose.   For God's sake,
Cronksey, do not fail me in this, do not betray this sacred trust
or let anyone know who the donor is; say a lover dying was
pleased to make such provision for her comfort.   *Promise me,*
Cronksey!" exclaimed Henry, wrought to a pitch of excitement
he could not control, rising to his feet and grasping the man by
both hands with the grip of a vise—"PROMISE ME! and I'll sign
your papers."

And Cronksey promised, chuckling to himself as he thought
how easily a promise may be given.

As the night was now advancing, and the objects of the interview had been accomplished, except the signing of Cronksey's papers, he rang a little call bell and instantly there appeared
the stylish coachman, divested of coat, cape and hat—in plain busi
ness suit quite a different man—whom Cronksey introduced as
Mr. Spideler, a Notary, ready to take his acknowledgment as required by law.   Each man eyed the other, and knew himself
not mistaken, but as before kept silence, and Henry signed the
name of Gerald A. Johnson, trembling like an aspen under the
penetrating glance fixed upon him from those dreaded eyes, and
his Mephistopheles affixed the proper notarial seal bearing the
name of Augustus J. Spideler, and while Cronksey placed the
two papers conveying so much valuable property to himself
carefully away in his safe, securely turning the lock upon them,
watched closely by a large mastiff, evidently one of the belong-
ings of that private office, Spideler and Johnson arrayed themselves for their drive to the depot, for train time was near at
hand, and were stiffly bowed out by Cronksey, who was well
pleased that the very important business of the night had been
so easily accomplished.   And so intensely satisfied was he over
the transaction that for hours he walked the floor of the little
study, unable to quiet his scheming brain or even think of sleep,
contriving how he should use his suddenly acquired wealth in
gaining more.

And as he paced backwards and forwards he would throw
up his head, which, by the way, was a very handsome apend-
age, not at all plebian, chuckling to himself, " Yes, when I find

her—*when I find her*, as if there wasn't plenty of old sweet-
hearts and pretty women near by. Oh! yes, when I find her,
to be sure!" For Cronksey had not the slightest intention Lucille should ever receive one atom of the proceeds of either the
lead or the gold mine. In fact, he never gave her another
thought until years after when she was brought to his attention
quite unexpectedly.

When Henry Armstrong was seated alone in Cronksey's
comfortable carriage being driven rapidly to the depot by Spideler, he began to think more quietly and composedly, yes, ration-
ally, than he had done since getting sight of those evil eyes; he
now seemed to himself like one just awakening from a dreadful
dream, in which he had been on the edge of a precipice, hanging over a fearful abyss, and rousing himself a dark and heavy
pall seemed lifting from his mind, his vision; and as he pondered, one might have heard the words ejaculated, " Buy him, of
course, *the little devil*, every man has his price, give him gold,
stuff him to the brim with gold. I have enough and to spare,
feed the little imp on gold, ha, ha!" And Henry took from
his pocket a well-filled wallet, and from his waist a belt quilted
back and forth, *solid with gold*, then examining carefully the
size of a roll of bills taken from another receptacle, holding
them in his hand he murmured, " Yes, this will do, this morsel
of gold will stop the brute's mouth for a time, and I can reach
my journey's end with these bills, when there'll be plenty more
of the trash awaiting me."

They were now at the depot, Spideler ready at the carriage
door; instead of alighting Henry grasped the man roughly and
strongly by the collar, and thrusting the wallet and belt into
his hand, said hoarsely, " Take *that*, and *mind no further word
must escape you*, you can have from me either *gold* or BLOOD,
which shall it be? *Your* blood understand! *your heart!* your
life! if you again betray me! Do you hear, man? Do you
hear?"

For it was now Spideler's turn, and he was quaking as in an
ague chill; the night was dark, the street obscure, no one near;
he knew Henry Armstrong might end the controversy then and
there if he liked and no one be the wiser until he was far on his
way and had made his escape. But Henry's heart was not
black enough to perpetrate such a crime, unless possessed by insanity or in self-preservation, and shaking the villain until his
teeth rattled, throwing the heavy belt across his shoulder, putting the wallet again in his hand, with the word, " *There, take*

that, and let it insure that you keep your oath, or you'll hear
from me again with the penalty, and a sure and bloody vengeance it shall be," and Henry let the miscreant go; leaping
from the carriage he boarded the train just arrived, and in a few
moments was leaving Bentonville most gladly behind him; ere
morning reaching New York, going directly to the steamer
which sailed for Australia before noon.

As we have seen, the main object with Henry had been all
along to kill old memories by excitement and change.   His
journey and contemplated residence abroad would serve this
purpose well, and he determined should the climate prove as
represented to remain for a long, long time, for he knew that
in the States he was liable to be disturbed at any moment.

A guilty conscience impelled him to flee from any one who
might recognize him in the wealthy gentleman, Gerald A. Johnson, Esq.

From one he could not escape, and bitterly did he regret
that Cronksey should know his secret, but for this misfortune
there was no remedy except such as gold could buy.

As the staunch Cunarder steamed down the Hudson, past
the wonderful city of New York, which has made Manhattan
Island one of the famous places of the world, down the sound,
past Long Island, Coney Island, Cape May, Newport, Long
Branch and other points along the shore, teeming with the intense civilization flowing from this vitalized center, from the
throbbiug heart of the great city; when at last they stood out
upon the broad Atlantic and were alone on the deep, Henry
Armstrong felt a relief he had not experienced for years.

Heretofore he had been under an irksome restraint and constant apprehenshion, because out of harmony with the requirements of social law, failing in its most essential idea, namely,
individual identity and responsibility; what had seemed a simple enough matter at first, entered upon to humor a doomed
man's caprice, had step by step grown into a complicated entanglement, from which he had been powerless to extricate
himself, but now he was leaving all this behind and 1 ounding
over the briny waves a free man.

Any one who has crossed an ocean knows how different
from any other experience the event is.   Being separated for
days and weeks from the rest of the world is of itself a novelty.
Isolated, encircled by the same circumstances, the oft-time dangers, the common amusements; all this engendering a strong
bond of sympathy, developing acquaintance, even life-long

friendships, and never to be forgotten attachments, during the short time consumed after leaving port before reaching a destination.

Dear companionships are sometimes severed and many a pair of lovers evolved from calm moonlight, tossing waves and breezy decks, have been rudely roused from the dearest dream of their lives when the cry, "Land, ho!" has sounded, and the craft with all on board, sailed up to her moorings. In rare instances the dreamers have continued dreaming on until two lives were fused in one; such was Henry's lot to outward seeming.

Unexpectedly, who should he encounter the morning of the embarkation, but the same little friend that had been entrusted to his care years before, when they traveled the length of the Erie Canal together; who but Miss Effie Stebbins? And again, matured and improved, Henry found the young lady a pleasant companion.

Shocked, she certainly was by the changed name, but he explained it as the freak of a dying man, an old friend, and begged her to secrecy.

Miss Stebbins was traveling to join an elder sister whose husband being succeesful in garnering wealth from the Australian mines, had sent for his wife a year before, and now for her sister.

Henry was disappointed that his identity should have been so soon discovered, but could only make the best of what could not be remedied by treating his young acquaintance with great consideration.

From the first day they were constantly in each other's company, with the result which might have been expected; one or both must fall in love. Miss Effie, dark-eyed, impetuous, but weak, forthwith did this very thing, she being one of those child-like women, never stopping to reason, but just loving every one good and kind, surely drawing others to themselves in return.

Like all women of her class, Miss Effie was not very constant or deep in her emotion; had fallen in and out of love a half-dozen times or more in her short life, and so far no one had been hurt, certainly not she.

Henry estimated the young lady at just about her proper value, but he enjoyed her society because she was sweet and simple, and as the days went by he surprised himself by enjoying her more and more.

During their frequent moonlight strolls about the decks, for the weather was exceptionally fine, it came to seem exactly the thing for him to take her hand, small, soft and pliable, as it lay on his arm, and the owner never objected that it should rest confidingly in his, large and warm and manly.

Some one says, " When a man grasps a woman's hand, he holds half her heart." Miss Effie Stebbins soon found, not half, but all, of this very susceptible organ of hers in the keeping, at least for the time, of her congenial friend; ere long, when a rough sea would give the ship a sudden lurch, Henry's arm supported her slender waist without reproof.

At last, as the wind was rising one evening near the close of the voyage, and the ship began to roll more than at any time before, little Effie really got a fright, and clung with trembling hands to her protector's arm; beseechingly her eyes met his, and with sudden impulse folding her in his strong arms, Henry pressed a kiss upon the pretty mouth the first any woman could boast from him since last he touched the lips of Lucille so long ago

But Lucille was married now, gone from him irretrievably, so thought Henry; and besides the die was cast, the advance made which could not honorably be retracted. The lady had responded gladly, without reserve; and really he did not care to renounce what he had done. Lucille, his true but lost love, was beyond his reach, why should he turn from this dear little woman even though he well knew she could not fill his heart as Lucille would have done. "No," Henry resolved, "I will accept this new love with all of comfort it may bring, giving the best I can in return, and will take to my forlorn heart and dreary life, an affectionate companion, man's choicest blessing if she be true and kind—a wife."

And this resolve he put into execution soon after arriving at the home of Miss Stebbins' sister, Mrs. Ferguson, who resided in New South Wales, Australia.

The courtship proceded smoothly without untoward incident, and the preparations for the nuptials as usual, until the day and the hour when the consummation was approaching.

On that day Henry arose from a night of disturbed dreaming, to a morning filled with strange forebodings, instead of joyous anticipations, as became an expectant bridegroom; his mind shadowed by sad memories, Lucille's image constantly before him, in her eyes a sad, reproachful look; until he was absolutely sick at heart, and trembled with fear and grief.

It seemed not only a memory which haunted him, but **Lu-**

cille's actual presence, and he could not dispel the delusion, if such it might be, or shake off the feeling for an instant. Every moment of the never-to-be-forgotten day was Lucille by her lost lover's side with utmost endeavor of pathetic attitude and tender gaze, drawing him back to her arms, to her heart. And he—held, restrained by circumstance, time, space; longing to bridge the gulf which separated them, finding it impossible; his very soul striving in agonized impotence to enfold her, but unable,—surely the bridegroom's plight was pitiful.

The bride, her family and the guests when they were assembled, noticed and upbraided poor Henry for his unnatural, distraught demeanor,

He could only answer them that he was not well—not well indeed—no more had he been on that memorable night at the claim, when, as he believed, he had looked upon Lucille, her husband and her child.

As the time arrived, and the to-be-wedded pair stood before the altar, Henry's indisposition increased until a deathly paleness overspread his face; suddenly every atom of color forsook his countenance, and as the words, "I pronounce you husband and wife" were said, with staring eyes and the ghastly expression of death upon him, the new made husband fell prostrate to the floor. For Lucille, bodily, had to all appearance, really and truly, come between himself and wife, her arms outstretched as though to clasp him to her heart, her eyes wildly beseeching, her lips moving as if to speak in remonstrance—what wonder Henry was overcome!

It was *so real*, as real to Henry as to Lucille, dreaming that same dream, seeing the same vision that summer afternoon as she dozed in the old arm chair, in the room where Myra died.

After a little, Henry recovered, "His sickness was caused by the unusual heat," they said, and the festivities were resumed.

When the climax had passed, Henry's trouble left him, and his usual cheerfulness returned, for he was fully resolved on making the best of what could not easily be undone. They were married now, himself and Effie Stebbins, she was his wife, he would be true and loyal until the end, whatever that might be; but as the years went by, bringing forth good and evil, he, bound with chords which could not be broken, regretted more and more that mortal eyes should lack the power of piercing into futurity.

CHAPTER XXII.

THE STALWARTS.

The war was long since over—the Union had been preserved—all the States remained united, the broad Mississippi flowed untrammeled from the Minnehaha to the sea, bearing upon its bosom the commerce of the North, West and South, and the grandest, freest country on earth stood undivided—because the Stalwart Republican party had, more than any other, fought against the fatal doctrine of " State Sovereignty " as opposed to National Unity; against the doctrine of human slavery, as opposed to human freedom; against the final absolute disruption determined upon by the southern " Secessionists," when they found they could not have their own way, regulate their State institutions as they claimed a right to do; though this right involved the cherishing of a deadly gangrene upon the body politic, even insisting in opposition to the expressed will of the majority of the whole people.

For this right they stubbornly fought—aided, abetted, *instigated*, as the sequel proved, by European Monarchies, aiming at an overthrow of our loved Republic—God's refuge land for the down-trodden and oppressed of all the earth; Monarchies whose progeny must, according to the Royal mind, be provided with necessary Thrones. These arrogant aristocracies, not content with setting the grinding heel upon the neck of honest toil in all the countries of the Old World, must needs endeavor to engraft their half civilized feudal systems upon the new.

Let us not be deceived, for even to-day are they nursing this wish in their heart of hearts, striving still to induce dissension in our midst; goading on capital to impose upon labor, and labor to rebel against organized authority; emptying cesspools of vice, pauperism and crime upon our land; exiling rankest anarchy to our shores, inaugurating the demon of misrule, certain to be followed, as they well understand, by the re-action likely to result in an established Monarchy or Monarchies.

Surely does our Republic need now, as during the civil war, a stalwart patriotism which shall boldly stand for American Independence and unity; driving every invader from our soil, be he Minister Plenipotentiary, heathen Chinee or exiled, self-imported agitator.

Not to any enslaved, toil-worn or distressed would we refuse shelter, but let us insist that *all*, be they high or low, shall while they remain conduct themselves as good *American* citizens, or at least as respectable, *honorable* American residents, and invited guests, not as spies, disorganizers and traitors.

The name of " Stalwart," which at first those staunch Republicans *gloried* in, who could be depended upon to stand by the Union, *never faltering* during the contest and immediately following the civil war; but which eventually, when the grand old party had degraded itself, as all parties too long in power are sure to do, into a mere machine for grinding the grist from which is manufactured the " pap " of our vicious " spoils " system wherewith avaricious leaders fill their hungry maws—came to be a term of ridicule and reproach, applying to those politicians who were known to be united "*solid*" for spoils only.

And at last it came to mean those who, not content with a double dose of the "one man " presidential power and patronage, would fain prolong the ruling dynasty even to a third term; how much longer, the Lord and those magnates across the water only know.

Finally the word was used to designate a paltry " 306," led by a still smaller number of designing men, crafty and wicked, who were determined, as their conduct fully proved, to ruin if they could not rule, and who were at the last as really in rebellion against the Government (which must always be in a Republic, but the "administration " installed for the time by the vote of the people),as were ever the southern "Secessionists," though perhaps not as honestly and openly, but *secretly, diabolically* and also impelled indirectly by the same foreign Monarchies, backed by the same foreign capital, controlled by the same foreign forces, as were they.

However, the civil war which had so nearly disrupted the union of our States was now an event of the past, and there were gathered in Chicago—our new Chicago—uprisen from the ashes and desolation of one of those great conflagrations the world sometimes sees, to be the most enterprising and progressive city on the Continent, an assembly of the best minds and most noted men of that party named Republican, which had grown out of those vital issues to which we have alluded, and which had agitated the country into the crisis of the war now deplored by all.

12

A war seldom equaled in its atrocities and sufferings, but settling forever the slave problem, and bringing about the emancipation of the colored race in our boasted free America; thus, evil being allowed that good might come.

For suffering can no more be eliminated from destiny than can the inevitable and indispensable discord from the finest musical instrument; life, no less than the grandest harp, being thus tensioned and attuned in the tightening grasp of a Power beyond control.

These leaders and representative men of this party, to whose original stalwart patriotism and unswerving constancy in the cause of justice and human rights was largely due the fortunate termination of the contest, and whose influence had dominated the country ever since its close, were now assembled to make their nomination for President and vice-President of the United States, to be submitted in the Fall elections to the vote of the people.

For many reasons, the little clique calling themselves "Stalwarts," which, though in the minority as to numbers, was an integral unit of the Republican Party difficult to displace, and seeking with utmost endeavor to dominate the majority, preferred as their nominee for President the renowned and popular General, who during the "late unpleasantness" had achieved the high place of Commander-in-Chief of the armies of the North, and to whom the General of the southern forces had at the close yielded up his arms.

This man who had become the most successful hero of modern times, was none other than the inveterate smoker, whose acquaintance Henry had acquired, and whose friendship he had gained years before in the lead mines of Galena. To the remarkable, steady persistency of this man in command, was due, in great measure, the final victory of the North.

At the beginning of the conflict, when the South, after many threats, had actually fired the first gun, opening upon Sumpter, men all over the North made foolish bets that the war would not last three months; but the fight continued with unabated fury, years instead of months.

The North all this time underrating the indomitable, passionate, fiery spirit of the South, and the willful determination to have what they believed to be their rights. But when this stolid General, who could neither be frightened or bought, and who had never been vanquished, but quietly puffed his cigar until victory perched upon his banner, the "smoking General,"

as he had come to be called, got a good ready and sat down before Richmond, their last strong-hold, his clear, grey eyes upon
that somewhat distant town, prepared for an all summer's
smoke, the South — Generals, army, people, concluded they
might as well succumb first as last, for they knew the "smoking
General" was sure to march into their capital, sooner or later—
and he did.

The enthusiasm at the North over the result had been boundless, and the treatment of his disarmed foe by the victorious
General such that even the South acknowledged him worthy
to be their conquerer.

At the first presidential election after the close of the war,
this General, well nigh deified in the minds of the grateful
people, was elected President of the country he had served so
well. And yet again, when his time of office had expired, was
he tendered the highest place in the gift of his fellow citizens.

The two terms of his presidency had proved so satisfactory,
his administration being wise and just, settling disjointed factions, and healing gaping wounds, that the North and the South
were forgetting their animosity, treating each other again
as human beings instead of as wild beasts; like brethren—quar-
reling a little perhaps, but as brothers quarrel, not as sworn
enemies.

As another election approached, and many had carried their
admiration and gratitude to the extreme of hero-worship, they
were determined a third time to nominate and elect the man
whom they felt had saved the country in peace as well as in
war.

Others, far-seeing, and wisely endeavoring to guard against
perpetuation of power in the individual ruler, which if continued long enough, must, even under a Republican form of
government, lead to Oligarchy—perhaps—*almost surely to a
Monarchy;* bitterly opposed the contemplated "third term" nomination of the General, and in this they were supported by the
people, ever jealous of any approach towards an established
dynasty, as were our forefathers, who refused to the father of
his country, the revered Washington, this honor.

The "third term" movement was defeated, and a good man
was nominated by the Republicans, and elected, who succeeded
in giving an administration of reasonable prosperity, entirely
pleasing to the majority. But these restless politicians,
who had for so long been recognized as Stalwart leaders, and
had come to consider themselves entitled to all the emoluments,

could see no opportunity for their own aggrandizement in a quiet, temperate, prosperous administration of affairs, in which they were ignored. They must have strife and turmoil for their purposes, also a hand in dispensing patronage, and were possessed of a dissatisfaction which they hesitated not to express.

Another presidential election was now near at hand, the prospective, possible and probable candidates had been canvassed by Republicans and Democrats, and both political parties were ready for action and to present their nominees to the people for their suffrage.

The General had, shortly before the assembling of this Republican convention we are considering, traveled round the world, his journey being a continuous ovation, ending in a series of receptions as he proceded from city to city on his homeward way across the continent from west to east, such as no other man uncrowned has received in modern times. When his party reached Chicago, the enthusiasm exceeded all bounds, certainly in this last grand demonstration continuing from days into weeks, greatness experienced its reward.

Encouraged by the respect and admiration evinced for this honored General and popular President, the Stalwarts, whose record entitled them as they deemed to special consideration, determined to place the great Commander again before the people, as the Republican nominee, committing the mistake of supposing they could be induced to raise him again to the highest office in the land, against their sober judgment.

However, as an alternate and dernier resort, Cronskey, the acknowledged leader of the Stalwart clique, had in reserve, should the General be defeated at the convention and fail of the nomination—one, J. G. Bamboozle, a blatant demagogue, full of tricks and sly conceit; who he believed would make a more willing, and *not unconscious tool*, as most surely would the General, if placed in the presidential chair. For this reason, as he had an end of his own to gain, Cronskey really preferred Bamboozle, if only the people could be induced to give him the necessary vote.

But, as is sometimes the case in this Republican country, this political schemer reckoned without his host; and the smooth and artful Cronskey found when the names were presented to the convention, even when backed by such faithful henchmen as Silas Smith, who after long disappearance from view, had risen to be a power in the country—a power as unscrupulous as his original character would indicate, and Spideler, not less useful and trusted, whom we remember to have met before, being fully as great a trickster as his master, with the help of their own special line of followers, both they and Cronskey failed to control the *dear people*, who when once aroused are quick to see through shams, and they could not be induced to place either the honored General or the demagogue in nomination for the highest place at disposal, as neither suited their mood, as indicated by those who held the hand and fingered the pulse of this same dear people.

When the time and occasion were ripe, the contention over the nomination being bitter in the Republican convention assembled within the immense Exposition building left standing near the shore of Lake Michigan, not far south from the spot where the Gascoigne and Grieveau families entered Chicago before old Fort Dearborn was torn away; there appeared a *man born for just that time and place!*

A man not then unknown; and as he rose before them, speaking of the points at issue, a hush fell upon the excited multitude while they listened eagerly to his powerful and melodious voice, discoursing calmly and wisely of men and measures over which they were battling.

Rather above the medium size, of generous proportions both mind and body, with a noble head and fascinating face, a soul capable of loving and of commanding affection and respect in return; a man of intellect and power to bear himself above his fellows. A man of Providence! A man of Destiny!

As he stood grandly before them and argued earnestly for his opinion, the attention of that vast assembly was intently fixed; reason triumphed, discord vanished, and at last both antagonistic factions withdrawing their candidate, agreeing to unite upon some other man, peace entered in and every heart was won.

Little thought the eloquent orator who had pleaded for amity and brotherly kindness that his would be the chosen name. But almost instantly—by acclamation—the fearless and winning speaker was declared the choice of the convention; so true are the instincts of the people—and a name destined to sound in echoes round a world before the end should come to him who bore it, was placed at the head of the Republican Presidential ticket.

The scheming Cronksey now realized that he was beaten at his own game.

With a long-headed treachery he had worked both for the
General and the demagogue, hoping in his heart should *they*
lose it the rich morsel of the Presidency would fall between
them into his own watering mouth, and when foiled, his wrath
knew no bounds although carefully concealed under a placid
exterior, only to burn as a raging fire within.

Soon he bethought him of a remedy, a partial revenge. His
old-time patron, the man whose secret he held, had returned
from Australia a year or two before, passing under the name of
Gerald A. Johnson; residing mostly in San Francisco and other
places on the Pacific coast, keeping well away from eastern localities, fearing recognition though much changed by time and
a foreign climate.

But for reasons best known to himself, moved by a lever
which Cronksey well knew how to work, Johnson, the millionaire, risking discovery, had met his former agent by appointment in Chicago, attending the convention. Cronksey, surmising that a necessity might suddenly arise for the use of extra
cash influence, had importuned him to be at hand, and now,
confronted by the emergency, had immediately indicated to
Johnson a desperate venture, which he had without consulting
anyone fully decided upon.

To appease his disappointment and secure co-operation,
Cronksey was quite sure the two factions would allow him to
name his man for the vice-Presidency; he well knew the party
could not afford to ignore his pleasure especially when furthered
by an abundance of money.

With the vice-President under his control, Cronksey was
certain that Smith, Bamboozle, Spideler and himself might
manage a deep affair they had in hand to defraud and weaken
the Government quite as successfully as though one of themselves were at the head of the Administration.

Cronksey's plan was, that Johnson, the man thrown into his
power by circumstances so that he held him body and soul, as
one does the insect between the thumb and finger of his strong
hand waiting to crush and mercilessly destroy when so inclined
—should take the vice-Presidency, and thus the proper man be
where, *if needed,* he could be used *even against his own will
without his knowledge,* in advancing the interests of these crafty
politicians and self-seekers.

At the thought of holding so prominent a position, almost
sure to result in an exposure of his secret, Johnson's blood curdled at his heart. He, the vice-President of the United States

might come to be *placed on trial for murder*, even though innocent, by the friends of the dead Wm. Smith. It was terrible.

And the one most to be dreaded after Cronksey and Spideler,
was the scoundrelly Silas Smith himself, and then the General
whom he had known years before, might remember him and
know he was passing under an assumed name—and query,
"Why?"—How could he hope if he consented to the nomination
to escape incognito through the campaign and his term of
office if elected? And he was sure some dark deviltry lurked
in Cronksey's mind inducing him to resort to such an expedient,
for his henchman, Spideler, and even himself might also be
called to give account for the mystery of that night in the
"Rockies," might possibly be accused of "compounding felony."

But notwithstanding all Johnson's remonstrances, Cronksey
remained inexorable, and declared he could manage the whole
business without disaster if left to himself, and would keep Silas
Smith (who now spent most of his time in London) out of the
way, and would prevent any meeting between Johnson and the
General if Johnson would obey orders, getting back to San
Francisco immediately and remaining there until wanted for the
inauguration. Pictures of the nominee for vice-President would
of course be sent over the country, but recognition would not
be likely to follow from such work as is usually furnished on
such occasions, and besides Johnson had very much altered in
appearance.

Finally Johnson yielded to Cronksey's importunities, more
afraid of present wrath than of any harm in the future, and
against his own judgment, the very marrow quaking in his
bones with dread and premonitions of evil, his name was placed
second upon the Presidential ticket, which after the usual campaign manœuvres was declared the choice of the people.

In due time the newly elected President and vice-President
were inaugurated into office upon the broad piazza of the beautiful white marble Capitol of the Nation in sight of a vast concourse of the so-called self-governed people.

During the campaign many strange coalitions had been
formed, and antagonistic elements fused in the struggle of the
Republican party for supremacy over the Democratic, but no
sooner was success assured than innate selfishness asserted itself,
and the victors began a disgraceful contest for the spoils of office,
the loaves and fishes of political power.

Before the end was reached the quarrel between the two
factions waxed bitter and fierce, and those who like Cronksey

had a special object in view scrupled not in adding fuel to the flame; only too anxious in keeping the contest raging for their own advantage, even to the imminent danger of again involving the country in the misfortune of civil war.

Many yet believe that such a catastrophe was only averted by a calamity as remarkable as dreadful; which, coming upon them as a thunderbolt from Heaven, had the effect of shocking these wrangling politicians into a sense of shame and remorse, causing each one to feel himself at least in a measure responsible for the horror of the climax, although it became necessary to use the *utmost endeavor to fasten the entire blame upon some-one else.*

CHAPTER XXIII.

A GIGANTIC SCHEME.

As has been stated, a few years before the events transpired last alluded to, Henry, as Gerald A. Johnson, had returned from his long sojourn in Australia to his native land, bringing with him his pretty though invalid wife, who had degenerated into this condition, considered by some people interesting, because she lacked force to be anything better. Her children were abortions for the same cause. She was amiable enough, and easily controlled—why not? Every desire gratified as soon as expressed, suffering but little pain, not possessed of an active mind, to chafe and grow restless under the weight of an aimless, helpless life, seeking only to while away the hours with as little exertion as possible. Effie was fond of Henry in her way, whom she of course always addressed as Gerald; and he regarded her as a feeble, pretty child, to be cared for certainly, and sometimes, to be sure, caressed; but as for the satisfaction and companionship a man should find in his wife, it was not there.

How intense grew the longing in Henry's heart all those years for his lost Lucille, only himself ever knew. He needed the daily help of her purity and steadfastness of purpose, her strong integrity of character, no less than the sweetness and loving-kindness of her presence.

As he remembered her, rather as she came to him, he thought, in very fact, there seemed more of her womanhood, both of body and spirit, than he found in his wife, or had ever recognized in any other.

Alas! was Henry sadly disappointed in the part of his life most essential to his well-being, and the trouble grew day by day.

Thus do men having their own way defraud themselves.

Through fear of some terrible catastrophe happening to her husband should his identity become known, Effie guarded well his secret, not understanding the particulars, but still loyal to the trust he had reposed in her.

Henry had so changed from his long residence abroad, there was little probability of any former friend even remembering

him; but, strive as he would, he grew more and more, as the
years went by, to dread the treachery of the only other one in
his confidence; for Henry well knew Cronksey would not hesitate for a moment in sacrificing a comrade, though ever so true,
or any servant however faithful, standing in the way of a desired end; and he was now the abject slave of the man—his
before-time agent—their places transposed.

Henry had often regretted having returned to the States at
all, the occasion of his doing so being the delicate health of his
wife, who pined for her old home. But since the further dilemma into which Cronksey had forced him, as narrated in the
last chapter, by insisting that he should allow himself to be nominated for the vice-presidency, Henry had innumerable times
wished he had remained in Australia, even at the risk of failing
health and lost life.

Running for vice-president may not so surely result in un-
earthing all a man's past experience as entering the presidential
race is apt to do, but Henry felt that he was risking a great deal
for small gain, especially as the benefit would mainly accrue to
another individual.

This man Cronksey, whom Henry so greatly dreaded, had
grown, as the years passed by, to be a remarkable character, as
strong as unique, as unprincipled as strong.

Although priding himself, not without cause, upon his antecedents and ancestry—for he came from one of the very best
old York State families—yet the man was what is called self-
made; that is, he had marked out an independent career of his
own, working his way steadily along with little help from others. He was, and had always been, as we have seen, a man who
would without doubt help himself to anything he wanted—
not hesitating, as was well known, even at defrauding his own
friend of a man's most jealously-guarded possession, the wife of
his bosom, the mother of his children—violating every principle of honor, all the obligations of hospitality, in consummating
his nefarious designs.

From the beginning of his prosperous days—they dating so
far back no one could remember when he had been impecun-
ious, but which really commenced with his charge of Henry's
Bentonville estate—Cronksey had been shrewd enough to understand the importance, to one who wishes to get on in the
world, of controlling the people with whom he comes in contact, either by fair means or foul, and in one way and another,

principally by dabbling in local politics, this he had succeeded doing early in his career.

By some influence which he alone understood he had bound to his service the man Spideler whose acquaintance we have made in former chapters, and whose snakey black eyes had seen *too much*, up in the "Rockies," and whose piercing glances had so disturbed Henry upon the occasion of his last visit to Bentonville.

The absolute devotedness of this man to his master's interests had, from the first, been so marked whether engaged in good or in evil work, as to call forth the comparison from those who knew them, of "My lord and his little dog." Some went so far, upon closer acquaintance, as to call Spideler a "Dirty dog," "a vile cur" "Just suited for such work as his master had plenty of," they sometimes added under their breath; for Cronksey was a man it did not pay his neighbors to offend.

And others, who knew to their sorrow even more of the man Spideler and his attributes, whispered still lower in the ear of some trusted comrade, "That *dog* was too good and noble a name; that it should have been Spider;" for in wicked machinations, net-weaving in dark corners, he surely was unexcelled by the most viperous of those busy insects — the blackest, most poisonous tarantula.

At times, when intent upon some special deviltry, he had a way of drawing his flat, shiny bald head, with its glistening little eyes and circling fringe of jet-black hair—the ears pinched tightly to the sides—back into the shoulders, extinguishing the short, thick neck, and poising his chunky body, bending those long, thin legs and wirey arms into a reaching, waiting attitude, restrained, but ready for the signal to pounce upon and grasp his prey; and then the bony hands, with claw-like fingers, would work nervously, as though impatient of delay.

This was Spideler's own self; but in presence of his master upon ordinary occasions, so habitually dominated had he become, the evil face and twinkling eyes had acquired an inquisitive, anxious look, impressing one as though he said, "What next, my lord?" Every motion of the impish little man would be alert to friskiness, as though inwardly fearing some duty left undone.

Unhappy Spideler! Many an angry frown and spiteful curse did you receive; only now and then was left you in your hideous den a loathsome morsel, requiting faithful service.

But Cronksey himself was quite another sort of man, at

least in appearance. Tall, dignified, and exquisite from the crown of his head adown to his very toes: the high white brow; the keen eyes and penetrating glance; the finely formed and knowing nose, always leading its owner to the exact point scented; the chiseled mouth with proudly curving though firm lips, surmounted by the imperial mustache; the handsome face, improved by the immaculate, flowing white beard and carelessly curling gray hair; the whole personality bespeaking in every look, tone and gesture the man of distinguished presence and attributes; always thinking well of himself; never deigning openly to low villainous deeds, whatever he might instigate in others; but also indicating a careful, shrewd calculator, and a schemer deep and unscrupulous.

A political trickster of the higher order, as Cronskey had long since become, needing without doubt some convenient party near at hand, willing to execute detestable work, which must not soil his own dainty hands—hence Spideler, in all but villainy, the contrast of his master.   *   *

After Henry's return from Australia, Cronskey continued the charge of the annuity designed for Lucille, but which she of course failed to receive; he also retained a general insight of Henry's extensive business, who at his suggestion traded heavily in stocks, often risking large sums in doubtful enterprises by his advice; Cronskey meanwhile keeping his own money chest safely locked, though reaping a handsome percentage upon his victim's investments if ending fortunately. It happened that in furtherance of these business ventures, Henry, Cronskey and Spideler were frequently together, and these conferences continued even after Henry was nominated for the vice-presidency, under the name of Gerald A. Johnson, although Henry kept well away from New York and other eastern latitudes where, if seen, he might be known.

Events coming about, contrary to usual experiences of life, that the General-in-Chief of the victorious northern army had been fully appreciated both as to honors and also money, and thus amassing a goodly fortune, more it must be said through the management of his friends than from any financial aptitude of his own; and being one of the "solid-moneyed-men" the General became to Cronskey a temptation, correlatively ending as a victim.

Having no more need of money-making than had Henry or any of the others, or even Cronskey himself, who all eventually became involved in a gigantic scheme, originating in the brain of Cronskey, and helped on—the two evenly matched—. by the only trusted counselor Cronskey ever possessed, or thoroughly confided in; the only man he had ever found who could equal himself in plotting villiany; a man no less remarkable in characteristics than Cronskey, and whom we shall show you further on, introducing another old acquaintance.

Not obliged to engage in any business for gain, but solely as a vent to their active, restless dispositions, were these men induced to enter into a speculation of which they knew little, by the intriguing Cronskey and his two trusted emissaries, and which caused them all much distress and grief before the end.

Pity such men could not be *forced* to knit their own stockings, or saw cord wood with the Wisconsin Norwegians, thus merging their surplus energy in a sweet content, instead of working mischief to their fellows.

Even the General was all right and in the accomplishment of good, *while he sat still* before Richmond—and smoked.

But Cronksey was a man who had the peculiar faculty of interesting other men in his plans, either for emolument or aggrandizement, and impelling them to accede to his wishes by the exercise of a strong will, not letting them know of his control in the matter. Spideler became in time a most useful accessory, and at last indispensible to his master. Cronksey had but to imbue Spideler with the thought that was in his own mind, the purpose to be accomplished, and forthwith the evil little man talked that idea incessantly—moved Heaven and earth, not mentioning Satan's dark abode, in arriving at the premeditated end.

Besides possessing this wonderful power over others with whom he came in contact, or to whom he could send his magnetized medium, Cronksey was a man who could brook no superior, and whose egotism and desire to rule over his fellowmen was boundless. Furthering his own preëminence, he was not content with being the acknowleged head of the leading political faction named "Stalwarts," but was continually on the aggressive, creating discord in his party, fatally antagonizing the two branches, and had conceived the idea of dominating the entire organization, and through it, the whole people, even to the destruction of cherished Republican institutions, not sparing the newly elected President from his dictation.

This man Cronksey had by slow but sure degrees advanced up the political ladder, until he had come to look upon himself as being, and his co-workers joined in the opinion, as though he were the great *I am*, his will the "Open Sesame" to any gate he chose to enter. Such a man aims at controlling friend and foe alike in his own interests; but soon after the inauguration Cronksey discovered that whatever he might accomplish with the intimidated Vice-President, he need not expect to overpower the newly elected President, against his honest convictions.

In the Vice-President Cronksey saw a man restless and dissatisfied, just in the condition to crave the excitement of ambitious projects, and whose long residence abroad under a Monarchical form of government had destroyed to a great extent his distinctive American and Republican proclivities, and he proceeded deftly to insinuate ideas into his mind, until at last he became a mere machine in his hands.

In the same way did he approach and eventually control the honored General who had saved the Union, and scores of others who were to figure in and help carry out the deep laid plot, deeper than any imagined, which his brain had contrived, and which he had determined to see through to its finality, no matter what or who stood in the way. For many years this man had been the power behind the figurative throne; he now proposed to place himself and friends upon a firmer foundation, and to this end had conceived a scheme intended to defraud and weaken, preparatory to revolutionizing the Government, and which required immense resources for the accomplishment.

Resources of political power and influence both American and foreign, a controlling monopoly of capital sufficient to buy up whole parties of men and wealthy corporations; a domination over the systems of mail service and telegraphic communication throughout the country, and also the Press, for the length of time required in ripening the scheme and producing the desired effect upon the popular mind.

It was at this point in his plan, as Cronksey realized the vast proportions of what he had undertaken, and the requirement of capital and influence necessary for the successful issue, that he bethought him of Silas Smith, whose acquaintance he had made a few years before in New York, where both had been engaged in the same extensive stock manœuvre, and in which Smith had vanquished Cronksey only by having unlimited access to London capitalists. In fact this *American citizen* had become more an Englishman than an American, by long habit of transient residence in London, and had become thoroughly imbued with the ideas of English capital and English aristocracy.

Smith had continued as at first when he tried to defraud

Uncle Tutty Swanson of his claim by deception and force—a grasping, hard-fisted, ugly customer, and had of course, gotten rich off from better men.

He had also naturally enough gravitated into New York and Wall street, and come to be one of the great men of that center of power long before his foreign experience.

From being at first only a speculator in stocks, he had come to own several American railroads and nearly the whole of the telegraphic lines throughout the country. By this ownership and other means, he often manipulated the news furnished to the Associated Presses and by them to the daily papers, and in this way molded public opinion as he willed, in the interests of any speculation in which he was engaged. He had long since ceased to touch matters not stupendous, and had become a king among capitalists both American and foreign, being the head and center of those vast intrigues which are sapping the foundations of free government, drinking the life-blood of the people, and enslaving them slowly but surely beyond hope of emancipation.

Such men as Smith and Cronksey and Spideler—born for evil work and to prey upon their fellows—drift into New York, this great, wicked city of our Continent, and come to the surface, making a stir in Wall street as naturally as the devil-fish, leviathan and dragon live and float in the sea.

Cronksey was in the great pool what the devil-fish is to the ocean—surrounding himself in impenetrable mystery, hiding from view in the black, slimy emanations of his own Satanic hideousness, while with long tentacled arms he reaches out under the darkened waters, drawing in his prey as surely and relentlessly as fate, to be reduced to finest atoms by concealed, grinding, sharp-edged instruments of torture; for thus does the monster live, placing all under contribution for his sustenance and pleasure.

But Smith was the Leviathan, spreading terror and dismay wherever his mighty strength and huge proportions became apparent.

While Spideler was the slimy Sea-serpent, living low down in the deep mire, stirring up filth at every movement.

Cronksey and Spideler had met Smith in New York during the years when Henry was absent in Australia, and they had been interested together in business transactions ever since and were fast friends.

To Smith did Cronksey in his emergency now go in person,

carefully and fully unfolding his scheme and all that might in any contingency be involved—receiving his promise of help and co-operation in any possible event.   Two villains evenly matched, pulling neck by neck for the same diabolical goal.

Only these two knew all, not even was Spideler trusted with the entire unfolded plan, his mission consisting only in working out blind hints as they were given him.

Others entered into the scheme as a *speculation*, putting in their money for gain only, upon representations conveyed through Spideler that it was a good thing, not dreaming they were being drawn into complications which would end in a terrible political tragedy.

CHAPTER XXIV.

JULES GRIEVEAU.—WHO WERE TO BLAME?

While the intense excitement preceeding the Presidential election to which we alluded in Chapter XXII, was at its height, among the frequenters of the New York headquarters of the Republican campaign, Spideler, as he thought fortunately, discovered a most peculiar and original character in the person of a little man impressing the beholder as of somewhat larger stature than he really was, who, though shabby and poor in appearance, was neatly and genteelly dressed, carrying himself always with dignity and as a gentleman.

Gaunt and hungry looking, evidently destitute, homeless and without remunerative employment, he yet had an air of attending to very important affairs. Every motion indicated a man earnestly pursuing some object to a desired end. What that object or the consummation might be, did not appear.

He seemed to be engaged in no legitimate business—unless hanging around politicians and noted men, offering advice and suggestions which passed unheeded, crowding himself obtrusively into the presence of the highest, might be called business.

Mischievously busy he was without doubt, as the sequel proved.

Such a character could not remain very long in constant attendance upon all the manœuvres emanating from the headquarters of a political campaign, without attracting the attention of the prime-movers. Soon inquiry was made from one and another, but no one could tell anything about the man, except that he was industriously distributing cards bearing the inscription "C. Jules Grieveau, Lawyer and Theologian," strange combination of professions surely. He also claimed to be a politician, and was never tired of lauding Cronksey, the great leader, to the skies, whenever any one would listen to him, and wanted his hero to the front upon every occasion. He had, it seemed, prepared a speech during the time preceding the presidential nomination when it was supposed the General would again be placed before the people, based upon this idea, and which he had altered in one or two particulars, suiting, as he believed, the change of programme, and he now wanted the managers of the

13

campaign to engage him on a salary to deliver this remodeled speech from the "stump" over the State. But of course they had no intention of doing any such thing; it would savor too much of the absurdity of preparing the eulogy for one man and then using the document in another's honor; and besides the paper was almost idiotic in composition. Strangely enough he took their refusal all in good part, although it meant starvation for him.

His good nature was absolutely foolish, he being apparently unable to comprehend a snub or an insult; accepting every slight or rebuff with indifference, going right along as though nothing had happened; no matter how coldly he was treated frequenting the Republican headquarters just the same. Poor fellow, it was the only comfortable, decent place where he could constantly visit with impunity without being interfered with.

Had that selfish, well-fed, scheming crowd known just how forlorn, hungry, weak and sick the man really was, how shattered his mind, and that he was utterly incompetent to provide for himself, compassion might have touched even their hearts, and he been placed out of harm's way to himself or others, and where he could have kind care and the treatment proper for those in his condition.

He had been for a long time used to starvation and snubs and insults, and did not himself realize how badly off he was; while restlessness kept him working persistently at something, even though resulting in no benefit to himself or others.

Occasionally he would secure a small sum of money, and upon this subsist, until the fund exhausted, want again confronted him.

Before his reasoning powers became so completely deranged, he had through the leniency of slack examinations in western states at that early day, succeeded in gaining admission to the bar—the fashion prevailing both in the legal and medical professions of allowing a man with slight knowledge a license to practice, that he might earn an honest living, as was said; he being expected by hard experience, both to himself and his patrons, to learn how afterwards.

And thus it happened that Jules, after spending a couple of years about the office of his brother-in-law, passing an examination when two out of the three Judges who constituted the board were off on a vacation—he answering only two of the three questions asked him, managed to slip inside the "bar," and was forthwith a full-fledged lawyer, entitled to all the privileges and immunities of the profession.

He then secured desk room got out some cards with good references which no one troubled to investigate, and being possessed of a gentlemanly, suave address, soon some slight items of business drifted his way, mainly the collection of small bills, and following the usual practice of older and more competent lawyers of his acquaintance, he never failed when collections were made, to retain the larger share.

In all this Jules exhibited a certain amount of shrewdness not uncommon with young men trying to make their way in the world unaided, and in their cases as in his, enabling them to slip along quite smoothly with apparent success for a time, only to end in utter collapse, if the sequal prove them lacking in sound knowledge, hard-headed sense, and integrity; qualities which alone can win.

As for Jules he had neither knowlege, sense or stamina, and disappointment and destitution were his fore-ordained portion. But even after he had stumbled and fallen, and scrambled up again in child-like impotency—time and again—and had wandered away from his original moorings, coming to the surface at last in the great, cruel city of New York, as a hanger-on of the Republican presidential campaign, he still made use of his old cards, they enabling him to pick up now and then a desperately bad debt for collection—so desperate no one else would touch it.

And somehow, by hook ·or by crook, he managed to worry a little money out of every one he tackled. He'd fasten himself on a man, and stick like a leech until *something* came, if he once started. A persistency which became a mania, until he believed himself *inspired* to the accomplishment of anything suggested to his mind as a desirable consummation.

His peculiarities, before his mind became entirely unhinged, rendered him a passably successful Insurance Agent, and he acted for different companies from time to time. Had he remained quietly at either the insurance or the collecting business, letting everything else go, he might have sustained himself perhaps, even with his unmistakably weak organization. But his diseased and malformed brain was leading him, year by year, into more and more erratic courses, and unfitting him for all usefulness. Finally he attended the "Moody meetings," and became in his own estimation a "theologian," and that ended it.

All this time even at the last, there in New York, during

the fateful summer of doom, little did those with whom he came
in contact dream that in the strange, intense, erratic but good
natured and apparently harmless man, there were elements of
discord and insane ideas evolving, eventually to culminate in a
deed as terrible and sudden as the rupture of a volcano, and which
should startle the world with the horror of its unreasonableness,
causing in its legitimate results, that sooner or later, the fair
goddess of Liberty must reel and totter, quivering in every atom
upon her pedestal, until only the strong hands of stern Truth
and evenly balanced Justice, could restore her equipoise and firm
stability complete as before.

Silas Smith, who, as we have seen, spent most of the time in
London across the water, came in one day and Jules handed him
his card, as he habitually gave them to everyone he met.
Smith, glancing at the remarkable announcement, " Lawyer
and Theologian," for it would attract the attention of the busi-
est man, and then pondering a moment, looking again at the
name, C. Jules Grieveau, abruptly inquired, " Are you the son
of Eben Grieveau, of Freelawn, Ill? "

" Yes, sir, that was my father's name," answered Jules.

Neither of the men said anything further, Smith not noticing him again in any way, indeed he never saw him, until the
day when the grievous fate of poor Jules Grieveau was consummated in Washington; but Jules, following an insane predilec-
tion for the adoration of supposed greatness, always after spoke of
Smith as " My friend Silas Smith, Esq."; only that subsequent
events proved the assumption extremely pitiful, it must have
savored of the ludicrous.

When his question was answered Smith knew very well
who the peculiar man was, and also his sad history or the beginning of it, and why he was so forlorn and erratic; Jules, of
course, having no remembrance of Silas Smith.

For several days at intervals of leisure, Smith cogitated over
the eccentric, cranky man, not to say insane, Jules had come to
be, and the possible use he might be put to with proper manipulation.

Cronksey had unfolded to Smith all that was in his scheme,
every contingency liable to arise; and Smith had finally mentioned Jules Grieveau to him during one of their confidential
conversations, with the suggestion that Spideler get him down to
Washington when the time should come, as he was evidently just
the man they'd need there in a certain emergency; Cronksey

afterwards assented, giving the hint to Spideler, who made short delay in acting upon it.

Thus did Smith, the rascally plotter, concoct his revenge for an old time grudge, at the same time with characteristic long-headedness, providing for his English friends whose capital was to aid him partial shelter, should their joint villainy in its consummation be exposed to the light; by selecting a man as the tool with which to accomplish the work, a man of French name and proclivities, and whose ancestors had surely been of the French Aristocracy, nearly allied to Royalty.

While Jules Grieveau had been hanging around the Republican headquarters in New York, Henry Armstrong, as Gerald A. Johnson the nominee for vice-President, had remained closely in San Francisco according to the plan, and thus it happened the two not chancing to meet;—again did Fate perform her mission, and play well her part.

Not many months elapsed before Spideler received the intimation that the time was near at hand, and immediately he proceeded to prepare the tool for a purpose dire as devilish.

First he went with Jules to a great revival-meeting, or, as it was styled, the "Moody meeting," which was in progress, where by well understood processes, the multitudes who flocked to hear the world-wide noted preacher were worked into a high state of excitement, and zealous enthusiasm was engendered. Spideler shrewdly opining that the intensely religious temperament of Jules might be worked to good advantage.

Jules had years before this attended these meetings in Chicago, and the talk he had heard in his father's house and in the "Community," had been largely of that insanely religious type just suiting his mental condition, and upon which he loved to feed.

He had finally become fully imbued with the idea of personal consecration, direct inspiration, Divine leadings etc., and under the excitement to which he was now subjected, he came to feel that he could do anything for Jesus, until, had he imagined any act or sacrifice was required of him by the will of Deity, that act would have been accomplished, that sacrifice made, even to the slaying of his dearest friend, even as Abraham was commanded according to tradition that he should slay his son, Isaac.

Spideler, too, became suddenly religious, talking often with Jules in the strain of this peculiar phase of his faith, causing his mind to dwell frequently upon it, until at last if he had not been absolutely insane before, he surely was so now.

As one of the links in the chain which the wily Spideler was busily riveting upon Jules, he one day introduced him to a fair widow, whom he chanced (perhaps) to come across at the meeting; she being also a devotee of the Moody type, immediately gained an unbounded influence over him.

Soon after this new coalition was formed, Spideler went with Jules down to Washington. Jules going ostensibly to look after some insurance business which Spideler had kindly thrown in his way—and Spideler himself going—well, for another purpose.

CHAPTER XXVI.

" I PREFER MURDER! "

During the few months intervening, when these intriguers were busy permeating the body-politic with the vile leaven of their own wickedness, until all was in a wrathful ferment boding only ill, and in readiness for the hour of doom, their needed tool was being prepared by Spideler. While the manipulation of Jules was in its incipient stage, the Presidential election had taken place, the inauguration quietly occurred, and the political machine commenced its work, installing one here, lopping off a head there, satisfying some, rendering others desperate with chagrin and disappointment.

At last, in the course of events, the scheme of Cronksey and his gang threatened to go awry.

In the new President they had encountered a man who had a decided mind of his own; who was determined to give the people an honest Republican administration—to unearth every fraud and political corruption. By his obstinacy their bubble was likely to burst, and there "was millions in it" for American speculators—perhaps American disruption, for jealous foreign capitalists and foreign dynasties. *Something must be done to avert the catastrophe.*

Silas Smith and Cronksey conferred together, and finally sent down to Washington their friend Bamboozle, who staid by the President's side constantly, apparently using his utmost endeavors and persuasive powers trying to induce him to stay his proposed investigation of alleged frauds in the mail service, Treasury reports, naval service, etc., which had at last attracted the attention of the people.

Dull and stupid as they usually are in regard to their own interests, they were beginning to inquire into the " Why? " of several things; they were insisting upon knowing the truth, and the President was helping them. The men who had perpetrated these frauds, hoping thereby to weaken the Government, stir up dissension, strife and possible disruption, this time more especially between the East and the West, between capital and labor, between honest toil and wealthy aristocracy—Cronksey, Smith, Bamboozle & Co.—saw that the new President was

treading dangerously near their individual toes, and were beginning to fear for the safety of their pet corns.   At last there was
an open quarrel between these men and their followers and the
new administration—a rebellion, if not a conspiracy, against the
President and the Government; and threats began to be made
against, and to the President.   The partisan press controlled by
Smith was vehement in its denunciations of the President's
course, and freely talked of the advantage to the country were
he only out of the way, declaring there was danger of another
civil war should he persist in antagonizing those obstreperous
"Stalwarts" who were determined to ruin if they could not rule.
At this stage of the contention Cronksey or Smith, no one
cared to say which, made a speech from the rostrum, which
was considered purely figurative by those who were ignorant
of what was going on, but by those who were inside the
"ring" known to mean just what the words implied—"that the
time might soon come when murder or suicide would be the
only choice;" and said the black-hearted villain: "*I prefer murder!*"   Their friends immediately denied the words in the public prints, and insisted political suicide, political murder was
meant; but it was too late to retract; the mischief intended had
been wrought; for the same evening the impeding President
was told in private conference, by those who were alarmed at the
fatal words—at midnight—*only the night before his assassination*—that he "*must desist;* that *he must stand back*, or something *dreadful would happen*, if he continued to persist in his
investigation."

But the President had steadfastly declared that he would "not
desist, but should proceed at once in the course he had marked
out for himself, no matter who stood in the way—no matter
who was hurt."

And this only a few hours before the shot was fired, instigated by rebels and conspirators, which ended his career; for
destiny was upon them all, and fate or Providence was bringing them through these devious channels and complications to
the final event, for which the stubborn President *and they all*,
no less than crazy Jules, was born.

When this deed, which Cronksey's friend had hinted at,
only suggested as *possible*, in his speech from the rostrum,
was finally decided upon in his own mind as necessary, for the
protection of himself, and also those who stood to him in the
relation of co-workers in political intrigue, and of clients, as well
as partners in speculation, he took measures secretly for the ex-

ecution of the threat—*not consulting with any one.* Giving his faithful Spideler the signal, the diabolical deed was perpetrated with what   villains   regarded complete success, without relenting.

While the quarrel between the two factions was waxing hot and bitter, the President and his supporters on one side and those interested in these great speculations as they claimed, but really *frauds* and conspiracies, on the other, from sheer necessity, Spideler had contrived to saturate the mind of Jules with the idea, advanced in the partisan prints—well paid for this work—that a civil war would be the result unless the Cronksey faction were victorious. Jules was also a devourer of newspapers, believing implicitly all the lies he read. Spideler also talked continually in his presence of the benefit to the country " If the President were out of the way, the disturbance would cease, and all would be well. The Vice President was a conservative, sensible man, and would make a better President than the one who was giving so much trouble. (Yes, trouble to thieves and villains!) If some good providence, some sickness or an accident should 'remove' him, everything would settle down, and there'd be no more talk of civil war." And besides, "Our friends," said Spideler—for he had continued to make poor foolish Jules feel that he was one of them—"will come into power, and I'll see that you get a consulate, or something better, and then you can marry the widow."

And thus was the poison injected, which in his crazy brain should breed unnatural imaginations ending in agony and death.

Little by little, day by day, did Spideler keep at his work, sowing the seeds and forcing the growth to the final terrible harvest, "Delays are dangerous, now is the accepted time;""Doing evil that good may come;" "Abraham was commanded to slay Isaac at the pleasure of the Lord God." These and other like canting phrases were poured from the mouth of Spideler, and filled the mind of Jules, until dwelling upon these ideas and the danger of civil war,—and he had not forgotten the sufferings of the struggle which had so recently taken place between the North and the South—combining with his desire to possess the widow, she, all the time encouraging the delusion as to the consulate and their marriage; he reasoning upon these things in a warped and crooked fashion, over zealous and devout, until finally the unbounded egotism of insanity over-mastering all else; at last the deluded man came to believe himself inspired, called of God to perpetrate as atrocious a deed as ever emanated from a sick brain, or was executed by a maniac's hand.

From the moment it took hold of him, that he was called of God to remove the President, it was to his mind "the Deity and me," who would set the affairs of the Nation right.

Surely, surely, poor Jules Grieveau was irresponsibly insane, but in view of all the facts and subsequent outcome of events, resulting in the final acquittal or escape of every one engaged in these "great frauds," some clear and powerful intelligence must have planned the whole scheme—must have been to blame.

CHAPTER XXVI.

AUNT DEBBY'S KITCHEN IN WASHINGTON; AND—THE CAT.

On one of the narrow, old-fashioned, stone-paved streets, bordered by diagonally laid brick sidewalk, in Washington near the Capitol—a neat, quiet neighborhood—stood behind a row of Linden-trees, a small brick house. Very modest and unpretentious was the snug home of Aunt Debby and Uncle Tut, who had followed the family of Gen. John A. Gascoigne to Washington.

Aunt Debby had softened down with advancing years, and having no children of her own, the natural yearning tenderness of womanhood in her old heart which she had all her life tried to crush out, exhibited itself to the extent that she allowed her domicile to become the rendezvous of all the children near and far, and had even come to tolerate a cat, their old " Tommy " being the pride and delight of Aunt Debby as well as Uncle Tut.

They were never tired of showing off the tricks that wonderful cat could do. He would jump through Uncle Tut's encircled arms; stand upon his hind legs, with paws crossed demurely before him and mew politely for his food; he'd open a latched door and come in, pushing it shut behind him, and quietly seat himself in his own cushioned chair; he'd walk leisurely around the cage of the canary as it sat upon the floor with open door, not offering to touch lively little Dick. You might go away and leave them alone if you liked without danger to the bird.

Aunt Debby declared " that cat had sense," and certainly he proved there must be a good foundation somewhere behind those yellow eyes, for the satisfactory results of the thorough education and cultivation of manners bestowed upon him by Uncle Tut.

Not the least of his accomplishments and the one in which Aunt Debby took special delight, was the ease and grace with which he sat at table upon a chair and ate from his own plate, lapping milk from the saucer without soiling himself or the cloth. A noble specimen was Tommy, his immense proportions covered by the finest fur, pure white, except a black spot at the tip of his tail, four jet black paws and a dark ring around his neck—" his neck tie," Uncle Tut said, and then " Tommy " had such a beautiful head, and large intelligent eyes—for a cat.

Besides the feline and the canary, Aunt Debby's clean kitchen just swarmed with youngsters both black and white. It would have done you good to see her laying the newly baked, warm, sweet cookies in the little aprons held to receive them, as she deftly lifted them one by one from the hot pan with the old-fashioned glistening steel knife.

The children could smell Aunt Debby's cookies and dough-nuts for blocks away, and her cream custard pies " well," as Uncle Tut would say, " don't talk," (he'd got so he *could* put two words together without stammering, when he kept cool); but the greatest treat was one of Aunt Debby's immense saleratus biscuits, (not baking powder) *hot* and spread with butter and the *real* white clover honey or genuine maple syrup, laid on thick; " oh! but they were good," the children said. Crazy Leonard too, who you will remember had insisted upon attach-ing himself to General Gascoigne's party when they started from Chicago, having been brought by them to Washington, forming ever since a part of their household, was, of course, now a frequent visitor in Aunt Debby's kitchen, and came in for a share of " goodies " with the children; so gentle and piti-ful a creature could not but appeal to the kind-hearted woman's sympathies.

Leonard's friends had succeeded in toning him down some-what as to dress, and his appearance was less grotesque than formerly, but he possessed an inordinate desire for decorating Uncle Tut's cat, and seemed to have transferred this propensity from himself to the patient animal, allowing Leonard to maul him about at pleasure, who, whenever he came was sure to leave a memento in the shape of some gewgaw fastened around Tommy's neck or on his tail. There was real danger the poor cat would be strangled, perhaps hang himself some day by the appendages attached to him. When Leonard was about Aunt Debby watched sharply, and if caught at any of his pranks, she gave him a dose of her tongue, if nothing worse.

" There now, you Leonard, let that cat alone I tell you, you'll be the death of that ar cat."

" No I won't, Aunt Debby, I ain't gwine ter hurt your cat, be I, Tommy?"

" Leonard's gwine to be a good boy, Leonard ain't lub struck no more, hi! hi! hi! Go bye, Aunt Deb;" and away he would shuffle as fast as his crazy old legs could carry him. But after he was gone Aunt Debby would find the invariable trinket tied to the cat every time, and he would manage to accomplish the feat so slyly she would not see him either.

It happened that one day Aunt Debby found tied securely around the cat's neck a small bundle of paper, well written over, signed very plainly with a name she too well knew. Showing it to her husband, as a dutiful wife should, consulting about any puzzling occurence, this little scrap of paper proved to be the missing clue necessary for unveiling a hidden mystery and in a measure righting a grievous wrong.

Thus did crazy Leonard, no less than the dumb brute, fulfil each their mission.

CHAPTER XXVII.

IF ONLY SOMETHING WOULD HAPPEN.

The family of General Gascoigne had resided in Washington since the war, with the exception of the summers spent usually on Uncle Tut's farm out in Illinois, or sometimes with Gertrude in Wisconsin.

Mistress Julia had improved her opportunities, developed her natural charms, and used her shrewd Yankee sense with such purpose as to become an acknowleged leader in the gay society of the Capital.

She had now a family of children, and daughters almost old enough to make their debut, but this did not hinder her from being a very fascinating woman, as fond of a quiet flirtation as ever, though not carrying mâtters to the extreme of disaster, as she had done in the inexperience of her early career.

However, she had lately come to think the new Vice-President the most charming gentleman she had ever met. His extended sojourn in Australia was somewhat unique even for a traveled man, and gave him great eclat; and the Vice-President although a recent widower, was quite the rage among the ladies of the capital, both married and single. His wife, who had always been a delicate invalid, had died during the early part of the political campaign preceding his inauguration; but what did it matter that his bereavement could scarcely be so soon assuaged, or that the ladies who admired him were many of them married? Not a whit—these circumstances are little thought of in Washington, and flirtations could be, for these reasons, only the more sympathetically indulged in and nothing serious expected on either side. Nothwithstanding the recent demise of the wife, there had already been talk of a union between the Vice-President and the daughter of a Queen, a rumor started, to be sure, for political reasons and as a sounder for the popular feeling, but which was so unequivocally frowned upon, as to be immediately checked. This rumor was speedily followed by a desperate flirtation with the daughter of a high official, carried on as a blind, to allay suspicion, for this foreign alliance was really a part of the plan of Smith and Cronksey for establishing a monarchy in our midst. But an episode occurred just here which drove forever from the Vice-President's mind all thought of a union with any woman but the one his heart craved, and she, too, was to be disappointed. Strangely enough, and much to her chagrin, Mistress Julia had found herself more deeply in love with the handsome Vice-President than she had intended; at last her heart was really captured, all there was of it.

Their acquaintance had not progressed very far, only a few weeks of intimacy such as society people indulge in, when Lucille returned from a visit to Gertrude who lived on her farm beside one of Wisconsin's beautiful lakes, and where she had been spending nearly a year, with pleasure to both.

On a sultry day in early summer, before congress had adjourned, or the fashionables closed their doors for a flight to northern climes, the Vice-President called to take Mistress Julia Gascoigne for a ride. As he sat waiting in the cool parlor, a lady passed through the hall, instantly their eyes met—a moment more and Henry had clasped Lucille in his arms, drawing her into the room; nothing could hold back the frantic man from the possession of his life-long darling. Now that his eyes again beheld her, he seemed as though he never intended to let her go. "Oh! Lucille, Lucille, why did you marry that man?" he cried.

"Marry? Me marry? Why I have not married."

"God in Heaven," exclaimed Henry, "is this true? Can it be true?"   *   *   *

The servant came forward announcing that Mistress Gascoigne was ready for the drive. Scarcely was discovery averted.

"Say I am at her service," responded the Vice-President; then turning again to Lucille, "I beg you to secrecy; say to *no one* that you ever knew me. I will see you soon and explain all. God bless you my own love, adieu," and he was gone.

Once again, after years of patient waiting, had Lucille been clasped in the arms of her loved one, looked in his eyes, heard his voice in endearing tones and words, felt his warm breath, his passionate kiss—and then he was gone! Heart-breaking mystery, when will it ever end? When and how?

For days, weeks, months, Lucille waited silently, sadly, with heart of lead, but Henry did not come as he had said. What could it mean?

Only that the man was entangled in meshes from which he could not break loose, and now found himself in the vice-like grip of Fate, whose hold loosens not, though woman's soul grieves in agony; though drops, blood-red, are pressed from the heart of the strong man, longing with passionate love to enfold her.

The Vice-President ended his flirtation with Mistress Julia Gascoigne that very day; why so abruptly, she never dreamed, but was sorely disappointed and brooded over the pleasure she had taken in his society, and the strange, sudden withdrawal from her presence, until a real trouble wranlked in her heart. He, preoccupied with his own difficuliies, scarcely thought of her again—such is life.

Henry now began planning in earnest to the end of reaching Lucille, but the more he revolved the situation in his mind the more hopeless it seemed.

First his unfortunate change of name, and the circumstances which led to it, confronted him; and then the political complication in which he was now involved;—every thing combining to thwart his desires. The trouble he was in was terrible, turn which way he would, black, still, despair confronted him. If only *something* would happen to break the deathly, suffocating calm; if only some change would come; *anything* would be better than the dreadful monotony of the long, silent, desolation and misery of their estranged and parted lives. And soon, very soon, the longed for sweet occurred.

One day Lucille sat listlessly thinking of Henry, when suddenly a din, a roar, as of a surging, angry, infuriated mob; and the cry, "The President is shot! The President is shot!" resounding through the air, flying from mouth to mouth, startles, shocks, stuns her. The commotion for a time is fearful—in the streets, in the houses, everywhere—each inquiring of every other, no one giving any satisfactory answer.

Before night Uucle Tut, who was a member of the Metropolitan police force, had heard a description of the would be assassin; for the president was not yet dead; might, it was said, perhaps recover; and who, after firing the shot, had exhorted the by-standers not to "Get excited," saying, "it's all right, the Deity and me's fixed it." And had then quietly given himself up as a prisoner. Uncle Tut had also heard his name, and, wonder of wonders, it was Jules Grieveau, Myra's strange boy, who had drifted away, and from whom they had not heard for years past.

Rumor said the prisoner was crazy. "Quite li-likely," stammered Uncle Tut, remembering Myra's condition before the boy's birth, and some of the peculiar things in his life.

When these rumors had been corroborated, and there was no longer any doubt that "*the assassin*," as he was called, was really Jules Grieveau, and that he was crazy; gently as possible were the sad facts disclosed to Lucille.

Surely now was her cup full, yea, running over; for once the woman who had endured so much without flinching was almost beside herself. If she could only get to him, do something to comfort him. " Poor boy! poor boy!" she moaned. But it was impossible, strong bars were between them; not for days, perhaps weeks, could she see him; not safely now could even their relationship be known, or that Gen. John A. Gascoigne was his mother's brother.

And during those months while the martyred President lay suffering, the throes of his agony pulsating from the sick-bed througn the hearts of myriads of watchers over all the land, even across the ocean and throughout the world, Lucille, Gertrude and all who loved the crazy boy for his mother's sake and because of his pitiful condition learned to be grateful for the strong bars, the prison walls, which were his protection from the unreasoning wrath of the grief-maddened populace.

And while the doctors probed and tortured the president, while the people wept and gnashed their teeth in the rage of sheer distress, while the crazy tool confined in his prison-cell, sometimes crouched despondently, oftener glorying in the deed he had perpetrated, as his moods changed; while the political schemers composedly looked on saying nothing; Lucille, Gertrude and the others, in dire apprehension, with quivering hearts and whitening hair and bated breath, held still and waited for the end to come.

And Henry, Gerald A. Johnson, the vice-President—what of him?

The blow had come at last unexpectedly, as great calamities always reach us, even while we look for them.

Henry had hoped against reason since meeting Lucille, that some way might be found out of the difficulty, the political quarrel.

Whatever his feeling of bitterness might formerly have been, his heart had softened since that day towards every living creature, he no longer wished any one harm, or cared for ambitious projects; his only conscious desire to finish his public career speedily as possible, finding happiness for the remainder of his days *anywhere* with Lucille. Just how this was to come about he had not thought.

14·

But now he feared he could never meet her more, for he too had learned who the unfortunate man was whom Spideler had so long been preparing for the *emergency*, when "Murder should be preferred to the political suicide of those engaged in the great scheme," and that the reputed assassin being the son of Eben and Myra Grieveau was Lucille's nephew. How could he now ever hope they should be more to each other than they had been?

The vice-President, whom a certain contingency would make the accidental President, seen visiting the family of the assassin? Never!

Henry, as Gerald A. Johnson, had now come to his bitterest portion, and was getting his full share. There was no escaping the difficulties pressing him down, for suspicion of high officials was in the heart of the people, vengeance was in the air and shrieked in every breeze; other bullets might come whizzing past; and the elegant vice-President, who so well knew how to enjoy the good things of life, had no choice but to shut himself in his own house a self-immolated prisoner, waiting for whatever might transpire; and he the more willingly submitted to this indignity and seclusion for should he venture to walk abroad or ride, he might meet Lucille and if thus encountered, what could he now say to her? How could he explain the mystery of his conduct?

CHAPTER XXVIII.

THE CHIEF OF THE SECRET SERVICE OF THE U. S.

The evening after the event had transpired which we have narrated in our last chapter, sending a shuddering thrill of horror through all the world, and coming near overwhelming our country in confusion, riot and bloodshed, Uncle Tut walked into Aunt Debby's kitchen with an unmistakable air of having something important to say.

Standing in the doorway a moment, he reached up his hand in his own peculiar fashion and beckoned Aunt Debby with his forefinger, as of yore; she, as a dutiful wife should, left her work and went to him, taking a couple of doughnuts which she was busy frying—for she knew Uncle Tut's weakness—but they proved no temptation; the man had a heavy trouble at his heart, and only hoarsely stammered some words into Debby's ear in a low whisper, which caused her to drop into the nearest chair, with the exclamation "Laws a Massa, Uncle Tut, what you been up to now? I declare to it, I never did see such another man since I was born; all'us getting into some kind of a mess, trying to help some poor devil 'stead o' minding your own affairs, you'll find yourself in hot trouble this time sure."

"Hu-hush Debby, ke-keep st-still, or it'll co-come true; if you do-don't," whispered Uncle Tut, fairly hissing out the words between his teeth, as his hard hand grasped her shoulder, and he stammered more than ever, in his suppressed excitement.

"I-I've *seen him* an-and I kn-know it's true, and he's no devil, bu-but su-sure enough poor My-Myra Greiveau's crazy boy," and Uncle Tut trembled and shook with emotion, and the tears trickled down his furrowed face.

"Myra Grieveau's boy! Oh! Uncle Tut, that can never be, you're not telling me the truth, some one has lied to you; it aint in the Grieveau blood, or in the Gascoigne either, to do such a dastardly deed, I *know*. No matter if he did stray away, and didn't get half brought up, after Eben and his sister Gertrude married and Lucille went to John's to live, I tell you, some one's lied to you."

"But Debby, I-I've—*seen him*," answered Uncle Tut again.

Still Aunt Debby protested vehemently; the while sobbing

and sighing, and wiping her eyes, and mopping her red face
vigorously with her always clean, blue checkered apron; that
"Some one had lied, she'd never believe the story about Jules
'till she saw him herself, she'd never believe Myra's boy would
do such a terrible thing."

But even Aunt Debby had to acknowledge at last that Jules
Grieveau was the man who had shot the President; and now
Uncle Tut wanted his wife's help in his efforts to save the crazy
grandson of his old friend Dr. Gascoigne, from his impending
fate. For the sake of the good man long dead, and his sainted
mother's memory, no less than to relieve the distress of Gertrude
and Lucille, did these two agree to use their best endeavors.
And Aunt Debby proved a useful ally.

Through the influence of Gen. Gascoigne, and from his
own aptitude, Uncle Tut had come to be a trusted member of
the Metropolitan Police of Washington, and had often worked
in the detective line; being from his efficiency and peculiar
characteristics, one of the men invariably sent for by the Chief
of the Secret Service, when coöperation was needed with the
regular force.

The day the President was shot, a message came to Uncle
Tut towards evening, that the new Chief, who had been appointed and taken charge only the day before, wanted to see
him, and he immediately repaired to the office of the Chief of
the Secret Service.

The change being so recent, it chanced that Uncle Tut had
not seen the Chief or heard his name. Being ushered into his
presence, our astonished policeman beheld a person tall, dignified, white haired and benevolent looking, upon every linea-
ment of whose face was stamped kindness of heart and honesty
of purpose.

His bright hazel eye of keenest glance, shadowed by heavy,
slightly arched brows, and the broad, high forehead, proving
him a man who could grasp every circumstance however minute,
and weighing all, arrive at a sound and just conclusion.

Chief Strong had in middle life been a lawyer, gaining
through a successful practice in criminal courts much celebrity.
His peculiar talents and quick sympathy causing him to engage
in the defense of various persons accused of crime, as he deemed
wrongfully, and making a masterly defense, his services had
come to be much sought after, sometimes by those who had
counted the cost before committing the crime.

From such men, ere convinced of the enormity of the offense

against society, he had received fabulous sums of money, working upon the established principle of law that a man must be supposed innocent until proven guilty. Like all earnest, forceful men, he did his best when once engaged on a case; but after the trial was over, his clients released "scot free" perhaps, or with only a nominal punishment; when the excitement of contest had passed away, Chief Strong's honest heart had oftentimes been troubled at the result to the body politic, and even to those whom his sober judgment condemned as guilty, and at last the astute lawyer had come to be the discerner and detector, instead of the excuser and defender of crime and of criminals.

And further, his innate sense of equity and kindness of nature, as well as keenness of perception, made him the quick discoverer of fraud, and the champion of those wrongfully accused, or who had been entrapped into vice by scheming villains and dissolute companions. To this field he had gravitated and settled, during years past finding ample scope for the exercise of his peculiar characteristics of mind and heart;—from being one of the most renowned criminal lawyers, and in the pursuit of his profession, a champion story-teller, he had risen to be the chief detector of shams, of frauds, of crimes, in places both high and low, where deepest, darkest villainy lurked, no less than among those rendered desperate by misfortune and hardship, or drawn into bad ways by unprincipled associates.

A detective whose financial circumstances rendered him independent of criticism, he was indomitable in perseverance, unsurpassed in quickness and insight, and while incorruptible, carrying a heart as kindly and tender as a mother for her new-born babe.

A man with scarcely a peer in all the land to match him in ability and grandeur of character—*the chief of the secret service of the United States of America.*

This man had examined the assassin, so-called, on the night following the firing of the cruel shot which had laid the President low upon a bed of pain, drawing to him the intensest sympathy of the whole world; and had reported the case to the Government as that of an irresponsibly insane man who should be tried by a commission in lunacy and not by civil process as a murderer.

And in this report the superintendent of the Government asylum for the insane, situated near Washington, concurred.

Neither of these men, the highest officials to whom the case could properly be submitted and to whom it *was* submitted in

the *very beginning, before the death of the martyred President
changed the administration,* ever in the slightest deviated
from this testimony, *their opinion remaining the same to the
end.*

As Uncle Tut looked upon the countenance of Chief Strong
he saw that time had softened and rendered beautiful the face of
his friend, but he could not be mistaken, and with unfeigned
surprise recognized the story-teller of the storm-tossed ship of
the olden time, which carried Gertrude, her mother and family
to Chicago years before; and whom since the trouble with Silas
Smith over his prairie claim, Uncle Tut had remembered grate-
fully; but after the death of Dr. Gascoigne the intimacy dropping, they had heard nothing directly for a long time, and the
name being a common one, did not know that he had been appointed chief of the secret service of the Government.

The men instantly extended each a hand, for the pleasure at
meeting was mutual and hearty; and then the Chief told Uncle
Tutty Swanson what he wanted, and how it came about that he
had so promptly sent for him.

" No sooner had I assumed the duties of my new position,"
said the Chief, "than the assassination occurred, and my attention was called to yourself as a man to be implicitly relied upon,
and likely to act with good judgment in any emergency. I remembered you at once as the friend of Dr. Gascoigne, at
whose home I had met you when you were having the trouble
with your neighbor Silas Smith, since become famous, out in
Illinois, and knowing you were the right man for the needed
work, I determined to ask your assistance in ferreting out the
terrible mystery which confronts us in the attempted assassination of the President—Jules Grieveau, the prisoner, who fired
the shot—"

" *Jules Grieveau!* not JULES GRIEVEAU! Oh! Chief
Strong, please sir, DON'T say it was Jules Grieveau! Not our
little Julius!" exclaimed Uncle Tut, springing from his seat,
white and ghastly as though himself instead of the stricken President were the victim; then, sinking down again, burying his
face in his rough old hands, sobbing aloud, "Juley, Juley, poor
crazy Juley, why didn't you come home to Uncle Tut and
Aunt Debby before this dreadful thing happened?"

Chief Strong rose, placing a hand kindly on the bowed head,
saying a few comforting words, and then Uncle Tut, raising
his sad face, composed himself as best he was able, listening to
all the Chief could tell.

" He has not tried, Mr. Swanson," proceeded Chief Strong, " to conceal his name; but rather glories in it and the deed, declaring himself ' God's man,' and that ' Deity inspired him to the act,' but while each look and every word the man utters proves him insane, to my mind, and he strongly denies the idea of a conspiracy or that he was instigated by any person, I still believe that there *is a conspiracy* against the present administration of the Government, even though the crazy tool be oblivious.

" Many are insisting he is not insane, even that he gave a fictitious name, it being so Frenchy and peculiar; but I remembering well both my old friend Dr. Gascoigne as of French descent and also a son-in-law, called Eben Grieveau, whose wife Myra, had died leaving a little boy named Jules, who when I was in Freelawn, was visiting at your claim with his Aunt Lucille, I have sent for you, Mr. Swanson, hoping you can and will tell me something reliable about the man and his antecedents."

" Certainly, Che-chief Strong. I-I will tell you al-all I can," and Uncle Tut related what he knew of the sad history, which was not much of late years—and when he had finished, begged the Chief to let him see Jules in his cell.

The Chief had already visited the man, and as he said, was fully persuaded of his insanity; but to Uncle Tut's request he the more readily assented, being anxious to try an effect upon the prisoner, by suddenly confronting him with the sight of an old friend whom he had not seen for years—since early youth —and then if possible, discover whether a mistake had been made in the diagnosis; whether after all the man knew more than he pretended, and was as some believed, shamming.

If such was the fact, he might be so startled upon recognizing Uncle Tut as even perhaps to show some soft-hearted compunction for what he had done, some remorse. .

Both the men agreed to this plan—for much as the Chief had respected the grandfather of the prisoner, Dr. Gascoigne— and desired for this reason if he were really crazy to save him, much as Uncle Tut had loved the little Jules, Myra's boy, both the men loved truth and justice better than any friend, better even than themselves; and they said if the man is sane who did this dastardly deed, whoever he may be, he deserves no help.

And of this mind they went together, the Chief and Uncle Tut, to visit the assassin in his cell.

CHAPTER XXIX.

THERE ARE OTHERS TOO.

The dusk of evening was upon them when, after a ride of a mile or more, taking them across the common and beyond the Congregational cemetery towards the Potomac Flats, about two miles from the Capitol, the two detectives came in sight, from a slight rise in the ground, of a massive brown stone structure.

Uncle Tut had seen the Washington jail often before this night, but never did it seem so gloomy, dark, *awful* to him; and he fairly shuddered as he thought of Myra's boy being there, friendless, alone.

They entered—the Chief and he—and after a few words spoken with the warden, a tall, military, severe looking man, who seemed as though he had known enough of horror to fill the days and nights of a legion of men with one long nightmare of regret, the three passed out through the large reception room entered from the warden's office, and thence to a spacious, open, stone-paved court.

Carefully locking the iron doors after him, the warden led the way across the court, past a large, circular, iron-railed corridor, inside which an iron staircase wound from the foundations down out of sight, up to the highest tier of cells.

After passing the corridor, the warden opened a grated door to the left of the jail as they entered, and then another just beyond, leading into a passage about four feet wide, and twenty-five or thirty long, perhaps ten feet high. On the left side of this passage were the cells, eight or ten feet long and four wide, a narrow window at the end, an iron bedstead constituting with the bedding the only furniture.

When the men reached the cell where Jules was confined, the darkness and gloom of night had settled within the jail, and only the tramp of the guards in the narrow passage, mingled with a strange, drooning sound from within, disturbed the stillness.

As the warden unlocked the outer door, the light from his lamp flashed through the grating, falling upon the figure of a small man stretched his full length upon the iron cot, lying flat upon his back, not yet undressed; his feet towards the window of the cell, his head near the door.

He did not seem to be disturbed in the slightest by the party entering the passage, but continued the drooning, monotonous song to which he was beating time with his feet against the wall, not stirring himself to investigate the intrusion; but when the warden started to unlock the door of the cell and was about to enter, the light falling upon his face, he roused up angrily demanding, "How dared they come there at that time of night, interrupting a gentleman in his meditations?"

And Uncle Tut beheld Myra's crazy boy; his eyes glaring and rolling in their sockets, with an incessant motion as indescribable as it was horrible; his face gaunt, haggard, distorted, but still the face of the little·Jules he had loved. The short, stubbed, unkempt hair as unlike the soft, silky locks he had so often stroked tenderly, as it was possible for time, neglect and hardship to make them.

As the real condition of Jules Grieveau dawned upon his old friend, and he realized the forlorn and abject wreck he was, when Uncle Tut saw the manacled hands trembling with rage, helplessly lifted together as Jules gesticulated fiercely—the same hands which had rested confidingly in his own, many an hour, as they strolled about the old farm on the Illinois prairie, long ago—*so long*, it seemed now to Uncle Tut, the sight was too much even for the rough, blunt man that he was, and his strong frame shook with grief, as sob after sob burst from the heaving breast, and tears trickled through the fingers of his toil worn hands supporting his bowed head.

All the tenderness of his manly, rugged nature yearned to take the crazy, friendless boy in his arms and comfort him, as he had done many a time when he was a baby.

Recovering, Uncle Tut spoke gently to Jules, calling him by name. There was no response; but his attention was apparently arrested by the voice, and he became quieter. Uncle Tut spoke again, calling him a pet name he had given him when a little fellow—"Juley, do yo-you know me?" The man stood still, hesitated, scowled and replied, "Yes, you're another old crazy tramp they've brought to tell me *not to do it*, but I *did* though. Did you 'spose I wouldn't when the Lord said I *must?* The Deity and me, we did a good job that time, I can tell you, if the confounded doctors don't spoil it all; but I guess they won't now. The Deity'll take care of that, and they know what they're about. Ha! Ha! Ha!" And with a wierd, in-

sane, nervous laugh, between a chuckle and a guffaw, the diabolically crazy man, with his manacled hands fastened together,
rolled helplessly upon his couch, stretched himself flat on his
back as before, and resumed the meaningless, monotonous song
accompanied by the same tattoo, exactly as though nothing had
happened to interrupt him.

The old Chief, with tears in his eyes, turned to Uncle Tut,
and grasping his hard hand, said, " Come."

The warden locked the cell door, and leaving the two
guards wearily tramping up and down the narrow passage as
before, the men sadly passed out to the open air.

When the Chief and Uncle Tut had entered their carriage,
the Chief turned and asked, " Well, what do you think of him,
Mr. Swanson?"

" Th-think! th-there's but one thing to think; he's crazy as
a loon," stammered Uncle Tut. " I knowed he'd never a do-
done such a dastardly deed if he wa-wasn't. Ca-can anyth-
thing be do-done for him, sir?"

" I fear not, Mr. Swanson. The populace are wild with
rage, the politicians who started the quarrel are scared out of
their wits, and determined to make him the scapegoat in order
to save themselves. I am sorry to tell you, the case looks hopeless.

" Both the Government asylum superintendent and myself
have reported the man insane, but some of the Government
officials, who, I believe are engaged in a great scheme with villains across the water, are determined not to recognize the fact,
and have placed the matter in the hands of the United States
District Attorney, who is also one of whom I am suspicious, to
work up a case against him.

" He has already sent for Greybeard, who manages an insane asylum, more of a prison than refuge, when he is not too
busy outside, giving testimony to run someone as sane as any
other man or woman into an asylum out of the way of somebody's interest, or in trying his best to have a poor fellow hung
who has unfortunately committed a terrible deed while in one
of the paroxysms of insanity—he can swear on either side, it is
immaterial to him if only he is well paid."

And this is as the case stood, just as the Chief of the Secret
Service in Washington stated it then within a few days of the
occurence—which had sent consternation and dismay over the
world—and just as he afterwards testified on the witness stand,
when he was sworn, in the trial of Jules Grieveau the so called
" assassin."

As the two men rode back to the city the Chief imparted some few of the strange things which he had found out since commencing to investigate Jules' case and also his suspicions, based upon the facts which he had gathered.

" And Swanson," said the Chief, " I believe there are others who are not insane, but only devilish—mixed up in this affair, and I want you to help me find them *all, everyone.*

" God helping me, I will, Chief, if it ta-takes me at all my life time, or even life itself," answered .Uncle Tut, " he-here's my hand," and when that honest hand clasped another it meant a great deal.

Said the Chief, further—" I have found that Gen. Gascoigne the son of my old friend, and even the vice-President are mixed up in this business. They certainly act strangely, and there are, I am satisfied, a good many *more in it too.*"

" Gen. Gascoigne has never met me, and my name of Strong is so common he will hardly think of connecting it now with the friend he has heard his father mention years ago possibly. We must watch these people, and everyone else to whom the slightest suspicion attaches wherever we can get a clue; they might perhaps suspect me were I to approach them, but you know the family and I shall leave this work to you." And for Uncle Tut as an obedient subordinate, there was no alternative.

Continued the Chief: " I believe the sequel will prove both the son of my old friend and the vice-President innocent of any wrong intention, but they are in some way mixed up with those who are aware, in their hearts, how this thing was done —and why—and Mr. Swanson, you and I must do our duty whoever stands in the way."

A hint of these things is what Uncle Tut had whispered in Aunt Debby's ear, and he wanted her to help him in finding out *why Jules did it.*

CHAPTER XXX.

THE PRESIDENT IS DEAD.

While Jules was lying sometimes stupid in his cell, or again glorying because "the Deity and he" had done it—while the doctors were working over the suffering president, probing honestly or otherwise, for the fatal bullet, until the tortured body was riddled with gaping wounds and the burrowing pus was draining his life away; while the civilized world watched anxiously with bated breath; while Silas Smith manipulated the wires, guarding well the interests of those engaged in the success of the "great scheme," receiving daily, even hourly, cypher dispatches from the bedside of the sick president, as his pulse went up with increasing strength or down with deathly weakness, a manœuvre which enabled these wily demons to control Wall Street stocks for their gain; while these things were transpiring, the Chief and Uncle Tut were doing their utmost to discover the hidden, mysterious "*why*" of the sad tragedy.

They had seen the decoy, and knew there must be game somewhere.

And the U. S. District Attorney, with a well selected corps of assistants, was endeavoring to establish the sanity of an unmistakably insane man, that he alone might bear the blame, which really belonged to others.

Finally, after weeks and months of excruciating suffering, bravely borne, the martyred President was released from pain, and went cheerfully, trustingly, to his home in the Hereafter.

As the midnight cry, "*The President is dead! the President is dead!*" resounded through the streets, every heart stood still, and all felt that one about whom their own lives were centered, for a time at least, had left them for the Better Land, and the people of his native country—of the whole world—grieved as for their own kin.

Never was known mourning so universal and sincere, intensified by the feeling everywhere acknowledged that events leading to his cruel death were still shrouded in an unfathomed obscurity and gloom. Those who, by the change in officials which was wrought, constituted the new administration, claimed, when the reputed assassin was placed on trial, that he alone should be blamed, but, for an unaccountable reason (?), were evidently afraid somebody would think this was not true—that somebody would withhold assent to their assertions.

And many did refuse to concede this view of the case; really, almost every one persisted in believing something else. Circumstances and the facts, when they could be *gotten at*, pointed so clearly to a different conclusion.

The discovery was made, after a time, that stupendous frauds had been attempted against the Government, looking to anarchy and destruction, and that, in the course of the investigation pending just before the President was shot, it became apparent that some of those who helped, by their money and influence, to elect him, were implicated in these frauds.

It transpired that some of the lawyers and officials who became cognizant of these facts went to the President and urged him to desist from the prosecution of those who claimed the right to assert themselves his friends. But the President was inexorable, and declared his intention of ferreting out the whole matter, whoever stood in the way, directing a certain attorney to go ahead vigorously, notwithstanding friend or foe; this man being accompanied by a high official of the administration, who was an honest, steadfast friend of the President, as after-developments proved, went—both urging, even begging, the doomed man to change his course towards those who had perpetrated the frauds upon the Government, and who at the time intended still worse doings; the lawyer going so far as to declare he feared something dreadful would happen if the President persisted in his offensive attitude towards them; and this, at midnight a few hours before the shot was fired which ended his career. Testimony, which was subsequently given under oath, upon this interview proved conclusively that it was " *cooked* " up, as a last desperate attempt to turn the tide of events, which they began to fear would engulph *them* instead of the Government, and they now wished, if possible, to save the President without sacrificing the conspirators.

It also transpired the same night, earlier in the evening, that some one was reported to have uttered these words? "*The time has come when we must choose between murder and suicide; and* I PREFER MURDER!" Whether this circumstance had any connection with the final catastrophe was never fully proven, but to the majority of the people, that sentence flying over the night wires to Washington, just before the midnight interview with the President, *will always be interpreted as the concerted signal, the shrill bugle-note of doom*, hastening on the fateful crisis—the shooting of the President occurring after he had given his last absolute, immovable decision on the matter in controversy, namely, that "He would not desist, would not stand back," but insisting that the " investigation of the 'great frauds' must proceed at once, whoever might suffer, be he friend or foe."

And this last official duty done, as he was about seeking the sorely needed rest from the anxieties which had harrassed him since the moment of taking his seat in the presidential chair to the time when he had hoped the contention ended by his an· swer, and he could now pass the remainder of the summer peacefully, the thunderbolt of destiny burst upon him, and a good President *fell*—ASSASSINATED BY A MONIED, POLITICAL, MONARCHICAL RING, TOO COWARDLY TO MEET THE ISSUES OF THEIR OWN SCHEME, OR EVEN PERPETRATE IN PERSON THEIR LAST DESPERATE RESORT.

To the trembling hand of a weak and insanely religious fanatic, worked upon until he believed himself inspired and directed by Deity to consummate their villainy by "removing" the President out of their way, was intrusted the execution of the final diabolism.

A few hours after the shot was fired, as the morning boat from Albany neared New York, bearing among others Cronksey and Silas Smith, the passengers noticed that when the startling news of the assassination was flying from mouth to mouth these two slipped quietly away, not seeming surprised by the dire announcement, locking themselves securely in a stateroom.

Upon landing, they got themselves speedily into a close carriage, driving rapidly to Smith's private residence, which he still retained in New York, where they remained secreted for a week or more from the populace until the excitement had somewhat abated—guarded (*or watched!* WHICH WAS IT?) all this time by a picked force of the city police and Government troops.

What could these men have been afraid of? Surely not the ghost of either the martyred President or of crazy Grievau! NOT THEM, for neither was yet dead!

But even at this early stage of the unfolding and disclosure of the plot, talk of conspiracy and foul play was bruited about, and the names of Cronksey, Silas Smith, and some others, were spoken in no soft whispers by the infuriated people. When projecting a skillful piece of strategy, the press was immediately flooded by Smith with stories of the infamy of the "vile assassin," as he was called, and popular attention being diverted from those in high places, all the wrath was turned upon this man, who had been used as their tool, *unknown to himself.*

Early in the progress of events the U. S. District Attorney, pursuant of the plan marked out, had prepared a statement from some of the facts in his possession, garbled to fit the idea of the heading, namely, "*He is sane!*" and sent it floating through the press. Everywhere the desired effect was produced, and the tide of sympathy for the man, which had been associated with the belief in his insanity, fast gaining in the minds of the people, was changed, and the feeling that he was a "vile assassin," a monster in human shape, *sane* and entirely responsible for his act, became paramount, and the needed "scape-goat" was ready at hand to be offered up for the political sins of others. All that fateful summer the *press of the world* was flooded with stories, too horrible to repeat, of the life-long wickedness of the "vile assassin," as he was everywhere called. Even from the pulpit, where men stand forth to preach the gospel of a loving Saviour, vituperation was heaped upon this doomed, well-nigh friendless lunatic, and maledictions were hurled without mercy.

At last, after the death of the President, and the change had taken place in the administration, preparations were made for the trial of Jules Grieveau, his reputed assassinator. Such terrible excitement possessed the people, such loathing of the accused man, it was difficult to secure a competent lawyer for the defense. Finally the husband of his sister Gertrude, although poorly prepared for the work—being ignorant of criminal practice, and never having tried a case of insanity, both requiring special talent and experience for a successful issue—announced his willingness to undertake the business necessary to be attended to upon the preliminary examination of the prisoner, and his probable indictment for the crime of murder, which the prosecution was determined to force if possible.

The friends of Jules Grieveau accepted this offer, sadly underrating the importance of every move in the preparatory steps of such a trial as this one proved to be, and expecting to secure associate counsel suitable for the importance of the occasion, even after the case was commenced, not knowing the difficulties in the way of such procedure.

Gertrude hoped, should her husband save her crazy brother—an easy matter as it seemed to her, lacking political and legal knowledge—he might also retrieve his own dilapidated fortunes through the renown he should acquire; and this idea was suggested at first by her husband himself.

Bitterly did she and the other friends of Jules have cause to regret this turn in affairs; for they found that only a lawyer with great political influence, well up in all the tricks and wire-pulling of the demagogues who rule the country and infest the Capitol, could by any possibility have won this case. Even though a man have truth and justice on his side, he cannot safely enter a contest in court, unless he is prepared to use the same means as are at the command of the opposite party in the case. Gertrude's husband, although a very good lawyer, was not versed in the sharp practices of criminal trials, or the ways that are devious and dark, peculiarly prevalent in the courts of the District of Columbia, and especially brought into requisition in this particular trial, for political reasons—aiming at the result of hanging their man, whether sane or insane. They also found that no competent lawyer will consent to take a second place in an important trial, under a man he knows to be inferior in knowledge to himself, and surely not after the case has been commenced, and perhaps poorly handled.

And thus it happened that this defender of the weak and penniless was, when the case came to trial, unevenly matched one against three—three competent, well-paid men, against one man, poor, overworked, and unpaid, struggling to meet the current expenses from day to day—Gertrude having mortgaged the little patrimony left to the family (inherited from Grandfather Gascoigne), for the means of making the trip and carrying on the trial in Washington.

Strangely enough Gen. John A. Gascoigne, the only one of the family who had influence and money, held himself entirely aloof from the defence of his sister's child; even shunned all association with those who, braving contumely and disgrace, quietly persisted in standing firmly by him to the bitter end. Chief in devotion Gertrude and Lucille; defending and protecting to the full extent of their ability, doing all they could, but proving a hopeless contest, resulting as might have been foreseen.

CHAPTER XXXI.

JULES' TRIAL.—THE VERDICT.

All efforts to have him tried by a lunacy commission having failed—Jules Grieveau had been indicted for the murder of the President, and the day set for the commencement of his trial was reached.

Gertrude, her husband and Lucille, with his few other friends were assembled in Washington to give their testimony in his behalf and help as they could—and the hour had come when the despised assassin was to be brought into court and before the judge for trial.

The Press for months had been teeming with bitterness—the air was full of threats and menaces—the guards had been doubled and trebled, that the law might take its course without interference from the mob.

At last the judge was upon the bench—a man of plain, kind exterior—with a marked fatherly manner, peculiarly captivating, and perhaps misleading to the prisoner and his friends; but who when the final decision came, gave it with the cold incisiveness of glittering steel.

The jury of twelve good men and true as was hoped were seated in their places to the right of the judge.

The counsel for the Administration, headed by the pompous little District Attorney, accompanied by his colored factotum Sam, were ranged beside a table near the jury for a reason which early in the proceedings, on to the end, became apparent.

Then came the counsel for the defense—one man—and the prisoner's friends—three women and a child—Gertrude's little Elsie—next her sat Lucille, a vacant chair between them reserved for the prisoner, who had not yet been brought in; and behind these a space for his body-guard, one of whom was Uncle Tutty Swanson; occupying the room intervening before the Judge—about two dozen news reporters.

As the court-room door opened for the entrance of Jules Grieveau, the hushed murmur, " There he comes," then all was still, every eye strained in the vast crowd—packed--not an inch of room to spare—appropriated by those eager to catch a glimpse of the " monster " as he had been so often styled.
15

When a little man cowering among his guards came rapidly along the passage cleared for him—his eyes rolling wildly in the incessant horrible way before described, his face that of a hunted animal, pursued to the death—the awed whisper spread from one to another, " Why, he's crazy! see! he's crazy! " and a shudder of horror, tempered with pity, transfixed and softened every heart in that assembly, where before had been only bitterest hatred.

The prisoner was brought past the jury and seated in the vacant chair between Gertrude and Lucille, the three policemen in their places standing guard behind them, little Elsie in front of Uncle Tut, beside Aunt Debby; and thus they remained side by side in that dreary, crowded court-room for three weary months, and as they sat and looked and listened, day by day, these women wondered if there was a God in Heaven or no.

During the highest excitement, when the prosecution were pouring in broadside after broadside of subborned testimony to prove Jules a sane villain instead of an insane tool, when threats of mobbing and shooting were freely spoken, and his violent death had been twice attempted; these brave women varied their position by inclining their bodies, so that bullets coming from either of the three accessible sides of the room must first hit them before they could reach him—believing no sane person would be found with a heart to shoot women down who were from day to day risking their lives in defence of a poor fellow too crazy to realize his own danger. And they were right, even the presence of the child Elsie was a protection.

Their anxiety for Jules' safety was partly that an opportunity might be had for proving his insanity, and thereby the stigma be removed from the honored name of Grieveau—also because they loved him as we all love our own, and besides they cared and labored for him, for his dead mother's sake.

After the first day was over and Gertrude and Lucille had seen Jules returned in safety to the prison van, and had themselves wearily gained the quarters secured for them near the court-room, as they waited a few moments in the little parlor, a pale, sweet-faced woman stepped up to them and said:

"Pardon my intrusion, but I wrote a bitter article for the papers yesterday about the man who shot the president; forgive me, I did not know until I saw him in Court to-day, that he was crazy." And the little news correspondent burst into tears. Such heartfelt sympathy greeted these sorrowing ones on every side, when the truth began to be seen as to the man's condition, which was apparent enough as he was uncontrollable from the first, and insisted upon talking every thing which came into his crazy head, without regard to advice or counsel. One of his favorite expressions being "I want the truth no matter who gets hit—*give us the truth Bloaty*," meaning the prosecuting attorney.

When all was ready, the government opening their case, after speeches on both sides were made, the real trial—the bringing of witnesses to prove the assertions of the indictment—was commenced. All the witnesses for the government had been well drilled, knew just what they were expected to say, their name was legion, and they swore him a sane villain. The defense to the accusation of murder were simply and solely insanity. After the history of the man's birth and life as herein narrated, had been proved, and a clear case of insanity made out, resulting from pre-natal conditions, and subsequent adverse circumstances, the government in rebuttal, produced a score or more of well paid asylum superintendents who swore that the crazy prisoner was perfectly sane and responsible for his act, and this, in the face of myriads of people who had visited the court room, seen the man, and *knew* that he was crazy, but dared not give their testimony in his behalf. Opposing the strong force arrayed against him by the power, money and influence of the administration, poor Jules could only bring the heart-broken women Gertrude and Lucille, the brother-in-law, between whom and himself there had been only antagonism since his boyhood—the mere sight of the man exasperating him almost to frenzy; and a handful of witnesses, including two physicians who refused to yield to the almost universal prejudice. A prejudice which had been assiduously cultivated by Silas Smith, in the interests of those engaged in the great fraud; through the medium of the Press of the country, since first the shot was fired, during all the months of the President's suffering, until now, the reputed assassin was on trial for his life.

A prejudice so strong and vindictive that from his native town, where his father and his mother had lived respected and loved, and where it was well known the boy had an unfortunate birth, witnesses were brought against him, who stated *privately* that they dared not give other than the testimony elicited, that they could not return among their old neighbors and dwell in peace—did they swear otherwise.

Even Gen. John A. Gascoigne pretended to believe Jules,

his sister's child, knew better than to do such a thing, though he was somewhat "cranky." The fact being he had been so long separated from the boy, he had lost his natural affection for him; besides he was tied hand and foot, and could not help himself, and in taking this position, thought he was choosing the smallest horn of the dilemma—perhaps he was for himself.

But Gen. Gascoigne was becoming a mystery to his friends, especially to Uncle Tut, such strange things were now coming to light through the investigation of the Chief and himself. They were sorely puzzled and distressed.

They had discovered that Cronksey was a cousin of Myra, the mother of Jules, the mother of Jules and the father of Cronksey being descended from the same English lord, and of course bearing the same relationship to Gen. Gascoigne, and that the General was in some way interested in the success of the "great scheme" they had an inkling of, and in which they knew Cronksey to have been the main plotter; also that Silas Smith, the Vice-President and Bamboozle were concerned in the same, and even the old and honored General, who so successfully closed the civil war, thus cementing the union, had allowed himself to be drawn in, not understanding its whole import.

They had discovered that Bamboozle was probably one of the men who went to the President and urged him to withdraw from the investigation the night before he was shot; also that himself and Spideler went to the depot in a carriage on that eventful morning, Spideler alighting and placing himself where he could fasten his magnetic eyes upon Jules, watching him intently until the deed was done, (it was even rumored that he actually fired one shot—the fatal one) and also being sure that the devoted doctor, who afterwards sent Silas Smith, his old-time friend of the western claim, the cypher despatches, had taken the fallen President into his exclusive charge, thereby ensuring that the murderous bullet should remain in its place until the patient was poisoned past recovery. Then at last Spideler walking slowly away, when out of sight increasing his pace to a run, soon overtaking the carriage with Bamboozle inside, which had gone by another route, Spideler getting in hastily and both driving rapidly away.

All these facts had been found out in detached items, requiring careful joinings to produce a complete mosaic, a connected chain of proof; and doing the best they could the work had been imperfect. Links of evidence were missing, blocks gone out of the mosaic, so that they failed to connect the certainty of a conspiracy to defraud, perhaps revolutionize the Government, with the agency of the conspirators in instigating Jules Grieveau to fire that shot upon the President, thereby removing him out of their way. That there was a connection they were sure, and the sequel proved them right—but hunt as they would, they could not get the proof of direct agency necessary to convict the real villains, and the trial of Jules progressed without interference to the end.

But at these developments the two men were in a state of turbulent excitement impossible to describe, and harder to bear because suppressed—amazement and grief were the dominating emotions—evenly balanced.

Cronksey, they had learned long before this, was undoubtedly capable of impelling his underlings to any desperate deed, in the accomplishment of an end.

As for General Gascoigne—when the Chief found the son of his old time friend involved in what he had come to feel sure was a conspiracy—his grief and chagrin were past all bounds; and he was debarred from proceeding one step in his purpose to ·save Jules and also the country from the disgrace of executing an insane man, unless he would sacrifice the son of his friend as well as precipitate the country in anarchy, riot, and, he feared, irredeemable ruin.

Slowly and cautiously moved the two disheartened men at this juncture, and they felt themselves treading very near the hidden fuse of a gunpowder mine, which might at any moment explode, perhaps rending the Republic to its foundations, destroying the confidence of the people in their rulers, overthrowing the stability of the Government; and they concluded their duty demanded the sacrifice of a wrecked and shattered life, rather than excite the people by an exposé of their discoveries and suspicions.

They did not believe that either Gen. Gascoigne, the Vice-President or the old General were cognizant of the villainy which had been concocted by Smith and Cronksey, and carried out by Spideler and the Doctor; or that Gen. Gascoigne had known of the relationship between Cronksey and his family, or that his nephew was to be their intended tool.

Only after the terrible deed was done, did the full scope of the scheme and all that had grown out of it dawn upon these entrapped men; and then dreading results which might follow a denouement—of excitement, riot and bloodshed—they had, with one accord, without consultation, held their peace; *struck dumb with horror*, giving no sign of the things they suspected, but of which they could not furnish positive proof.

Gen. Gascoigne, and the man who had by an accident, as was said, become the President, showed in their haggard faces how deep their trouble was.

A hint of the suspicion in the mind of the Chief of the Secret Service, that there had been a conspiracy resulting in the removal of the President, had escaped into the air, and the same talk which had flown wildly the first day or two after the shooting, before Smith had gotten entire control of the wires, began again to be whispered about.

The defenders of Jules were threatening to attack the administration under the new President from this very standpoint.

The associate lawyers of the prosecution were anxious to evade such a turn in the case, and to refute the theory which was creeping into the defense that Jules, even though insane, had been made the scapegoat of designing villains, who, for some cause, had conspired to remove the President.

For this reason they wished to place the men to whom popular suspicion pointed, on the witness stand, that their testimony might show this theory to be untrue.

But both sides found it well-nigh impossible to get any of these men into the case; especially did Cronksey, Smith and Spideler shun Washington; in fact Cronksey and Smith hied themselves speedily across the water on board the latter's swift yacht. Neither the famous General of the war, or Gerald A. Johnson, the new President, or Gen. Gascoigne, the uncle of Jules, all of whom were believed to know something of the matter, not one could be gotten into court. An unseen power seemed to shield them from the ordeal. Certain newspaper men were also supposed to be *well informed*, but refused to know *anything*. This was noticeable of the editor of a leading stalwart Washington paper, the one of which a prominent "Star-Router" was part owner, and from whom the administration, about this time, bought his interest, thus making, as was said, an "administration organ" of the paper, dipping liberally into the U. S. Treasury for the purpose of furnishing this generous fund wherewith to defend himself upon his approaching trial. As if the paper had not been an "administration organ" all along, both through the previous and the "accidental" dynasty. These sort of editors can turn their coats in a twinkling when a man or measure is *dead*, either figuratively or actually.

But, however, this fine handsome editor, reminding somewhat of the loved and honored Logan, was put upon the stand, and, under oath, declared he knew *absolutely nothing* of the political situation, although his paper had *at the last, just before the change*, been most rabid in affirming that the country would be better off if some sickness or an accident should remove him; but while he lay ill played an old trick by professing extreme sympathy, bitterly denouncing the assassin, but no one was deceived, and now, that the Martyred President was dead, and everything had changed, this editor had straddled back into the stalwart traces, and was ready to curry favor. Although the files of this man's paper for May and June of that year were insisted upon for use in the trial of Jules, the Judge did not order them brought into court, and this editor had *forgotten everything*, yes absolutely.

Another important witness was about this time spirited away. In the upper tier of cells over those where Grieveau was confined, was quartered, quite comfortably during a part of the same period, a short, thick-set man, unmistakably a seaman probably a captain, by the cut of his jib you'd say he was English.

This man's case was on the same calendar for trial with that of Grieveau, just ahead of his by the call number; as was the case of those who had been indicted for complicity in the " Star Route " steal, and whose case, it will be remembered, was when called set back and continued indefinitely, as was said, to give way for the speedy trial of Grieveau. The fact being they dared not bring these men to the front until they had first disposed of Grieveau's crazy, rattling tongue. For the moment their names were canvassed in the public prints, Grieveau's quick eye and acute brain was sure to divine, as by an intuition, things in connection with this matter and the names of his friends as he believed them, which would be to himself no less than to the " dear people " a revelation. And they knew too, full well, that did the idea once take hold of his erratic mind, that a fraud had been perpetrated upon him, or upon the people, *whom he loved* with a patriotic fervor few can understand—no power short of death could have closed his mouth from exposing all he knew or imagined; for if there is one thing a Grieveau detests, whether crazy or sane, that thing is *trickery, deceit, fraud;* this hatred is a part of, and inseparable from the

Grieveau blood, coming down from Huguenot forefather. No, they dared not bring their men to the front for trial while Grieveau lived. They did not know how much he knew, but they feared. They did not know that he had given to Gertrude a list in his own hand-writing, unmistakably his own, of the names of his friends, those who were to stand by him in his trouble, with the injunction that she go to them *herself*. "Tell them," said he, " that money is needed for my defense, that they *must furnish it*, or *I'll make it hot for them*, mind now, *go yourself*, tell each one individually what I say—*consult no one*, but go yourself, and you'll get the money." But she, knowing his insanity, thinking he did not fully realize all his words implied, did consult with her husband and others supposed to be engaged in his defense. She afterwards, when *too late*, felt the force of his injunction.

Especially when after her brother was gone some of the names written proved to be those of the leaders in this "Fraud" who were put on trial and of course acquitted everyone. But theirs were not the only names—Oh! no! There were others much better known, higher up in national affairs, much higher, who have not yet come before a human tribunal—though some of those most noted, and most surely guilty, have been called to give an account to the Judge of all the earth. But the sea captain whom we left after introduction to you my readers, in his comfortable cell, with wine and cigars liberally provided, requires a little attention. He is quite a different man from Grieveau. No danger that *he'll* ever go crazy over any religious, fanatical idea of Divine inspiration and leading, or from fear of any danger to the body politic which he might strive to avert. No, there is no sign of intellect or spirituality about him, but just a good heavy liver, honest enough perhaps in his intentions, but easily managed by superiors. A man to whom the comforts of life, including good wine and cigars, *was all*; articles for which Grieveau had no use whatever, only contempt. Give him pen, ink and paper, he was happy. While Grieveau could not, crazy as he was, be bought at *any price*—this man would sell himself for a mess of pottage. However, he had come to know a great deal about the corruption in the Naval service, had himself pocketed a big steal. What he knew of some other things has never transpired, for while Grieveau was on trial securely guarded n'ght and day, this man proved (How) easily the prison (gate) may be lifted by slack officials when they are so inclined. As easily and in a similar manner to the case of one of our Chicago " boodlers," who only went home by appointment to meet the opposing attorney, in company with an official, to smack his wife and take a bath—but actually had the impudence *when given every opportunity* to go clear away to Canada, without thanking or saying by your leave to the (Mat) over which he walked out; or even looking back at the people's custodian who stood (Grinn)ing behind the door. These same honest and conscientious officials had to make themselves very zealous for the people afterwards to set themselves right, and they found a case near at hand upon which to exercise their energy, for other criminals were to be tried, and the people had been, by a suborned press, worked up to the desired state of wrath —as no money was at stake—and they were free to act according to the demands of popular clamor—which they did.

However, in the trial we are now considering—one J. G. Bamboozle, a sly and experienced old demagogue, was at last put upon the stand—evidently as the safest spokesman for the crowd, and who contrived to solve the problem of how not to tell the truth. To be sure, he was obliged to contradict himself point blank, as to the dispatches he had sent to Europe the day after the President was shot; saying, as will be remembered, that " the deed was the sole work, without doubt, of a crazy man," while he now testified him to be a perfectly sane villain, wholly responsible.

But then it was no worse perjury than was committed by a celebrated Chicago lawyer and popular Republican orator, who was never known to be dashed by so small a thing as a black lie. * * *

As for the new President, he would have forfeited his life, rather than face Lucille in that court room, and have *her* know the real connection between himself and the trouble poor Jules was in. And then, his appearance before her would have revealed his changed name, and have thrown greater suspicion upon him, and he feared he had already more than he could successfully battle with. Fortunately just at this juncture he was taken suddenly ill, and before he recovered it had been argued and decided that an attachment against a President of the U. S., bringing him into a Court to testify against his will, could not hold. Both sides had been insisting upon the President's appearance, but now the effort was abandoned, and thus it happened that the new President sent his elegant, black-edged mourning letter with excuse and regret, which was accepted strangely enough, in lieu of his important testimony, and he was not again asked into Court, or urged to the unpleasant predicament of facing either Lucille, or crazy Jules; who it afterwards came to light, had expected great things,—*sure relief and a rescuing hand* from the new, stalwart President. But the dignified and elegant black-edged note, read from the witness stand, was the only message ever received by the poor, trusting tool, from *"his friend, the President."*   *   *   *

The Doctor who had attended the dead President, he who had sent the cypher dispatches, was not allowed to escape as easily, but was brought into court, and so painfully terrorized did he appear under oath, that it was remarked, "one would have thought the Doctor himself was on trial for the murder of the President."

He turned out to be the old-time "chum" who had been on the western "claim" with Silas Smith and perhaps a greater villain than even he—the man they called "Doc."

As the trial progressed, it became more and more apparent that Jules Grieveau was doomed; that the prosecution—and this meant the administration—were determined to execute the man whether sane or insane, and were evidently acting upon the theory that dead men tell no tales. The district attorney saying in one of his many *side speeches to the jury (it will be remembered they were seated conveniently near the prosecuting counsel and the paid experts)* after Jules' friends had proved his insanity, and been denied by the court the introduction of their *nine best witnesses,* reserved for sur-rebuttal of the expert testimony—"Well, if he is a crank, then we will hang him for *being* a crank; *a crank has no business to live."*   *   *   *

The whole trial from beginning to ending was a masterpiece of legal chicanery; but no one who watched its workings, ever believed the pompous, strutting little district attorney, or even his able associates, capable of the work as a connected, finished whole.

The prosecution—both Judge, jury, witnesses and lawyers— were too palpably under the direction of an indomitable controlling brain; more than one person suspected, indeed was *convinced* long before the trial ended, that Cronksey, the shrewd, unscrupulous lawyer and political schemer, was that invincible master-mind. And the sequel to the whole business, the sham trial, at last, of those concerned in the great frauds, which was conducted ostensibly by the same pompous district attorney, assisted by the lawyer relative of the Doctor, who sent the cipher dispatches from the bedside of the dying President; and

the final acquittal of every one; a consummation, completing
the achievement undertaken by the same unconquered will, in
the end confirmed that suspicion.

The administration, the prosecuting lawyers, the judge, the
witnesses, poor Jules himself, were all, no less than those in-
veigled into complicity with the great frauds, but puppets in the
show, revolving as the master pulled the wire—a long time
elapsed before the showman was himself shown. Only one
other legal mind and political schemer in all the land could have
matched, conquered and forced the black-hearted pirate sooner
to unfurl his true colors before the world; and by fraud and
trickery he was excluded from the case, *for the end was not yet.*

After all the tedious, sometimes pitiful scenes of one of the
most remarkable criminal trials of modern times, it was now
drawing to a close.

The prosecution had bullied the crazy prisoner, his witnesses
and relatives; the Judge had been carefully watched, lest he
might give some ruling in favor of the defense; doubtful
points and exceptions referred to, and decided from day to day
by the judges who were to constitute the Court in banc, upon
appeal for new trial; thus unjustly and unlawfully cutting off
the prisoner's last resort.

The jury besides being manipulated in low spoken "asides"
from the prosecuting attorney, intimidated by an ever present
mob admitted to the court room on the *"red passes"* furnished
by the prosecution to the administration employees, and various
well known means, had been terrorized by the Masonic signs
of warning and exhortation transmitted, from time to time,
through one of the lawyers of the prosecution, himself a Mason
as was also the foreman, and at least two other jurymen, all
belonging to the same lodge with the martyred President, and
bound by their oath to avenge his death. The fact that both
the father and grandfather of Grieveau were Master Masons,
might have helped his case, had this idea been pushed, but the
brother-in-law lawyer of the defense, not being himself a Mason,
refused to consider the importance of this point.

And further: a newspaper full of distorted, rabid utterances
and unmerciful threats towards the prisoner, and even the jury,
should they fail to convict, had been found in their room at the
hotel where they were secluded, scribbled round with the written
names of every juryman on the panel, in their own hand-writing, indicating that they had read and digested its contents; certainly increasing their prejudice and fear, rendering their ver-

dict, whatever it might be, illegal.   The tide was setting strong
against him; but one thing more remained to be done in poor
Jules' behalf, a desperate alternative, so reckoned in all criminal
practice, namely, putting on the stand in his own defense, the
crazy prisoner.

His friends considered him so plainly insane upon the subject of "the removal" as he called it, always insisting that "Deity"
inspired him to the deed, and that "Deity" was well pleased
with the result; they reasoned it could not hurt his case to let
the jury see his insanity just as it was, believing they would
honestly bring in a verdict according to their convictions.

And Jules Grieveau was placed upon the stand under oath
to tell the story in his own way; which he did, relating it honestly and pitifully.

The counsel selected for the work of coss-examination being confined in his hotel undergoing a three days' course of
opium and whiskey, in order to fit him for the exploit, and when
brought up to the desired pitch of unfeeling blaguardism and
debauchery, this oldest, wickedest, vilest man of all the lawyers
of the prosecution, was put to the task of trying to force other
than the truth from the prisoner.

Any but a heart of stone must have been moved to hear crazy
Jules Grieveau striving to have the court and jury understand
"how it happened."

"You see, I noticed Bamboozle and the President going about
together, always talking in a low tone, but could sometimes
catch a word, and would hear him urging the President to *crush
the Stalwarts*, and I knew *they* wouldn't give in and we should
have another civil war, sure.   Finally it came to me that the
Lord wanted me to 'remove' the President and prevent it."

Why he should not "remove" the man who was advising the
victim *contrary to the instructions* of those who delegated him,
as his coadjutors afterwards hinted, declaring "he had wrecked
a President in furtherance of his own two-faced, treacherous
selfishness," or why he was not "inspired to remove" the chief
contestants on the other side of the quarrel, and thus, by either
course prevent a war, is a mystery never solved in the mind of
any but those who instigated the deed; *they* knowing full well
that an *entire change of administration* was needed as *their
only safety.*

Certain it is, that whatever influenced Jules Grieveau, "malice
prepence" was not the motive, for he constantly averred "The
President never did *me* any harm, he was a fine man, and

a good fellow, I guess; but the Deity put such a grinding pressure upon me, *I had to fire that shot*, if I had been torn in pieces the next minute."

And then to hear the wily lawyer try to wring from those pale, thin lips, some expression of remorse for the deed, some word that would prove his reiteration of "The Deity and me" to be but an afterthought, and that he was only shamming.

But for two days Jules Grieveau sat under the most persistent, scathing, *cruel* cross-examination any shattered creature was ever subjected to—his answers, no less than his distorted, blighted, partially paralyzed features, expressing only honesty of purpose to "Tell the truth no matter who got hurt," as he said again and again.

Sometimes under what was to his sensitive organization, a *real torture*, his lips would quiver, and his face blanch and twitch convulsively, as he strove to remember the minutiæ of the dreadful thoughts and feelings which only the insane ever experience, and which had haunted him night and day for weeks before the final climax of the deed he felt impelled to do, had given him rest and peace. As he told how he prayed night and day that the "*Diety would let him off*," because he "*didn't want to do it*," how once when he thought he had a message from Deity the night before to *do the deed that very morning*, and hearing the President was to take the train, he went to the depot, the fatal firearm ready, but the sight of the wife hanging on her husband's arm, deterred him from executing the Divine command, for Jules Grieveau had a tender heart. And then how for two weeks more he prayed and prayed that "the Deity would let him off." Poor fellow, he did not understand that the *time was not yet ripe*, that he must wait until other minds consummated their desires, and laying hold of his own crazy brain, should hypnotize him in a way to *impel* him to the *final issue;* that he must wait until Cronksey was ready, and the doctor in his place, and Spideler stationed where his magnetic eyes could give the required courage, could nerve the trembling arm; no, Jules Grieveau did not understand all this, or the workings of his own insane imaginings. He only knew what he *believed, what he felt, what he suffered.*

But the most expert lawyer among them all, perhaps in the country, failed to mix him up in the slightest upon his testimony; as this lawyer stated the evening after he closed his cross-examination, to an acquaintance, the editor of several small, newsy, daily papers: "I never got hold of such a witness, I could not

shake him in the least, his *delusion is so strong*, he thinks the
Deity commanded him to do it, I am certain." Though this
was afterwards denied when it might have saved Jules Grieveau's life.

And thus right through, from the beginning to the end, from
the first examination of the prisoner in his cell by the Chief of
the Secret Service, the night after the shot was fired, and by
the Government Insane Asylum Superintendent, through all
the subtle means used by the District Attorney and the Judge
to entrap him, through all the surprises sprung upon him during
his trial and on the witness stand, in his speech to the jury, all
through, his dominating idea was "the Deity and me, we did it,
and it's all right," nothing could dislodge him from this position, and herein was his insanity.

But all the efforts made in his behalf, even the truth itself,
when *proven*, availed nothing, it was *fore-ordained the man
should die*.

Certain of his insanity, and that the jury had recognized the
fact, the friends of Jules were altogether unprepared for the
result which followed the close of his trial. Confident of the
ending, when the jury, led by their foreman, filed into that dingy,
shabby, old court room on that dark, stormy day in mid winter,
just at the dusk of evening, every friend who had stood by him
on to the last, Lucille, Gertrude, Aunt Debby, Uncle Tut, even
the brother-in-law who had defended him as best he could, assisted at the last by a lawyer, versed in criminal practice, who
had volunteered for the defense; (or prosecution, which was it?)
even Jules himself expecting, if he could be said really to expect anything, an acquittal.

When amid breathless suspense the foreman solemnly announced the verdict of " *Guilty*," poor Jules, who had trusted
in the judge and jury—they seeming kindly enough disposed
towards him during the trial—almost as implicitly as he did in
" Deity," when he understood, though but partially, what had
happened, and felt that they were against him, were not now
friendly to him—stared vacantly at first, turning from one to
another in a dazed sort of way; as though amazed beyond the
power of speech, as a devout believer might, who getting a
glimpse of Heaven, should find there no God.

And then, as the idea came to his darkened brain more
clearly, of what they had done, that they had played him false,
gone back on him as he reckoned it, that they did not mean to
let him go, but to send him again to his prison-cell, his rapidly

moving eyes glanced fiercely upon them, in the dim, dusky light of the now fast waning day; and as the thought of the injustice of the verdict grew stronger in his mind, he found speech, and poured out his wrath upon all who were as he thought concerned in the wrong. The judge, jury, witnesses, lawyers, the administration, even the new President, calling Heaven and Earth to witness that the " Deity " would punish them for that verdict, punish each one, and strangely enough the curse pronounced that day, by crazy Jules Grieveau, came true every word—and that ere long.

As the guards roughly hurried him exhausted away, Lucille, Gertrude and Aunt Debby followed, out to the prison-van—with a look of death on their faces.

No frenzied shrieks, or hysterical sobs and tears, betrayed that the glittering steel had entered the heart—the blow had been too sudden, sharp and deep, for noisy demonstration—but the ashy greyness of the corpse-like visage, the deadened eye, the thin drawn lips, and the unsteady gait, marked the palsy of despair within.

Extraordinary measures had been taken for the protection of the prisoner during what every one felt would be great danger when the climax came, however the verdict might be; but after all, the poor fellow's real protection consisted in the silent company of those devoted women. Everyone knew of their steadfast love which nothing could intimidate, and all respected them for it, and they said, " If he were our brother or kin we'd stand by him, too, notwithstanding all."

When it had become known that a verdict was soon to be brought in, a vast crowd gathered about the Court-House square, and when the news flew from mouth to mouth, that the foreman had announced a verdict of " *Guity*," every element of fierce revenge, every desperado, every vagabond, black or white, in all the city came rushing there until a sea of heads met the eye from the broad steps.

A seething mass of human beings, now muttering low, threatening, menacing, and again cursing loud and deep, until the din became a roar of fury. Anew were the dreadful sufferings of the martyred president remembered, and an eager thirst for the blood of him, whom they had been taught to believe and whom the verdict now declared to be his assassin, possessed them.

But when the rumor gained credence, that his sister Gertrude, and Lucille, the sister of his dead mother were to march with him to the van sharing his danger, every imprecation was stilled, and as the party issued from the lower entrance under the main portico, with the little man feebly cowering in their midst, a hush of awe pervaded the vast crowd to its utmost limit.

Slowly, with measured tread, the three devoted women and Uncle Tut, marched two on either side of the guards down the long passage cleared by the police. Quickly was the transit made, for such an unnatural calm could not last. As the women parted with Jules at the door of the van, Lucille and Gertrude lost their self-possession at the thought of the crazy boy a condemned murderer, and throwing their arms around him, tried to hold him back—" Oh! Jules, Jules," they cried, " we won't forsake you, we'll do all we can to save you yet."

Almost roughly he shook them off. "I don't want any women folks crying around me, "he said. " You needn't worry about me, I'm all right, you'd better go back and look after that judge and jury, the Deity's down on them, ha! ha! ha!"

And as the prison-van rattled away surrounded by its mounted guard, the colored footman at the door, poor Jules' horrid crazy laugh died on the chilly air.

The crowd quietly dispersed, a few of the more sympathetic ones gathering around the now well-nigh fainting women, assisting them kindly to their rooms near by; and soon in the grey dusk of that bleak winter evening, no one could be found near the late scene of so much excitement, unless some belated unfortunate, hurrying past against the blinding storm which had been coming on all day and now increased with vicious fury, as though the elements, too, were filled with unrelenting wrath.

As the sleety wind came down from the cold North, soughing through the trees about the square, it seemed that the demons of the air were let loose among their branches, and with long skeleton arms were in wierd frenzy reaching out seeking to find their escaped victim.

CHAPTER XXXII.

"I AM GOD'S MAN."—JULIA'S PUNISHMENT.

After the first shock of the adverse verdict had passed, the friends of Jules Grieveau set themselves about contriving some way to save him, if possible, even now.

A new trial was asked for and elaborate arguments prepared on the motion, but, of course, the prayer of the defense was refused.

Then came efforts for the commutation of sentence of hanging, to life imprisonment, or a stay of sentence until congress convened and a law might be passed, establishing an asylum for the safe custody of insane criminals; a needed institution as has been often proved.

In pursuance of this end, a petition to the President was prepared, and signed by many of the medical profession, a majority being intensely disgusted at the course of certain Asylum Superintendents, subpœnoed by the government, also lawyers who had watched the case without prejudice, and knew Jules had not been granted a fair trial; these with many ministers, collegiate men and other people, more or less prominent, both men and women, sent in their names to be affixed to the petition, until the number reached up into the thousands. As a part of this effort, Gertrude, by the advice of friends, tried to arouse the sympathy of the people, herself appearing before them, stating his case truthfully and asking their signatures. She gave several lectures which were well received, but no impression was made upon the masses, although names were secured sufficient to have turned the scale in an ordinary case; but in this, only an overwhelming, spontaneous, popular demonstration would avail. And here, as in every attempted benefit for Jules Grieveau, his friends were checkmated by some unseen, mysterious power, working mainly through the various news channels which centered in Washington, and throwing out at every pulsation of the great throbing citadel, a stream of vitiated and corrupted influences and perverted facts, blackening the thought, corroding the sympathy, paralyzing the will of the people throughout the land.

The same power which had been discovered manipulating

16

the stocks in Wall Street as the dying President sank down in utter weakness, or rallied with renewing strength, using his martyrdom for their gain, during weary weeks and months of suffering seldom equaled, heroically born until death's reprieve.

The same power which planned the "removal" of the dead President, and also the trial of Jules Grieveau, the "scape-goat" and reputed assassin, carrying it through to the desired end of conviction and proposed execution.

The same power which contrived the escape of at least one, and afterwards planned the trial of the others interested in the success of the great frauds, and carried *them* safely through to a *virtual acquittal* of every one.

And with this influence, this power, whatever it was, their weakness was unable to cope, in staying the current or turning the tide so fiercely setting against the doomed man.

With despairing sadness, the friends of Jules Grieveau at last made up their minds that, as he expressed it, "he must go."

They had expended every energy, done the utmost anxious hearts could devise, made all effort their feeble means would allow, had put in a brave fight for his defense against desperate odds—naught availing.

Nothing remained but the heart-rending task of preparing themselves and him for the horrible ordeal of a barbarous execution.

A punishment under any circumstance, which is a disgrace to civilization; but when, as in this case, visited upon a deluded man believing in his soul, that God and his country received good service, when that fatal shot was fired; deluded because his mal-formed and diseased brain gave only the ability of drawing so warped, crooked and crazy a conclusion from the premises; then such an execution is worthy the intelligence of a hundred years ago, when even in proud England, the naked skeletons were left swinging in the breeze from the road side gibbets, to be removed as the judges went their yearly rounds, making room for the newly sentenced victims of three-score petty crimes, punishable with death.

As for Jules, it was still in his mind only the "Deity and me" who were concerned in the matter, and having no compunctions of conscience, he was fully reconciled to his fate, even impatient of delay in reaching what he considered his just and sure reward for obedience to the Divine command, and which he had come to believe attainable only as he should pass over the river of death. "Because of the wicked perversity of men who should have been instruments in the hands of the Lord for my release, they refusing," said he, "I must suffer, but the Lord will punish them, every one, and prove to the world sooner or later, that I am *God's man*,' called to execute His will, and the men who stand by and see this wrong done to me, shall be cursed from Heaven;" woe unto him through whom the offense cometh, saith Holy Writ. "I am ready to go in five minutes, but I dread the retribution of the Deity on the American people. Make no mistake; it is not Grieveau who is in trouble, it is the people of the United States who are on the brink of a crime. I was inspired by Deity to remove the President, Grieveau, the patriot, is all right; but those who hang him will wish they had never been born." He continued to the last to resent the theory that he was insane; and the success the man who now installed himself as his confessor had in winning his confidence, was due to the fact that he humored his whim in this regard.

On the Tuesday night before the execution, this confessor has reported that Grieveau pointed to a verse he had been reading, "Except ye be converted and become as little children, ye shall not enter the kingdom of Heaven." "And," added the confessor, "Grieveau was the *happiest* man last night, positively that I ever saw." He said, "He was counting the hours until he was to die and be done with mundane things." During the same conversation he said, "Confessor, you are going with me to the scaffold and you'll stand by me there, and I shall look up to where God is waiting for me, reaching out His hand to me, and when the time comes, I think I shall be so near to God that when I let go of your hand I shall be able to take hold of His." Oh no! it was not Grieveau who was in trouble now, whatever he may have suffered during his sad, earthly life.

To his sister, for whom he retained a special affection, he said at their final interveiw, "Yes indeed, I'll be glad to leave this place, no matter how; Paradise's a great improvement on this world. There's nothing *here* that *I want.*" And as she alluded to the probable meeting with his mother in Heaven, he answered, "Yes, I'll be glad to see her when I get there. If she had lived I shouldn't have had so much trouble. I don't remember much about her, but I'll be glad to make her acquaintance. I guess she'll be glad to see me, too—" half crying.

Jules' indifference did much to reconcile his friends to the inevitable; as they pondered over his sad, unfruitful life, they ceased to wonder that he should anticipate with eagerness almost any change. * * *

The terrible tragedy through which they were passing had for the time being absorbed Lucille's every thought and feeling, and she had scarcely wondered during the first days of intense excitement and dismay following the shooting of the President, why Henry had not returned, or at least written an explanation of his strange conduct.   Surely he had given the proof of a true and passionate love which neither separation or time could quench, and this complete assurance comforted Lucille and supported her through days, weeks, months of grievous trial; it was a boon beyond estimation she thought, the knowledge that Henry had been, in his heart, true to his love for her, even though she never saw him more.

But as the weeks passed into months and she heard nothing from him, after the suffering and death of the President, after the trial, conviction and sentence of Jules, now the ordeal of his execution and the ignominy unavoidably endured and shared with him by his relatives, confronted them; partially recovering from the shock of the unjust verdict, and beginning to revolve in her mind the feasability of plans whereby to save him if possible, her thoughts turned anew to Henry, and she could not understand how affection which she believed equal to her own, could be estranged by any calamity or why he had not come forward as a staunch-hearted man, helping her, even though ever so little.

And when one and another not as near in friendship offered their sympathy and assistance—for there are some whom the wildest storm will fail to unsettle—then, steadfast, patient Lucille began to waver in her trust, and indignation filled her heart, that a man for whom she had suffered so much, and whose love had after long years again asserted itself, should keep aloof from her when in trouble; because, as she concluded, he lacked the courage to stand by her even against the world.

At last poor Lucille drank the dregs of her bitter portion; after all those years of self-sacrifice to this ideal lover of her youth, whom she had cherished sacredly, carried in her heart of hearts; after the chasm had been bridged and they two stood face to face united—alas! she had found he was unworthy of her devotion, of her life-long love—now she would tear his image from her heart and trample it under foot.

Could she?   Verily she could not; the idol had been too long enthroned, worthy or not worthy, whether pure gold or only dross; in the inmost recess of her soul Henry Armstrong must remain enthroned—entombed if you will, to Lucille's dying day; this she felt, and grieved as of yore; even more sorely than ever before.

All the long years of the past it had been only the memory of the young love of her girlhood, the memory of a man scarcely more than a boy, the memory of an inexplicable mystery; but now they had met in the full prime of maturity, every attribute, every atom developed to the utmost of which pure, loving manhood and womanhood is capable. Had met and been clasped in each other's arms, her tortured heart at last lay upon his own, his protecting arm around her, his warm breath upon her cheek and life, passionate, loving life, had been eagerly absorbed and freely given back from off dewey lips, and then—he was gone—his last words:

"I beg of you say you never knew me; I will come again and explain all." And now months had elapsed, and he had not come.

This was all she knew, and she believed he did not come because of the terrible disgrace which had since fallen upon her, and for his cowardice she tried to hate him, but could not.

True love never turns to hate, but sometimes into indifference when the adoration is gone. Lucille was passing through this transition she thought, otherwise she must have sank overwhelmed.

John having refused help and co-operation in the defense of his sister's child, a coldness had come between himself and the friends of Jules; but Lucille still continued for a long time visiting her brother's house occasionally, with the hope of again meeting Henry; in this she was disappointed.

For Henry Armstrong kept entirely away from the home of his old friend, Gen. John A. Gascoigne, for several reasons; one, that he wished to avoid Lucille until he could make an explanation, which was now impossible without compromising others; another, that he determined not to give Mistress Julia an interview under any circumstances, and still another grave reason made it inexpedient if not dangerous.

The rumor of conspiracy had not entirely died away; (although the Vice-President had been quietly installed in the place made vacant by the death of the President, *secretly at midnight*, on the day of his demise), and there had been just the faintest whisper of a hint that himself and Gen. Gascoigne were in some way connected with it, and safety dictated that at this juncture these politicians should become estranged from one another. Somehow as only intriguers can accomplish their designs, it was bruited about that Gen. Gascoigne was jealous of attentions bestowed upon his wife by the fascinating " accidental President," especially since his bereavement, and which had called for remonstrance from Gen. Gascoigne, who, the gossips averred, oft times had occasion to look rather sharply after his gay wife.   In this manner was the public deceived as to the real intimacy between these men high in official position, and thus it transpired that Gen. Gascoigne no longer spoke the name of the new President in his home, and forbade his wife the privilege.   This command would have annoyed Mistress Julia less could she have continued her flirtation with the handsome widower President, but one cannot flirt all alone, and *he* ignored her existence.   For the time the passionate, fickle woman was desperately in love with her new flame, and would have braved a scandal; disgracing husband and children for his sake, and was now deeply chagrined and puzzled to account for the sudden coldness.   She did not know there was another woman in the case, and that herself was getting a taste of her own medicine, which she had forced upon many a true wife ere her own retribution came.

CHAPTER XXXIII.

LUCILLE'S LETTER TO HENRY.

Jules was now a closely guarded felon under sentence of death.

One day Lucille and Gertrude were returning from a visit to his cell; as they were passing on foot past the Capitol, after their weary walk of an hour across the common, who should Lucille discover coming down the broad marble steps, but Henry Armstrong. One quick glance, to which there was no apparent response, and she passed on, with feeble, grief-stricken step, and head bowed down.

He recognized her at once, and had Lucille seen the concentrated, passionate love of years, which came unbidden and in spite of a strong man's will, into the eyes that hungrily sought her downcast face—a passion, a love, leaping like liquid fire from the throbbing heart, burning through every vein and fiber, though suddenly, *instantly* repressed, crowded back into the secret sanctuary of the man's hidden life, mastered by a superhuman force; but leaving those glorious, warm brown eyes *burnt* and *scared* and *changed*; forever after of an ashen, dead, blue-grey hue, so unlike those of the Henry she had known—had she seen this, the positive assurance thus unwittingly given, of a love as unquenchable as her own, it must have comforted Lucille's breaking heart. And if the noble-looking, imposingly handsome, altogether exquisite gentleman, had been *shot* then and there, he could not have turned to a more deathly pallor, or shown greater trepidation, for an instant—only an instant, so quickly did he recover himself.

Without haste or further apparent emotion, he came down the steps with a party of noted men accompanying him, taking seats in a carriage waiting for them. Yes, it was the President's liveried carriage, Lucille could see; although she came near falling in a faint with the shock of surprise, grief and consternation which overpowered her.

Certainly the gentlemen in his company gave him precedence—what could it mean?

He must be an influential man, a friend of the President, his private carriage placed at his disposal.

" No wonder," thought the sad, crushed little woman, " he could not come to me, or keep up his acquaintance with Gen. Gascoigne, both now known to be relatives of the despised 'assassin.' " And Lucille thought she had solved the mystery, and for the first time *fully* realized what a terrible calamity had befallen her sister's child and all who should be connected with him down to remotest time.

She felt now that fate had *her* in its iron-vise, relentlessly pressing the life current from her bleeding heart—and that no earthly power could save.

And Henry Armstrong, the " accidental " President, what of him?

How he reached the end of that long flight of steps, composedly continuing the conversation, and chatting gaily with his friends as they rode together to the White House, quietly maintaining his equilibrium until he could finally dismiss them and be alone, was past his own comprehension; and certain it is, from that day, whenever the beautiful and imposing Capitol of the Nation came within view, his heart sank and sickened, and he could see Lucille exactly as she appeared to him then, and he felt again just as when he had passed her by without the slightest sign giving proof of his love, or even that he ever knew her. Passed her by—the woman he would have died to possess as his own, with not so much as a glance from his eyes, and hers cast upon him with such a desperate, hungry look of longing, not the least reproach or anger, at what anyone must deem his outrageous treatment; but only surprise, and love beseeching and inexpressibly tender, expressed in every line of her sad, worn, pale face.

And the struggle of those few hours which he spent alone, when his friends had left him, the strong man never forgot.

His life would not have weighed a feather in the balance, could its forfeit have gained for him, and for her, one quiet hour of companionship and happiness in the complete possession and ownership of love.

But others besides himself were involved in the tangled thread of their destiny, and this could not be. How he longed to take the weary little woman in his arms and comfort her aching heart, but at present it was absolutely impossible to communicate with her in the slightest. They must continue as though they had never met, until the revolving wheel of fate brought some propitious changes. Whatever this might involve Henry had no idea, but that some event or events would transpire whereby Lucille should be his own in fact, as she was now in feeling and desire, he believed. The possibility of such consummation depended upon persistent avoidance of recognition, on this point his mind was clear, further into futurity he did not penetrate.

As for Lucille, accustomed to shocks and griefs and suffering of almost every kind, figuratively knocked down so many times before, she only gathered herself up wearily, and sick with despondency, dragged along her homeward way, carefully helped by Gertrude, to whom she explained her condition as the effect of intense heat and fatigue.

Reaching her quiet room she sat herself down to think of all the long, dreary past, of the present, and of the unknown future.

Sadly and anxiously pondering over the whole situation, Lucille resolved upon writing a letter, not in her own behalf, but interceding for Myra's crazy boy, with Henry Armstrong, her old-time lover, and now certainly, she thought, the intimate and influential friend of the President.

She had lately considered the plan of going herself to the Chief Executive, begging his clemency, trying what she could do by personal appeal; but this would be better: yes, much better, she would write to-morrow.

On the morrow, as Lucille had resolved, she wrote to Henry Armstrong, directing her letter in the care of Hon. Gerald A. Johnson, His Excellency, The President of the United States. She had seen Henry but twice during her residence in Washington, and concluded him to be merely a visitor, and with the President's carriage at his disposal, she argued a letter sent through his hands would reach its proper destination.

Henry begging Lucille not to disclose their acquaintance, when leaving her at Gen. Gascoigne's, she had refrained from making inquires regarding him of her brother or his wife, and not meeting him there again, was corroborated in the idea that he was an occasional visitor at the Capitol, accidentally, perhaps, securing an introduction to her brother's family, knowing, as she did, Julia's predeliction for cultivating distinguished strangers, in which category Henry surely seemed to belong. She had heard the rumors of jealousy on the part of her brother towards several gentlemen, the President included, and doubted not the gay Julia had given ample occasion; probably Henry had been one of her casual admirers and come under the ban of John's displeasure; this would account for his continued absence;

or possibly he wished to avoid herself, and thus the discovery of their secret. Fortunately or otherwise, on the day of the encounter, at her brother's house, when the servant came in view, Henry and Lucille had taken the alarm and were standing one on either side of the room, each cold as an icicle, entirely self-possessed, their trouble safely concealed in their own hearts.

After that interview, Lucille was positive, whatever the mystery influencing Henry's past and present conduct might be, his heart was true to her, and that he would now respond to her request, and try his best to induce the President to commute the sentence of Jules Grieveau to imprisonment, and thus they, no less than himself, might be saved from the disgrace of his execution, as she had come to consider the world would estimate.

Until recently, his friends, absorbed in the anxiety and grief of the situation, had given no thought as to how they were regarded in their relationship to the "vile assassin," their first aim being to save Jules from a cruel and unjust fate. But during the time intervening between his sentence and its execution, they were considering the importance to themselves as well as Jules, of averting it if possible.

They believed that time, the softener of all bitterness, would in a measure, right the wrong by allowing the truth of his insanity, and that history would excuse the deed in him, placing the blame where it belonged; but remembering it were always better to prevent, than to depend upon correcting an evil, they redoubled every effort to avert the catastrophe.

With this view the following letter was sent to Henry Armstrong in the President's care, by Lucille, as her final attempt in his behalf:

WASHINGTON, D. C., June 29th, 18—, Thursday.
To the Hon. Henry Armstrong,

My Friend of the Olden-time:

With emotions inexpressible, an uncertainty bred from ignorance of your position, a mingling of doubt, chagrin and sorrow, but withal of love, which, since our meeting at my brother's I am free to confess is boundless and unutterable; I address you, not in the capacity of any high place or influence you may hold, but as a *man* with the sense of right, the feelings of humanity common to good men everywhere.

Not in my own behalf; too many years has self been crucified—as between you and me all is mystery unfathomable—sometime—somewhere—God grant it may be solved.

My request now is, for my dead sister's child, Jules Grie-

veau, " the assassin." I yesterday visited him in his cell, or
rather outside the grated door, not being allowed to enter, but
kissing the lips dear to me, taking the warm hand in mine
through the bars. He was at times so violent they dared not
open the grating into the corridor. I was unprepared to find
him in this wild, crazy condition, for much of the time he is
quiet and reconciled to the inevitable in the strong belief that he
is " God's man," as he expresses it, and will be cared for either
here or in the Great Beyond, having no anxiety about himself,
it is immaterial to him whether he remains in his cell or goes
" to Paradise," as he says, of the two preferring Paradise.

But yesterday he was in terrible excitement over something
—" the making of a will," said the confessor and the lawyer,
both employed as I am informed and believe by the administration to protect itself and its co-workers in iniquity from any
scheme Jules may at the last moment perhaps reveal, though
inadvertently, in his insane ravings, likely to criminate any other
than himself. Whatever he may know or imagine of concealed
villainy, he was yesterday pounding his cell door until it rang
even louder than his voice as he denounced the warden, the
President, the Stalwarts, in curses loud and long, saying God
would punish every one because they had gone back on him,
leaving him to suffer while they had " a good time outside," as
he made us understand, in spite of the confessor, who, inside the
cell, was vainly trying to quiet him with soft words and endear-
ments, his arms about his neck, so anxious was he to keep back
any revelations.

I have tried to picture Jules to you as he appeared to
me, that you may more fully understand his case and condition
and where the real blame lies; and I entreat you to use your
utmost endeavor with the President for the commutation of his
sentence to imprisonment. What good to society or to him
can be accomplished by the execution of this insane man I am
at a loss to understand. Why not stay the sentence procured
by an unjust and unfair trial, and appoint a competent commission to examine his case from a medical, not from a legal or
criminal standpoint?

Surely could the President be acquainted with the facts divested of prejudice, he would interfere and the country be saved
the disgrace; himself, the remorse of allowing the execution of
an irresponsible man.

A petition will be sent to the President to-day signed by
hundreds of the best people in the land, physicians, lawyers,

men and women connected with educational institutions and others, of refinement, intelligence and thought, who have gone below the surface in this matter, forming just conclusions which time will confirm.

You have no need to be ashamed of their company. Will you for truth's sake, for justice's sake, for the old love's sake, for *my sake*, if happily this can move you, join them, and intercede with the President, whom I judge to be your friend, when the intimacy places his private carriage at your disposal; for the reprieve of one unjustly condemned?

Oh! Henry, my friend of years gone by, will you not use your influence for the rescue of Myra's boy from his impending fate?

Think, Henry, of his sainted mother, you who knew her pure and lovely life, remember the boy's unfortunate birth, entailing years of suffering upon her, finally ending in her early death; a birth proving only a calamity to himself and his friends.

You who knew his ancestry, respected, upright, honored, tell me, must all this be lost, and we as a family go down into the depths of shame?

Oh! Henry, my beloved! for I *will* say this now, even though you cruelly passed me by yesterday without the slightest notice, for I know you love me still notwithstanding your strange conduct; and I am sure you can help me in this dire distress. Will you? This is my last appeal. Will you help me save Myra's boy, Jules Grieveau? ·

Should success attend your efforts, the undying gratitude of poor Jules' friends will be yours, not least in value perhaps to you may be that of   LUCILLE.

CHAPTER XXXIV.

PLAYING FATHER CONFESSOR.—ONE OF THE 306.

Lucille's letter was delivered immediately to Henry; the petition he never saw. Somehow by the manipulation of the same invisible power, before referred to, it remained tied up in the White House "red tape," and never came to light until long after Jules Grieveau had opened his eyes in Paradise.

The agony of mind and heart endured by Henry upon the perusal of this letter, was beyond anything he had before undergone; but for reasons already explained, he could not respond, or help Jules in the least degree. An interference on his part, or of anyone connected with the administration, would be regarded by the people as corroborating the vague rumors of a conspiracy still floating through the air, of which Jules was said to be the unconscious, deluded tool; they had not forgotten the suffering and death of the martyred President, and could hardly settle down to the belief that only crazy Jules Grieveau was to blame.

And some unseen intelligence seemed to fear the friends of Jules would claim after his death that he had imparted to them more than they made public; and for this reason both were closely watched.

The new President's most intimate counselor, a wealthy minister and renowned politician, one of the 306, being sent to sleep on a *cot in front of the cell door*, and for weeks before his death watching "the assassin" night and day lest a word or hint should escape of which they were not apprised.

His spiritual advisor, the confessor and politician mentioned, taking care to gain the confidence of Jules, who, being of an affectionate disposition, this was easily accomplished; by flattery and sympathy he was encouraged to communicate, and every word uttered, carefully noted by the devoted confessor; not less devoted than was the dead President's most devoted doctor; these two, by faithful service to the cause, certainly earning an exceeding great reward in the interest of virtue or villainy, which was it?

The transcript of his sayings which accumulated during the last weeks of Jules Grieveau's life were preserved by the con-

fessor, he omitting any objectionable hints or passages, any al-
lusion to the Stalwarts; he intending, should the necessity arise,
to give all a thorough revision, publishing the revised work as
Jules' statement of all the facts in his possession, thus exonerat-
ing and protecting those who sent him to do the work.   Jules
had invariably insisted when questioned that " The Deity and
me" had accomplished the deed, and denied any knowledge of
a conspiracy to save the men interested in the success of the
great frauds from prosecution and punishment, by "the removal " of the President.   Deceived, deluded tool, although he
knew not the hidden hand which was using him, often in his
rattling, crazy talk, he verified the adage, " Children and fools
tell the truth."   Hence the precaution practiced as to his sayings,
writings and finally his execution, forever stilling his excited,
feverish brain and babbling tongue.

The unseen intelligence engaged in manipulating his case,
also encouraged him in writing, for it would never do to let the
claim be made that he had been deprived of the privilege of
promulgating all he knew.   Therefore a book was prepared
and published after careful supervision, Jules believing a second
trial would be granted and the sale of the book which was called
by the taking title " The Truth, and The Removal," would enable the payment of suitable counsel for his defense.   Jules was
also given to understand that the notes and papers bequeathed
to the confessor by virtue of a bogus will, *void and of non effect*
wrung from him at the last moment—*concurred in under protest,* by his sister as his heir; for thus only could she secure a
final interview with her brother; should be used just as received
from him in compiling another book, to be a complete vindication of his act, and prove that he was inspired of God to " remove " the President, and thus prevent another civil war; which
he fully believed the truth, and expected his name after the
publication to " go thundering down the ages," not as *Grieveau
the assassin,* but as GRIEVEAU THE PATRIOT and savior of
his Country, beside those of Washington and Lincoln and
Grant, as he classed them.

This project pleased him beyond measure, as he was extremely sensitive upon the point of his insanity, always resent-
ing the imputation angrily; calling the working of his mind
which culminated in the shooting of the President, inspiration.
But withal the rest of his strange make-up, possessing in some
directions the quick-witted cunning common to the insane, he
would sometimes admit, both in speaking and writing, that such

manifestations constituted *insanity in the law,* "*Abraham's insanity,*" he would say, with his chuckling, crazy laugh. This was one of the ideas which cropped out after the lawyer before referred to as working with the confessor, both covering up tracks, had gotten into the case for the defense, gaining unbounded influence over Jules, and injecting this, with other like ideas, into his crazy brain for a purpose.

He also bitterly resented the thonght that he could do so dastardly a deed as murder a fellow-being in cold blood from selfish motives. He said: " *The President was a good fellow, he never did me any harm, but he was wrecking the Republican party, and sure to bring on a civil war,* and the Deity put it upon me to 'remove' him, and I had to do it if I had been shot dead the next minute. I prayed and prayed for weeks to be let off—but the pressure of inspiration was on me, grinding, *grinding,* GRINDING me down, and I could not escape; I *tell you I had to do it,*" he would sometimes yell out in thundering tones. " I would not go into that crowd of people at that depot and fire that shot again, not for a million dollars. I was never so unhappy in my life (and I'd had trouble enough before), as I was that spring when the Deity was putting it upon me to do that thing; but when it was done I was all right, and told the folks so—told them to go home and keep quiet; the Deity and me had fixed it, and everything would be all right now and no more trouble, and I was happy and contented after I gave myself up and the officers got me safely into my cell. I could *sleep then,* for I knew I'd done the Deity's work, and He'd take care of it. I hadn't had a night's rest for weeks before I fired that shot, and I tell you it seemed good to get into a quiet place, with my mind easy and nothing to trouble me." [These, and all quotations attributed to Jules Grievau, are my brother's very words. F. M. N.]

Poor fellow, he did not understand or recognize the fact that the grinding pressure was an influence from without, persistently exerted with malicious intent, for weeks and months, until the time came when for their own protection, murder was to be preferred to political suicide, and the *hypnotized tool held as though by an iron hand, was at the right moment* (as he expressed it in his testimony upon his trial) "projected upon the President," and the desired end accomplished by those who willed the deed.

How shamefully his " spiritual advisor," the confessor, deceived him in every particular, and especially as to the use he

intended making of the knowledge gained through intimate association with him and from his writings, happily Jules Grieveau never knew.

  · Neither did Lucille know why Henry Armstrong failed to
answer her appealing letter, or did anyone know outside the
ring, why nothing more was heard about the petition to the
President after it went to the White House in the hand of the
same trusty and most devoted confessor; he having, with wily
tact, ingratiated himself with the friends of Jules, thereby learning all their plans, that he might frustrate them, they believing
from his manner of treating both Jules and themselves that he
was using his utmost endeavor trying to save the boy; meah-
while doing well his work of watching and revising, even to the
scaffold speech and prayer.

  The queer, pathetic, crazy death-song written by Jules
Grieveau, early upon the morning of his execution not being
exempt from the pious confessor's sacreligious meddling; but
even so, the little story based upon the thought which came to
Jules with the first light, as in the early dawn of his last day
upon earth he read from a book of poems presented to him by
C. J. Griffith, of Baltimore, as inscribed therein, a hymn, which
his sister found marked in his own writing after his execution,
—namely: "*I shall be there soon*," of which this is the first
verse:

> Beyond the smiling and the weeping,
>   I shall be soon;
> Beyond the waking and the sleeping,
> Beyond the sowing and the reaping,
>   I shall be soon.
> Love, rest, and home!
>   Sweet hope!
> Lord, tarry not, but come.

  In conversation with his confessor, following the thought he
said, "Before to-morrow I shall enter the kingdom; it is the
Lord's will or it would not be permitted. *I am satisfied*, it's
all right. As a little child I will go to Him, nothing doubting,"
and this thought suggested Jules Grieveau's Death Song, "*I
Am Going To the Lordy*."

> I am going to the Lordy,
>   I am so glad;
> I am going to the Lordy,
>   I am so glad;
> I am going to the Lordy,
> Glory Hallelujah! Glory Hallelujah!
>   I am going to the Lordy.

I love the Lordy with all my soul,
  Glory Hallelujah!
And that is the reason I am going to the Lord,
  Glory Hallelujah! Glory Hallelujah!
    I am going to the Lord.

I saved my party and my land,
  Glory Hallelujah!
But they have murdered me for it,
  And that is the reason I am going to the Lordy.
Glory Hallelujah! Glory Hallelujah!
    I am going to the Lordy.

I wonder what I will see
  When I get to the Lordy,
I guess I will weep no more
  When I get to the Lordy,
    Glory Hallelujah!

I wonder what I will see
  When I get to the Lordy,
I expect to see most splendid things,
  Beyond all earthly conception,
When I am with the Lordy,
  Glory Hallelujah! Glory Hallelujah!
  I am with the Lord!

The thought and the pathos of it, even thougn marked unmistakably by insanity, must touch a tender, sympathetic chord
in every heart wherever it shall be read.

CHAPTER XXXV.

READY! GLORY!

The hours were rapidly passing, and now unfortunate Jules
Grieveau must ascend the scaffold.   On the morrow, so soon,
was the execution of the unjust sentence to be consummated;
his friends were allowed a parting interview, and sadly, with
tear-dripping hearts, Lucille, Gertrude and the others, led by
one of the guards, passed through the large outer room where
had gathered a crowd of the curious, into the narrow way leading to the cell of the "assassin."

When they reached the door Jules was heard denouncing
the " accidental " President, whom he styled an " ingrate and a
villain," implying that he expected some favor from him, and
had been disappointed, saying that " Deity would curse him,
and every one concerned in this judicial murder.   I spit upon
this death warrant, this execution," he said.

" You can hang me if you want to, you can put my
body in the ground, it is all you can do; but I'm God's man
and you'll find it out yet.   God'll curse you for this, *I'm not
afraid to die.*   Paradise's a great improvement on this place.
I'm God's man, he'll take care of me, I'd rather die like a man
than be shut up like a dog.   Put me in the insane asylum! ha!
ha!"   Again that laugh.   " That crazy sister of mine is trying
to get the President to put me in a lunatic aslyum.   Me, a lunatic! ha! ha! ha!   Guess I know what I'm about.   The Deity
and me's all right, but the President's a villain to keep me here
so long while he's having a good time outside, and he won't let
me go now when I've got my satchel all packed to go to Marsailles, Consul to France, you know where our folks came from.
I wouldn't care only they promised me.   I'd rather go to Paradise anyhow, but now my lady's waiting for me in New York
ready to take the steamer, you know—we were going to be
married," and he gave a significant look towards Gertrude and
Lucille who came up to the door just then.   " But the President
won't let me go now, after all, he's an ingrate and a villain, he'd
never have been a President if it hadn't been for Deity and me,
and God will curse him for this, I'm God's man, and I'm all
right, but I'm sorry for the President, he'll get punished yet,

and you'll all find out that I'm right. And you're a villain too,"
turning and noticing the warden. " You pretended you'd let
me go when the time came, and now you won't; I don't care,
but I hate deception and trickery and meanness, it's nothing to
me though, what you do any of you, the Deity'll take care of
me, and take care of every one of you villains yet, too."

And as the crazy man talked loudly in his excited, wild, in-
coherent manner, he pounded the bars of his cell door until they
rattled and resounded through all the jail.

Lucille and Gertrude spoke gently, lovingly, trying to quiet
him with pleasant allusions to a boquet they had before sent in,
by the warden's son John, and to his mother dwelling for long
years past in the Better Land. The confessor within the cell,
having every appearance of the watchful English mastiff, laid
his hand on Jules' shoulder, not roughly; and speaking kindly
the desired effect was produced, and he became for a few moments docile as a child with its mother, and turning, laid his
head affectionately on his keeper's neck, throwing his arms around
him, saying, "Yes, confessor, I'll be quiet; I'll do as you say, I
suppose it's all right, you know best; but don't forget the book
and the record, and my vindication, *Grieveau the Patriot!*
that's the way I want *my* name to go 'thundering down the
ages,' mind you don't forget, confessor, don't forget what you
promised me. The Deity'll get down on you if you do; I don't
care what they do with *me*, I'd rather go to Paradise anyhow;
there's nothing in this world that *I* want; they are all a mean
lot down here anyhow; the Stalwarts, the President and all of
you, all but the Lord's men. It's all right if the Deity wants
me to go. I'd rather sit on one of those thrones up there than
to be President, or get married and go to Marsailles. Paradise
is a great improvement on this place anyhow."

Trying to divert his attention from the theme which exasperated him, the confessor reached for the flowers before mentioned, taking them from the ledge of the little window,
which had been bricked up to within four inches of the top for
protection his friends insisting, after one of his own guards
had fired at him, instigated by authorities. For in every way had
the administration, *after conviction*, tried to avoid hanging a
man they knew to be insane, and this by trickery; well knowing
a pardon or even reprieve to Grieveau, would be their own death
warrant, so suspicious were the people of the Stalwart President. Handing the boquet to Jules, he smelling it, said, "Yes
they are very nice; I haven't had any flowers before for a long

time; but I'll have all the flowers I want when I get there *to-morrow*." Lucille catching this moment when he was calmer, spoke again of his mother. "She'll be glad to see you Jules, she's waiting for you up there, she's—" but a sob uncontrollable broke the sentence. "Yes," he answered, not taking notice of her grief, "I don't remember much about her, I suppose she was a very nice woman. It's a long time since I've seen her, I don't suppose she'll know me, but I shall be glad to make her acquaintance again; I guess she'll be glad to see me too," becoming excited again. "I was all ready to go to France, where our folks came from you know, but the President won't let me go, *he's a villain*. I don't care only the lady'll be disappointed you know. I'd rather go to Paradise anyhow, for the confessor here says the Deity wants me up there; but the *President's a villain!*" screaming and yelling at the top of his voice, pounding the cell door until it shook and rattled, he not minding the work of the cruel iron on his bare fists.

At last Lucille and Gartrude could endure no more, and Gertrude said, weeping, "Jules, you know I always loved you, no matter what you did, will you kiss me good bye?"

"Kiss you! kiss you? Yes, kiss me through the bars; let it go thundering down the ages that my sister kissed me through the bars. Ha! ha! ha!" and the parting kiss and the crazy laugh were inseparably intermingled.

Bidding him again a final farewell, in their hearts commending poor Jules Grieveau to the care of that God who looketh upon the sparrow in tenderest compassion when it falleth, his devoted friends, every one with streaming eyes, turned sadly away; believing that in the balance of the Most High, this man, who to-morrow must meet an unjust fate, was of more account than many sparrows, or than those who had ensnared him, men sound of mind, black of heart, devising only evil; and in the Great Hereafter each should find meted out to them equitable judgment.

June 30th—on Friday, between the hours of twelve and one, by the prison clock, Jules Grieveau, the unfortunate offspring of untoward circumstances, gave up his sad and unprofitable earthly life.

When marching to the scaffold, impatient of delay, he urged the escort and accompanying friends to greater speed, and reaching the place of doom, after a short address to the crowd assembled inside the jail, a prayer followed by the little hymn "I Am Going to the Lordy," prepared in the early morning, all rendered in his own peculiar, insane fashion, pathetic yet triumphant, dropping a white paper by preconcerted signal, from his pinioned hands, at the same time shouting loud and clear until the words rang through all the jail, "READY! GLORY!" In an instant, *painlessly, without a struggle, hardly a tremor of the body*, the spirit of Jules Grieveau had entered the realm of the Unknown, where are gathered the sheaves of the Great Harvest Home of Humanity; and not with more tenderness and compassionate love, was he welcomed by the angel mother who had bestowed his earth life, than by the Father God from whom he now received immortality. His "Faith accounted unto him for righteousness."

In this belief, Lucille, Gertrude and all who, knowing his sad history, were moved to pity and grief, were comforted, and they said, "When our time comes may we be 'ready,' and as sure of reaching 'Glory.'"

Immediately after the barbarous execution, and while the old guards who had discharged well their trust in conveying crazy Jules to and fro from the prison van to the court room in safety, thus earning the gratitude of his friends, were gathered around the carriage in which were Lucille, Gertrude and Aunt Debby with Uncle Tut, offering their honest, sad-hearted condolence to the women convulsed with grief, expressing admiration of their brave steadfastness, wavering not to the bitter end; inside the jail was the horror being finished.

At the time of his execution, the insanity of Jules being a a mooted question, the parties involved in the dispute agreed that an autopsy should be performed, examining into the actual condition of that abnormally developed, unevenly balanced, queerly constructed brain, which had worked out such dire results to himself and others.

Scarcely had the throbbing heart ceased to beat, the quivering nerves to vibrate through all their substance in the birth-throes, as the liberated spirit took its flight, ere the work was commenced, at the instigation of cruel, savage science, eager to catch the ever eluding secret of the why, the wherefore, the how, a soul can influence matter, working out the will, the thought, the desire, through the delicate, complex, wondrously formed tissues prepared for this end. So delicate, that however little the space intervening between the state we call life, and the state we call death, it seems to obliterate in greater or less degree, according to the time elapsing, the connection known to exist, the impression disappearing, so that it is impossi-

ble to determine, even by actual sight, by actual handling,
whether a given brain carried out a sane or an insane thought
or desire, unless the brain tissue is markedly diseased, the con-
struction of the organ decidedly abnormal and mal-formed.

Hence the haste, regarded by those not understanding its
importance unseemly, that this particular brain should be carefully, quickly and thoroughly examined, in the cause of science,
justice and mayhap vindication, either for the departed man, or
for those who had defrauded him of bodily life.

The government having the power, had appointed their own
experts for this work, and to make the report to the Press, so
that the people might as usual be deceived.

The friends of Jules Grieveau had done their utmost in securing the attendance of two physicians at the autopsy, whom
they hoped would report truthfully, whatever they saw, though
not officially, and thus a record might be kept of the real facts,
available for future corroboration of their assertion in Jules' behalf.   One of these men, the confessor before mentioned as a
noted Divine, was also a most unscrupulous politician, being one
of the steadfast "306," and withal a medical professor, who,
exhibiting a wonderfully affectionate interest in the welfare of
Jules while living, they supposed could be trusted to act at least
not adversely to his cause after he was dead, but the outcome
proved him determined, as he stated to Gertrude, "To stand by
the President and the administration, even though the Heavens
fall." Faithful henchman, Time should hasten your reward.

The other physician upon whom these sorely tried ones depended for achieving tardy justice, was the superintendent of
the Government Asylum for the Insane. A good and true man,
incorruptible, who having been requested officially at the beginning, while the President still lived, and before the changed
administration came into power, to examine "the assassin," had
reported him "undoubtedly insane, a man who should be tried
by a lunacy commission, not as a murderer," and since watching
the case persistently, attending the trial from day to day for
his own edification, instead of changing, he had repeatedly
averred himself firmly grounded in his first opinion   This
physician, more competent than any one accessible, had purposely been left out of the afficial appointment for the autopsy,
and purposely kept from the witness-stand during the trial; the
Government knowing his report adverse to the view of the
case taken by the prosecution, and that his testimony would be
the same.

The defense, because he was under Government pay and patronage, not understanding or being acquainted with the man's nobility of nature, feared to call him, not daring to trust their cause in his hand; herein was their most grievous mistake. At the last moment his position was understood, but when subpœnaed in sur-rebuttal, his testimony with that of eight other most important witnessess, was not admitted, being ruled out by the judge; the only reason given being urged by the prosecution, "*this case has already taken too much time, and must be closed.*"

Now of his own accord this physician offered his services in attending the autopsy of Jules Grieveau, which he did in the capacity of a privileged spectator, afterwards reporting the facts to the man's friends, and incorporating the result in a little book issued soon after the execution, named "Two Hard Cases," comparing this and a similar one coming under his observation. In relating to Gertrude the sickening occurrence constituting the finale of Jules Grieveau's tragic end, the good doctor, waxing warm, said, " The moment the man's brain was stripped," using medical parlance, " undoubted insanity caused by pre-natal and subsequent conditions, was indicated; but although every man present knew this was true beyond question, the Government will if possible prevent the knowledge coming to the people. Their experts will defer the report for a month or two, fixing up a scientific diagnosis for the newspapers which no one but a professional can understand, and conveying by the heading and italicised phrases as they well know how, the idea to the minds of the people, that 'the assassin' was not crazy at all or irresponsible, but only 'cranky,' whatever that may be. There never was a surer instance of mal-formed, diseased brain; but what I tell you these fellows will do," said the doctor, full of wrath. And they did, everyone agreeing to promulgate what they knew to be a falsehood.

CHAPTER XXXVI.

ON THE SCENT.—CORRALING THE CONSPIRATORS.—FICTION.

As the vast crowd gathered around the jail, was dispersing, who should Uncle Tut discover with those sharp, twinkling eyes, but his old-time enemy, Silas Smith.

He was getting into a carriage accompanied by a gentleman, and carried himself with the pompous dignity, and magnificent ease, of a man to whom the world has been forced to bow by his imperious will and undoubted ability; but Uncle Tutty Swanson, the detective, recognized him instantly. Aunt Debby knew him too, although her eyes were still wet from weeping. Astonished, Uncle Tut saw that the man with whom Silas rode was none other than the elegant Cronksey, just returned from a European tour, and who had been pointed out to him by the Chief only that morning.

Uncle Tut and the Chief had by untiring diligence and endeavor, nearly succeeded in fastening the infamy of planning and instigating, indirectly, the "removal" of the late President, upon this man Cronksey and his co-workers, but there were missing links, which hunt and ferret as they would, could not be found, and without which the chain of evidence, even circumstantial, necsssary to convict, was incomplete.

Uncle Tut now said to himself, "Here's another of these villains; we will get them all yet."

Leaving Aunt Debby with the other women to the care of Gertrude's husband, who had just come upon the scene, he followed the carriage closely, impeded as it was by the crowd; when coming accidently upon Chief Strong in his private conveyance, Uncle Tut tapped on the glass door, which quickly opening, he entered and in a few words related what he had seen and all he knew of Silas Smith. The two men drove close in the rear of Cronksey and Smith among the people huddled together, who with unappeased curiosity, elbowed and tiptoed and pushed, straining every sense and energy, in the vain endeavor to compass still more of horror.

At last, leaving the rabble, the old jail full of tragedies, the stretch of common, the Congressional Cemetery and the Park behind them, driving on past the Capitol, down Pennsylvania

Avenue, the carriage containing the suspected parties persistently dogged by the Chief of the Secret Service and his aid, though circuitously, finally drew up in front of one of the old historical hotels of Washington, known as "Willard's."

The pursuers arriving just in time for Uncle Tut, alighting, to overhear the order given Spideler, (who had been called out) in a low tone at the carriage door, to meet them in an hour at the house of General Gascoigne, bringing with him J. G. Bamboozle and the Doctor who had so devotedly attended the wounded President.

They then drove to the Court House where Jules was tried and sentenced, calling for the District Attorney who had prosecuted the case in so malicious and vindictive a manner, and who had a few moments before returned from witnessing the execution of his victim. He, much to the Chief's surprise, brought with him one of the lawyers who had volunteered for the defense during the latter part of Jules' trial, remaining as devoted to his interest apparently, as had the confessor, or as had the probing Doctor at the bedside of the martyred President. Taking his seat beside the driver, the party proceeded to the White House, when the lawyer hurriedly alighting, ascended the broad steps, the carriage going round to the secluded side of the mansion, the lawyer soon emerged, accompanied by a heavy man with iron-grey hair and beard, carrying a cane upon which he leaned for support as though feeble from age, assisting the old man, both hastily entered the carriage.

The Chief and Uncle Tut following at a safe distance, were again surprised to find themselves going in an opposite direction from Gen. Gascoigne's house.

Uncle Tut was sure he heard aright, for he stood not a foot away when Spideler received the order. At last, after making several turns they came up to the house by an unfrequented street, thus avoiding attention, and coming leisurely up the grand driveway, entered from the front, while Chief Strong and Uncle Tut, who were now in dead earnest, being sure they were on the right scent, were coming from the back, in through the garden, piloted by crazy Leonard, Uncle Tut making him understand there was no nonsense about their errand.

Leonard would do anything Uncle Tut bade him, and he now conducted them to the library, or rather to a small closet between this room and the one adjoining, which was a study or office used by Gen. Gascoigne exclusively for private business. This closet was situated at the end of a narrow hall, into which both apartments opened, leading into the garden, the shrubbery and vines coming close up to the door.

The two men hastened along fearing to meet any one, and hurriedly entered the closet just as the others passed from the front into the study, soon being joined by Spideler and the two he had brought with him from the hotel.

Leonard remained with the men in the closet, for they dared not trust him outside. He was well content to cuddle down in the darkest corner and keep still, while Uncle Tut, to whom he was much attached, was near. "Yes, Massa," he whispered, "Leonard'll be a good boy—he'll keep still, hi! hi!" he giggled.

"Well ke-keep st-still then, wi-will you," stammered Uncle Tut under his breath, while he alternately applied an eye or an ear to an aperture no larger than a knitting needle, through the wall dividing the closet from the study, by which observations had been taken before this, being prepared by Leonard at Uncle Tut's suggestion, for if crazy, he understood enough to take a hint when the service of a friend came into the account.

Many a disjointed bit of information had Leonard carried to Uncle Tut and Aunt Debby from the house of Gen. Gascoigne, as well as from poor Jules, who had been regularly supplied from his Uncle John's kitchen, with comfortable meals, carried every day across the common by Leonard, in one of the tin cupboards contrived for transporting hot meals by the cooks in Washington, where so many transients dwell in rooms, their food served by colored men.

This privilege Gen. John A. Gascoigne insisted upon, for himself and for his sister's child, from the authorities, for, although pretending to believe with the populace, that Jules was responsible for his act even if a "crank," and deserved at least some punishment, he did not propose to have him ill-used or poorly fed. His pretense as to his nephew's responsibility was of course assumed to shield himself and others from the complications and dilemmas, which they could not otherwise escape; but he never dreamed his luke-warmness in the defense, or rather refusal to defend him, would do more perhaps than any one thing to help along the final catastrophe. Gen. Gascoigne up to the last moment, never believed they would *dare* execute his crazy nephew, any more than he and the others associated in the great frauds, the scope and purport of which they did not understand, finding themselves forced to seek shelter from the President, who prying into hidden schemes, was crowding them from their holes—dreamed, when they placed their desperate case in the hands of the great *I am*, the unconquerable and unscrupulous Cronksey, that he would resort to measures resulting in assassination.

They learned, when too late, the danger of trusting vital matters to the sole management of any uninterested person, either tried friend, spiritual advisor or legal counselor. Each must give their special business careful attention if they would escape disaster. By shirking responsibilities, we are often obliged in the end to shoulder greater. This is true in a paramount degree of leaving affairs entirely to the option of those long and successfully engaged in the legal profession, the first maxim instilled into the aspirant's mind being SUCCEED, no matter by what means, only so that you succeed and accomplish the end sought.

Many a noted lawyer looking at his processes from the standpoint simply of a man, would shudder, in contemplating his own inhumanities. Why is this? Why have these things come to be? Because the technicalities of law, or rather of legal decisions, and the practice of the courts all over Christendom, have so warped and corrupted the channels through which justice should come to us, that the side possessing most power, either of mind, money or influence, will, as a rule, win without regarding equity.

Hence, those involved in law from any cause must employ such means as are at command, or they will likely suffer whether in the wrong or in the right. And likewise a good lawyer' taking cases expecting to carry them through to a successful issue, when his mettle is up, scruples at nothing, and is sometimes forced by circumstances to go further than he first intended.

To return, our party was now snugly ensconced in Gen. Gascoigne's private office; after a hearty hand-shaking and an introduction or two, for all had not before met, while the gentlemen were disposing themselves about the room, mine host unlocked a little closet built in the end of the massive fireplace, where were stored choice wines and cigars, which, offering to his guests, they proceeded to enjoy themselves, at the same time conferring together.

An incident here occurred which attracted ths attention of the two detectives, each watching through his own loop hole, for they had made a second, with the strong wire left on the floor by Leonard after the previous operation. The sight which met their astonished gaze was the performance of the gentle-

man who had entered the carriage at the White House, deliberately laying aside his cane and the heavy over-coat, which
gave him the figure of a portly old man, carefully removing
his long grey beard, his mustache of the same color, though
not so white, also his iron grey hair, straightening himself and
at the same time his beautiful brown mustache, the man was
seen to be none other than the elegant Gerald A. Johnson, the
"accidental" President of the United States.

No one present exhibited the least surprise, if we except Silas Smith, who, when the President was removing his disguise,
first eyed him curiously, then enquiringly, and at last *knowingly*,
with a gleam of malicious hatred and sullen vengeance flashing
from his snakey little eyes.

Aside from this episode, which perhaps boded some unpleasantness, but was unnoticed even by the President at first,
the party of jolly fellows seemed very comfortable sipping their
wine and inhaling their fragrant cigars, chatting the while
earnestly and cheerfully, with now and then a joke.

Comfortable?   Well, yes, almost comfortable, even gay,
notwithstanding several of them had so lately witnessed the execution of poor Jules Grieveau whom every one of them knew
to be irresponsible and insane, long before he fired the fatal shot
upon the President; and every one of them knew now, if they
did not then, *why he did it.*   Every one of these men was
aware the deed had resulted in shielding them from harm; pol-
'iticians, capitalists, lawyers, doctors, plebians and aristocrats
who had become involved in the "great scheme" which had
been contrived to defraud the government, which they now
understood the dead President had been determined to investigate, and to punish the wrong doers whether friends or foes,
and they were also certain that nothing short of his "removal"
had saved them.

They were before this almost sure in their own minds,
though they dare not say it, who had planned the dreadful alternative for their protection; who it was had carried the poison
of assassination, and deftly but surely inoculated the crazy brain
of Jules Grieveau with the terrible inspiration which ripening
and bursting forth, had horrified and sickened the whole world
by the vile abomination.

But now they were almost comfortable, although they could
hardly forget so soon, that at the last moment the poor fellow,
by an insane intuition, had divined their treachery and denounced
as villains and ingrates those who had deceived him, declaring

that Deity would curse them for their cruel treatment of "God's man," curse every one.

Yes, almost comfortable, though in their ears was still ringing loud and clear, Jules Grieveau's brave death cry, "Ready! Glory!" Quite well satisfied; they knew no pains had been spared by the confessor and the devoted lawyer (who both attended him at the last), in keeping the doomed man quiet, and preventing the revelation of any knowledge he might possibly have acquired, of the real benefit resulting to those engaged in the "great frauds" by the "removal" of the President.

He had been at their headquarters before the election, and around the hotels where they congregated, even in their private rooms at hotels and boarding houses, both in New York and Washington, and just how much Jules had picked up, they were in ignorance; but they dared not risk any future disclosure.

They were sure no one had voluntarily trusted the strange, erratic man with momentous secrets, but after firing upon the martyred President, Jules Grieveau had also sent a fatal shot into their camp, when he had shouted, "I am a Stalwart of the Stalwarts." From that moment every Stalwart involved sought only safety for himself, and Jules Grieveau's fate was sealed. He had also said, "My friend Johnson will now be President;" and continuing with an impressive gesture, "keep quiet, friends, keep quiet, it's all right, the Deity and me's fixed it, there won't be any war, you can all go home now, I'm going to the jail until the excitement cools down; you'll all understand it when you see my account of the affair in the morning papers," for he had left his documents with the Washington agent of a Chicago Stalwart organ. "Good bye, friends, till I see you again, you'll understand my motives then, they are for your good, my friends, good bye," as the officers hurried him away from the gathering and infuriated mob; he, after the climax and achievement of his insane impulse, the calmest man among them.

This assumption that the leaders of the Stalwart clique, and the man who afterwards became the "accidental" President, were his friends, and would save him in the end, (an assertion which his real friends could not restrain him from reiterating, for they knew it would hang him, and it did,) resounded through all the land, arousing in the popular mind a suspicion of *the truth*, causing the nerves of every one of the infamous crew to tingle and vibrate with fear. An assumption resulting on his part, partly perhaps from insane egotism, and Spideler's indiscriminate pandering to his vanity; a fear causing those who were so desperately trying to cover their tracks, to act in a manner which only confirmed the suspicion; showing by the vindictive, unjust prosecution and execution of their "scape-goat," that they dared not let him live; they knowing that a hint of any of the real facts in the case, had he discovered them, would be fatal.

But now *Jules Grieveau was actually dead*, his white lips forever sealed beyond any possibility of divulgement, and if the people, the only power feared by politicians in this Republican land, could be made to believe that the man who was undoubtedly insane, and from his peculiar make up and condition, exactly suited for their use, was, after all, a responsible, sane villain, who had himself alone planned and executed the deed, the entire work undertaken might be said to have been successfully completed. Hence, the care taken at the autopsy to cover up the truth; and they were now assembled at the house of Gen. John A. Gascoigne, in spite of his protest (for they had him in their power) for the purpose of hearing the report of the confessor, momentarily expected; and if necessary that any change should be made in their program, after the result of the examination of the brain and other visera of Jules Grieveau, the "assassin" was known, they would then perfect their final plans.

Yes, these men were really quite easy and comfortable at last over the situation, but yet needed a few bottles of choice wine, and a mild cigar or two, enabling them to overcome the intense heat liable to occur in Washington the latter part of June, also the nervous strain and depression to which each had been for so long a time subjected. During the year past all had been annoyed, especially the President, by a series of unpleasant events, and as they sat smoking and drinking, waiting the arrival of the Confessor, they complacently planned how the remainder of the summer should be spent now that the business of changing the administration, (though they had got no further,) and the final disposal of poor Jules Grieveau had been accomplished; and they decided upon giving themselves a long holiday; for the present dropping all ambitious schemes.

Cronksey and Smith, accompanied by Spideler, were to start immediately upon a European tour; the doctor thought likely he would soon follow them.

While Jules lay in prison, Cronksey and Smith had remained most of the time in London, they getting away on Smith's fast yacht immediately after the assassination, deeming a foreign climate advisable, should by any accident a denouement occur. Not having been in Washington since, until now, it chanced that

Smith never had seen the "accidental" President until the meeting at Gen. Gascoigne's. All he knew of him was the information volunteered by Cronksey, that he "Was an old friend who could be trusted, that he had spent several years in Australia, returning long enough before the election to be eligible for nomination to the vice-Presidency."

The President was evidently annoyed and depressed, even more so than Gen. Gascoigne, the uncle of Jules, and he plainly betrayed his deep trouble, for he was very sad at the outcome of events. Neither entered freely into the conversation, although the President expressed a desire to visit the Rocky Mountains, through which he had passed many years ago, he said, "In mid-winter when the 'California fever' was first raging, and it would require more gold than any mine contains to induce me again to undertake the same experience; but I am told the trip is delightful in summer." At this, Smith, who had from the time the disguise was removed, been casting upon him occasional sharp glances, now eyed the President intently, disturbing him not a little.

The President knew very well who Silas Smith was, and when they had met; but hoped Smith would not recognize him. Now he began to fear he had or would.

This contingency was talked over between Cronksey and himself, when the conference at Gen. Gascoigne's had been decided upon, and, as many times before, he yielded his own judgment to the other's importunity, consenting to risk the encounter.

The worst that could happen he thought would be a discovery of the man supposed to be Gerald A. Johnson as none other than Henry Armstrong; and Lucille, her brother, Gen. Gascoigne, and the rest might find out the deception practiced, but he hoped by some explanation as to the changed name connected with the inheritance of property to delay further investigation for a time at least.

Cronksey had somehow learned that Silas Smith was in possession of the fact of the murder of his relative Wm. Smith, years before in the "Rockies," and that a man by name Henry Armstrong, had taken charge of his will and effects, also assuming his name, but he did not know that against this man Smith held an old grudge, even more personal. Of this circumstance Henry was cognizant though not of the other, fearing only should his identity becomes known, a murderous attack from Silas Smith, but not the disclosure of his whole secret;

Cronksey deeming it inexpedient to inform Henry of what he had ascertained, and as to this part of the difficulty Henry remained ignorant.

Both trusted Smith would not recognize his enemy in the President, and here they rested, Cronksey hoping in any event he would estimate the great secret they were now engaged in hiding as of immeasurable importance, compared with any merely personal spite. Even Cronksey failed to realize the hoggish, wolfish nature of the man, and reasoned that now they were involved in a scheme requiring concert of action for self-protection, it did not much matter if he knew the whole affair with every complication; not one of the three, any more than did the others assembled, guessing the ramifications of the net in which they were entangled, or what the result would be when it began to unravel.

They had been so closely watched since the assassination, the President, even before the change of administration being subject to an irksome surveillance, which had not yet decreased on the part of the ever suspicious people, with the result, that neither himself, Gen. John A. Gascoigne or the doctor who attended the dead President, had dared absent themselves from the capitol lest an intention of escaping detection should be attributed as the motive; and Cronksey, Smith and Spideler, even more certainly marked than they, had cautiously refrained from approaching the dangerous district.

During all the months of the martyred Presidents suffering, ending in his death and a changed administration, while Jules Grieveau, the crazy fool who persisted in saying *too much*, lay in prison waiting upon his doom, these men wisely kept apart, not risking close proximity by venturing a conference; messages sent by inconsequential persons who being in the "ring" *could be trusted* from self interest; and the cypher dispatch, being their "denier resort." But on this memorable day so many visitors congregating in Washington, these wary schemers concluded upon meeting quietly as possible immediately after the execution of the assassin, at the house of Gen. Gascoigne, which being situated in a retired quarter, they hoped to elude notice, as the mind of the public, especially of the omnipresent reporter and news-monger was sure to be fully occupied. These starvelings, who, vulture like, subsist by devouring the vitals of those unfortunates upon whom they light, having this day for once, their maws, their heads and their hearts (if they have any) and eyes and ears, and hands full; obviating the necessity of breaking into any private residence, or prying open sacred secrets, or defaming anybody's character, breaking hearts and wrecking lives, in the ravenous hunt for items.

As the whole infamous business was at last finished, except the sham trial soon to follow of those who had been engaged in the great frauds, and which could now be easily managed by placing a relative of the devoted Doctor in charge, and who had purposely been kept in the back-ground for this service, to be associated at the proper time with the ostensible prosecutor for the government, by collusion, thus saving them, every one; certainly in view of all that had passed, no less than because of liabilities in the future, a careful consultation was advisable at this juncture, they must plan for a conclusive, final showing in their interest, to the people, providing for every contingency, and agree upon a satisfactory settlement among themselves, each hereafter going his own way, carrying a terrible secret, only partly understood, certainly, undivulged to the end of his career, if happily conscience should not too hardly smite them, and remorse wring from some a confession.

Surely, sober deliberation was necessary, but before they were aware, important issues were foolishly and irretrievably betrayed by weakly yielding to the demoralization of the mocking wine.

Only Silas Smith and the President realized the need of moderation; Silas was on the scent of an enemy, and the President felt himself watched, and he knew he must be cautious. However, the tipsy crew waited patiently for the arrival of the confessor.

CHAPTER XXXVII.

THE CONSPIRATORS IN CONFERENCE.—MORE OF FICTION.

On the way from Pennyslvania Avenue, across to the upper street, upon which was situated the White House, as the President's mansion is styled, and also at the further end of which, quite in the suburbs, Gen. Gascoigne resided; the Chief had stopped at the Metropolitan Police Headquarters, and given an order for a squad of picked men to surround the house of Gen. Gascoigne, as secretly as possible, so sure were both himself and Uncle Tut that they should now bag the game for which they had so long been on the hunt.

To Uncle Tut the fact that Siias Smith was around, gave conclusive evidence that some desperate villainy was being, or had been concocted.

In all their searching for the hidden, mysterious WHY, of the terrible deed which had been committed, and of the subsequent conduct of those who had heen placed in power by the change it had wrought, they had not until now encountered him, or mistrusted any connection on his part in the work.

They knew of Smith's prominence in financial matters pertaining to the government, his gigantic speculations, rather frauds, and that occasionally in his interest apparently, some mysterious power manipulated public opinion at will, through the medium of the press associations; and although they had recognized a similar influence, working adversely to Jules, both before, during and after his trial, from the fact of Smith being much of the time in London, choosing that citadel of capitalists as a center of operations for his schemes, they had not connected him in their minds with the trouble, supposing the enemy had his lair nearer home among the political tricksters with which this country is infested.

But now that he had been discovered in the intimate companionship of one whom they could almost prove to have been the prime mover of the plot, they wondered at their own stupidity in not before suspecting his agency, at least in the control of telegraphic matter, as it was well understood he held a monopoly of the lines of communicatioh throughout the United States.

Now that their attention was directed to him, they were quite sure his personality had permeated the whole diabolical mystery from the beginning.

Just here, for a moment, the Chief and Uncle Tut were diverted from their observation of the men in the little study, by the arrival of Lucille, Gertrude, Aunt Debby and Gertrude's husband, in the private carriage of Mistress Julia Gascoigne, which she had kindly sent that morning to take them to the jail, as they insisted upon being as near as possible to poor Jules, in his trouble at the last. His Aunt Julia had done all she dared from the first, all she could, without compromising her husband in the position he had assumed.

Driving in through the garden, the ordinary entrance for the family, the party were welcomed in silent grief by Julia, and taken directly to the library where they were to rest a short time for condolence and sympathy before retiring to the rooms which Julia had begged that Lucille and Gertrude should occupy during the remainder of their sojourn in Washington.

· Little Elsie came rushing in from the nursery where she had been left with the children, (upon hearing her dear mamma had arrived) and throwing her arms about the neck of one and then another, tried to comfort with her childish philosophy. "Don't cry Mamma, Uncle Jules gone straight to Heaven, sure, he said the Lord would take care of him, and that he'd punish those naughty men, don't cry, he didn't want to stay here, he wanted to go to the 'Lordy,' don't cry," and the little girl patted and stroked and kissed their wet faces, until the weeping eyes were finally dried, and they could talk composedly, of the poor dead boy's life, of his mother and dear old Grandpa Gascoigne, both gone so many years. Happy Jules had met them in the Better Land, seen them face to face, even while those who loved him for their sakes, were grieving over his sad fate.

Said Aunt Debby, who was an old woman now, " I declare to it, Gertrude, if that Elsie o' yourn ain't the complete picture of yourself when you were her age, just the same golden hair, and the same eyes; wouldn't good Dr. Gascoigne have doted on the little pet? Come here, honey," taking the child on her lap, " tell me about your kittens, I know you've got at least a dozen, you wouldn't be your mother's girl if you haven't, you must come over and see my 'Tommy,' he beats any cat you ever *did* see." And thus, so soon was the trouble passing out of mind to live only in memory.

The eyes and ears of the Chief and Uncle Tut were again intently fixed upon the men in the study; the Confessor had arrived, and gathering around him they listened to the report of the autopsy just completed at the jail.

The wine, too, was beginning to make them talk freely, and it was of the utmost importance to know what they were saying.

The Confessor reported that the uncovering of the brain had shown one side much larger than the other, strangely developed and out of shape, that the substance itself had undergone changes indicating disease, especially the covering showing chronic inflammation, the autopsy proving conclusively malformation at birth, which could only have resulted in insanity; that the man had been more or less insane all his life because of pre-natal conditions.

The autopsy was carried even further at the insistence of the superintendent of the asylum, at Washington, who as the Confessor pettishly said, "Sat watching us like an old grey eagle ready to pounce down at the least provocation. I tried to stand so he could not see, but he deliberately left his position and came over examining everything carefully, crowding himself in without invitation. We dared not remonstrate, for the old Doctor is independently rich, and cares neither for Government patronage, the criticism of the Press or the snubs of his fellow professionals when he gets on a scent. If you'll believe it, he deliberately declared the man unmistakably insane, and towering his full height, his keen eagle eyes fairly piercing us through, he turned full upon us and said, ' Gentlemen, every one of you know that man to have been from birth tending to incurable insanity. Now, gentlemen, let us finish this work properly, that there may be no question as to this fact; examine his heart and lungs,' actually directing the remaining examination himself, when the President had requested me to act in special capacity for his protection, though I was not, of course, officially appointed; that would not have answered the purpose. Grieveau's friends might have insisted upon some other physician being present had they suspected me.

" But what could I do? The old doctor would have floored me in a minute had I remonstrated, and all the others too; he's a giant in size and a terror in strength when he starts in. We just had to let him have his own way. He found the heart enlarged, the lungs hepatized and with tubercular deposit, the spleen atrophied; thus contradicting the testimony of our experts on the trial, who swore every one that the man was perfectly healthy. Of course all this must in some way be kept from the people. It will never do to let them know we have hung a crazy man after all. They'll think there is something wrong then, sure. I told them all to keep still and mysterious, and use some confoundedly long, unknowable, supposed to be medical term, in talking to the reporters who'll flock around us, and tell them we'd give them a written report in a few days. In the meantime we can contrive something among us which even the most learned professor of medicine will be mixed up and puzzled over, and which no ordinary reader can interpret, and we'll head the paper, " *The Assassin was sane,*" and that'll end the whole disagreeable business, thank the Lord. The worst of it is that old grey eagle threatens to write a book giving an account of ' *The Trial and the Autopsy, the truth as I saw it,*' he will call it, and if he does all our. fine plans will be knocked into ' pi;' *but it will take some time to get out a book, we may all be dead before then.* If he'll only keep still and write his book we're safe enough; the people will forget about this business soon and be after some other craze."

And thus these villains consoled themselves.

Spideler, not being used to high living, as it would unfit him for his master's service, was beginning to talk more than Cronksey cared to hear, but he found it impossible to control him.

Coming up familiarly to the elegant Cronksey, Spideler, slapping him on the shoulder, broke out with, " I say, Cronksey, we did a slick job that time, didn't we? About the best, hey? "

Cronksey winced visibly, but dared not repulse the disgusting little imp in his present mood, too many of his secrets were stowed away in that round, shining pate.

" I sa-ay, Cronksey," holding on by the lapel of his master's immaculate broadcloth, staggering and stammering drunk, " I sa-ay, Cronksey, you ought to pl-plank hic-down an-hic-nother ten thousand for-hic-me on that. Everything-hic-all right and safe now-hic-mum's an-hic-oyster. He'll never sq-hic-squeal now. Oh! no, he'll never sq-hic-squeal now, the doctors have been-hic-clean through-hic-that crooked head-hic-of his, you bet he'll never squeal-hic-now. I say, Cronksey, gi-hic-give me your check while the-hic-thing's fresh-hic-strike while the-hic-iron's hot, is my motto; de-hic-delay's dan-hic-dangerous, dang it, gi-hic-give me-hic-your check-hic-I say, or hic-I'll squeal-hic-my-hic-self, I will, dang you."

And to quiet the man, Cronksey took out his check-book, tearing a check off the stub, handing it to Spideler. The man, though drunk, knew more than Cronksey thought he did, and taking the check to the window, scanned it closely, leaning against the casing for support; looking where the signature should be, and not finding the name, Spideler called angrily to Cronksey with an oath to come over by the window, in front of which the writing table stood and sign the check.

Hoping to appease the irate man, Cronksey crossed over to the table, intending if necessary to sign the paper, but before he could do so, his hand was arrested, his eye riveted—paralyzed by a most appalling sight. * * *

While this scene was transpiring between Spideler and Cronksey, Silas Smith was tantalizing the President to the point of torture.

He would commence a conversation leading by slow degrees up to the night of the fight at the claim, and the President as persistently, would politely but decisively, by his answers lead away from it; Silas, the while eyeing him as a cat when she has the rat in her power, or as a tiger toying with its prey before making the final spring.

With Silas Smith the desire to satisfy a bloodthirsty, cruel spite, was stronger than the instinct of self-preservation. He would have visited vengeance upon this man who had so nearly been his death that night of the desperate fight years ago, even if himself sure to be killed in the encounter.

Revenge was sweeter to him than aught that life contained, even than life itself.

After the report of the Confessor had been listened to, and during the lull in the proceedings, each waiting for some one else to make a suggestion as to the future conduct of those present, Gen. Gascoigne and the Confessor, not noticing the others, were talking soberly and sadly together of poor Jules' last hours, his implicit faith in Deity and his own inspiration, amounting to an insane delusion; his loving confidence in his Confessor, who said "I tell you, General, I really became attached to your crazy nephew, and I can't have the heart to deny his last and constant request, that I should embody all his writings and sayings in a book, which he imagined would set him right 'in history,' but I'll have to go over them all carefully, and expunge anything detrimental, (to the book I mean, of course,)" said the Confessor, giving Uncle John a knowing look which they both evidently understood, "for we must stand by the cause and the Administration if the Heavens fall. After a while when I have time, I'll take the papers he left, which you know belong to me under the will signed and corroborated by yourself and sister, (another exchange of glances) "down to Florida, they'll be safe there on my plantation, and I can look them over and prepare the book at my leisure."

"All right, all right," answered Gen. Gascoigne. "I leave all these matters to you," only too glad was he to shirk the responsibility and dismiss all thought of his dead sister's wronged child from his mind. Surely was he in pitiable trouble.

Still another conversation was going on between the two lawyers and the doctor, who did so much of that cruel probing after the bullet had lain undisturbed, until nothing could benefit the sick man.

"I suppose, Bloaty," said the doctor, "there'll be no slip about my getting that twenty-five thousand dollars for my services, just as soon as Congress convenes in the fall? If I can be sure of it, some of my friends will advance $5,000 or so and I'll be off to Europe with Cronksey and Smith, for I'm sadly in need of rest. Fact is I am completely exhausted. I'd no idea the President would hold out as he did, it was wonderful the grip that man had on life. I tell you his constitution and endurance were astonishing; nothing but the poison of that bullet could have done the job. Poor fellow, how he suffered. I did all I could to save him after I came to know his noble nature, but the business was done before the first twenty-four hours had passed, and no hope for him then. I wouldn't undertake another such case for one hundred thousand dollars, no, not for a million! It was terrible, terrible." And the worn and debilitated doctor wiped his smooth, intellectual brow with a sky-blue silk handkerchief and sighed.

And the pompous little attorney, who prided himself upon his remarkable physical likeness to the great Napoleon, answered without hesitation, "Certainly you'll get it according to understanding. The people surely will not refuse to requite suitably the devoted physician of their dead President. Leave that all to me, I'll see it through when Congress meets and send you the check for the amount if you'll leave your address with colored Sam my factotum. Sam and I'll attend to it. You needn't delay a day on account of the money, you'll be sure to get it, all in good time."

But although the pompous, self-sufficient little bloat, nothing doubted of his own ability to compass an end, some people remarked *when Congress met,* that it required rather more than one little man, even possessed of a factotum to run the whole country, and that the people had something to say about paying the worthy doctor's little bill; at any rate in the manner he wished and expected, but he received his pay in the end surely.

"And," chimed in the disinherited lawyer, who had been so ready with his services on the defence, "how about my fees, Bloaty?"

"You mustn't forget me. I'm not sure but those devoted friends of the 'vile assassin' would have gotten him into an asylum after all, at the very last, if it hadn't been for me and the Confessor there, we both worked hard that last week I can tell you. That little sister of his had secured a string of names a yard and more long, signed to a petition for the President, asking him to commute the sentence to life imprisonment, life imprisonment, ha! ha! his life would have been short, I reckon. which she was bound to take, *herself* in *person* to the President. A pretty kettle of fish we should have had then, don't you think so? Ha! ha! we had to tell her all sorts of stories, false as hell of course, to keep her away from him, myself, the Confessor and her Uncle John. She's a holy terror when she gets started on a track she thinks is right; about as crazy as her brother Jules on matters of conscience, but we managed her among us all, and that confounded petition never saw the light or got near the President, the Confessor and I took care of that.

"He's soft-hearted you all know. Look at him now, he's as pale as a ghost and trembling from head to foot as though he actually saw Jules Grieveau or the dead President come back to him. We feared if the little sister or lovely Miss Gascoigne got at him with their imploring, beseeching ways, he'd cave after all, and give us all away, but it's over now, thank the Lord or the Devil, as you please, and we can breathe easy."

"Yes," said J. G. Bamboozle, who seemed by natural fitness to be the spokesman of the party, and had faced about, drawn down his face, not forgetting his leering, "evil eye," and hemmed and hawed in the vain endeavor to clear his throat of a lump which threatened to annihilate his voice. "And now if you are ready we will attend to the business for which we are assembled. Gentlemen, this solemn occasion upon which we meet, the memorable day when we have witnessed the execution of 'the assassin' of our beloved and lamented President, calls for————"

CHAPTER XXXVIII.

WHAT MIGHT HAVE BEEN.—THE MOB.

" Henry Armstrong, as I live! Now, you villain," cried
Silas Smith, " I'll have your blood and your life, as you tried
years ago to take mine! "

And before anyone, even the President, mistrusted his intentions, Smith had made a spring for Henry's throat.

As they grappled, Gen. Gascoigne heard the name Henry
Armstrong—the name of the man who had defrauded his beautiful, noble sister Lucille of her best young love, had wrecked
years of her life; and *he* there, the " accidental " President was
Henry Armstrong! Surely no honorable man would have received the suffrages of a great people under an assumed name,
under *false colors.* And this man, this Gerald A. Johnson, was
the one who had been instrumental in getting him into the toils
of the conspirators, as in his own mind Gen. Gascoigne had
come to regard his associates, into the meshes of a net of steel
wrought chains, from which he found it impossible to free himself, even though his dead sister's crazy boy had been sacrificed.

Surely this Henry Armstrong, this Gerald A. Johnson, must
be a double-dyed villain; and upon the impulse of the moment,
as insane perhaps as the delusion of poor Jules, Gen. Gascoigne
fired, and Henry Armstrong, who was getting the better of
Smith, fell bleeding from a ghastly wound in the head, inflicted
by the General's sure aim; and he did not stop at this, the one
insane, reckless deed, sent him into a frenzy of excitement, for
stung by remorse, and with a sudden premonition that now
retribution was coming upon them all, that the curse of Jules
Grieveau was to be verified—he placed the muzzle of the pistol
at his own heart and fired again.

The shooting and the instant confusion ensuing scarcely attracted the attention of the two men at the window. Spideler
was stupid with wine, and only stared vacantly, mumbling to
himself, stammering, and with the drunken hiccough, about the
check. " I'll sq-hic-squeal, I will, Cronksey, dang you." And
Cronksey, whose eyes now beheld from the open window
where he stood spell-bound, frozen, paralyzed; a sight which
blanched his face till it was colorless as white marble, and his

brow was clammy with the dew of fear, would at that moment
have signed ten thousand checks, even the whole of his immense
fortune, away, could it have procured his escape from that spot
where were centered upon him wrathful glances, menacing
swift vengeance, from the congregated seething mass of humanity outside.

The people having somehow heard the rumor, that a party
of the much talked of conspirators had been discovered holding
a conference at the residence of Gen. Gascoigne, the assassin's
uncle, a mob was gathering in front of the house, and Cronksey well knew his time had come, and that there would be no
respite.

Some little time before the attack of Smith upon Henry
Armstrong, the Chief, leaving Uncle Tut with crazy Leonard
in custody, to watch, himself slipped out, hidden by the vines
and shrubbery, through the garden, joining his men stationed
around the place in ambush; and seeing the mob gathering, had
dispatched orders for the whole available police force to report
at once on the grounds of Gen. Gascoigne.

Soon after, Uncle Tut, hearing the shots, and seeing the
commotion in front through a crack in the door which had
been left for ventilation, no longer able to restrain his impetuous
nature, had rushed out from the hiding place into the study,
just as the women came running, screaming in alarm, from the
library across the hall, aiming also for the scene of the disaster.

Rushing past those who were striving to come out, not
knowing what they wanted except to escape from violence,
blood and distress, Lucille was the first to enter the room, where
she was encountered by the appalling sight of Henry her lost
love, lying apparently dead before her, upon the floor. One
thought only possessed her, to go to him, raise him in her
arms, clasp his bleeding head to her heart, while she implored
him to speak to her, look at her. Slowly the wounded man
opened wide his eyes, and with a deep sigh of happiness, murmured, "My darling, my life—" sinking instantly away again
in a faint like unto death.

Gen. Gascoigne, who had but succeeded in wounding, not
killing himself, gazed upon his sister and her lover with a dazed
expression, as though he were losing his mind, but he was quite
too weak to express his astonishment; Julia was now bending
over her husband, oblivious to the surroundings, and in real grief
at his sad plight.

When the police heard the sound of firing, they suddenly

appeared like the locusts of Egypt, everywhere, and before anyone knew what was happening, the supposed conspirators and all in the room were under arrest.

Uncle Tut had already tackled Silas Smith, and Aunt Debby seeing her husband through the open door in the midst of the melee, had tried her best to rush in and rescue him, but being encumbered with little Elsie in her arms, Aunt Debby was for the first time in her life too slow, and the door was closed against her.

But crazy Leonard, quicker than Aunt Debby, catching a glimpse of Spideler, sprang through, and with the exclamation, "Bless de Lord, dar's my ole massa at last, shoah, let me eat de debil," Leonard leaped upon the man, who, drunk as he was, knew enough to try to escape from danger, and had reached the threshold of the room; as a wild beast springs upon its prey, and before any one could could prevent him, Leonard, in his frenzy, had bitten Spideler's nose clean off.

There is no telling how much more of his individuality would have been sacrificed upon the shrine of vengeance, had not the men of the force taken Leonard away.

The reinforcement ordered by the Chief had now arrived, and numberless men, mounted and on foot, were on the premises ready for any emergency, and as it proved in good time, for when those on the outside heard the shots within, they made a rush, and every man, woman and child must have met a fearful fate, had not the police restrained the unreasoning wrath of the mob.

Sooner than it can be told, the Chief had surrounded the house by a force strong enough for their protection as well as safe-keeping. Only Cronksey came to any real immediate harm. Beset upon all sides, partially recovering from his trance like state of fear, trying to shun the danger, every moment growing more imminent, he foolishly jumped from the open window to the ground, which the mob seeing, broke pell-mell through the garden, breaking down shrubbery and even small trees, in their haste to get at the man whom they believed morally guilty of all the deviltry enacted in connection with the great frauds, and the assassination of the President. Upon him for the time was concentrated all the hate felt for a Benedict Arnold, who in the first revolution had tried to betray us to the English, for an Aaron Burr, a Jefferson Davis, for every traitor who has sought to overthrow our government, be he erring countryman or foreign potentate.

In this desperate strait, Cronksey endeavored to evade his pursuers, by secreting himself among the shrubbery, but soon ten men stood in the places of each, bush, vine and tree destroyed; being thus hardly pushed, rushing from cover to cover, as a hare hunted to its death, the wretched man essayed to scale the wall, but in this attempt also he failed, for reaching the top, hanging on by the iron spikes set closely together along the edge, those nearest in the crowd dragged him fiercely down, not heeding the lacerated, bleeding hands used only to dainty, gentlemanly work. At last the rabble had him in their clutches, hesitating not to end his life in the roughest, most precipitous manner.

Before the corpse was finally left dangling from the convenient lamp-post, the elegant and altogether exquisite *Cronksey* that was, had been utterly despoiled of every attraction, and none who had known him in life would have recognized the hideous cadaver, above whose head was placed the words, "Be it thus to all conspirators and traitors forevermore."

Crazy Jules. Grieveau made a better appearance when the doctors had finished their work and composed his remains to rest, lying peacefully in that upper room of his prison home, dressed neatly, with the placid smile which had settled upon his face when the spirit took its flight; and keeping him company, the fair flowers which Gertrude and Lucille had placed above his breast; than did the man of wonderful intellect but depraved heart, whose dead body hung helplessly there that night in the ghastly moonlight, wierdly swinging to and fro in the midnight breeze, with a look of hate and terror imprinted upon the distorted countenance, the last impression left upon the inanimate clay by the sin-steeped soul, departing to meet its God.

When the mob which had gathered at Gen. Gascoigne's, (as the rumor at first whispered, and then flying wildly from mouth to mouth, spread and was corroborated, that the men suspected of complicity in the "removal" of the martyred President, had been discovered while in conference and heard to confess to one another their scheme, and that their arrest was about to be made,) had satiated their fury upon Cronksey the typical conspirator and traitor, they dispersed contentedly, leaving the others to the care of the police and the troops, who had also been called into requisition.

After the turmoil subsided, surgeons were sent for, and Gen. Gascoigne, Henry Armstrong and Spideler, who was certainly one of the wounded, were removed to comfortable quarters in the General's residence, and placed under care of the doctors and women, but of course as closely guarded prisoners. .

Lucille begged to remain with Henry, who, recovering from his faint when the flow of blood had been stopped, and was now able again to speak, suplemented her request. The consent of the guards was readily obtained through the interposition of Chief Strong, who had disclosed himself to the stricken family of his old time friend, Dr. Gascoigne, assuring them that the course his oath of office required him to take towards them, had been a great grief, still continuing, and further, he hoped that when they came to the examination, Gen. Gascoigne, the President, and perhaps some of the others under arrest, would be able to prove their innocence of actual crime, either in the first or second degree; time and evidence must determine this point, his duty now was to the commonwealth, in the exercise of his prerogatives, he would deal as gently as possible with those in his charge, especially with the wounded men.

It was found that neither the President or Gen. Gascoigne had been fatally injured, and as Lucille nursed Henry through that long illness, so painful, and which several times came near ending in death, such perfect happiness and peace came to both, as is seldom experienced by mortals, and Lucille was fully repaid for all she had endured.

They conversed when Henry was able, of what each had experienced during the long years of sadness and trouble, and as Lucille recounted her longings, her sorrows and her fears, his love for her grew to adoration. He was never tired of watching her as she moved about the room, arranging every minutia with regard for comfort, convenience and taste; and his eyes would follow her beseechingly if she did not come near enough to his bed-side every few moments, that he might grasp her hand in silent caress, and she had no choice but to leave what she was doing, and go to him.

Lucille's mature but soft and loving touch would quiet his pain when opiates failed, and he could only sleep restfully while her hand lay upon his brow.

Many an hour did she sit stroking tenderly the aching head, or pressing lightly the feeble pulse, watching closely every symptom, when the patient was at the worst, but in spite of sickening dread, fatigue and anxiety over-powering, Lucille had never been so supremely happy and contented in all her life. Certainly, Henry's countenance now that he was canvalescent, indicated only joy when his eyes rested upon Lucille, though there was still a look of deep trouble when she was not near.

John too lay for weeks upon a bed of pain, and Julia tended her husband faithfully, if not with the absorbing love of Lucille's ministry at Henry's bedside.

When Julia understood that in the elegant Gerald A Johnson, who had captivated her fancy and temporarily aroused her passion, Lucille had found her lost lover, Henry Armstrong, she ceased to regard him as other than Lucille's affianced husband.

Women such as Julia, take a desperate liking for various men, and are, for the time being, in earnest, but they are incapable of a devoted, lifelong, enthusiastic affection, enduring through poverty, sickness and adversity, through evil repute, sometimes even in spite of unkindness.

But although naturally of a vain and frivolous nature, Julia was coming at last to appreciate her husband in some degree, now that she had seen his patient good temper, during a long siege of pain and discomfort; and these two felt themselves growing together as they traveled life's pilgrimage side by side.

Julia's honest passion for a man so lovable as Henry Armstrong, had softened and sweetened her character; for even a disappointing love is better than none at all, and besides the real grief she had passed through of late, had made her more considerate towards all with whom she came in contact.

CHAPTER XXXIX.

GEN. GASCOIGNE'S STORY.—CONSPIRATORS INDICTED.

As the wounded men were now recovering, the minds of all reverted to the causes producing the catastrophe which had befallen them, the assassination, the rumors of conspiracy, the execution of the crazy scape-goat, the unwise meeting for conference, and finally the arrests; and Gen. Gascoigne was glad to relieve himself from the distressing strain of self-imposed secrecy, by relating to the Chief all he knew of the bearing of recent events upon the points at issue.

He made a clean breast of his connection with the great frauds; how for a long time, he, with many others, did not understand that they were frauds, but had been enticed into these speculations, as they were called, by the smooth tongues and blandishments of Cronksey, Silas Smith and Spideler, drawing them in little by little, until all their available capital was invested, and ruin was upon them unless the scheme could be pulled through. "But" said Gen. Gascoigne, "I, long ago, withdrew from the whole business, and am a poor man to-day."

With flashing eye, the gallant General related how these men spared not even the honored General-in-Chief of the army, who had led the country on to final victory in the late civil war, and should have been exempt from their sacreligious touch; how by their mercenary machinations, he was induced to squander the competence secured by his friends for an old age coming fast upon him; and besides, his connection, though indirectly, with them, had cast a blot upon his fair name, which could hardly be removed, and "For this injury to him and to me as well," said the General hoarsely, "no consideration can ever atone."

Gen. Gascoigne recounted too, how, finding themselves unable to cope with the magnitude of the venture, and realizing their desperate predicament, they had with one accord, assented to the suggestion of Cronksey and Smith, conveyed through Spideler, that they leave the whole affair to them, they managing it their own way; *their way*, resulting in blacker villainy than any had imagined possible. How, when too late for a remedy, although *mistrusting* what that wickedness was, having no actual proof upon which to bring those they believed

guilty to justice, and dreading an epoch of dangerous public
excitement, should a disclosure be attempted, they had, with
one accord, waiving consultation, decided upon remaining passive, and deeming it futile to beat against the current, hopelessly
drifting with the tide, as a sure result which might easily have
been foreseen, they had struck at last upon the rocks.

Not one had been willing to take the responsibility of casting a fire-brand into the minds of the already suspicious populace, for a terrific explosion was almost certain to follow, which
might rend into fragments the republic, and although this was
exactly what Smith and Cronksey had planned, the others were
not ready for any such outcome.

"It were better that Myra's crazy boy should suffer an ig-
nominious death unjustly, than that such a crisis should occur,"
said Gen. Gascoigne.   Chief Strong and detective Tutty Swanson had felt this truth, as they proceeded with their investigations, and they, as well as the guilty ones, who knew the real
state of the case, trembled from day to day, fearing that Gen.
Gascoigne or the President, whom they by some means had
ascertained was formerly acquainted with the family of Jules
Grieveau, should reveal all they knew or suspected, in their
endeavor to save him.

During the whole time from the firing of the shot until the
execution, these two men were as closely watched as Jules himself, by their own friends; but not before the denouement, did
any know that the Chief of the Secret Service, seconded by
Uncle Tut, the detective, was also keeping over them a strict
espionage.

Even now that the arrests were made their vigilence did
not relax, and while Cronksey had met a retribution as swift
as terrible, and Silas Smith, the Doctor and the others were occupying fellon's-cells, these two, Gen. Gascoigne and the accidental President, were also prisoners awaiting recovery only to
encounter the ordeal of a criminal trial.

The speaker of the house had been installed President pro tem,
in the interval of that official's disability, and the machinery of the
government was moving along smoothly. But the dear public, especially the news-mongers, were still in trouble, as to the mysterious shooting which occurred at Gen. Gascoigne's on the day of
the arrests.   They at first attributed the tragedy to jealousy on
the part of the General towards the handsome President; but
when through the garrulous Leonard it transpired that Gerald
A. Johnson was really an old-time lover of Gen. Gascoigne's

beautiful sister Lucille, (at the age of forty accounted one of the handsomest women in Washington,) this lover, strangely enough, whom the General had never seen, and therefore did not recognize in him the Henry Armstrong who had jilted his sister, in years long gone, until Silas Smith, who also counted him an enemy, had spoken his real name. When they learned about the horrible episode in the Rockies, causing him to pass for years under an assumed name; when the rumor gained credence that the old love and engagement had been renewed, and that Miss Gascoigne was devotedly nursing the President through his dangerous illness, although now he was under suspicion and arrest on account of recent events, and must, if he recovered, stand trial with the others; when these items had been corroborated, the prying gossips were just wild with excited curiosity to know all the rest.

As to Henry and Lucille, and why Gen. Gascoigne had assailed the President, it was plain when the mystery of the changed name was unraveled; but for what reason had he shot himself?

This was never made clear to the public, for only the Chief and Uncle Tutty Swanson and Gen. Gascoigne's immediate friends knew the remorse which for so long had been straining every nerve, rendering existence a burden, and culminating in the attempt upon his own life. The inference at last was, that a taint of insanity existed in the Gascoigne and Grieveau families after all, which was liable to develop upon any sudden excitement.

These, wise in their own conceit, did not stop to consider the fact that both Lucille and Gertrude had been under greater intensity of anxiety heightened by grief, than Gen. Gascoigne had ever known, and *that without losing their equilibrium*, the difference being caused by the possession of a *satisfied*, as against a *guilty conscience.*

But the news-gathering public were sure they understood the whole matter fully, and desisted in their search.

As the President and Gen. Gascoigne were recovering rapidly, the country was alive with expectation and excitement in view of the developments likely to occur at the approaching trial of the men who had been arrested on suspicion of conspiracy to defraud the government, if no worse.

Just why the party of gentlemen who had been found at the house of Gen. Gascoigne, enjoying themselves, on the afternoon of the execution of Jules Grieveau, had been so roughly dis-

19

turbed, no one but themselves, Uncle Tut and Chief Strong, as yet altogether knew.

The rumor had started when the police were ordered to surround the house that a discovery of conspiracy had been made, which seemed probable enough, the General being so nearly related to the "assassin;" and it was said also that Cronksey was one of the party, and the people believed that were a conspiracy proved, this man would without doubt be found to be the "ring-leader;" and lately it had been acknowledged, as had been asserted, that Cronksey was own cousin to Myra, the mother of Jules Grieveau; Cronksey's father and Jules' mother being descended from the same English lord. This fact exerting a peculiar influence over the boy, who, being by nature a hero worshiper, thought his celebrated relative the crowning glory of the family tree, and one of the greatest men the world ever saw, and under his leadership, willing to go to any extreme.

Putting these items together, when the house of Gen. Gascoigne was surrounded, the mob seeing Cronksey, whom they hated on general principles, they made a rush destroying him in a twinkling, for the time satisfying their revenge; since when they had been quietly waiting for further developments and for the law to interpose its powerful arm.

In the proper course of events the men who had been arrested, President and all, were brought into the same court-room where Jules Greiveau had been arrained, tried and sentenced; and after a preliminary examination, those who were found with suspicions confirmed by adequate proof were held for trial.

Such excitement was never known, but the well trained force under the control of the Marshal of the District, who had been an intimate friend of the martyred President, held the populace in check until a thorough investigation was had sufficient to bring an indictment.

The people were not in a mood for trifling, and watched every movement made, determined that no truth should be suppressed, no villainy left uncovered. At this point the slightest mistake, blunder, or trickery would have, if discovered, brought about an uprising of the people, clamoring wildly, unreasonably perhaps, for justice, for vengeance.

Had they seen a disposition on the part of the authorities to keep back any fact, or to shield anyone suspected, no power could have controlled their wrath, and a wave of anarchy, riot and bloodshed must have swept over the country, getting its impetus from Washington, the center of Government, such as has never been experienced on this continent; distrust, reigning suspense, every man's hand against every other, until our loved Republic sinking under a military dictatorship must have gone down, as sank the Roman Republic, as all Republics since the world began have disintegrated and disappeared, and the fair goddess of Liberty despoiled of her rightful home, defrauded of her children, gone weeping through all the Earth, homeless, childless, dying.

Happily for the present and the future, for ourselves and for posterity, was this calamity prevented. In this instance those having power were as honestly in earnest to discover the truth, and have absolute justice measured out to the guilty and the innocent alike, as were the people themselves.

The Chief of the secret service with the power, the facts, the case, in his own hands; had no intention anyone should escape deserving of punishment, or that any should suffer, being innocent.

Such confidence had the people in this man and his integrity, as well as ability, they waited patiently while the facts he had accumulated were being unfolded and the guilt placed where it belonged.

By this man's wisdom and careful prudence at this critical juncture of national affairs was the excitement controlled, distrust removed, confidence in the Government restored, and disaster for the time at least averted.

It was found that although these with others had blindly placed their money in the hands of Smith and Cronksey, to be used in the furtherance of the great frauds, meaning only to invest in a legitimate speculation, no one knew of what was in the mind of Cronksey except Smith, the doctor his old friend of the western claim, and Spideler.

Mob law had already disposed of Cronksey, and it only remained to be seen what should be done with the doctor, Smith and Spideler.

Spideler soon settled the matter as to himself by turning States evidence. Since Cronksey's demise Spideler seemed to have come to himself, and to have recovered the slight degree of manhood originally belonging to him, at best very little, but quite as much as could be expected of a man who would treat his faithful servant as Spideler had used poor Leonard.

Even with this added testimony, the proof brought before the Grand Jury upon the preliminary investigation could not be construed as criminating anyone living except Smith and the doctor; Cronksey being dead and Spideler giving evidence which could not be dispensed with, only Smith and the doctor were finally arraigned for trial.

It turned out that the accidental President and the others had allowed themselves to be thrown into a state of *morbid fear* of the *populace* although really *guilty* of *no crime* or *complicity with crime, but only frightened at the connection which they knew could be shown between themselves and two men whom they suspected of the blackest villainy;* a hint of which getting into the popular mind would they feared bring dire results. The suspicion had already lodged and hence the extreme caution, even to the disguise of the President when going to attend the conference called by Cronksey.

When the announcement was made that *Silas Smith* and the *doctor only* were indicted, one as an instigator, the other as accesory to the "removal" of the late President, the people were well satisfied, cheer after cheer went up, nothing could stop them in the manifestation of wild exultation.

As for the General in Chief of the Army, he had long been the idol of the people and they would believe nothing ill of him.

Gen. Gascoigne was scarcely less a favorite, and all Washington at least adored the handsome accidental President who had by a sad tragedy been made the Chief Magistrate.

As for Bamboozle, there was no direct proof against him, although Cronksey had once accused him openly of "wrecking a President," supposedly by failing to win the man who stood in the way over to their side of the contest, thus preventing an investigation; a work for which he had been detailed by Cronksey and Smith, and in which they long afterwards came to believe he had played them false; but the people hated him for a sly, tricky, double-faced demagogue, full of fraud and deceit, and after a little, finding it very cold over here at home, he departed for more congenial European climes, and was never heard from more.

The confessor and the attorney who had deceived poor Jules Grieveau, suppressing the truth for the sake of the pay received, though no criminal process could be brought against them either, yet in the minds of the people, they forever after remained under a ban of reproach.

CHAPTER XL.

TRIAL OF THE CONSPIRATORS.—SPIDLER'S CONFESSION.

The usual time elapsing, and the necessary legal formulas having been obeyed, Smith and the doctor were brought before the same Judge who sat upon the bench when Jules was tried —a Judge, who against his will, had been overpowered by popular clamor and the strength of the prosecution, giving rulings adverse to Jules Grieveau.

A jury was empaneled and the new district attorney, (appointed in the place of Bloaty, who had died suddenly of an excruciatingly painful disease brought upon him by dissipation,) assisted by the Attorney General, also newly installed, they commenced the prosecution of Smith and the doctor.

Spideler being sworn told how Cronksey had hinted, the only way to save his clients, the men engaged in the great frauds, was by changing the administration, and putting the Vice-President in power. Said Cronksey, "I can manage him easily enough, I've got a screw on him, ha! ha! and he's very ambitious too; but the man at the helm now will ruin the whole business; we can do nothing with him, I've had Bamboozle and two or three others working with him for a month; but he's as stubborn as a mule. They've even threatened him, and told him plainly that *something terrible would happen*, if he did not desist; but it's no use, he won't budge one inch, but says he's bound to go straight ahead—go to hell—he will." And said Spideler, "I saw what was wanted, and soon after, I got a notice to go down to Washington and look around and report which way the wind was blowing, and see what had become of that 'crank' we'd sent on that insurance business; see if he'd got crazy enough to blow his own brains out yet, &c. Well," said Spideler, "I took the hint as intended, and went down to Washington and talked 'removal' and 'inspiration' to cranky Jules Grieveau, and showed him the Stalwart newspapers, which were full of the idea that the President ought to be out of the way, until he thought of nothing else night or day; finally he announced that the 'Deity and me' would fix everything up all right; and then I knew he'd go along persistently until he had accomplished the needed 'removal,' for you see nothing could stop him if once he got a notion of doing a certain thing, and he'd do it his own way too. He would never allow that any one could advise him, much less dictate. 'He always knew what he was about,' he would declare; he'd never own to any 'boss,' unless possibly 'Deity,' he always called himself 'God's man,' and seemed to regard the 'Deity' as a sort of senior partner in some great business they two had undertaken together. But he was a man who could be influenced, to anything, if you went at him right, not letting him know your purpose, but just filling his mind full of the idea, and then making him think he was doing it alone, that the thought was the outgrowth of his own wonderful brain, for this was his estimate of himself." Spideler did not know this was the *egotism of insanity* afflicting all disordered brains, unless the dementia tends to the stupidity of idiocy, when the same thing shows itself in the willful, stubborn ugliness so hard to deal with; instead of, as in the case of Jules Grieveau, in good natured elation and extravagance of ideas and schemes, often leading to most unexpected and cruel deeds; being regarded by. the insane perpetrator, as eminently suitable and proper, often glorying in the accomplishment.

All this Spideler did not understand from the medical view of the case; but as he said, continuing his testimony, "I saw from the first that he was just the man for our work; and the best of it all was, he'd be sure to claim the whole credit himself, and be so fearful of not getting it all, he would never acknowledge that any one had even so much as hinted such a thing. Knowing him as I did intimately for months, the only wonder was that he was willing to divide the glory of the deed even with the 'Deity' Himself; ha! ha!" laughed Spideler; but this unseemly merriment was instantly checked by the court.

" He was such a kind of a girl-boy," said Spideler, "never having practiced any manly exercises, not knowing how to swim, or ride, or shoot a gun, more afraid of a revolver than of the Devil himself, that I feared he'd never get up courage enough to fire the shot after all. At last I hit upon the thought of the ' Deity and me ' theory and filled his mind full of this, until he believed that God Almighty wanted the President ' removed ' to save the country from a civil war, and that *he* was God's chosen instrument for the work. This was all right so far, but now another trouble suggested itself; how was I to get him in training so he'd ever hit the mark when the time came? If he missed after I got him worked up to the point of firing the shot, the whole business would end in failure, and I knew there wasn't one chance in a thousand of our finding another 'crank' just in his condition, *just fitted for the occasion.* And besides, when I received the signal, the thing must be *done forthwith,* without *delay,* without *mistake*—with no *possibility* of failure—for there were millions of money involved, and danger of a prison cell to hundreds of our men, should the Government probe into their secrets, which the incumbent President had avowed his determination to do, and unless he could be dissuaded from his purpose, he must *go.* *This was my order* from the 'Boss,' there," looking towards Smith. At this pointed disclosure from Spideler—a low, muttering growl, ending in a venomous hiss, long and sharp and menacing, came up from every part of that packed court-room, and for a few moments it seemed that the prisoners were to meet the fate of Cronksey. But it proved that almost every tenth man was a policeman, so thickly were they scattered among the crowd, besides the uniformed force about the prisoners, the Judge's bench, the jury, the witness box, and the doors.

The Judge, rising to his feet, brought his gavel down stroke after stroke, until the resounding noise diverted the attention of the angry mob from the prisoners and from themselves, to the Chief of the Secret Service, who calmly standing by the Judge surveying the crowd, addressed them, " Gentlemen, I trust you will obey the order of the court, and the decorum of this important trial, remaining quiet and patient to the end, letting the law decide this case according to all the evidence produced; remember we have heard only the testimony of one man. I appeal to you as good citizens, not again to interrupt the Court. *I give you my word,* based upon my oath of office, that the *truth,* whatever it may be in this case, shall be *fully shown,* so far as I have been able to secure the witnesses for the use of the prosecution." This was enough, the tumult subsided, and the Judge, turning to Spideler, said, "Let the witness proceed."

" Well, as I said, the man, Jules Grieveau, didn't know how to *hold* a revolver, much less *fire* one; but I got over the difficulty by suggesting that in case we did have a war, or an uprising of the people, every man ought to know how to defend himself if attacked, and told him he ought to get a revolver and practice shooting at a mark, which he finally did, I going with him, selecting one sure to hit within a foot of anything it pointed at. And then he went down to the bank of the river and shot at fences and finally willow trees, until he got so he could hit one. At first he complained of the noise hurting his head, and

as I watched him from behind the fence the first morning he
went 'out hunting,' I laughed until I burst my jacket buttons,
to see him jump when the iron went off. The next day I told
him to stuff some cotton in his ears, which he did, and got along
all right after that. I kept him practicing at a mark for about
two weeks, and he could hit fairly well at the end of that time.

But there was too much at stake, and I was getting nervous
myself at the last. I had got notice that when the message
came over the wires, 'that murder was to be preferred to suicide,' I might know the time had come and I must be ready at
the depot the next morning at nine o'clock with my man. As
I said, I feared Jules wouldn't hit in a vital place, if at all, and
so at the last moment I decided to fix the bullets so if they got
in at all they'd do the work, and I made up my mind not to risk
the 'removal' to Grieveau's blundering aim, but I just provided
myself with a good shooting iron, and when the time came, after
he had fired twice as I told him to do, one shot hitting the President, and the other a poor dog which happened to be passing,
while Grieveau was shouting and claiming all the glory, I
just quietly put in a shot myself aimed at the heart from the back,
and only that the President was actually sinking to the floor at the
time, my shot would have finished him; as it was the backbone
was grazed, and they said the bullet passed down into the ab-
domen where it lay encysted, doing no particular harm, until
the surgeons found it after the man was dead. I don't know
how that was but my bullet struck nearly opposite the heart.
But the bullet I had fixed for Grieveau, although not touching
any vital part, did its work too, the *poisoned bullet* I mean. To
make the thing sure—*sure to stay*—I had to secure the services
of the doctor there, but it took some money for that though, I
can tell you. The doctor's a great fellow for money, but I
fetched him, and had him at the depot all ready on time too.
And he stuck by to the end, although it was a longer job than
any of us reckoned on. We'd all been glad to have backed out
before we got through, but we couldn't—the die was cast—
there was no retreat. It was a terrible piece of business from
beginning to ending. We never really thought it would have to
be done; at any rate we hoped the President could be won over.
It was all Bamboozle's fault that he wasn't. While we were
depending on him more than anyone else to bring this about,
he was playing traitor to the cause, and just putting the
President up to be more contrary than ever, 'widening the
breach.' You see he hadn't got over his spitefulness towards the

leaders, for throwing him overboard at the Chicago Convention, and nominating the man who was elected, and he meant to get even with them by manipulating the President and running the administration to suit himself. You see it was next thing to being president. This is what the leaders mean when they say 'he wrecked a President'—and he did.

" I guess this is about all there is to tell, only I forgot to say that I told Grieveau he'd better leave all his papers and manuscripts at the news stand, for that agent connected with one of the Chicago stalwart papers before he fired the shot, and that I'd see him set right before the people if he did; and the poor fellow obeyed my advice for a wonder, for he'd got mightily attached to me, he was very affectionate. You see I didn't know what he might have been scribbling, and meant to get possession of his writings. And then it was me suggested his going to the jail for safe keeping. I didn't want to see him torn limb from limb before my eyes.

" He wouldn't consent at first, he didn't like the idea at all, and I had to hire a carriage and let him go down and see what a nice, clean, comfortable place it was, not at all like the old Toombs prison, in New York, where he had once been kept longer than he liked on a charge of vagrancy—not at all. He finally agreed to give himself up, immediately after firing the shot, and go quietly to the jail until the people could be informed of his inspiration and be made to understand the matter. It was actually ridiculous the way he looked at the whole affair, only that anyone knowing how simple-minded he was could not help pitying the poor fellow.

" I believe this is all I know about the business, all there is to say."

At any rate it was all Spideler ever had a chance to tell; for when the guards were taking him back to prison that night for safe keeping from the mob, who had declared their intention of lynching the little dog, as they called him; when opposite the Capitol, just where a rascal protected by those in power had tried to kill Jules during his trial; they surrounded the prison-van, as the vehicle was styled which carried him, just as it had so many times conveyed poor Jules Grieveau; and they tore him roughly out, calling him a traitor even to His friends! A murderer! Using means fit only for a savage, or a slave-driving and torturing " Legree! " Exasperated to frenzy at the thought of all his diabolical deeds as a slave-owner and seller, as a sneaking, cruel, plotting murderer, as the entrapper of the crazy, foolish tool with which he had accomplished the work, and all for gain, from the lowest, most mercenary motives; the mob deeming the little imp too low and vile even for their touch, wrenched the iron spikes composing the fences in the vicinity wherever possible from their fastenings, and lifting the terror-stricken, abject creature not gently upon them, they tossed him from one to another to and fro, batting him about, applying heavy brogans not unfrequently as the spirit moved them to rougher work—heaping all manner of abuse and indignity upon him, as they had a few months before done with Cronksey.   Master and servant ending their worse than useless lives in a similar way, each unmourned, unregretted even by their compeers in crime.

CHAPTER XLI.

THE FAIR EVANGELISTIC WIDOW. — HER STORY. — THE CONVICTION.

A sensation was produced next day upon convening of the court, by the announcement of Spideler's fate; and also by the appearance of another voluntary witness for the prosecution, whom a quickened conscience had driven upon the stand, in spite of the reward which the witness of the previous day had received for his testimony, given with the intent of shielding himself from merited punishment; which the people understanding, had taken his case into their own hands.

The new witness proved none ôther than the woman who had been with Smith on the "claim" long ago out in Illinois, passing as his wife, being for years since until quite recently his mistress. She was also the "fair widow," whom Spideler had introduced to Jules Grieveau for the special purpose of working upon his imagination and passions, thus hastening the climax of insanity.

The woman had it seemed, been honestly converted at one of the Moody meetings, and truly repented of any wrong she might have done in the past, and of the part she had unwittingly played, in influencing the mind of Jules Grieveau to commit so dreadful an act, as firing upon the President of the United States.

She now came of her own accord to Washington, offering to tell all she knew of the assassination, in the cause of truth and justice.

Her testimony was mainly against Smith, and being placed upon the stand confronting him face to face, this under oath, was her story:

"Years ago I met the man Smith, there," pointing with trembling finger and flashing eye at her victim, "in what was then the far west. I was young, perhaps attractive, surely honest and loving—he won my heart—myself—body and soul, under a sacred promise of immediate marriage, which was never fulfilled; but instead he took me with him out on a desolate prairie, where he had staked a claim and thrown a few boards together which he called a cabin. In this home I was installed.

"I remained because I could do no better. Shame prevented

my returning to my own home.   My friends thought I had
been married before going with him, and being an orphan, living with distant relatives who had little sympathy for me, I
dared not return to them with my story, they never would have
believed me, and I should have been turned away disgraced—
and besides, I loved the man," said the woman, tears now streaming from her eyes.

" We continued living together as man and wife for years
after, he drinking a good deal, I following his example to
drown my troubles.   Finally after a desperate brawl, into which
he drew me trying to jump another man's claim, and in which
he came near losing his life, after forcing me to swear falsely in
a lawsuit over the dispute—when he had partially recovered,
we left the country together still as man and wife.   I lived
with him for years, he sometimes treating me kindly, many
times otherwise; but persistently refusing to give me a legal
right to bear his name or call him husband.

"After a time when he became rich and powerful, he began
paying attention to other women, as the fancy took him, and—
and"—here the woman's trembling voice and tearful face proved
her emotion, ending in convulsive sobs, "he—he shook me off,
he broke my heart, wrecked my life, and now, I don't care what
becomes of me, or what you do with me—for I love him still."

Regaining her composure, she proceeded: "After refusing
utterly to have anything more to do with me, he advised me to
'try some other man,' as he expressed it; and I did try to form
attachments for other men, but I could not.   I had for so many
years regarded this man as my husband in fact if not in law,
my whole existence being bound up in him and his affairs.
He can be as lovely as an Angel of light when he chooses, and
as ugly as Satan too, when he likes," said the woman, her eyes
flashing again.

"Although I felt all the ownership any wife can have in her
husband, he cunningly avoided establishing a marriage holding
good in law, by refusing to live with me long enough in one
place or allowing me to bear his name; thus making me a respectable—self-respecting married woman.   All these years I
was only his mistress; that most degraded of all slaves to the
passions of men.   His mistress!   And I would have given my life
for him," sobbed the woman.

"At last," she said, drying her eyes again, "I thought if I
came across an honest, kind-hearted man who wanted to marry
me, (for I was still an attractive woman,) even though he was

not so smart or so rich as that villain Silas Smith there, I would unite myself with some one and try and forget my past life.

"Well, about this time I met a gentleman to whom I was introduced by the name of Mr. Jules Grieveau, a lawyer, as was said, poor but honest, religious and a gentleman, and I assure you he *was* a gentleman before he got so crazy.

"I had been grieving and grieving for a long time over my dreadful trouble, when one day in New York I wandered into a place called 'the Tabernacle,' an immense structure erected for the holding of 'revival meetings,' as the gatherings congregating to listen to the ministrations of a noted Evangelist, were styled.

"I had been going about the streets all day, trying to forget myself, and being attracted by the sound of a thousand or more people singing together, old fashioned Methodist revival hymns, not caring much what I did, but very tired, I went in and sat down.

"After the singing, which from the number of voices and the hearty enthusiasm was soul inspiring, a man of magnificent physique and powerful voice, eyes large, black and penetrating, arose, and clasping his hands, kneeled before the great congregation, fervently invoking the Divine blessing.

"While the people were recovering their breath almost taken away by the impetuosity of the short appeal, a slender man, a complete contrast to the other, with fine features, noble brow, loving eyes of purest blue, a mouth tender and delicate as a woman's, came forward; seating himself at a little parlor organ, and touching the keys with his long, white fingers, after a short prelude, the marvelously sweet, far-reaching, spiritual voice with which the singer was endowed, entranced those hundreds of eager people, as though by some Angel descended from on High.

"The words, simple enough, were fervid and appealed directly to the heart, 'Jesus Lover of My Soul, Let Me to Thy Bosom Fly.' When the sweet singer had finished, tears were streaming from many eyes in that vast assembly; my heart was melted even before the wonderful sermon was commenced. A sermon denouncing sin but not the sinner, calling upon those who had done wrong to repent and flee from the wrath to come, from the fire which consumeth, to come to Jesus—Jesus who died to save—died that we might live. At the close, hundreds in response to the final invitation crowded tearfully about the altar, I among the number.

"The man who had so stirred our hearts came down to the

altar rail, and passing from one to another gave each a message
of admonishment, of warning, of entreaty, of love—the love of
Jesus. The magnetism of the man was wonderful. I would
have died willingly for Jesus then, or done any deed for Jesus'
sake, so enthused was I by the thought that Jesus was the lover
of my soul; that He offered me love pure and unselfish, not the
disappointing human love, but the love immeasurable, satisfying,
infinite and Divine, offered freely without price, asking only
love in return.

"After this I went to the meetings every day, three, four
times a day; feeding upon the excitement which I found there.
One day I met the very last person I should have expected to
see in such a place. A man whom I felt to be a villain of so
deep a dye that scarcely could the blood of Jesus even make
him white. A man whose sins I knew to be as scarlet, for I
had often heard Smith and himself and a man they called Cronksey, talking over their plans together, and I knew they never
mentioned any but their mildest schemes in my hearing, and
that they were engaged in worse deviltries than I ever heard or
dreamed of; at any rate I was quite sure neither of the three
were saints or likely to become such, and here was little Spideler in company with a man who any one could see at a glance
was a regular devotee, and honest too; and Spideler was attending a 'revival meeting' with this man—what on earth could it
mean thought I. Soon Spideler saw me, and my astonishment
was not greater than was his evidently; however, with a quick
change of countenance, a peculiar expression which I had never
noticed before coming into his face, he watched his chance,
edging around the crowd, and just as the meeting was breaking
up, he managed to get near me at the door, and stepping up
with his companion, introduced him without asking leave, as
Mr. Jules Grieveau. He seemed a gentleman and Spideler being on intimate terms with the man I regarded as my husband,
frequenting our room before I left him, took a liberty perhaps,
but not an unusual one for him.

" Whenever I went to the meetings after that day, invariably
Spideler and Mr. Grieveau would meet me near the main entrance, a consummation seeming to come about by design; but
as I found my new acquaintance honest-hearted, kind and agreeable, I had no objection; in fact, I soon came to feel under obligation for the introduction, for I was becoming attached to my
friend, Mr. Grieveau.

" He was so entirely different from any of the men I had

met. Absolutely there was not a particle of the villain in his nature. Other men with whom I had become acquainted through my relations with Smith had been nearly *all villains* through and through.

"After Spideler had established an intimacy between us, he seemed satisfied to leave us mostly to ourselves. We talked much upon different subjects, and I found him passably well-informed. He had some unusual theories, and his mode of reasoning was peculiar; but somehow he would arrive at pretty fair conclusions generally—by instinct it appeared to me—but one day he made such a queer remark about something after there had been great excitement at the meeting, that I was really startled.

"From that time I could see that the intense excitement of the meetings was injurious, and I tried to disuade his constant attendance, but to no purpose. He grew more strange each time we met, and finally I could see that he was absolutely insane upon certain subjects.

" The idea of Divine direction had taken possession of his mind, and he refused to attend to the slightest matter until he had first prayed over it, and he carried this to a ridiculous extreme.

"Once, when I remonstrated, he became indignant and declared, that ' If in answer to prayer he got the inspiration that Deity (as he called God) wanted him to kill anybody, he'd do it sure, if he was shot dead the next minute.'

" This, and some other things, opened my eyes to the fact that I was becoming attached to a lunatic, and I soon broke off the intimacy; but I never thought he would harm anyone, he was always so kind and affectionate.

" When I began to repulse him, he was greatly distressed, and at last followed me around as a child does its mother—surely he was growing rapidly worse—more insane each day—but so quiet and apparently harmless. I really pitied, but could do nothing for him, except, as he seemed very poor, I often gave him money; indeed, I now believe he must have suffered only for the kindness he received from myself and Spideler.

"" After making some provision for his immediate wants, by depositing a considerable amount in the hands of Spideler for his use, I left New York to be rid of him. I knew no other way out of my foolish entanglement.

" I heard nothing more of Mr. Grieveau until the late President was shot, when recalling his condition, and the remarks he had made, I cannot say the news that he was the assassin very much surprised me although I was deeply grieved. Immediately I set myself to the task of helping him out of the trouble he was in, and endeavored to have him tried for lunacy instead of murder; but I soon found I had undertaken more than I or anyone could accomplish.

"Being known as the mistress for years past, if not the lawful wife, of so influential a man as Silas Smith, I was not without power with a certain class, and after a second trial was refused, I succeeded in securing many names to be affixed to the petition for commutation of sentence to life imprisonment, which was prepared to be sent to the accidental President, but which I afterwards understood he never saw.

" In the course of my investigations, which were commenced early in the history of the case, I found out that Smith and Spideler with someone behind them, had been for a long time, even before the nomination of the lamented President, working a desperate venture to defraud the Government and the people, a scheme which contemplated involving the country in a foreign, if not perhaps also another civil war, and that the predicament of poor Mr. Grieveau was the outcome of a contingency, which had all along been considered probable, in the course of events liable to produce an emergency.

" Smith had years before this initiated me in the duties of a detective, and I had helped him work many a crooked transaction.

" I had mistrusted at the last that the infernal scoundrel lately known as A. J. Spideler, Esq., had introduced me to Mr. Grieveau for the purpose of working upon his passions, and thus hastening the climax of an insanity all his life slowly developing, and which was nearing the point at the time our acquaintance commenced, when some catastrophe must occur. Bitterly I regretted my blindness, for certainly when I first met Mr. Grieveau no one would have thought him more than queer, more than fanatical, and I now firmly resolved, if possible, to save him from a cruel death.

" With this thought I went to Washington, and saw Jules Grieveau in his cell. I had no difficulty in securing this privilege as those in charge seemed to know the name of Silas Smith, even the warden and the underlings of the jail, and of me as his former mistress and confidential agent. Up to this time I had no quarrel or formal break with Mr. Smith, although I ceased to live with him after my conversion, and giving his name as my credential, it proved the necessary 'open Sesame' to the assassin's cell, although at that time admittance was refused to ordinary visitors.

"How the change which I saw in poor Jules Grieveau shocked and horrified me I cannot describe, and can never forget; those incessantly rolling, quivering eye-balls glaring wildly at me, that worn haggard face, those manacled hands, haunt me still. Oh! it was horrible! horrible," and the woman, again overcome, covered her face with her hands and wept aloud. Soon she went on:

"After the first encounter and the excitement produced by seeing a new face, whether friend or foe, he knew not, had passed, Jules seemed partially to remember me, at least he liked me and trusted me as he did no one else, for, previous to my visit he had learned to distrust every one who came near him. This was long before the advent of the Confessor, and before his sister or Aunt Lucille had seen him; for them also he seemed to have an almost natural affection.

"The authorities of the jail allowed me free access, supposing I was a detective acting especially in the interest of Silas Smith and the 'Ring.' Smith being abroad in London had no idea of what I was at, and those in the secret who knew of my movements believed me working with them; for there were two others pretending friendship who were paid detectives. One a former acquaintance of Jules, in Chicago, whose name, no less than his character, was so nearly allied to Raynard the fox, and who, when Jules was on trial for his life, basely swore to utterances which never came from the lips of the accused at all, but which this man, well rewarded by the prosecution, declared he had received from the prisoner in the first gush of confidence upon meeting one whom he had known in better days. Utterances which established the theory of the prosecution, that Jules was a sane villain, himself only to blame. Even in Washington, during the trial, they dubbed this man 'THE SPY.'

"And there was still another, who, if he did not steal money from the unfortunate, friendless prisoner, a commodity of which he was destitute, he was certainly guilty of "larceny as bailee," for he took notes of his case in shorthand, from which he prepared an article for a New York paper, *devoid of truth*, receiving for the same $500. An article intended to work against the then utterly defenseless man. Afterward those notes were turned over to the prosecution to be used as evidence against the

20

prisoner, but upon examination there was found so much that would help instead of hurting his case, they were destroyed. This same Bailee swearing afterwards upon the witness stand that he 'had destroyed his notes,' for he knew they would contradict his testimony. He, too, was made to feel the finger of scorn pointing at him derisively from that court-room, for it was said no one who heard believed his story, and that he went from the stand with red, confused, abashed count-enance, as did many another witness for the prosecution.

"However I went every day to see Jules, and at last gained his confidence; as we talked, I found that some one had assured Jules certain protection, that he should be cared for, exonerated, and lauded as a hero if he would go quietly to the jail, after firing the shot upon the President. He had expected to be petted, visited and made much of by his 'friends outside' as he said, and 'his friend, the President,' as he called him; especially depend-ing upon this man, himself for a long time under duress, though not actual arrest; watched even more vigilantly than Jules Grieveau, both before and after he became President. Jules did not at first know the wounded President still lived, and evi-dently thought '*his friends*' had come into power.

"But in all this expectation, poor Jules Grieveau was doomed to bitter disappointment. Not being apprised of the true state of the case, not knowing why the promises given him had not been kept, he had come to distrust every one who approached him.

"But at last by slow degrees I gathered that Spideler had been the go-between who manipulated the crazy man for the fatal work.

"He said, 'Spideler told me this, Spideler said that,' and I got at the fact that Spideler had for months before the catastro-phe been filling the poor fellow's crazy brain with suggestions of the very thing which happened; even directing him as to the minutia, Jules not recognizing this, but thinking himself had received the commission direct from 'Deity,' believing the Most High was inspiring him from day to day in all the 'modus op-erandi,' when, pitiful to know, it came from that vicious little black Spideler as direct as any man's thought and desire can come to another.

"Finally I succeeded in getting Jules to write the things Spideler had said to him, and then in Jules Grieveau's peculiar hand-writing impossible to imitate, for it was in no two words alike, I went to Spideler with his own statements and suggest-ions, and told him an exposé should follow if he refused to help me save Jules from his cruel fate. 'Very well, Madam,' said Spideler, 'I'll do as you wish about it, if you'll agree to save me harmless; but you will have to take your choice, either Smith and Cronksey and the Doctor must hang or crazy Jules Grieveau. You say, which shall it be.' And I answered, let it be the man to whom neither life or death can make much difference; the man whose insane fanaticism will carry him glorying and happy into Eternity; he who will be surely by death the gainer—but not the man steeped in sin, whose soul must sink in perdition, not the man I have loved truly for so long, not him—not him!"

And the woman stopped her story, sobbing and moaning and wringing her hands with grief uncontrollable.

Even Silas Smith, the time-hardened villain, shed tears, and was visibly affected, and in the court room were very few dry eyes, every heart seemed touched by the proof of a love which none could doubt.

"And" continued the witness, "I gave the paper Jules had written to Spideler for *safe-keeping*, as he said, and discontinued my investigation and my efforts to save Jules Grieveau, but the remorse I have since suffered God only knows; that haggard face, those rolling eyes are with me night and day, and his outraged spirit walks ever before me with imperative gesticulations imploring to be avenged.

"I never thought that they'd *dare execute* their victim; but they did—the villains! And now I have told all I know about it, and that's not much without the paper; if I'd only kept the paper, justice might yet be done, and the ghost of crazy Jules Grieveau no less than our martyred President at last be appeased."

"Has the witness anything more to say?" asked the Judge.

"Nothing," answered the woman faintly, and a moment after she was borne in the arms of friends from the court room, overcome and in a deathly stupor.

A murmur of sympathy surged through the crowd, and then profound stillness supervened as the Judge called the Chief of the Secret Service of the Government to the stand.

"Let Mr. Strong be sworn," said the Judge turning to the clerk of the court

And as the venerable Chief lifted his penetrating eyes, and that thin white hand, holding so much of power and of fate in its grasp, up to high Heaven, with solemn invocation taking the oath to tell the truth, the whole truth so far as he knew it, and nothing but the truth, a feeling of awe fell upon every heart, and a sickening dread upon the guilty ones before him, until they trembled and quaked with the premonition of doom.

" Have you anything to introduce in evidence, Chief Strong?" asked the new prosecuting attorney.

" Only a few scraps of paper," answered the Chief, " corroborating the testimony already given.

"One was picked up on the floor of Gen. Gascoigne's study, near where the Confessor had been standing, by Mr. Swanson, just after the shooting and the arrest, and which we had a moment before seen the Confessor take from his pocket, showing it to Gen. Gascoigne. It confirms the testimony given by the last witness as to certain vague promises made to Grieveau by somebody, supposed to be Spideler, and which the Confessor procured at the last from him as his whole statement of the case. But the sequel has proved that he either could not, or did not try to get the whole story from the doomed man.

" The second paper, also the third, which I shall introduce in evidence, were torn by Leonard, pocket and all, from the coat of Spideler, upon recognizing and attacking his former master, by whom he had been so cruelly wronged.

" The first of these papers taken from the pocket of Spideler confirms his testimony as to the doctor; being a contract in regular form, signed by both, stating that for certain indefinitely described *services* to be rendered the late President the sum of twenty-five thousand dollars shall be paid by the said Spideler when those services are satisfactorily completed.

" The second paper taken from the pocket of Spideler, is the writing secured from Jules Grieveau by the former mistress of Smith, and which she declares she afterwards gave to Spideler at his solicitation.

" It is a statement that ' Spideler told him not to be afraid, but to follow his inspiration and go ahead and do the thing the Deity wanted him to do, and that Spideler had promised him that Cronksey and his friend Silas Smith, Esq., would see him through, and that he should have at least a foreign consulate, and then he could marry the widow,' as he thought her.

" The fourth paper which I shall introduce in evidence was found on the floor of Jules Grieveau's cell, by Leonard, when cleaning up after serving his dinner as ordered by Jules' Uncle, Gen. Gascoigne   Leonard had a propensity for picking up scraps of paper and rags, ' to light the fire,' as he said, and often took them to Aunt Debby Swanson.   He also had a strange habit of decorating the cat named ' Tommy,' upon his frequent visits, and for some unknown reason he fancied tying this particular scrap on Tommy's neck. Aunt Debby, soon after his departure, finding it and knowing the hand writing and signature of Jules Grieveau, very properly saved and handed it to her husband.

" It was a scribbled letter from Jules to Spideler, threatening dire vengeance from ' Deity,' unless Spideler should come to the rescue of ' God's man,' as he had promised, hinting that the ' accidental ' President, Cronksey, Gen. John A. Gascoigne and several leading politicians and officials had made promises they had failed to fulfill. Though the paper contained no direct proof of guilt, it was valuable as giving the first clue we had received as to the proper course our investigations should take. And from that day, Spideler, Cronksey, the President, Gen. Gascoigne and others were closely watched, but the denouement did not come in time to help poor Jules Grieveau."

" I believe you have stated that you received these four papers from the hand of Mr. Swanson, the detective, Chief Strong; is this correct? " asked the prosecuting attorney.

" Yes, sir, that was my statement," said the Chief.

" Let the papers referred to be produced," said the Judge, " and have Mr. Swanson sworn."

This being done, Uncle Tutty Swanson identified the four papers as the ones he had turned over to the Chief at different times as he had come into possession of them.

" The first one described by the Chief," said Uncle Tutty Swanson, " I myself secured, picking it up from the floor of Gen. Gascoigne's study after the arrests were made, as stated by Chief Strong. The second and third were handed me by my wife on that day, in the evening, upon my return home, she telling that Leonard had brought them to her.

" The fourth was given me quite early in the summer, shortly before the execution of Jules Grieveau, by my wife also, she finding it on the cat's neck after one of Leonard's visits."

Finally, Mrs. Swanson was put upon the stand, and stated that she received the second and third papers from Leonard, on the day of the terrible doings at Gen. Gascoigne's, as he said "To kindle a fire with." " And a fire sure enough we should have had then, had I not sent them by my husband to the good Chief there, for the people were like tinder that day, and a fire ending in an explosion might have occurred, destroying the guilty and innocent alike, had not the Chief kept all quiet until the excitement cooled.

"The fourth paper referred to, I received also from Leonard in an indirect way, as has been testified to, and he told me how he came by it." "That will do, Mrs. Swanson, we cannot take hear-say evidence which cannot be confirmed," said the Judge. "If you have told all you know of your own knowledge, we will excuse you."

Leonard could not of course be sworn, as the testimony of the crazy or idiotic is not admissable in a court of justice.

The woman who had lived for so many years with Smith as his wife, and had finally, conscience smitten, given her testimony against him, having partially recovered from her swoon, was again called into court, and under oath, identified the second paper referred to in the testimony of Chief Strong and the other witnesses, as the one she had "Seen Jules Grieveau write and sign, and which she had afterwards given to Spideler at his request." She also swore, "That Spideler did not deny making these statements to Jules, or that he had influenced him to do the dreadful deed of shooting the President, or that he was at the time working in the interests of Cronksey and Smith.

"All I have stated is true, so help me God!" exclaimed the woman falling headlong from her seat in the witness-box. She was found to be *dead*—gone beyond recall; her last earnest words still sounding in their ears.

This episode delayed for a short time only the business before the court.

Upon the testimony which had been produced, the case was allowed to go to the jury by the prosecution. No defense was attempted except the point blank denial of the two men accused, which went for naught both in the minds of the jury and the people.

Had the verdict been returned of "not guilty," so enraged had the populace become, the accused must surely have suffered death before they reached the court house portico.

When the announcement was finally made of "guilty," Silas Smith as the instigator and the Doctor as accessory to the murder of the late President, the vast crowd dispersed, well satisfied, to their homes.

The incumbent President, Gen. John A. Gascoigne, the honored General-in-Chief of the army, and others more or less mixed up in the intrigue; who at the last had weakly allowed themselves to become enthralled by the horror of the situation, not daring bravely to face the popular clamor in the interest of truth and justice, thus averting a wrong; were long ere this verdict was rendered, excused in the minds of the people from any supposed complicity in the terrible tragedy perpetrated without their actual knowledge.

But the Confessor and the Attorney, who united in so shamefully deceiving poor Jules Grieveau, his friends, and the people no less than they, in the endeavor to conceal and cover from view the slimy track left behind him, of that political serpent named "the Stalwarts;" and J. G. Bamboozle as well, whose double-faced treachery helped *"wreck a President,"* were each and all ever after under a ban of reproach, because of their nefarious conduct; and finding the climate of the United States uncomfortably cool, they wisely departed for foreign parts, remaining permanently abroad.

After the usual preliminaries, legal and otherwise, had transpired, everything possible being done to delay the event which could be devised by the two felons, who, notwithstanding all, still commanded great wealth and influence; they were executed, both Silas Smith, the typical intriguer, and the typical Doctor, on "black" Friday, but a few months after Jules Grieveau's brave death cry "Ready, Glory!" had resounded from the same scaffold.

They came pinioned from their cells, quaking with fear, begging piteously for that mercy which *they had not given;* but the time had come, there was no reprieve.

As the secret hand pulled the hidden rope, launching their sin-burdened souls upon the sea of Eternity, all who remembered the gambling in Wall Street stocks, as the cypher dispatches informed of a dying victim's fevered vibrating pulse; and the horrible persistent probing, torturing a Martyred President to his death; could not but feel that a just retribution had been visited upon these who were certainly to blame, whoever else may have been concerned in this wrong to individuals and to the Nation.

But still let us believe, that from the beginning was foundation laid of some plan, whereby every creature, even though grievously sinning and heavily chastened; yet in the rolling cycles of the ages, coming at last to recognize the GREAT LOGOS the LOVING MEDIATOR from Everlasting to Everlasting, and finding repentence, surely also forgivness, and the Infinite blessing of Jehovah's peace.

THE END.